SWORD-BOUND

A Novel of Tiger and Del

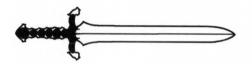

JENNIFER ROBERSON

DAW BOOKS, INC.

DONALD A. WOLLHEIM, FOUNDER

375 Hudson Street, New York, NY 10014

ELIZABETH R. WOLLHEIM
SHEILA E. GILBERT
PUBLISHERS
www.dawbooks.com

First Hardcover Printing, February 2013
1 2 3 4 5 6 7 8 9

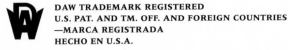

DAW TRADEMARK REGISTERED
U.S. PAT. AND TM. OFF. AND FOREIGN COUNTRIES
—MARCA REGISTRADA
HECHO EN U.S.A.

PRINTED IN THE U.S.A.

For the readers

Prologue

"**D**OMESTICITY," my son announced, "has blunted you."

He stumbled back from me, nearly stepping outside of the circle. Like me, he wore leather dhoti, no tunic, no sandals; we were dressed for sword-dancing. His skin was tanned, like mine, and, remarkably, clean of scars. *Un*like mine. Well, that would change.

Overhead, the sun burned. In the Punja—the most deadly of deserts—it would drive a sane man to seek the nearest shade, to carry plenty of water, to cover his body with a hooded burnous of nubby silk. But this was not the Punja. This was a place of water, of grass, of high canyon walls that blocked the sun, except when it was directly overhead.

It was directly overhead now, and it was hot.

My son, my opponent, stood upright, breathing hard; sweat ran down his dark hair, dripped onto his shoulders. He had grounded his sword in the sand, resting his palm on the pommel, fingers loose. I stared at him, momentarily speechless.

Domesticity.

I stood up straight as well, also breathing hard, but did not ground my sword. In fact, I waved it at him, right wrist flexing, supported by musculature developed over decades of practice. Sunlight flashed off the blade.

"Sharp enough to take you," I pointed out. "Three dances,

three wins, and I've just about got this one. Or *had* this one, before you decided to distract yourself from that fact by opening a topic about which you know nothing." I waved the sword again. "Blunted, am I?"

"Your sword isn't," he clarified, wary of the exceedingly sharp point. "*You* are."

"*I* am."

"You are."

I wasn't certain we'd make any progress this way. I squinted at him. "Domesticity?"

"Yes."

I said something short and sharp, and it elicited a snicker. "In what way am I blunted?"

"You used to have adventures," he said. "Now you stay at home and *teach* sword-dancing, instead of doing it yourself."

It stunned me. "You think I'm not dancing anymore? I do it every day, Neesha! I teach *you*, even, and I don't notice you've left to go off on any *adventures*."

"I'm thinking about it," he said, "and I thought you could come with me. Father and son. You know. Bonding."

"Bonding," I muttered between my teeth. Bonding. Bonding? What in hoolies did that mean?

"Maybe even Del could go."

I blinked. "Del?"

"Sure. The three of us together."

I frowned. "Del's got Sula to look after. She's only two."

Neesha smiled. "Do-mes-ti-city."

"*And* she teaches, too," I pointed out, meaning Del, not Sula. "When's the last time you danced with her? Afraid she'll defeat you?"

He grinned widely, white teeth flashing in a tanned, handsome face. (I had to admit I'd sired a good-looking kid.) "I'm *sure* she'd defeat me. But that's not what I mean. Why not dance for real again? You could leave Sula here with Lena and Alric. They've got so many kids now running around like chickens that they wouldn't even notice another. Besides, Sula stays over there while you and Del are teaching. You know they'd be happy to do it." He shrugged.

"Alric's domesticated, too, but he seems happy that way. I don't think you are, and I know Del isn't."

It was a stab in the gut. "Del isn't?"

"She adores Sula," he said, "and she loves you. You stay here, so will she. I'm just saying it would do both of you good to get away for awhile. Accept challenges. Guard a caravan. Get away." He watched me avidly, then grinned. "Ah-*hah*! I saw that look on your face. It appeals. You hid it fast enough, but oh, it appeals."

Maybe it did. I wouldn't admit it to him. "I have students."

"Right now you have me. Everyone else has gone off to see families or whatever, remember? "

This was true. Apparently all seven students had gotten itchy feet at the same time—or else the challenges of my discipline had chased them away. Some would come back. I'd left my shodo three times before I finally committed to sticking it out.

Neesha grinned. "What harm would it do for the great Sandtiger to go out and practice again what he teaches? You would add luster to the legend."

Luster to the legend. Like my legend needed any.

He shrugged. "You'd probably attract more students."

Probably. But. "Del and I have enough."

"Have more."

I sighed. "Neesha, you can go any time you like. Neither I nor Del would suggest you stay here. You've learned a great deal in two years."

He nodded, but his eyes, as they met mine, were intent. "What level?"

I shrugged. "Third."

He shook his head, lips compressed, tips of damp dark hair brushing his shoulders. "Third's not good enough."

"It takes seven," I reminded him. "And usually a minimum of ten years."

"But of course you did it in seven. Seven levels in seven years."

"So I did. But you came here with some skills, and third level in two years is not what I'd call slow." Now I grounded my sword and, as he did, rested my palm on the pommel with fingers loose. "Go. Leave. Make and accept some challenges, Neesha. Sort out what you want, then come back for more teaching."

His eyes met mine and did not waver. "Come with me."

I lifted my sword, set the flat of it across one shoulder, turned my back on him, and began to walk away.

"Think about it," he called. "And ask Del!"

I didn't need to ask her. I knew what she'd say.

Chapter 1

"YES," Del said.

Pretty much what I expected. Still, "Did he *tell* you he planned to suggest it?"

"No."

She sat on a bench outside of our little mudbrick house. Scattered nearby was a litter of kittens and their indulgent mother, slitty-eyed in the sun; a handful of chickens pecking for bugs; Alric's moth-eaten old yellow dog, yipping in his sleep. And our two-year-old daughter, seated in the middle of it all, picking up dirt and flinging it into the air.

I sighed and sat down next to Del, leaning the sword against the wall. Sula was too busy making a mess to notice the blade. I had learned, once she began to walk—well, more or less walk—that she was worse than a puppy at getting into things. I had eventually trained myself to put the sword and harness up high on pegs pounded into the hand-smoothed wall. For now, I kept one eye on her.

Which reminded me . . . "He says I'm domesticated."

"Yes."

I turned my head with a snap. "*You're* saying it, too? And do you plan to say anything in words of more than one syllable?"

Del smiled. "Maybe."

I scowled.

"Two syllables," she said, lifting one shoulder in a slight shrug.

I sighed deeply and set the back of my skull against the mudbrick. "Maybe he's right."

"The Sandtiger is not domesticated, regardless of what his son says. The Sandtiger is teaching what he knows, which is substantial. That's an honorable thing, Tiger. When Neesha's older, he'll recognize that." She patted me on one thigh. "You're older, now, yes. You need not go traipsing all across the Punja looking for jobs."

I suppose she meant that in a positive way. I *was* older. So was Del, but we'd met when she was twenty, so she wasn't exactly old. But I didn't require being reminded, necessarily, of what I was told each morning when I arose. Creaking bones were noisy. "He says you should go, too."

She didn't respond, merely watched our daughter now attempting to sneak up on Alric's dog. On hands and knees, and filthier than ever.

"He says you could leave Sula with Lena and Alric," I observed idly. "And he's right: She's over there half the time." 'Over there' constituted a mudbrick house very like our own, though larger, approximately two hundred long paces away from ours. Alric and Lena had a litter of kids to go along with the litter of kittens.

"He says I could add luster to the legend. Not that it needs luster, I don't think." I paused, waiting for a reply. When it didn't come, I asked, somewhat aggrieved, "Do you think it needs luster?"

"I think," she said finally, "that a shodo could—and perhaps should—venture forth to refine his skills so he can best teach his students what new techniques there may be."

" 'Refine his skills'," I echoed with no intonation that might be interpreted as my being upset.

Del said, "You're upset."

"Do you want to go?"

"If you want to."

"Is that a roundabout way of saying you'd like to go?"

"It's a way of saying I'd go if you want to."

"Gah," I declared, thudding my head against the wall.

"The same thing applies to me, Tiger."

"What applies to you?"

"I teach, also. I could—and perhaps should—venture forth to refine *my* skills."

I eyed her sidelong. Her white-blonde hair was loose and curtained part of her profile. I couldn't see her expression. "Are you sure Neesha didn't address this with you?"

"Neesha has been muttering about wanting to go for awhile. It started when everyone else left."

"I told him he could go!"

"He didn't suggest anything to me about you going. Or me."

"Oh, he suggested to *me* that we both go with him."

"And so we are back at the beginning," Del said. "And you had best put up the sword, because Sula is on her way."

So she was, still on hands and knees in the dirt but crawling in our direction. Apparently, for the moment, she found it easier than toddling. I picked up the sword and held it high over my head. This technique resulted in my daughter standing up against my knee, clutching flesh, reaching as high as she could in pursuit of the sword.

"There's no question," I observed, "what she will be when she's grown."

"A wooden sword," Del suggested, "and the blade perhaps padded so when she whacks you on the shin, you won't come whining to me."

I gently but with determination directed Sula aside with a hand cupped over her skull, and stood, once again resting the flat of the sword against my shoulder. I headed for the door. "I think she's due for a bath."

Del said, "Your turn."

I paused in the doorway and glanced back. Our daughter, deprived of my sword, was once again sitting in the dirt, stirring up dust. "All right," I growled. "We'll go with Neesha."

Del smiled serenely. "I thought we might."

Sword safely in harness on pegs against the interior wall, I gathered up the bag of lumpy soap, washing cloth, and the folded length of sacking we used for drying our daughter. Went back outside. Scooped up Sula and headed down past the multiple circles pegged out in the earth—as well as multiple footing surfaces for sword-dancing: sand, dirt, grass, gravel, a mix—and took her to the natural pool in the wide stream that ran through the canyon. Alric and I had, over the last two years, built up the edges with mudbrick and rocks, mortaring all into something akin to a fire ring surround, except much larger, and its contents were water, not flame. Everyone at this end of the canyon used it for bathing but also for fishing. On hot days, the dog used it for swimming. It was a very accommodating pool.

Despite the warmth of the day, the brightness of the sun directly overhead, the water was cool. I stepped over the surround and into the shallow-edged pool carefully, still barefoot and therefore attempting to miss rocks beneath the surface. I planted my butt just on the edge of the bank, lowered Sula, and tolerated the usual squeaks and shrieks as her lower legs made contact with cool water. One big hand clamped onto a small arm, I dumped the bag of soap and fabric out onto the bank, then stripped off Sula's tunic. This occasioned more squeaks and shrieks, and vehement protestations involving a squirming, naked body.

She was lovely, my little girl, if loud. Prior to her arrival, I had never spent time examining small children. Or infants, or even older children. Children were—other beings. Eventually they became men and women, but for years they were simply—other beings.

Sula, of course, was not and never had been an other being. She was mine. Del's. Ours. Oh, Neesha was mine as well, but he had arrived in my life a young but fully grown man. No soiled loin wrappings. He could even bathe himself.

I sluiced handfuls of water over my protesting daughter, top to bottom. She did have a vocabulary—two languages, no less; Southron and Northern—but it was relatively limited as yet and often consisted of *"No,"* if in two languages.

"Yes," I said. In one.

She was a blend of us both. Not as dark as I, nor as Neesha; eyes were blue, hair was blonde but not as pale as Del's. Del said it would

likely darken as she grew. Del also said it had my wave, and tended
to stick out in bizarre sculptural shapes after naps.

Suds. Wash. Sluice.

Domesticated.

Yes.

I swore. Then told Sula she shouldn't swear and inwardly swore
again that I had done so outwardly. Dammit.

The Sandtiger, the celebrated seventh-level Sandtiger, infamous
throughout the South, sat on his butt on the damp bank of a stream
soaping up, scrubbing down, and rinsing off a two-year-old girl.

I swore again. But very quietly.

And Sula was shrieking anyway, much too loud to hear me.

"Of course," Southron-born Lena said, as she squashed dough on a
flat wooden square Alric had adzed and rubbed smooth for her. The
kitchen consisted of a small mudbrick fireplace, rounded like a bee-
hive but boasting a gaping mouth that allowed access to the turnspit;
cleverly, a narrow chimney forced smoke out of the daub-and-wattle
roof. There was also a barrel of water and a narrow plank workspace
snugged up against one wall. Alric was somewhat handier than I, and
he had built something identical for Del and me in our smaller house.

"Of course," Northern-born Alric said, watching his wife work.
The children were, as usual, tearing in and out of the house. I'd
given up trying to count them.

"Go," Lena said.

Alric nodded. "Go."

"No trouble," she told me comfortably, flour to her elbows.

"None," Alric agreed, flour on his nose.

I looked at each suspiciously. "Did Neesha talk to you?"

They both turned genuinely puzzled faces to me. In unison:
"No."

And so our daughter's immediate future was settled. And also
my son's; I need not, after all, have a discussion with him about
speaking out of turn.

Not that it would have stopped him.

Alric smiled. "I believe you would do well to have some ale. Apologies. I have no aqivi."

I waved a hand. "I'm not much for aqivi any more."

"Just a memory from your youth, is it?" He laughed in genuine amusement when I scowled at him. Then he gestured. "Come on. I've got some jugs soaking in the pool. We'll go sit by the water and exchange memories of what we once were."

"Stop with the suggestions we're aging!" I followed him out of the house and fell into step beside him. "Hoolies, Alric, we're not that old!"

"But our best days are behind us."

"No, they're not!" We strode comfortably together. He was a Northerner, tall as I was. We could look at one another eye to eye. "And I'm beginning to think Neesha *did* talk with you about this."

Alric shook his head. Blond hair, pale as Del's, brushed his shoulders. "Truly, he did not. But he's been fidgety of late."

"What do Neesha's fidgets have to do with me? In particular, what do Neesha's fidgets have to do with age? My age, specifically?"

"The sap is running in him. Running fast and rising."

I glanced at him sidelong. "Why are we speaking of trees?"

Alric laughed. "It's a saying we have in the North."

"You have a lot more trees in the North," I said, recalling thick forests. And cold. And snow. "We don't have that saying down here."

"Our sap," he continued, "yours and mine, is somewhat more sedate now."

"My sap is not sedate!"

We'd reached the stream. Alric stepped over the pool surround, bent, found the pegged out twine, and pulled a jug up from the water. As one, we sat down and leaned against the sun-warmed bricks, swigging down cool ale. After a few substantial swigs, I felt somewhat more companionable.

"You may be sedate," I noted, "but not me."

"Then let's say we're wiser than we used to be, and somewhat more deliberate in certain movements."

It was true I didn't leap out of bed in the morning. But then, Del was in it.

"We don't spend ourselves unnecessarily," he added.

I grunted. For all my denials, I knew very well what he meant. I even knew what sap was, despite my protestations. I took the jug as he handed it over and swallowed deeply.

"But you may have to," Alric said.

I took the jug away from my mouth, savoring the robust taste. "May have to what?"

"Spend yourself." He retrieved the jug from me. "Just come home again in one piece."

It was true I'd lost a couple of pieces before: the little finger on each hand. I didn't even notice they were missing anymore. I'd found that by going inside myself, in summoning absolute belief, I *felt* the fingers when I danced.

"How old are you?" Alric asked idly.

Glumly, I said, "Forty-two." Which I only knew after my visit to Skandi, where I learned a great deal about myself. And lost two fingers. "What about you?"

"Thirty-four."

I looked at him sharply. "You're joking." I'd thought him nearer my age.

He shook his head, smiling faintly. "Having children keeps you young."

"Not when you have a litter of them, like you and Lena."

"Another's on the way."

My mouth fell open. "*Another* one?"

"We're hoping for a girl."

"You have several girls."

"Another would be nice."

"Alric, you don't have any boys. Wouldn't a boy be nice for a change?"

He shrugged. "I guess."

I hefted the jug, shaking it. Nothing sloshed. "Is there more where this came from?"

"Of course." Alric picked up the twine and hauled another jug out of the pool. He unwound the loop from the narrow neck and handed it over. This one sloshed nicely. I uncorked it and poured ale down my throat. It was a heavy brew, with a sharp tang to it. Not aqivi but more than drinkable.

I felt a presence behind us. "Uh-oh," Del said.

I cranked my head around to look at her. "Why uh-oh?"

"You're drinking."

"Why, yes. So I am."

"You've had nothing to eat."

"No, not when I'm dancing. Neesha and I were in the circle."

"But you're drinking on an empty belly."

"Why, yes. So I am." I held the jug out. "Want some?"

"No." Del was never one for drinking much. "You'd better come up and I'll fix something for you to eat before you keel over."

I grimaced. "Very domestic."

"And you can bathe Sula again while I do that."

"*Again?* I just bathed her a while ago!"

"She's dirty."

"She's always dirty."

"She got into dog piss." Del paused. "Fresh dog piss. In the dirt."

Beside me, Alric snickered.

A thought occurred. I smiled up at her. "I'd best not. I'm drunk."

Del narrowed her eyes.

"Drinking on an empty belly," I reminded her.

She glowered at me, hands on hips. "Then *you* fix the food. That, you should be able to accomplish without risk of drowning our daughter."

As she walked away, I sighed and thrust the jug at Alric. I got to my feet, as Alric laughed. "Ah, yes. Domestication."

I said something extremely impolite and swung around to follow Del but stopped short as I nearly ran into Neesha.

"Well?" he asked.

"Well, what?"

"Are you going?"

"Going where?"

"Out." He waved a hand. "Out there. Out wherever."

I scowled at him. "Yes."

"And Del?"

"Yes."

Neesha laughed, sounding unconscionably pleased. "Hah! I knew you would. That bit about adding luster to the legend . . ."

But my mind was on other things. "I'll have to go into Julah . . . pick up supplies, let Fouad know we're going." Fouad was a partner in the cantina Del and I had accumulated along the way. "He'll be on his own." Which usually resulted in less income for us and more for him.

"I'll tell him," Neesha offered. "I'll take the wagon and team and pick up supplies. I wanted to go to town anyway."

Of course he did. He'd accomplished what he'd set out to accomplish. Dryly, I said, "Do examine the latest batch of aqivi, won't you?"

Neesha grinned. "The only way I know how. From the inside out."

I watched him walk away: tall, lithe, limber. From behind me, Alric noted idly, "He'll do."

So he would. Smiling, I headed for the house. Feeling the ale, I took a couple of off-balance steps. Empty belly. And I'd danced three and one-half dances with my lithe, limber son. Food would be welcome, even if I had to fix it myself while Del bathed Sula.

Two baths in one day. Well, it was better than the three required two days before. Our daughter managed to find the messiest, smelliest things to get into. I suggested once that we put a lead-rope on her and tie her to the bench, much as one would a horse, but Del's frosty stare suggested the jest wasn't appreciated. Of course it was only *half* a jest, but I didn't tell Sula's mother that.

Even in the desert, Del could freeze a man.

Chapter 2

THE FOLLOWING EVENING as the sun climbed down from the sky, my lithe, limber son walked into the house with an odd expression on his face. Then I saw his left forearm was tightly wrapped with a bloody length of cloth, and the tips of his hair were dried into stickiness. Now I knew what the expression meant: embarrassment.

Del was putting Sula to bed; I'd lighted lanterns. Two hundred paces away, beyond our window, Alric's windows glowed. Twilight gave way to increasing darkness. In the desert, night comes quickly.

I finished chewing and swallowed the final bite of mutton, arched brows, asked mildly as I waved my meat-knife, "One of the ladies did not appreciate your company?"

Neesha went to the kitchen barrel, unwrapped his forearm, wet a rag and began sluicing blood over the ewer on the board. He said nothing.

"Or was it a man who didn't appreciate you stealing his woman?" Of course it wasn't that Neesha set out to steal anyone's woman; they just seemed to like him better the minute he stepped into the cantina. Any cantina. Any woman.

He muttered something indecipherable against the sounds of splashing water. I rose, shoved back the bench, looked over his shoulder. A slice through the layers of skin, but the muscles were untouched. It wasn't pretty, the wound. But it wouldn't kill him, either.

"Hmmm," I said. "Sword."

Neesha stopped cleansing and examined his arm. He bobbed his head briefly, acknowledging my observation.

"Not a dance, was it?"

Grimly, he said, "It was."

"And from the tone of your voice, I'm assuming you lost."

He muttered confirmation.

"Was it your challenge?" I thought it likely; he wanted very much to test himself against men other than his sparring partners here. Other than me.

That brought his head up. He turned to look at me. "No. His." His lips were compressed. "Some comments were made about 'a sword-dancer who came to town in a wagon.'"

"So they knew you on sight. You were in harness." Only sword-dancers wore swords sheathed across their backs.

Blood welled up. "Yes," he answered, distracted as he washed the arm again.

He wasn't wearing his harness now. "Where is it?"

"In the wagon."

Several comments occurred to me. I said none of them. But he knew very well what I wanted to say about a sword-dancer who removes his harness after a dance. Especially if he puts the sword and harness in a wagon.

"That," I said, "wants stitching. Let me get the kit, and I'll do it."

Neesha grimaced. "I'll just wrap it again. Two days. Three. It will heal well enough on its own."

"If you were a horse," I observed, "you wouldn't say that."

No. He would not, and he knew it. He'd grown up on a horse farm and took exquisite care of our mounts. Even the stud tolerated him.

"I'll do it." Del had heard us; she carried the kit in her hands. "Sit down, Neesha. And don't protest, or I *will* let Tiger do it. You know perfectly well my hands are defter than his."

Well, that was true. Neesha went directly to the table and sat himself down. So did Del, and pulled the lantern closer.

"So," I said, "who was this sword-dancer?"

Neesha's gaze flicked up to mine, then returned to Del as she threaded a curved needle. "No one I knew. But then, I haven't been out much, have I?"

Ah, accusation. "Perhaps I accorded you a level you haven't yet reached."

That told. He glowered at his arm as Del prepared to stitch, ignoring my comment.

"What does he look like?"

Neesha's head snapped up. This time he met my eyes and didn't look away. Color rose in his face. Between gritted teeth, he said. "Don't you dare."

"I'm just curious." I shrugged. "I might know him. That's all."

"That's not all—*ow!* Ow-ow!" He sucked in air between his teeth. "That hurts."

"Of course it does," Del said matter-of-factly. "I'm sticking a needle through your flesh."

"Ow!" Then he glared at me. "I know what you're thinking. Don't do it. Don't—*ow!*"

"Did you pick up the supplies?"

Color bloomed in his face again. "No."

"Then I'll be taking the wagon into town tomorrow." I paused. "That is, if you still think we need to go *out there*—" I waved a hand, as he had earlier, "to find adventure."

Del glanced up at me, then studiously returned to her stitching. Only rarely did she take part in the arguments between son and father, unless we were too loud, at which point she told off the both of us.

Neesha muttered, "Yes."

"Well then." I shrugged. "We still need supplies. In the meantime, I'll go unhitch the team."

"I did that."

Of course he had. Horses came before his own welfare. "Then I'll bring in your harness and sword."

He looked away from me, eyes latched onto Del's work. He was embarrassed. Ashamed.

I smiled. Two things had been accomplished: Neesha had lost a challenge, and he'd gained his first scar. Both were necessary, were he to name himself a sword-dancer.

Or, for that matter, my son.

Come morning, as the sun rose, I stuffed bread and eggs down my throat, swallowed all with goat's milk, took down my sword and harness, and slipped into the leather straps, buckling myself in. I wore leather dhoti and sandals, no tunic, and pulled on a faded green-and-orange striped burnous. I made sure the triple-stitched slit in the shoulder seam accommodated my sword hilt, and then I went out to hitch the team.

Neesha, as expected, was nowhere to be seen. Since he was a student like the others, he called one of the small mudbrick cells, built against the canyon walls, his own. A length of somewhat tattered blue cloth was still pulled across the low doorway. Usually he was up with the sun, milking goats, collecting eggs, pulling vegetables, tending the horses in the small pole corral, and limbering up for training. There were mornings he slept in, leaving Del or me to handle the chores, but I didn't think this was one of them. He was very likely wide awake, listening to me hitch up the team.

Well, I should give him the opportunity, so he wouldn't continue to assume I was overprotective and intent on teaching a lesson to the sword-dancer who'd defeated him. I strode across grass kept short by the goats and went straight to his cell. I accorded him his privacy and spoke through the rough curtain.

"You coming?"

There was no sound for a moment. Then he pulled the fabric aside. He, too, wore a dhoti. "To town?"

"That was the plan, yes."

I saw him think it over. A myriad of fleeting expressions crossed his face. He finally settled on a mild bemusement. Would I invite him along if I meant to challenge the man who defeated him? What would happen if he accompanied me? Would the sword-dancer challenge him again? He had a legitimate reason to turn down a challenge, but would he? It wasn't part of the codes to dance when injured.

"Arm hurting?" I asked, to remind him of the codes.

He could save face with that. Besides, I knew exactly how much it hurt. He wouldn't want to do anything with that arm for some time, though of course, he'd insist on doing so. Del had wrapped a soft cloth around his forearm, warding the stitches, and I noted that fluid had seeped through.

Neesha glanced at the bandaged limb. "Well," he muttered, "yes."

I noted his red-rimmed eyes. "Didn't get much sleep last night, did you?"

He twisted his mouth. "None."

"That's to be expected." Even without a sword in my hands or a circle around my feet, I felt like a shodo. "This won't be the first time, so you'd best get accustomed to it."

"Or else become quicker? Better?"

I smiled. "That helps. In the meantime, have Del look at it again, rebandage it. She's got some salve that will help the swelling." I paused, then asked the question he'd been waiting for. I kept my tone even, putting no emotion into it. "Why did you lose?"

He very nearly flinched. But he did not avoid the question, nor the lesson I was teaching. "I slipped."

"Barefoot?"

"Of course." Sandals could turn on a foot, interfere with motion. Before a dance, they were always removed, as was the harness. We danced nearly naked, clad only in a dhoti.

"Footing?"

"Dirt."

"Where?"

"In front of the cantina. Your cantina."

"Why did you slip?"

It took him a moment to answer. Color crept into his face. But he did not avoid my eyes. "A puddle," he said, "of horse piss."

A puddle of horse piss. It appeared both of my children had an affinity for such puddles. "Why on earth was there a puddle of horse piss *inside* the circle?"

Neesha sighed. "I let him draw the circle."

"So he knew where it was, how to avoid it, and how to force you into it."

He nodded.

"Well," I said, "you've learned to always be certain of the footing before the dance commences."

His tone was grim. "I have."

I nodded. "This happens, Neesha. It's all part of being a sword-dancer. You'll get cut. Even stabbed, sometimes. And you will lose."

He nodded, not meeting my eyes. Then, realizing that I might infer from it something he didn't want inferred, he raised his head and looked me square in the eye. "I'll see Del."

"It won't interfere once it's healed," I told him. "It's flesh, not muscle."

His tone was dry. "I guess you would know."

I smiled crookedly. "*Oh*, yes."

With a lifted chin, he indicated the sword hilt showing above my shoulder. "You're in harness."

"I'm often in harness when I go into town."

He couldn't argue with that, much as he wanted to; it was true. His eyes narrowed. "Don't."

One might observe that made no sense, except I knew exactly what that single word meant. It was less an instruction than a request. Maybe even a wish. "I'm going for supplies and to talk to Fouad. I don't want him robbing us blind while we're off on our adventure."

He wanted to say more. He did not.

"Go see Del," I reminded him. "Have some breakfast while you're at it. Healing wants fuel." And before he could reply, I turned on my heel and left him.

Of course I wanted revenge. What father wouldn't? But I knew very well I should not seek it out. Neesha needed to learn to defend himself, which he had not, in this instance, done very well, unfortunately. But only a fool believes he will remain undefeated. I'm no fool, and I've been defeated.

Though not often.

I'd left the canyon behind. Now the sun burned, unhindered by high walls. It was never cool in the South except for nights. In what we called winter, a desert could be downright cold once the sun went down. But whenever I was moved to complain of the chill of some nights, I kept my mouth shut. I'd been to the North. *That* was cold. Winter there was full of snow and ice.

Though it was early morning, the rattle of the wagon upon the rough track and the jingling of horse harnesses lulled me into a desire for more sleep. Maybe what I should do, once I reached Julah and the cantina, was appropriate one of the rooms in back for a nap. The girls wouldn't be needing the rooms till evening.

Del was not happy about the "cantina girls"—women who spent nights with men for coin. She'd argued about it in her firm, deliberate, logical way, saying it was not necessary to make coin from women. But she was outvoted by Fouad and I. We explained that this was how cantina girls supported themselves, and they'd just go to other cantinas if we turned them out. At least in our establishment the girls were not beaten or required to work when they didn't wish to, and though the cantina took a cut of their earnings, it was a lesser cut than elsewhere.

Not entirely convinced—she said we were men and thus were biased in favor of slaking our desires (I'd never heard it put that way, but decided it was accurate)—she took the girls aside and discussed the matter with them. I don't know what was said, but though Del still disapproved, she said no more about it. I guess she'd been reminded that women in the South had few choices, and this choice was theirs.

Over the past two years, the route to and from Julah and the canyon was used more frequently and was therefore more passable. Mehmet and his aketni—his religious sect—went into Julah regularly, as did Alric and his family, as did Del and I as well as our students; traders happened by now and again. Because of the improved footing, it was now a matter of half a day's drive in a wagon. Less, if you rode a horse.

I reached the old lean-to, still in use by others now and again— I couldn't help but smile wryly. Much had happened here. Del had been attacked by a sandtiger, nearly losing her life; that she hadn't was more thanks to Neesha's care than to my own, though at the time neither Del nor I had a clue he was my son. Like me, she still bore claw marks as souvenirs. And I'd been kidnapped by Rafiq, back when Umir the Ruthless had placed a bounty on my head. Since I was no longer considered a true sword-dancer and thus worthy of the honor of the circle—I'd sworn *elaii-ali-ma*, breaking all of the oaths sworn at Alimat, where I had learned my trade—I was merely a valuable captive to whomever managed to catch me and haul me off to Umir's place.

I'd been hauled, all right; dirty, sunburned, sick from my own share of sandtiger venom, leather tied around wrists and throat, and delivered to fastidious Umir for what was and what wasn't a sword-dance. Umir didn't care about Alimat or honor codes; he just cared about hiring the best and figured one way to find the best was to hold a tournament of sorts, sword-dancer against sword-dancer. Whoever won would face me—to kill me, of course, to kill the man believed by many to be the best sword-dancer the South had ever known. (Though, as might be expected, some disagreed with that.) Nonetheless, plenty had wanted to kill me just to do it, and a fair number because of the codes and oaths I'd broken. The problem was, none had succeeded. *I'd* won the dance. And departed with all alacrity, Alric riding with me.

Now here I was—here *we* were—living less than a day's ride from Julah. It had been a peaceful two years, as these things go, with much to be taught and learned: a daughter taught to walk, a son to dance, a man to be a father, and a woman a mother.

But still.

I looked at the lean-to, let the memories flow and wondered, then, whether the man in Julah who'd challenged Neesha had done it because Neesha was my son or just because he believed it would provide entertainment. There were sword-dancers who were bullies, who might well think it amusing to challenge a young man who wore a harness and sword but rode into town on a supply wagon.

Which was precisely why I wore a harness and sword but rode into town on a supply wagon.

Chapter 3

IN MY YEARS, in my myriad travels, I'd seen numerous towns and settlements established throughout the South. The guiding force was not geography so much as it was water. The deadly Punja desert was pocked by oases and domains claimed by various tanzeers, yet welcome settlements sprang up on the edges of the Punja, surcease from the remorseless sun and crystal sands. First water was always welcome; after crossing the Punja many were afraid to stray far from water ever again, and so towns slowly appeared as people remained. Wells were dug. Fields were claimed out of scrubby brush and tough desert grasses. Seed was planted. Streets were not so much built as shaped by frequent use, pathways carved out of dirt. Julah was an old town, well-settled. Trade caravans, guided strings of wagons carrying people on their way elsewhere, came through as well as lone travelers. Occasionally people stayed on, adding to the population.

Julah now boasted more than one road as entry and exit. But the ruts mingled with the hoof prints laid down by occasional wagons traveling to and from the canyon and Beit al'Shahar—my version of a training school similar to Alimat, where I had learned—made the track difficult to see unless you were familiar with it. Now and then travelers turned the wrong way and ended up at the dwellings of Mehmet's aketni. They watered their mounts and teams, sometimes spent the night, but departed the next morning with Mehmet's directions to Julah. No one new, it seemed, wished to listen to Mehmet preach. Those who had accompanied him across the Punja, however, were devoted to him, their unwavering faith bound to his conviction that I was a kind of messiah. Had I not turned the sand to grass?

Well, no. Magic had done that, when it brought the high, circular tower of stone tumbling down and split the earth asunder, forming a canyon. With grass.

With me.

But nothing was ever said of our canyon, the hidden extension of Mehmet's, except when young men arrived who wished to learn or to refine the sword-dance. Mehmet and his people had come to recognize and welcome them. To them, Mehmet and his aketni provided directions: Follow the wide stream to the stone shoulder on the right, where it tilts down from the canyon's rim, and enter a second canyon. Smaller, steeper, surrounded by high walls, save for the narrow entrance. And so they came upon us, looking for learning. Looking for me.

For some time, I drove up and down the narrow byways of Julah: Street of Weavers, Street of Dyers, Tinsmiths, Apothecaries, Renderers, many others, and of course plenty of cantinas. Now and again I stopped, inspected items, bought bags of flour, beans, onions, tubers, sugar, salt, and other foodstuffs. I bought medicaments and herbs, canvas and twine, colorful nubby silk and thread, new-made botas for water, leather saddle pouches, dried meats. I even threw in sweets for Sula.

By the time I was done, I'd been noted by several young men wearing harness and sword. All but one watched me incuriously; they lounged outside cantinas, filled benches, drank spirits, talked among themselves, challenged one another just to pass the time, wagered on the outcomes. When I pulled up in front of Fouad's, wagon rattling, bits and chains chiming, I became an object of attention. A few horses were tied to the hitching post Fouad had built, but no other wagons. Mine was the only one.

I jumped down, ground-tied the team with a weighted length of leather thong, headed toward the door. There, I paused a moment as if undecided about whether I should go in. A simple matter of delay, allowing bored sword-dancers to see the sword rising from my shoulder. The set of the blade told its own story: a man, though in harness, was buying supplies as if he were a farmer. No self-respecting sword-dancer did such a thing. It made no sense. Perhaps it was arrogance, a farmer attempting to make more of himself than he was. Perhaps he deserved to be taught a lesson.

Young men, all. I heard the snickers, the muttered comments, a few scattered jests, the disdain of healthy, physically gifted young men who fancied themselves above the common man. They could dance. They served tanzeers, hired on as outriders with caravans, challenged one another to keep fit and fast and judge each other's skills. They did not drive wagons.

Fouad's was the first stop. It would be most convenient if Nee-sha's challenger were here; otherwise I'd be going into every cantina in Julah to down at least one drink. And if I were challenged at the last cantina, it would be a half-drunk Sandtiger he'd face.

But only half.

Fouad was in the midst of serving customers a light midday meal. Most didn't order food; they were there to drink. But Fouad felt it a courtesy—and a source of income—to make food available, and Del and I, now having the majority say in such things, con-curred. Besides, before Del entered my life I'd spent many a day in Fouad's drinking aqivi, passing the time with cantina girls, and eat-ing his food.

He saw me come in and opened his mouth to speak, but shut it when I gave him the tiniest shake of my head. He went back to serv-ing men at tables, but he was clearly curious about why I did not wish my name spoken in front of the others. As for the wine-girls, there was no need for any of them to address me by name; besides, if they took their attention from the men with whom they shared drink and food, they might well make the men jealous enough to dismiss them.

Eight tables. And a plank bar. Walls built of mud, a slurry of mortar, and tough desert grasses were six feet thick to beat back the sun. Window sills were deep enough that one might sit in them, and often the girls did if between men. Sometimes men did. I had. Shut-ters were folded open, as no simoom or rain threatened. A small

beehive-shaped fireplace built into one corner warmed winter eve-
nings, though it was empty of wood now. Behind the plank bar was
a thin lath wall, hiding the oven; a narrow hallway led from the
common room through the kitchen and to the small back rooms
barely large enough to contain a bed and a clothing trunk. Fouad
had kindly knocked out the wall separating the last two rooms so
that Del and I, when in town overnight, had more space. He kept
himself to one of the small rooms, which left five for the girls.

I slouched up to the bar and leaned there on one crooked elbow
waiting for Fouad to return. He did so, dropping the tray onto the
divoted wood. His rising eyebrows asked the question. "Aqivi," I
said. Then, as he poured a quarter mug as I indicated, I very quietly
asked if Neesha had been in the day before.

As quietly, Fouad said, "He was, yes."

"And you know he was challenged."

Fouad put the pitcher away, mouth crimping at one end. "Yes."

"Here?"

"Yes. But the man isn't here now, if you've come to kill him."

"I did *not* come to—" But broke off as my voice rose. I tamped
it, muttered between my teeth, "I didn't come to kill anybody. Hoolies, Fouad, you know better than that."

He narrowed dark eyes at me, drawing himself up. "I know
nothing of the sort. You have done so before. How am I to know
what mood you may be in?"

Well, it was true. I had indeed killed in Julah; hoolies, I'd evis-
cerated a man. Hadn't been planned, but circumstances demanded
it. Now and again, you couldn't escape that. At least, I couldn't. "I'm
not in a *mood*." I filled my mouth with aqivi, felt its familiar bite,
swallowed. In fact, I felt it all the way down; it had been a while
since I'd had any, and my innards knew it. I cleared my throat. "And
I didn't come to town to kill anyone. I came for supplies."

"Then you've got the wagon."

"I do."

"Ah," Fouad said in dry wisdom. He took up a rough sacking
towel and began to wipe down the bar.

I opened my mouth to defend my son, who had lost the dance,
and got cut in the process, but I closed it before speaking. Neesha's

battles should be his alone. I had no place interfering; the gods knew that, when I first left Alimat and my shodo, no one had ever attempted to defend me or to punish someone for cutting me. It was foolish. The desire to punish was perhaps natural, but such things should be curbed when a young man was learning his way.

All I had to do was climb into the wagon and go back home. I need not seek out anyone to pay him back for what he'd done to my son.

And so I didn't, drinking down aqivi. The man sought me. And found me.

He was not alone. Two young men flanked him. Sword-dancers all, in harness and dhotis, unencumbered by burnouses probably left with their horses, wherever hitched or stabled. Typical Southroners, dark of skin and eyes, shorter and lighter than me, but undoubtedly quick. I'd learned to respect the quickness of Southroners, and in the meantime, my fellow students had learned that I was not to be underestimated because of my greater mass. Six-foot four, two-hundred and twenty pounds, much taller, and broader through the shoulders than Southroners. But I, too, was quick.

The one in the middle, of course. The one striding into the cantina a step ahead of the others. The one who dominated his companions merely by his arrogance. He saw me, smiled; a slight sideways twitch of his head indicated the other two should find places along the wall. They did so. He glanced over the interior, marking the men and their positions. No one was eating, no one was drinking. All they did was stare, first at the young sword-dancer, then at me.

Fouad sighed loudly in resignation, making sure I heard it.

"When we get to the dance," I said quietly, "you can hold the wagers."

"I always do," he muttered. Then he raised his voice. "Welcome, Khalid. What are you and your friends drinking?"

The bully had clearly spent several days here if Fouad knew his name. I didn't recognize it, but I couldn't know every sword-dancer in the South, especially as so many young ones had sprung up in the last few years, while I wasn't looking. This one was young but no innocent. There was confidence in his eyes and posture, not bluster; confidence that came from success. He'd won dances. Neesha was only his latest opponent not his first, nor, probably, even his tenth.

"I'll drink after," Khalid answered, not looking away from me. "Mere moments, only."

I wouldn't give him meek. I wouldn't give him arrogant, though certainly there had been a time when I would have. And I wouldn't give him the poised expectation of a dance; I gave him a man minding his own business, glancing at the latest customer without much interest before turning back to his drink.

"Am I to believe you're a sword-dancer?" Khalid asked, weighting a raised voice with the right amount of disdainful wonder. "Or just a man who wishes to be one? Wishes others to believe he is one?"

Ignoring him was not an option, precisely as he intended. I turned toward him slightly, brows raised, one hand on my mug as if not expecting to move away from the bar. "Me?"

"You." He made a gesture indicating the sword jutting up from behind my shoulder. "There's a harness and sheath underneath that burnous."

I nodded agreement. No meekness. No arrogance. Merely matter-of-fact concurrence.

He very nearly sneered. "I don't know a sword-dancer alive who rides into town in a *wagon*."

It amused me that he relied on such a flimsy excuse to begin a dance. First Neesha, now me. Why not a straightforward challenge?

"Well," I said, "now you know *me*."

Not what he had expected. After a moment of consideration, he said, "You're a farmer aping our ways. You dishonor our codes, our oaths. You demean us."

I looked at his two friends, then back at him. "I'm sorry. I don't mean to."

This was not going the way Khalid expected. Brows knitted briefly.

I raised my mug. "Aqivi? It's better than most. I'll even buy."

"Prove it," he said, not meaning aqivi. "Come into the street and prove it."

Still holding my mug in the air, I let him see only a confused and slow understanding. "Oh. Is this a challenge?" I set the mug down on the bar. "I'd thought to head back home after I finished my aqivi."

"Don't worry," Khalid said. "You'll be on your way soon enough."

I watched them file out, the three young men who believed themselves invincible. I looked at Fouad, who was shaking his head and muttering, "Foolish, foolish, foolish."

"It's how they learn." I smiled. "I'll finish off the aqivi when I'm done with the boy."

"*Fool*ish."

I walked outside to discover Khalid's two friends digging through my wagon. Already they'd cut open the flour sack and spilled the contents into the street. Beans littered dirt as well. It was added provocation, of course, though unnecessary. I'd give Khalid his dance even if the supplies were untouched.

"Wasteful," I commented, then stepped out into the center of the street where Khalid waited. Already, onlookers gathered. Sword-dances are always entertaining; something to break up the day.

I unbelted, unhooked my burnous from the sword, pulled it off, bundled the cloth, and tossed it aside. I unlaced my sandals and tossed them aside as well, followed by the empty harness. Now it was just me, my dhoti, my sword.

Khalid had drawn the circle. I inspected it, then grinned at him. "No. Over there. *Away* from the puddle of horse piss." Probably one very like it had tripped up Neesha.

But Khalid didn't look at the circle or the puddle. He stared at the cavity in my side, a fleshed-over chasm carved out by Del; at the claw marks in my face. He raised his eyes to mine. I looked back cheerfully.

While he watched, I occupied myself drawing a new circle, one lacking in horse piss or dung, or anything that might affect our footing. Upon completion I placed my blade in the very center, then walked back to the line, stepped over it. I turned to face him.

He didn't move. I read the thoughts passing through his eyes.

He was young, but I was indeed a legend, as Neesha reminded me that morning. Khalid thought he knew me. He thought I might well be that man.

Onlookers murmured. Many, just passing through town, didn't know me; certainly the residents did, but as a teacher, a shodo, not an active sword-dancer. I hadn't danced in Julah for more than two years.

I watched Khalid arrive at the conclusion that I was indeed the Sandtiger. He calculated his skill against the legend and came up lacking. Acknowledgement was bitter. Then again, I was older now. Undoubtedly slower. Not what I once was, probably. He looked at my hands, mentally counted the fingers. The first realization, the first waning of confidence, dissipated. Older, slower, that terrible wound in my chest and side that undoubtedly bothered me now, at my advanced age; and only three fingers on each hand.

Khalid smiled. Khalid bared his teeth. Khalid walked to the center of the circle, halted, as if to set down his sword next to mine. But he did not. "You're not a sword-dancer," he said. "Not anymore. And I don't have to obey any codes, or dance any dances. I just have to kill."

And then he came at me.

Of course.

Chapter 4

FOUAD'S WORDS: Foolish, foolish, foolish. I ducked the first swing, dove to the dirt and rolled to my feet, sword in my hands. Khalid had not expected it. He swung to face me hastily. Saw the sword in my hands, the readiness in my posture. And he hesitated.

I poked one finger into the air and crooked it repeatedly, gesturing invitation. Asking him, mutely, to come closer. To continue the dance.

He did so with a rush.

Swords sang as we clashed. The dirt beneath my feet was packed from footprints, hoof prints, and wagon wheels. No puddles, no droppings, nothing that could interfere. But then this was not a sword-dance, according to Khalid; we need not confine ourselves to the circle.

Yet I did. I made Khalid come to me. I wanted this to be a traditional dance, so Khalid and his friends could see how it was done, could see what it was that had made me great. Speed, despite my size. Power, because of my weight. Strength, because of my fitness. I had spent two years teaching students. I was as well-conditioned as a man could be, who was active on a daily basis, who used skill and muscle memory. But above all, I had the mental focus that came from years of dancing against the best. From years of *being* the best.

But I paid him the honor of not being complacent.

I used the sun. I used my shadow. I used my green-eyed Sandtiger's stare. I used his inexperience. The kid was good, and he'd be better. But not today.

I smashed the sword out of his hands with a twist that sent it wheeling out of the circle. I drove him to the ground, flat on his back. I placed the point of my sword in the hollow of his throat. "Call off your dogs," I directed, knowing full well that because I'd broken all the oaths and codes, his friends might decide to attack me together. "We're done here. You and your boys can walk away, can ride out of Julah. In fact, I think you'd better." I tapped the sword point against flesh. "You're good, Khalid. You'll have a successful career, since I'm leaving you alive. That's my gift to you. But you're not ready for me yet, and don't fool yourself into believing you are." I glanced at his two friends, watching me as if transfixed. But it was Khalid who maintained my attention. "Now," I said, "tell your friends to replace everything they destroyed and repack my wagon. Until they do, you'll lie here in the dirt with my blade at your throat."

After a moment, Khalid croaked an urgent "Go!"

I smiled down at him. "Good boy."

Afterward, Fouad freshened my mug with aqivi to the rim. I started to tell him I'd only planned to finish off what I'd left behind prior to Khalid's challenge but decided I would enjoy more than the few remaining swallows—especially since there was backwash in what I'd left.

My eyes adjusted to the dim interior as I blinked. High sun outside; cool in the cantina. I'd sheathed the sword after wiping it down, laced up my sandals but dropped the burnous across the bar top. I leaned casually on one elbow set against the plank, watching men file back in. All took note of me: sandals, harness, dhoti, and twinned silver rings in my ears. Bigger than Southroners. Oh, and claw marks on my face, a crater under my ribs, stumps where my little fingers had once been. Quite a picture, if I do say so myself. And it all served a purpose. You didn't take me for granted.

Well, at least, you shouldn't.

There was quiet talk about the dance as customers resumed their seats, but in my presence none of them raised their voices. I turned to the bar and smiled into my mug. Sometimes it was just plain amusing to see what effect I had on others. Of course Del would say that was me being egotistical, but hey— I was what I was. As Khalid had found out.

Fouad, on the other side of the bar, said quietly, "You may have made an enemy today."

"No 'may' about it. I definitely made an enemy today." I swallowed aqivi, set the mug down. "But they are all my enemies, Fouad. I broke every oath, flouted the codes, dishonored my shodo, dishonored Alimat, and therefore dishonored every sword-dancer in the South. I *expect* that kid to come after me again."

That kid, once I permitted him to get up from the dirt, had noted that I stood with the hilt in my right hand, blade resting lightly across the crook of my left elbow. It would be a simple matter for me to swing the sword backhand and lop off a limb. Khalid briefly matched my stare but not my casual smile. He inclined his head to acknowledge my victory, a muscle twitching in his clamped jaw, then turned, gathered up his sword and sandals, and walked stiffly away. His friends fell in beside him, though I suspected he wanted no part of them at that moment. As he departed, wagerers gathered around Fouad as he paid out.

Now he asked, "But if it restores honor to kill you, how is it you have students who want to learn instead of kill?"

"It's not guilt by association," I explained. "Yes, learning from me will undoubtedly result—and maybe already has resulted—in an additional challenge or two, and probably some very bad words and nasty accusations, but my students haven't dishonored anything or anyone. What I started at Beit al'Shahar isn't Alimat; we swear no oaths. There are no rituals." I shrugged. "I'm just a teacher, not a true shodo."

"And others like Khalid?" Fouad asked. "Will they come, too, to challenge you?"

"Khalid didn't challenge the Sandtiger. He challenged a man for no other reason than to show off. He'd already defeated Neesha, and he underestimated me."

"But others *will* come."

I shrugged. "A few already found their way to the canyon. Two I had to kill." It was two years before, and one of the dead was Abbu Bensir. We'd finally laid to rest the question of who was better, though I damned near bled to death in the doing of it. "Three others I defeated badly and gifted them with cuts that required enough stitching so they'd have impressive scars to show other sword-dancers; an understated warning from me to others that I won't go down easily. We haven't been bothered of late." One-handed, I turned the mug idly against the bar top. "Swearing *elaii-ali-ma*—the repudiation of all my oaths and commitments to the honor codes—did not erase any of my skills, you know. But I admit it will be easier for anyone bent on killing me to find me, now that we're leaving."

Fouad's eyes widened. "Leaving?"

"Temporarily." I sighed in resignation. "Neesha managed to convince Del and me that we should go out and have *adventures*."

His brows arched high on his forehead. Then he observed dryly, "You had an adventure today."

"Well, yes."

"And your son believes it's worth it to place you at risk?" Fouad shook his head. "There's no need for you to go, Tiger. You are you— still. Everyone knows it. Such risk is not necessary."

I narrowed my eyes at him. "Are you suggesting I can't hold my own against other sword-dancers? Just against Khalid?"

"Oh, I believe you can hold your own against anyone," Fouad answered promptly. "But that doesn't necessarily mean you'd actually be alive at the end of the dance."

I weighted it with irony. "Thanks for the vote of confidence."

Fouad shrugged. "We've been friends for how long? Ten years? I've been witnessing you dance in Julah for a decade. I know how good you are."

Friends. Hunh. Interesting he would say so. Fouad once sold out Del and me to a lethal and lunatic female tanzeer a couple of years before. Admittedly he'd done it under pain of death—a very painful death—but still. I didn't consider us friends. We were friend*ly*, but that's different. When you're the sellee, not the seller, you hold different opinions. And that was how Del and I had come to own one-third of the cantina each. Recompense. Reparation.

"So," I continued, "you can give the two-thirds share of the profits to Alric. He and Lena will be looking after Sula, and there are no students at the moment. They'll need the coin."

Fouad nodded, looking everywhere else save at me. "And if something should happen to you?"

Hah. I figured we'd get around to that. "There's Del."

"And to Del as well?—though the gods forbid it should be so."

He seemed a little happier to assign death to me, rather than to Del. I glared at him. "Then there's Neesha."

"And what—"

I cut him off. "If the gods see fit to wipe out all three of us, there's still Sula. She inherits."

His face fell. He'd forgotten about her. Ten years before, when I'd first come to Julah, eventually making Fouad's cantina sort of my headquarters, I'd been traveling solo. Now I had a family of four.

I grinned at him, then drank more aqivi. "Sorry, Fouad. One way or another, you're stuck with us."

Gloomily he said, "I suppose it could be worse."

"Yes," I agreed cheerfully. "I might have killed you instead of merely taking shares of the cantina."

That set him to coughing into his aqivi. When he could breathe normally again, he noted nervously that it was time for him to see to his customers.

"I'm a customer," I reminded him. The aqivi was having an effect. Hot sun, sword-dance, hours past breakfast, meaning a mostly empty belly. "I need food . . . and *water*. And a bed." I usually stayed overnight when I went into town. But generally I didn't drink so much aqivi. It had been a long time. If anyone challenged—or came at—me now, I would probably lose.

Fouad was startled. "A bed? It's only afternoon."

"*Late* afternoon," I emphasized. "And since when is it disallowed for a man to take a nap? A man who just faced a much younger man in the circle? And won?"

He considered that a moment, couldn't find an inoffensive response, and nodded. "I'll fix a tray. The bed you can find yourself, since you're in it often enough." Fouad turned away, muttering in disgust, "The Sandtiger . . . drinking water. *Going to bed in the daytime.*"

Yes, the Sandtiger wanted water. And food. And a bed. A bed empty of wine-girls.

Hoolies, I *was* domesticated.

Rudely awakened by loud knocking at the door, I flung myself out of bed and grabbed my unsheathed sword, coming up ready to fight—until I realized it was unlikely that anyone who wanted to fight me would do me the favor of knocking first.

"It's me," said a male voice I recognized.

Not someone come to kill me. Swearing, I opened the door with the sword still in my hand. "What in hoolies are you doing here? And what time is it?"

"Sundown," Neesha said, answering my last question first, "and I'm here to complain that you've treated me like a child."

Now that my body realized it was not required to defend itself, my heart slowed. Skin prickled as knee-jerk preparedness and tension bled off. I scowled at him as he stood in the narrow corridor. "Couldn't we have this discussion at home?"

He scowled back. "No."

"Then how in hoolies have I treated you like a child?"

He did not moderate his tone or accusation. "You challenged that sword-dancer. After I told you not to. After I practically *asked.*"

Still bearing my sword—the gods knew when another sword-dancer would come for me—I stepped into the corridor, pulled the door closed. "If we're going to discuss this, let's take it into the common room. At least a man can get a drink as he explains the details to his son, who's entirely incorrect." I was still without burnous. Still in sandals—which I'd neglected to take off when I fell into bed; still in dhoti, harness, earrings, and scars.

Neesha let me pass and followed me out past the kitchen. "Fouad said you'd already had a fair amount of aqivi."

"Yes, I have. Did. But a mug of ale would go down nicely right about now." Neesha wore a belted burnous. I saw him consider taking his off as well, so he could show off his harness and well-conditioned body, but he decided against it.

"Get whatever you want," I said, "and bring a mug over to me. I'll find us a table." At sundown, there were plenty of men scattered throughout the common room. No tables available, but I carried a sword and looked rather intimidating. As expected, two men got up from a corner table almost immediately and retired to one of the deep window sills. I liked it when they did that.

I hooked out a stool and sat down, putting my back to the angled walls. Fouad had lighted the table candle cups in preparation for nightfall. I balanced the sword across my lap beneath the table.

The wine-girls were out in force. They knew better than to approach me—they'd given up on that, thanks to Del—but Neesha was a different story. He politely declined two of them while waiting at the bar for Fouad's attention; after that, disappointed, they left him alone and found other companions.

He came back with two mugs of ale, foam slopping over the rims. He'd never been much for aqivi. He thumped mine down in front of me, sloshing liquid to the table, and found himself a stool. "Fouad said you fought that sword-dancer."

"Did Fouad also say I didn't do the challenging?" Neesha's brows ran up in surprise. "Ah, you didn't bother to ask. You just *decided*."

My son, delaying a response, drank down several gulps of ale. "Well . . . I thought that was why you left for town."

I owed him the truth. "Yeah, sort of. Kind of. But mostly, really, it was for supplies. I just thought I'd deal with both."

Puzzled, his observation was part question. "But you didn't challenge him."

"I did not."

After a moment of consideration, he asked. "Why didn't you?"

I smiled. "Because I decided you need to dance your own dances, and learn your own lessons. Such as being certain there're no horse piss puddles in the circle. Or rain. Or spit. Or anything else wet. I thought I'd taught you that already. Did you forget?"

He had the grace to look abashed. "He annoyed me."

"He made fun of you," I translated. "I know, because he tried it with me, too."

A corner of his mouth jerked wryly. "But you won your dance."

I sucked down ale, wiped the foam from my upper lip. "You'll win plenty. Hoolies, next time you come into town in harness—on a wagon—you might just prevail over the fool who annoys *you*."

He shifted on the stool. "Well, at any rate, I have a suggestion for the school."

Neesha was always full of suggestions. Some of them, occasionally, were even good ones. "Yes?" I asked warily.

"You need to offer a circle with piss puddles in it."

I blinked, then laughed aloud. "Well . . . yes. So I do."

Neesha's smile faded. "Did you tell him? That sword-dancer?"

More ale slid down my throat. "Tell him what?"

"Who I am?"

"What, that you're my son? No. He didn't even know who *I* was, until he saw the bits and pieces and knitted them together. Scars. Missing fingers." I shrugged. "You know. I was just a farmer in harness driving a wagon, aping sword-dancers."

"That's what he said about me," Neesha observed gloomily.

"Yes, well, I don't think Khalid is exactly original. But at any rate, he probably won't make fun of anyone resembling us for a while."

Tension flowed out of his body. "All right. Good. I'm glad you didn't challenge him. It would have been hard to swallow." His attention began to wander. Ale was no longer worth his concentration; neither, apparently, was his father.

"Go on," I said. "One thing I don't need to teach you is how to charm the wine-girls. Or how to lure them into bed. One glance from those eyes of yours takes care of that." He had melting eyes, did Neesha; a warm ale-brown and fringed with thick lashes.

He grinned at me, showing lots of white teeth against his tanned face. And got up laughing as I shooed him away with a gesture. Two of the four wine-girls attached themselves to him at once. I saw scowls tossed Neesha's way by the newly unattended men.

Ah, yes, my son. Definitely my son.

Come morning, I was outside the livery, hitching the team to the wagon and making sure supplies were packed safely. I'd just completed my tasks when Neesha arrived, looking the worse for wear. Dark hair was sticking out here and there, and he moved with a little less grace than usual. Overnight stubble shadowed the angles of jaw and cheekbone. He was in harness, but the burnous over it had been belted haphazardly.

I grinned to myself as I climbed up into the wagon. "Satisfying a woman all night is a taxing job."

He shot me a baleful glare. "Not something you'd remember. With wine-girls, I mean."

Definitely out of sorts, my son. "Are you coming home with me?"

Neesha nodded. He changed course and went into the livery to get his horse and tack. In the meantime, I told my team to be patient and grabbed a full bota. When Neesha came out, leading his horse, I tossed him the bota. "Aqivi," I noted. "Hair of the dog."

He caught the bota and unstoppered it. "You're taking aqivi with us?"

"It has its medicinal qualities."

Neesha grunted and squirted liquor into his mouth. A couple of big swallows, and he restoppered and tossed it back to me. But even somewhat hung over and worn out, his grace in mounting his horse didn't waver. Growing up on a horse farm will do that. Everything is second nature.

"Let's go," I said. "We're burning daylight."

Neesha squinted at the lightening sky. "Does it qualify as daylight yet?"

"Close enough." I clicked my tongue at the team as I took up the reins. "Since you're so all fired up to go on adventures, we should make as many preparations today as possible, so we'll be ready to go tomorrow."

Neesha brought his horse up to ride beside me. "You've changed your tune," he observed. "Now you're in a hurry."

It was true the promise of leaving the canyon for a while appealed now, as it hadn't when Neesha first brought it up. I didn't feel stifled by my duties as a teacher, but it would be nice to get out in the world again. I suspected Del felt the same—or would, once she got over leaving Sula behind. In two years, other than visiting Julah, we hadn't gone anywhere, certainly not with a baby in hand. But Sula would be fine with Lena and Alric. I think she considered them as much her family as Del and me.

We rattled out of town, following the ruts that led toward the canyon. The route was no longer quite as direct as when Del and I first discovered it. We had wanted to avoid the Vashni, a decidedly hostile tribal clan whose territory edged near the nascent road, but we had to approach the boundary to reach the lean-to atop the bluff. One never knew when shelter, or simply a rest, for humans or horses, would come in handy. I thought it possible the Vashni left us alone because Del's brother was their Oracle—they had, after all, accepted him as one of their own. I'd had my dealings with them as well, when one tried to turn me into a dream-walker. But it wasn't wise to be complacent about the appearance of amity. One never knew what the Vashni might do. And their idea of hospitality was to boil uninvited guests in a cauldron.

Through the riverbed that hadn't held water for as long as I knew, then up the bluff to its small plateau. A horse was tied in the thin shade of the trees that edged the bluff. I figured it was a good place to water the team.

Just as I began to climb down from the wagon, a man walked out of the lean-to. Sword-dancer. No burnous, so there was an expanse of abdomen and shoulders naked save for a harness, and bare legs below dhoti. Also bare feet.

And I knew him.

"Challenge," said Khalid.

Oh, hoolies.

I jumped down to the ground. "So now you're giving me a chance to meet you in a circle instead of simply attacking? I thought I had no honor and wasn't deserving of a dance in the circle. Or words to that effect." I'd halted the wagon in the thin copse of trees, near what must be Khalid's horse. I went about the business of getting canvas buckets out of the wagon and two fat botas.

"*I'll* dance with you," Neesha announced to Khalid.

I glanced at him, startled. But Khalid demurred, looking at me. "You're not good enough. I want him."

"Hah," Neesha said. "Afraid to risk losing to me."

This time Khalid looked at him. "There's no risk of that. You were soundly beaten."

Neesha glared at him. "I was beaten because I slipped in a puddle of piss. That's all."

"I don't want you. I want to dance against the Sandtiger."

I unstoppered the botas and poured the contents into both collapsible waxed buckets and placed them close to the team. I slung the botas back into the wagon, then unlaced my sandals, stripped out of my burnous, unbuckled the harness. I placed everything in the wagon. "All right, let's get this over with."

My son was startled. "You're not!"

"I am." I looked at him. "Draw the circle, Neesha."

Khalid started to object, but one glance from me silenced him. He'd already drawn two of them in Julah. Our turn now. He got out of his harness and tossed it into the lean-to, keeping the sword with him.

Neesha jumped down from the saddle and looped reins around a bush. Like me, he watered the horse first, then walked out to the most level section of ground he could find. For my benefit, he made a production out of testing footing. Rocks were kicked aside, wood was tossed away, twigs picked up and deposited elsewhere. Then he took off his sandals and walked the area, muttering something about no puddles. Finally satisfied—though not looking happy about it—he drew his sword from the sheath at his shoulder and set the point into the dirt. He wasted no time; he knew, as did I, as did Khalid, how to draw a circle quickly and accurately. Then he stepped away.

I looked at Khalid. "You're sure you want to do this?"

"Yes."

"Absolutely sure?"

"Yes. I said so."

"Well, as you said to *him*—" I gestured to Neesha with a jerk of my head, "'you were soundly beaten.'"

He put up his chin. "I know that. I—"

I overrode him. "And you want a dance to the death?"

He closed his mouth.

"Remember," I noted, "I let you live last time."

"That was a death-dance. Well, no, it wasn't really a dance, since you have no honor, except you stayed in the circle anyway. It was—"

"I know exactly what it was," I interrupted. "It was an attempt to humiliate a farmer aping sword-dancers. But then you figured out who I was, and the stakes changed. I'm fair game to any sword-dancer because of what I did. And how better to establish yourself than to kill the Sandtiger? Instant credibility." Gripping the hilt, I rested the flat of the blade against my shoulder. "Last time I had a bounty on my head, thanks to Umir, but—"

This time he cut me off. "You still do."

I stared at him.

"You do," he said defensively, as if he thought I didn't believe him.

In exasperation, I asked, "Don't tell me it's Umir again!"

"It's Umir," Khalid said. "Whoever he is."

This annoyed the hoolies out of me, enough that I articulated a rather long litany of swear words. Umir the Ruthless, a very wealthy and powerful tanzeer who liked to collect unusual things—even people—had put a bounty on my head to be taken alive for his little competition. He wanted to hire a sword-dancer, and decided the best way of finding the right man for the job was to hold a competition. Winner got the job of dancing against me. I was supposed to be dessert to the main course. "Umir already paid. He paid off Rafiq," I said. Rafiq and his friends had actually captured me, sick and weakened by sandtiger poison, right here by the lean-to, and delivered me to Umir. "And I killed the winner. And then escaped." Neither of which was what Umir had in mind.

Khalid shrugged. "There's a new bounty, then."

Neesha, who had once been Umir's captive in order to trade him to me in exchange for a book of magic in my possession, swore beneath his breath. "Is he *ever* going to give up?"

Del and I together had once been his so-called guests, too; he'd wanted to add Del to his collection. I began to think Umir had been put on this earth just to annoy me.

I turned and stalked to the trees skirting the edge of the bluff, staring northward toward the Punja. "Umir," I muttered. "Umir. I'm *sick* of Umir!" I swung back around to face Khalid. "You're sure about this. That it's him."

He shrugged. "That's what I was told."

It sounded just like something Umir would do, putting yet another bounty on my head. It had worked before. He'd caught me, but he couldn't keep me.

I wished him to hoolies. I turned and walked back toward the circle, muttering and swearing between gritted teeth. I wanted to hit something, preferably Umir's face. But I did have Khalid to beat up on. That was something.

"In Julah I wanted to kill you," Khalid explained, oblivious to my frustration, "But now I just want to dance. Because if I win, you have to go with me."

"Go with you where?"

His voice rose. "To Umir's! Where do you think?"

Neesha started to answer angrily, but I gestured him to silence with a lifted hand. My attention was on Khalid. "What do you know about him?"

"Just what the sword-dancers told me. That he's a rich tanzeer. But that's why I've decided not to kill you. It's about some kind of a book." He shrugged. "I don't know why a book matters so much, but it does."

"*The Book of Udre-Natha*," I told him. "It's a grimoire, a book of magic. But Umir *has* it. What in hoolies does he want me for?"

"He can't open it."

This was pure aggravation. "Of course he can't open it! I put a spell on it so he couldn't!"

"Well," Khalid said matter-of-factly, "he wants you to take the spell off. At least that's what they told me. So he's put a bounty on your head."

"Wonderful," I muttered. "Half the sword-dancers in the South want to kill me, and the other half want to haul me off to Umir's. Again. Umir and his bounties. It's ridiculous. It's stupid. It's annoying as hoolies."

"Maybe you should just kill him," my son said.

I glared at him. "Umir doesn't dance. He doesn't even fight. He hires people for that. So you're saying I should just ride in there and lop off his head?"

Neesha, clearly defensive, brushed a nonexistent smudge of dirt from his burnous. "Well, it was just an idea."

Khalid raised his voice. "So if I win the dance, but don't kill you, you have to come with me to Umir's."

"Good gods," I said in disgust, "are you a lunatic? Why would I do that?"

"It's stupid," Neesha interjected. "Only a fool would agree to that."

Khalid flicked him a glance of pure venom, then looked back at me. "So, will you swear it?"

"Swear to go with you if I lose?" I very nearly laughed at him. "Why would you want me to swear to anything? I have no honor, remember?"

Khalid remembered. He chewed briefly at his bottom lip. "Then no swearing. Agreement would work."

"And why would you trust my *agreement* any more than my oath? Khalid, you can't win this argument. If you want to dance just to dance, we can do that. But it will have nothing to do with Umir."

He thought that over, then finally nodded. Bounty or no bounty, defeating the Sandtiger was probably worth more in bragging rights.

One should always assess his opponent. I registered Khalid's physique, his posture, the steadiness of hands and eyes. He was somewhat taller than the usual Southroner, somewhat lighter in skin, his eyes were a green-gray color, and his hair was brown, not black. I thought it possible there was some Borderer blood behind him. He looked about the same age as Neesha, which placed him around twenty-five. Young enough to be my son.

Hoolies, I already had one of those. But I had only known about *Neesha* for the last two years. "Is your father really your father?" I asked warily.

Khalid did not know what to make of that. Baffled, he said, "What?"

"Is your father really your father?"

"I don't know!" he declared, clearly frustrated. "Why in hoolies do you care? And what has this to do with a sword-dance?"

"I'd just like to know. I'm curious by nature." A glance at Neesha showed me a somewhat stunned expression. He'd wanted to dance against me, too, before he got around to telling me who he was. I could see him doing the math.

"He wasn't around for my birth," Khalid replied flatly. "Nor ever after. So, I'm a bastard. Does that matter?"

"No," I told him. "So am I. So is my son." I tilted my head in Neesha's direction. "Him."

That startled Khalid. "He's your son?" Then he looked at Neesha. "You're his *son*?"

Simultaneously, Neesha and I answered: "Yes."

Khalid shook his head slightly, clearly in disbelief. Then he cheered up. "So. I defeated the Sandtiger's get."

Neesha glowered at him. "Let's make it two out of three. You've got the one."

"I'll save you for tomorrow," Khalid said airily. "I've got your father to beat today."

It was fixing to be a lengthy dispute between two cocky young men. Sighing, I walked to the center of the circle and set my sword down. I knew this time Khalid wouldn't come after me. He'd dance. I walked back to the edge of the circle. "Any time," I said lightly.

Khalid walked to the center as well and placed his sword next to mine. Once he'd taken his place opposite me, he looked at Neesha. "Say it."

Neesha said it. "*Dance.*"

Chapter 5

IT DIDN'T TAKE LONG. During the second engagement I smashed the sword out of his hands straight to the ground, then butted him just under the ribs with the pommel of my blade. Khalid went down hard, all his breath gone.

It's a scary thing, that. You think you're dying. But then breath begins to come back, after you whoop and gasp for a while. And as he was doing that, I returned to the wagon and sheathed my own blade, laced up my sandals, yanked the burnous over my head, worked the slit over the sword hilt. By the time Khalid was breathing normally again, I was up in the seat, reins gathered and ready to go.

Khalid got slowly to his feet. "You cheated! You're not supposed to do that!"

"What, employ a part of my sword other than the blade? You keep forgetting . . . I'm a man with no honor, and I'll do whatever I like." I glanced at Neesha, who was in the saddle again. "Now," I said firmly, "I don't want to see you again. Ever. We're done. It's over. You're not good enough to even step into a circle with me. I'll beat your ass every time, in any way I can. Do you understand?"

Khalid picked up his sword. "I'll go wherever I want."

I ignored him and looked at Neesha. "You ready?"

At his nod, I clicked to the horse and slapped the reins lightly on their rumps. The way was narrow here; Neesha rode in front while I rattled down from the bluff, heading west.

From behind me, there came a shout. *"I'll go wherever I want!"*

Neesha twisted in his saddle to look back at me. "That was very impressive."

"I meant it to be."

"I've never seen any man disarm an opponent so quickly."

"I was feeling magnanimous. I gave him two engagements, instead of one, before dumping him on his butt."

Neesha laughed. *"That's* humble."

"The Sandtiger," I said decisively, "is never humble."

He quoted me, " 'You're not good enough to even step into a circle with me. I'll beat your ass every time, in any way I can.' "

"He's not, and I will."

"He may not believe you."

"He'd better."

"He's young and stupid."

"He's your age, or close to it."

"But I'm not stupid."

"Look out for that branch."

Neesha whipped his head around, leaned sideways so that the branch only slid over his shoulder, and turned to look back at me. "You could kill him. Then he wouldn't be around to bother you anymore."

I was incredulous. "What *is* it with you? You've become bloodthirsty all of a sudden. Kill Umir, kill Khalid. I don't want to kill anyone!"

"It just seems to me it would solve two problems."

"Well, yes, so it would. But that's not how I'm made."

Neesha grinned. "I didn't think so. Good. I don't want a father who kills without compunction."

"You know me better than that."

The track was wide enough now. Neesha dropped back to ride beside me. "Actually, I don't, you know. It's only been two years since we met, and all you've been doing is teaching. That's only part of the measure of a man."

"And another measure of a man—of *me*—is that I don't just kill people."

"Unless they try to kill you."

I had to agree with that. "Well, yes. It does provide a little motivation in that regard."

"You'll do it again."

"Kill?"

"Kill."

I waved a dismissive hand. "Only if they insist."

Del stared at me in shock. "Umir? *Umir?*"

I pulled a large bag out of the wagon and shouldered it. "That's what *I* said."

She grabbed a smaller bag and followed me into the house. "Umir?"

"Yup. At least, that's what I was told." I set the bag down beside the kitchen wash basin. "I have no reason to disbelieve the kid who told me. Umir's done it before."

"I thought we were all done with him when you traded the book for Neesha."

"So did I. But he is once again making himself a thorn in the ointment."

Del's expression was one she wore whenever a Southron saying was alien to her Northern upbringing. "Ointment doesn't get thorns."

"Thorn in our sides," I amended. "Fly in the ointment." The wagon was now officially unloaded. Neesha had undertaken seeing to the team. "Maybe it's just as well we're going to visit other environs for a while. I don't think it's a secret anymore, where we live." Not now that sword-dancers had come to visit, intending to kill me. Umir's bounty would dedicate even more of them to finding me. Though at least Umir didn't want me dead. "Where's Sula?"

"With Lena. Alric's off hunting dinner."

I grunted. "She's over there so much she may not even miss us."

"Well, I guess that's a good thing if Umir captures us," Del said dryly. "We'd best go practice."

"Practice what?"

She took her sword down from the high-set pegs. "Sparring.

You and me. Students are not what we'll meet in the Punja or even up by the border."

I was still in harness, myself, so I stripped out of my burnous, out of leather and buckles. I unsheathed my sword and hung the harness on one of the pegs. "Why would we go up near the border?"

She already wore her leather tunic. It bared most of long, muscled legs to go with long, muscled arms. "I had a thought."

"Always a dangerous thing."

She ignored my comment, which is about what it was worth. "Neesha's been here two years. I thought maybe it we could go north and visit his mother. The horse farm is near the border."

I followed her out of the house. The suggestion left me speechless. It had never crossed my mind. Visit Neesha's mother? She was the first woman I'd had, on my first night of freedom, away from the Salset and no longer a slave. See her again? The idea made me uncomfortable. I was a long way from the boy she had met. I'd been considerably younger than Neesha then, all of seventeen. Twenty-five years had passed. And Neesha had left her and come to me.

Del's sidelong glance told me my silence had piqued her concern. But my Northern sweetheart, my *bascha*, knew when to let me work through something in my head. She wouldn't suggest it again. She wouldn't even mention it until I'd sorted out my feelings. I'd learned to do it with her as well, though it went against my nature to keep my mouth shut.

"Which circle?" she asked, since there were several.

"Oh, grass I guess. I've danced on dirt twice in the last two days." I unlaced each sandal one-handed, switching the sword from one to the other. "My feet will thank you. And so will you, when you land on your butt." That would make twice in one day. I smiled at the idea. Though I admitted to myself that it would be considerably more difficult to dump Del.

It wasn't a dance, exactly. We didn't place the swords in the middle of the circle, we didn't run on someone's signal to snatch them up. It was sparring. We simply assumed a position opposite one another and began.

As always, it was a long session, with blades flashing in the sunlight, the clangor of metal on metal, the swing of a white-blonde braid, the dazzle of blue eyes utterly focused on me. Del was not distractible. Whomever she met in a circle, in any kind of fight, had her full attention always. Both of us sweated, both of us sucked air, both of us took turns coming out on top for the space of a second or so, before being back in the thick of the session.

I drove her nearly out of the circle. She returned the favor. Never had we settled the question of who was better. Abbu Bensir and I had finally arrived at a conclusion when I killed him, but Del and I just traded victories. The closest we'd come to the real thing was in the North, up with Del's people; we had nearly killed one another. I bore the scar, the lumped tissue and cavity beneath my left-side ribs. Del claimed nearly the same scar on her own body, thanks to me.

My blade met hers. She shifted. For that instant, that tiny, un-remarkable instant, I was just slightly off-balance. I moved a foot to recover it, came down with the ball of my foot on something hard that abruptly rolled sideways; I'd committed my body and went down, landing hard on my butt. The sword fell out of my hand.

Laughter. Loud laughter. The sound of applause. "Hah!" Neesha cried. "A-HAH! Didn't inspect the circle, did you? Didn't make sure nothing would hinder you. Didn't do anything you should have done to prevent that, did you? Hah!"

I looked for it and found it. A stone, about a fourth the size of my fist. It had been hidden in the grass.

"You're dead!" my son exulted. "*You're* dead! The Sandtiger's dead!"

I lofted the stone at him, which he promptly caught. "I'm so glad to provide entertainment for you." I looked at Del, standing in the middle of the circle. Her expression was curiously blank. I'd seen that before. "Oh, go ahead and laugh, bascha. I know what it looked like."

Del forbore to laugh, but she did grin. "And lo," she said, "the Sandtiger is brought down by a stone. An inoffensive, innocent stone, just sunning itself in the grass. What a rude awakening for it, to be stepped on by the greatest sword-dancer in the South."

I pressed myself to my feet, brushing grass from my dhoti. "I suppose this means I have cooking duty."

Del smiled cheerfully *"And* clean-up duty."

Swearing, I grabbed my sword out of the grass and marched myself toward the house. I overheard my son say, "That was beautiful."

"That," Del said, "was luck. But yes, luck can be beautiful when it tips in your direction."

Later, after dinner, as twilight began its downward journey into the canyon, Del joined me outside on the bench beside our door. She handed me a mug.

It wasn't ale. "You found the aqivi."

"I did." She sat close beside me, thigh against thigh, arm against arm. She'd never been fond of aqivi, saying it made me foolish. But now she said, "It has medicinal qualities."

I grinned and drank.

"So, Umir wants you to open the book."

I swallowed aqivi. I was accustomed to it again; and no, it did not make me foolish. Well, maybe too much of it, but I didn't do that anymore. I mean, the last time, in the cantina, I went to bed, which is never foolish. Especially when you don't take a wine-girl to that bed. That *would* be foolish, with Del at home. Also unnecessary. Maybe worse than foolish, in fact. Possibly dangerous where my head was concerned.

"Umir wants me to open the book."

"But you used magic to lock it. To make it so he couldn't open it, couldn't use it."

I sighed deeply. "So I did. At the time I considered it a very clever idea."

"It was. But . . ."

"But?"

"You don't have magic in you anymore, thank all the gods. *Can* you open it?"

"No." I'd poured into my sword all the magic ioSkandi—with its stone spires and collection of lunatic mages—had awakened in my bones, and then I broke it. Left it. Far as I knew, Del's sword and my sword both lay inside a collapsed chimney-like rock formation outside the first canyon where Mehmet and his aketni lived. I was empty of magic. Being so was what I very much preferred; it freed me to live many more years than ten. IoSkandic magic and madness killed a man too soon.

The first stars crept out of the deepening twilight. A glow on the high rim of the canyon promised moonrise. Before us, in the fire ring, embers glowed. The scent of roasted venison drifted into the air as the spit dripped leavings. I had never in my life known such peace as I did in this canyon, at our Beit al'Shahar. Once, I'd have denied any suggestion that I would settle, raise a family, stay put in one place. The long view I'd held promised me only sword-dancing interspersed with occasional caravan guarding, other temporary employment. I'd expected to die in the circle one day. It was what all of us did, eventually. Or got hurt badly enough that we had to stop dancing, a death in itself. Few of us died in bed.

"You're of no use to Umir if you can't open the book," Del said quietly.

Dryly, I observed, "Well, that presupposes he manages to catch me first and learn that. I, of course, am counting on you to help prevent my capture."

"I'm your bodyguard."

"So you are."

Del's voice hardened. "He needs to be dead."

I sighed, peering into my mug to see if an insect had drowned itself in the contents. I tipped the mug toward the firelight to capture some light. "You and Neesha. I have somehow surrounded myself with bloodthirsty people."

"He keeps capturing you."

"I'm not the only one," I said, aggrieved. "He captured you, he captured Neesha."

"Yes. And to prevent any more capturing, he needs to be dead."

This was aggravating. "As I told Neesha, I am not going to just ride in there and lop off his head. He's too well-guarded. I'd have to make my way through an army of sword-dancers to get anywhere near him. Head-lopping would be difficult. Hoolies, I might even get *my* head lopped off."

Del said with some asperity, "Well, I'm not suggesting you do the head-lopping by yourself. There's me. There's Neesha. We could probably even borrow Alric."

"For head-lopping?" I shook my head. "Lena would never let him go. And he listens to her."

"More than you listen to me," she observed. "But then, he's a Northerner. Northern men are more respectful of women. They listen to their women."

I ignored the provocation. I'd learned I could never win those debates. "Alric's got to stay here to help Lena. They'll have our daughter, remember."

"Well, yes." Del thought things over for a moment. "All right. Three of us. We'd have two who claim to be the greatest sword-dancer in the South, and—"

I interrupted. "Two? Who's the one besides me? Abbu's dead."

"Me. I may be a Northerner, but I live in the South. And there's Neesha. He's doing well, Tiger. Someday *he'll* be the greatest sword-dancer in the South."

"Well, not yet!"

"I said 'someday,' did I not? But in the meantime, one of us should really kill Umir. He's a thorn in our ointment."

I laughed. "Such a kind, gentle woman, my bascha."

"Oh, I don't think so, Tiger. That would be very boring."

Chapter 6

NOT LONG AFTER DAWN, as morning mist lifted, I carried the littlest of us out of the house. Del and I had let Sula sleep in our bed with us for a bit, the night before. She was still sleepy, with mussed hair and a crease-line running down the right side of her face. I held her against my chest, and she set her head on my shoulder as I walked toward Alric's and Lena's.

"Will you be good?" I asked.

She didn't answer.

"You have to be good," I told her. "You'll be a guest of the house. Guests must have manners."

She lifted her head, rubbed the side of it with a fist, and met my eyes with her mother's eyes, though blurry with sleep. Then she said something that was totally incomprehensible and laid her head back down against my shoulder. I just grinned and carried her onward.

Del walked up from the creek, carrying freshly filled botas. She placed them on a bench, by a door very like our own, and put out her arms. I passed to her the dead weight of our daughter, a dead weight that weighed hardly anything. You could blow her away like a dandelion.

In a low voice Del spoke to Sula in Northern, her lips very close to the tangled hair. She was clearly torn by the prospect of going back out into the world we'd known for so long, and leaving her daughter behind. But there was no place for Sula in this. We weren't caravaners. We were sword-dancers and ran the risk, all three of us, at any time, of being killed.

Lena was in the doorway, smiling as Del wished her daughter good health—and good manners—while we were gone. In Southron, now, she explained to our drowsy offspring that we would come back to her, back to the life we had built within the confines of a beautiful canyon. Back to our home.

It was Lena's turn to take her. Sula did not object to being passed from one to another to another. It was true she looked on Lena and Alric as parents almost as much as she did us, to the point of making a wobbly break for next door if Del and I found it necessary to discipline her. She was certain Alric and Lena would rescue her, though they never did. She was ours to chastise. Ours to love.

Del cupped Sula's head in her hands and gave her a kiss on her forehead. Then she gathered up the botas, slung them over her shoulder, and strode back to our house. I smiled crookedly at Lena, whose expression told me she knew all too well what Del was feeling.

"Go on," she said. "Sula will be well. Del won't be for the first couple of days. But it will lessen a little as she's distracted." Lena smiled crookedly. "Some of the time."

I nodded, leaned close to give Sula a quick kiss, then turned my back on them both. I felt a twinge of regret myself and a faint undertone of anxiety. There was so much to live for now. So much more to live for. More than I had ever expected to reside in my heart, my soul.

Then I told myself to get to work. We were burning daylight.

Well, to be completely accurate, we were burning dawn.

Del, Neesha, and I haltered our horses and led them out of the pole corral. Del still had her white horse, but no longer did he wear a wine-girl's scarlet tassels to shield pale blue eyes against the sun. She had made a headpiece out of soft indigo-dyed leather strips, quite fine and narrow, almost like long fringe. It also served to keep the flies away from his eyes.

My horse needed no such thing. My horse sported a rather luxuriant black forelock to do that work. He was dun with a dark line running down his back from withers to rump. At the end of that line over his rump was a coarse black tail that just at this moment was being whipped back and forth with some force. The stud, as always, had an opinion. Especially in the mornings.

Blanket, saddle, saddle pouches packed with supplies—he bore all these without complaint as, one by one, I attached them to him. He made no complaint when I swapped out halter for headstall, bit, and reins. Then the halter on top, customary for journeys. One might be glad of his quiet acquiescence, except I knew it did not bode well.

Neesha was already aboard his dark bay horse. He was grinning in anticipation. I shot him a scowl and was rewarded by a wider grin. In fact, he swung his right leg over the saddle pommel in front of him and took his ease, arms crossed, knowing his own exceptionally well-trained horse wouldn't do anything except stand there quietly, waiting for directions from its human.

Sighing, I led the stud out, away from the house and corral. I swung the left rein up over his neck and stuck a foot into the stirrup then pulled myself up and over, reins gathered short, and steeled myself.

The stud didn't do anything.

"*Oh* no," I said. "You're not going to lull me into a false sense of security."

He pulled against gathered rein, stuck his head down, and shook it. Then he shook everything else, including me. I hated that. It hurt to have my head, spine, and neck snapped inside out.

He stood still. I waited. Finally I ventured a question "Are you done?"

Of course not.

He stuck his head up in the air, dropped it, bent his spine upward, tail slashing back and forth, and proceeded to back up rather swiftly. Which was not the direction in which I wished to go. "Quit," I said. I glanced over my shoulder to see if we were approaching anything, person, or horse—possibly even a house and furniture—that might trip us up. "*Quit.*"

So he stopped backing up and moved forward, stomping as he went, trying to yank the reins out of my hand. Horses are powerful, and stallions more powerful yet. It was always a fight to control a snuffy stud-horse. Especially this one.

Eventually, as I applied pressure to the bit, he hopped up and down. Stiff-legged. Which caused me to swear most vehemently.

Then Neesha appeared. He leaned down from his saddle, caught one of the stud's reins to control his head, and quietly asked, "Is this any way for a well-mannered horse to act?"

Well-mannered, my ass.

"We discussed this," Neesha continued. "This is not the way to treat the man who feeds you. And his bones are old. They'll break."

I gritted my teeth. But Neesha had grown up on a horse farm, and he'd conquered the stud the first day he met him. He conquered him now. The stud blew out one tremendous, breathy, damp snort, and settled. All the protest died out of him. I could feel it go.

"My old bones still have a lot of life left in them," I muttered, "and I had him under control, thank you very much."

"*I* know that. He doesn't." Neesha released the rein and sat upright in his saddle again. "So, where are we going?"

"This was your idea," I reminded him sharply, still disgruntled. "Don't you have a place in mind?"

"Well, no. I didn't think you'd agree to go."

I glanced at Del, who'd finger-painted black circles around her horse's eyes to cut down on the sun glare. Now she was in the saddle, blacking pot tucked away, saying nothing. Her face was expressionless. She just waited to see if I'd settled on her suggestion or ignored it utterly.

I looked back at Neesha. "Let's go north. Let's go visit your mother."

His mouth fell open. "My mother?"

I used Del's argument. "It's been two years."

"Yes, but . . ." He trailed off and ruminated a moment, frowning faintly, eyes gone blank. Finally he came back to himself and met my eyes. "All right."

A sudden thought struck me. "She wouldn't try to beat me up with a shovel, would she? Or hit me over the head with a stool?"

"No." He was utterly baffled. "Why would she do either of those things?"

"Well, I slept with her one night, then left the next morning. And she'd never been with any man before. I'm sure she had better dreams than that for her first time."

Neesha made a dismissive gesture. "Oh, no, she understood. She told me about that. She didn't expect you to stay. Admittedly, she didn't expect to conceive, but she did, and she said I was worth it." He paused. "I am."

"*That's* humble," I said, echoing something he'd said the day before.

Neesha laughed. "Oh, but the Sandtiger's cub is never humble."

Del observed, "If we stay here any longer, we may as well go back to bed."

I made an expansive gesture. "Lead on."

She rode by me on her white, blue-eyed gelding. The stud reached out to bite him. I smacked him on top of his head. "Don't be rude."

The big oasis was a popular stopping place for folk of all kinds, from single families to caravans hauling goods and people, nomadic tribes, merchants, any number of others on business of their own, guides hoping to be hired, and sword-dancers also looking for work as caravan outriders or settlers of disputes. Tanzeers knew to send servants here to find such sword-dancers. It was a place of palm trees weighted with heavy ribbed fronds, dripping dates in season; trees with frothy limbs, wide canopies, thorns, spiked bark; succulent ground vegetation, such as alla plants, growing in the shade; catclaw, creosote, cactus; even tough, webby grasses rooted so deeply that sand didn't block their growth. Shade was sought and treasured, but the most significant attraction was water. Here, an underground stream bubbled up between a drift of half-buried stone, surrounded by a short man-made wall built of rocks and mudbrick.

I had been here countless times on my own, and occasionally with Del; with Neesha, once, when we rescued him from Umir by trading him for the *Book of Udre-Natha*—part of Umir's eclectic collection of things for which he conceived a desire, though perhaps *obsession* was a better word. Once, that had been Del. I, on the other hand, he merely wanted to kill.

It was near sundown, which meant that sites beneath almost all of the trees had been claimed already by various travelers. The smell of roasting meat, yeasty bread, spices, and pungent liquor blocked other smells. We rode the path through the oasis and fetched up at the spring. All three of us swung off our horses, but Neesha held back as Del and I led our mounts to the spring. There wasn't enough room for all of our horses; another burnous-clad man watered two oxen on the other side. He marked the swords jutting up behind our shoulders, saw clearly that Del was a woman, and immediately goaded his oxen from the spring.

I turned to tell Neesha there was room to water his horse, but he had disappeared. Likely looking for an acceptable area to bed down. We wouldn't need shade at night, but it would nonetheless be nice to have a tree of our own.

"I wonder," I commented, "if our friend with the oxen departed because we are sword-dancers or because you're a woman."

Del shrugged as she allowed the gelding to dip his head down into the water. "Probably because of me. I'm foreign to Southroners still, *and* I wear a sword-dancer's harness. How dare I? How dare I go against everything they've ever been taught? How dare I take on a man's role by stepping into the circle?"

No longer was there bitterness is her tone when she spoke of such things. Del had not—and would not—accept that every woman in the South was expected to serve men, but she also had learned to pick her battles. One woman at a time.

I brought the stud in next to the gelding, and leaned down with a gourd scoop to bring water to my mouth. "Of course it could be me. People do recognize me."

"It's the scars," a male voice said. "And missing fingers. And the Northern woman who rides with you."

I looked up, then violently dashed the contents of the gourd back into the water. "No," I said. "*Oh*, no. Not again. Didn't you learn anything? Don't you recall what I said?"

Khalid's jaw was tight. "That I wasn't good enough to even step into a circle with you."

"Yes," I declared, seriously exasperated. "That's exactly what I said. I meant you to heed it."

Though the sun was going down, I could still see his face and his expression. He glared at me. "I don't want to step into a circle with you."

I blurted a rough laugh. "Well, that's the first smart thing I've heard you say. But why in hoolies are you here?"

With some belligerence, he said, "It's an oasis. Anyone can come here. And I told you I'd go wherever I wanted."

I shook my head in disgust. "What did you do, run your horse all the way to get here before us?"

Del's voice was very quiet. "Who is this fool?"

And I remembered that she had never seen Khalid. Only I had, and Neesha. "This fool," I said, "challenged Neesha to a dance. And he cheated. He—"

"I didn't cheat!" Khalid, stung, raised his voice over mine. "I tricked him, yes, but that is something all of us can do, who dance. *He* was the fool for not examining the circle before we began."

"Well," Del observed, "then it's not entirely accurate to accuse him of cheating, Tiger."

Khalid looked at her warily, not certain if or why she was agreeing with him.

Neesha appeared out of the setting sun, leading his unsaddled, unpacked horse. His tone was exquisitely dry. "Are we inviting him to dinner?"

Khalid sneered. "I wouldn't eat with you."

"Then why are you here?" I asked. "Neither of us will dance with you, so it makes no sense for you to follow us."

"I've danced with him." He meant Neesha. "And I've danced with you." Now Khalid looked at Del. "This time, I challenge her."

"No," Neesha and I said simultaneously.

"Excuse me," Del said pointedly. "I accept or reject my own dances."

"He's a fool," Neesha blurted.

"Sandsick," I said.

"A fool, sandsick; neither matters." Del met Khalid's eyes. "Tomorrow.

Khalid inclined his head. "Tomorrow." And then he stalked away.

"Well," Del observed, "at least one Southroner doesn't care if I'm a woman, only if I can dance. Progress."

I scowled at her as I backed the stud away, leaving room for Neesha's horse. "Beat his ass, bascha."

"Of course," she said matter-of-factly.

Neesha had found us a tree. There was even a fire ring beneath it, but it wasn't lighted since there were no coals, and we didn't feel like kindling a flame for cooking. We had perfectly good food in our saddle pouches. We ate the fresh meat first, rather than the dried and salted supply from the house stores. All of us were greasy-fingered within moments. Del used a rag to wipe her mouth. Neesha and I resorted to the backs of our hands.

"How far do we have to go to reach your mother's place?" I asked around a finger as I sucked fat from it. And its neighbor.

"Two days, unless the weather stops us," Neesha answered, wiping his chin. "There's another stopping place, though much smaller. We can reach it tomorrow night, if we push."

I gnawed on the joint bone, then leaned over to spit out gristle. "Well, it depends on how quickly or how slowly Del defeats our friend tomorrow."

"I won't waste time."

I'd told her, in great detail, how things had gone, first with Neesha then with me.

"We'll make Neesha's stopping place," she said.

"It's much smaller," Neesha noted. "There won't be as many people, if any. But there's good water."

"And I take it you've got water at the horse farm."

He nodded. "It's close to the border. More water, lusher vegetation, good grass. My stepfather raises horses of a quality many people travel to see. And if they've got the price, they buy."

"If they're anything like the one you ride, indeed the quality is good," Del told him.

Neesha smiled proudly. "I raised this one from a colt. He's eight now and ready to be serious. My father—" he caught himself, "my *step*father said I should not grow too attached, because the colt would likely be sold. But when a buyer asked for him, my mother said he wasn't for sale. My stepfather wanted to argue, but of course you don't do that in front of a buyer. Afterward, when the buyer had taken a different horse and my fa—*step*father addressed the topic with my mother, he lost the argument. And so the horse was mine." Neesha glanced over at the hobbled bay, who nosed contentedly at grain and grass.

"That man raised you," I said briefly. "And if you called him 'father' for all of your life prior to finding me, you should continue to call him that."

My son stared down at the bota in his lap, giving away nothing in his expression. Then he looked up to meet my eyes and dipped his head in a nod.

"Good." I washed down the meat with a slug of bota water, then said I was turning in. I mentioned that Del might want to as well, considering she had a dance in the morning. She was willing, and Neesha said he'd check on the horses.

It wasn't necessary, but Del and I both knew why he did it. We unrolled our blankets, flattened folds, and lay down, burrowing together for warmth. In the distance I heard the scream of a sandtiger, the yips of desert dogs.

"That was well done," she said very quietly; the horses were not picketed particularly far away.

"What?—oh." I spoke as quietly. "Well, the man is more his father than I am."

"Neesha has much to think about. He has found you, found his dream of wishing to be a sword-dancer."

I couldn't argue with that. It was far safer living on a horse farm than dancing, but being safe was not what aspiring sword-dancers desired. Neesha might well have sought the life even if he weren't my son, but he was, and he had tracked me down. He'd taken a handful of lessons from Abbu Bensir, when Abbu stopped over at the horse farm, and had spent much of his life practicing the forms; first those he made up, then those Abbu taught him. But I had beaten him in the circle, my son. Beaten him badly.

Which put me in mind of another young man who'd danced with me and lost. I shifted closer to Del, speaking very softly. "You don't think he's my son, do you?"

It startled Del, though she spoke as softly. "Neesha's your son!"

"No, no—not Neesha. The fool. Khalid."

"Why would you think he's your son?"

"Because he's doing very much what Neesha did, insisting on dancing against me. And now that I know Neesha's in the world, there could be more offspring scattered throughout the South."

"Don't brag, Tiger."

"Hoolies, Del, you know as well as I do that before I met you, I wasn't exactly chaste."

"You weren't chaste even after you met me. I remember the caravan and Elamain."

"Who?"

"Elamain. The woman we guarded on the way to her wedding."

It took me a moment. It had been about six years since Del and I met. "Oh. Her."

"Yes. Her."

"I was a fool, bascha. And then I wasn't anymore."

"No. You gained wisdom, once I beat it into your head."

I grinned into darkness.

"Go to sleep," she whispered. "Neesha's coming back."

I wished her goodnight and allowed myself to fall off the precipice. Sleep is a good thing.

Chapter 7

DEL WAS UP AT DAWN. I woke up when she threw her covers back, but did not immediately join her. I knew what she was about.

The forms. The sheer grace of preparing a body to dance. Muscles warmed, loosened; the body's agreement that it would do what it was told. When she was done, Del smiled. A sidelong glance told me she knew I was watching. She raised her brows in a question.

"Yes," I said. "All right. You approve or reject your own dances. Point taken. And, I daresay, you will put that boy on his butt."

"I've decided to teach him a lesson," she said. "Nothing done too quickly. Nothing done so hastily that he can't understand what's being done to him. He needs to learn what it is he needs to learn."

Before I untangled that, Neesha poked his head out from under blankets. He rubbed one eye. "What did I miss?"

Del smiled.

"Everything." I flipped the blankets all the way back and stood up from my bedding. "I assume the idiot will be here soon. I'm going to go visit a bush now, so I don't miss anything."

"Oh," Neesha said. "Me also."

And as we moved with alacrity around the wide-canopied tree, the stud let loose a river to remind us of what we were about.

She moved beautifully, did my bascha. Her feet sluffed through the sand with the soft, seductive sibilance of bare flesh against fine-grained dust. Wisps rose, drifted; layered our bodies in dull, gritty shrouds: pale umber, ocher-bronze, taupe-gray.

Dawn had passed. All was clear now, in the newborn sunlight. As I drew the circle, the news was passed: a woman danced against a man. Some men, Southroners, laughed, disbelieving it. Khalid had walked over naked except for dhoti. And he carried an un-sheathed sword.

The dance began as all dances do: two swords in the center of the circle, a sword-dancer on either side. This time, I was given the task of telling them to begin.

I watched her move. I watched the others watch her move. All men. No women here, at this moment, under such circumstances; never a woman.

Except for Del.

Admiration, as always. And pride. Two-edged pride. One, that the woman brought honor to the ritual of the dance within the circle, and two, that she was my right hand, my left hand; companion, swordmate, bedmate. Pride is always a two-edged blade. When it concerns Del, the second edge is the sharpest of all for *me*, because for the Sandtiger to speak of pride in Del is to speak also of possessiveness. She'd told me once that a man proud of a woman is too often prouder of his *possession* of her, and not of the woman for herself.

I saw her point, but . . . well, Del and I don't always agree. But then, if we did, life would be truly boring.

"Gods," Neesha said in wonder. "I've never seen her like this."

I nodded. "You've seen her spar in order to teach. This is Del dancing."

I watched the man she faced in the circle. Khalid showed more skill than he had before, and Southron-style: dip here, feint there, slash, lunge, cut, thrust . . . and always trying to throw the flashes and glints into her eyes; ordinarily, a shrewd ploy. Khalid displayed some experience. But while another opponent might have winced or squinted against the blinding light, giving over the advantage, Del didn't.

I knew she could kill him if she wished, though Khalid didn't. He hadn't realized it yet.

Few men realize it when they enter the circle with Del. They see only the tall Northern woman with thick white-blond hair braided back, and blue, blue eyes; her perfect face with its sun-gilded flesh stretched taut across flawless bones. They see all of that, and her magnificent body, and they hardly notice the sword in her hands. Instead, they smile. They feel tolerant and magnanimous, because they face a woman, and a beautiful woman. And because she is beautiful they will give her anything, if only to share a moment of her time, and so they give her their lives.

But she wasn't here to kill Khalid.

She danced. Long legs, long arms, bared to the Southron sun. *Step. Step. Slide. Skip.* Miniscule shifting of balance from one hip to the other. Sinews sliding beneath the flesh of her arms as she parried and riposted. All in the wrists with Del. A delicate tracery of blade tip against the afternoon sky, blocking Khalid's weapon with a latticework of steel.

"Hoolies," Neesha whispered. "She's playing with him."

"She's not," I told him. "This is a lesson. Whether he will heed it is up to him."

Neesha shook his head, spellbound.

"You did wager on her, didn't you?"

Neesha's mouth twisted. "I thought it might not be polite."

"To wager on Del while everyone else—except me, of course—is wagering on Khalid? Hoolies, kid, Del and I made a living for nearly a year doing this. I thought you were smarter than that!"

Neesha scowled. "Apparently not."

I agreed wholeheartedly. "Apparently not."

"Sword-dancer?" The question came from a man who stepped up next to me, slipping out of the crowd to stand closer to me than I liked. "Sandtiger?"

I glanced briefly. Young man. Copper-skinned. Swathed in a rich silk burnous of melon orange, sashed with a belt of gold-freighted bronze. A small turban hid most of his dark hair, but not the fringe of dark brown lashes surrounding hazel eyes.

"Sandtiger?" he asked again, hands tucked into voluminous sleeves.

"Sandtiger," I agreed, still watching the dance.

He sighed a little and smiled. The smile faded; he realized my attention was mostly on the circle, not on him. For just an instant, anxiety flickered in his eyes. "My master offers gold to the sword-dancer called the Sandtiger."

There was a time I'd have given him my full attention at once. But now Del and I owned two-thirds of a cantina, and earning coin by dancing wasn't quiet as vital as it had been. "Can we talk later? I'm a little busy."

"Of great urgency, my lord Sandtiger. My master waits to speak with you."

I didn't answer at once. Too much noise. All the indrawn breaths of the onlookers reverberated as one tremendous hiss of shock and disbelief. Well, I could have warned them . . . I glanced at Del, automatically evaluating her condition. Her face bore a faint sheen of sweat. She was sun-flushed, lips only slightly parted. Her breathing was even. Khalid hadn't offered her much at all. He lay sprawled in the sand, dust sticking to every inch of bared flesh. His chest heaved as he sucked air.

"He'll never live this down," Neesha observed. He looked at the robed, turbanned man. "What business have you?"

"With my lord Sandtiger."

I couldn't help but grin at the expression on Neesha's face as he was dismissed so swiftly.

Del turned and looked at me. The sword hung loosely in her hand. She hunched one shoulder almost imperceptibly—a comment; an answer to my unspoken question on whether she was all right—and then she nodded, only once; an equally private exchange.

I turned back to the messenger. A servant, I was certain, but not just any servant. Whoever his master was, his wealth was manifest. And in the South, wealth is synonymous with power.

"Yes?" I asked.

The hazel eyes were fixed on Del as she cleaned her sword. Onlookers huddled and muttered among themselves, settling bets. None were winners, I knew—not even my foolish son. Only the one wise man who knew her better than most. Many drifted away from the circle entirely, away from the woman who had defeated a man in a supremely masculine occupation with supremely "masculine" skill.

Khalid got up, shook sand out of his hair and, red-faced, inclined his head. Del nodded back, accepting his retirement from the circle.

I smiled a little. The servant looked back at me. He didn't smile at all. "A *woman*," he said. Two words full of disbelief, shock, a trace of anger as well. Underlying hostility: *a woman had beaten a man.*

"A woman," I agreed blandly. "And what is it you wish to speak to me about?"

He pulled himself together. "My master extends an invitation for you to take tea with him. I am not authorized to inform you of the employment he has to offer. Will you come?"

Tea. Not one of my favorite drinks. Especially effang tea, gritty, thick, offensive, but customary in the South. Maybe I could talk the man into some aqivi, now that I was drinking it again. But it wasn't entirely my decision.

I glanced at Neesha, who shrugged. "The horse farm will be there when we're done. And this might be an adventure."

I laughed, then looked back at the short man. "There are three of us," I said. "Including the woman."

He was torn. Utterly torn. "Will you come without her?"

"I will not."

He sighed deeply and began to turn away. Then he swung back. A hint of desperation showed in his face. "The woman comes."

"And me," Neesha added.

The servant barely looked at him. He gestured expansively, one smooth hand sweeping out of its silken sleeve. "This way, my lord Sandtiger."

I grinned at Neesha as I followed the man.

Rather than Umir's sprawling brick palace, this tanzeer currently occupied a series of elaborate tents. And we did not see him immediately. Well, *we* didn't see him at all—only I was given the honor of stepping into the man's presence. And what he desired of me might indeed qualify as one of Neesha's adventures. But I didn't think it was one we could accept.

When I was guided back to the guest tent, I found Del and my son ensconced comfortably on low divans, nearly buried in colorful tribal pillows, picking black grapes off a cluster and eating pale green melon chunks.

"You started without me?" Half of me was serious. I sat down on the edge of Del's divan and began dining on various kinds of fruit. Wine was also offered in a ceramic carafe. I tasted it and nearly spat it out; too sweet for me.

Neesha had no patience. "Well?"

I ate a little more. Then sighed. "He's the tanzeer of Hafiz, which is where we are. A small domain, yet wealthy; next door to Dumaan, also small, but not wealthy." The South was full of domains large and small. Basically, it depended on who was strong enough to keep his patch of dirt and sand. "But there might be a slight problem with this. We might want to consider continuing our journey to your mother's place."

Neesha frowned. "Why? Coin is coin. Does he want us to kill someone?"

I shook my head.

"Well then," he said, "what's the problem?"

"He's a khemi."

"*Oh*," Neesha said after a moment. "Uh-oh."

Del frowned at us both. "What? What do I not know?"

I sighed. "It's a religious sect. An offshoot of the Hamidaa faith. Hamidaa hold majority here in Hafiz."

She nodded acknowledgment, but the frown didn't fade.

"Khemi are zealots," I explained. "They take the word of the Hamidaa'n—the sacred scrolls of the Hamidaa—rather literally."

She narrowed her eyes. "And what does the Hamidaa'n say?"

I cleared my throat. "That women are abominations, unclean vessels that should not be touched, spoken to, or allowed to enter a khemi's thoughts."

Silence. Neesha stopped chewing, waiting for Del's reaction.

"Pretty conclusive," she observed after a moment. "Can't be too many khemi left, if they don't have congress with women."

She was taking it better than I'd expected. "I imagine they've figured out a few loopholes, since the job involves a son. Ordinarily I'd have turned it down, of course, since I do have *some* sensibilities, after all, but, well, it's not entirely up to me."

Neesha was puzzled. "Just what *is* this job?"

"We are expected to negotiate the release of this son, who was kidnapped two months ago."

"Negotiate." Del nodded. "That means steal back. Who, how, and when?"

"Name's Dario," I said. "Soon as possible."

"Of course," Del said dryly. "But that's the who and the when. What about the how?"

"Haven't gotten that far. I wanted to leave something for you and Neesha to contribute."

"Hoolies," Neesha said, reaching for the wine carafe. "I have no idea. Steal back a kid?"

"We stole you," I reminded him.

"You *traded* for me," Neesha clarified. "I'm worth a book."

"You're worth a grimoire," I said. "A book of magic. Better than just *a* book."

"Ah," he said. "Certainly it's better if my life is worth more than *a* book."

Del smiled briefly, but she was more interested in the central topic. "I imagine this khemi had an explanation for why his son was kidnapped in the first place."

"Claims the neighboring tanzeer of Dumaan took the boy to force trade concessions. And Hafiz is more than willing to pay handsomely." I pulled the leather purse out of a pocket in my russet burnous and rattled the contents. "Half up front, half after."

"Sounds easy enough," Neesha observed. "When do we leave?"

"About a half hour ago."

Chapter 8

REZ WAS A SMALL ENOUGH TOWN, capping a domain not much larger. No wonder the tanzeer of Dumaan had deemed it necessary to go to such dramatic lengths as kidnapping to get concessions from Hafiz's tanzeer. Hafiz was a rich domain. Hafiz had wealth to spare. Dumaan wasn't and didn't.

Del, Neesha, and I did a careful reconnoitering of Rez, locating the puny palace and paying strict attention to the comings and goings of palace servants. It is the servant population that forms the heart of any tanzeer's palace; subsequently, it is the servant population that forms the heart of any city, town, village. You don't see a tanzeer without first seeing his loyal servants, any more than you break into a tanzeer's palace without first figuring out how to get past his loyal servants.

A day spent taking turns loitering outside the ramshackle walls of the dilapidated palace with the rest of the bored petitioners gained us a little information. We now knew one thing was certain: Rez's tanzeer didn't subscribe to the same religion Hafiz's did. Or there wouldn't be female servants on marketing expeditions. And there *certainly* wouldn't be harem girls.

It was Del who came up with the idea. Neesha and I mostly watched the silk-swathed women spill out of the palace gates, giggling among themselves like children. Hoolies, for all I knew they *were* children; the silk burnouses hid everything save hands and sandaled feet, and the hands clutched at bright draperies eagerly, unwilling to share with the petitioners what the tanzeer saw any time he wanted. They were accompanied by three men in correspondingly bright silks and turbans; eunuchs, I knew, judging by bulk and Southron custom.

As we watched, Del considered. And then she guided us off into the labyrinthine market stalls and explained her plan.

Since she wouldn't let either of us talk, I did, in silence, what I could to dissuade her. I shook my head repeatedly, vehemently rejecting her suggestion. Neesha looked from one to the other of us.

Finally, Del stopped and glared at me. "Have you a better idea? Or *any* idea at all?"

I scowled. "That's unfair. I haven't had time to think of one."

"No. You've been too busy ogling harem girls. Both of you." She motioned us to be quiet and stay put. "Wait here while I get the things we need." And she was gone.

Disgruntled, I waited in the shade of a saffron-dyed canvas awning, out of direct sunlight. The Southron sun can leach the sense from your head if you stay in it too long; I wondered if it had finally gotten to Del's Northern brains.

Neesha moved up beside me. "I don't see how this will work."

"You should have said so," I observed sourly.

"She wouldn't have listened to me."

I grunted. "Half the time she doesn't listen to me."

"Oh, that's not true."

I scowled at him. "Whose side are you on?"

"Oh, neither side," Neesha said. "I learned it's best for me to remain in the middle if you two argue."

Del came back a while later lugging an armload of silks and spent several minutes laboriously separating them until she had apparel sorted out. And then I began to understand.

"Del—"

"Put the clothes on. Both of you." She plopped a creamy silken turban down on top of the pile in my arms, then thrust amber-hued clothing, and turban into Neesha's chest. "We're going into the palace as soon as we're dressed."

I gritted my teeth. "You want us to masquerade as eunuchs."

Neesha was startled. "You do?"

"Neither of you can masquerade as a harem girl, can you? You're too tall. You have to be eunuchs."

"You're not a whole lot shorter, you know."

"Ah, but I have breasts."

Neither Neesha nor I could come up with a good riposte to that.

A smile curved the corners of her mouth. "Get dressed. We'll be in and out in no time with Dario in tow. And don't forget to use the veil to cover the bottom half of your faces. Eunuchs don't have beard stubble."

"The khemi may have the right idea about you women," I muttered in disgust, staring at the clothing in my arms.

Neesha asked plaintively, "How does a eunuch act?"

"Probably not much different from the Sandtiger or his son." Her words were muffled behind the multitudinous robes she was bundling herself into. "Ready?"

Neesha and I hadn't even begun to put on the bright silks.

"Hurry," she urged. "We have to insinuate ourselves into that flock of Southron sillies. And they're due to come by here about— *now*. Tiger, Neesha—come *on*—"

Silks whipping, tassels flying, Del hastened after the women as they bobbed and weaved their way through the narrow stallways on their way back to the palace. Hastily we jerked on our eunuch's robes, slapped turbans on our heads, hid swords in silk, exchanged glances of resignation, and went after her.

We passed guard after guard on our way into the palace. Del fit in with the other girls well enough—though a head taller than most— but *I* felt about as innocuous as a sandtiger in a flock of day-old goats, and Neesha clearly didn't believe we could pull this off. Nonetheless, no one paid much attention as we paraded down the corridors of the musty old palace.

I wasn't certain I *liked* being taken so easily for a eunuch.

I watched as Del in her rose-colored robes allowed the other girls to move ahead of her. Now we brought up the rear. I saw Del's quick hand gesture; we ducked out going around the next bend and huddled in a cavernous doorway.

"All right," she murmured. "We've passed four corridors. I overheard that Dario's supposed to be in a room off the fifth. Come on."

Sighing, I followed as she darted out of the doorway and headed down the appropriate corridor at a run. Neesha was behind me. I *didn't* run, but only because I decided it was not in keeping with a eunuch's decorum.

We caught up to her outside yet another doorway. This one bore a large iron lock attached to the handle. "Dario?" I asked.

Del shrugged. "This is what I heard one of the women say."

I glanced around the corridor uneasily. "Fine. *You* trust them, then. Did they slip you a key as well?"

"I already had one." She displayed it. "I borrowed it from the same eunuch who donated his clothing to you."

"Can we hurry up?" Neesha asked nervously. "Our luck can't hold forever."

The kid obviously needed more experience with adventuring, if this was going to bother him. I mean, the likely punishment, were we caught, was being turned into real eunuchs.

Now *I* was nervous.

She turned and inserted the key into the lock. Iron grated on iron; I wished for a little fat to oil the mechanism. But just about the time I was opening my mouth to urge a little more care, the lock surrendered and the door was ours.

Del shoved, but nothing happened. Neesha and I leaned on it a little and felt it move. Rust sifted from all the hinges. But the door stood open at last.

The room, as we'd hoped, was occupied. The occupant stood in the precise center of the little room—cell, really—and stared at us anxiously. He was, I judged, not much past ten or twelve. Dark-haired, dark-skinned, brown-eyed, clad in silken jade-green jodhpurs and soiled lime-colored tunic; two months had played havoc with all his finery. He was thin, a little gaunt, but still had both arms, both legs, his head. Rez's tanzeer, it appeared, didn't want to injure Hafiz's heir, only to arrange a more equitable trade alliance.

And now the leverage was gone.

"Here, Dario." Del, smiling encouragingly, reached under a couple of layers of silken harem robes and pulled out more clouds of the stuff. Orange. It dripped from her hands: a woman's robes. "Put these on. Use the hood and modesty veil. Walk with your head down. Stay close to me and they'll never know the difference." Her warm smile flashed again. "We're getting you out of this place."

The boy didn't move. "Hamidaa'n tells us women are abominations, unclean vessels placed upon the earth by demons. They are the excrescence of all our former lives." Dario spoke matter-of-factly in a thin, clear voice. "I will touch nothing of women, speak to no women, admit nothing of women into my thoughts. I am khemi."

After a moment of absolute silence in which all I could hear were the rats scraping in the wall and Neesha's breathing close behind me, I looked at Del.

She was pale but otherwise unshaken. At least, I thought she was. Sometimes you can't tell, with her. She can be cold, she can be hard, she can be ruthless—out of the circle as well as in. But she can also laugh and cry and shout aloud in an almost childish display of spirits too exuberant to be contained.

She did none of those things now, but I thought, as I watched her looking at the boy, she had never met an opponent such as this son of the Hamidaa'n. And I thought, She is at a loss for what to do and how to answer for the first time in her life.

Slowly I squatted down in the cell. I was eye to eye with the boy. I pulled down the veil so he could see the beard stubble and know I was not a eunuch. "Choices," I said casually, "are sometimes difficult to make. A man may believe a choice between life and death is no choice at all, given his preference for staying alive, but it isn't always that simple. Now, something tells me you'd like very much to get out of here. Am I right?"

His chin trembled a little. He firmed it. "My father will send men to rescue me."

"Your father sent *us* to rescue you." I didn't bother to tell him his khemi father had no idea one of my partners was a woman.

Neesha spoke quietly. "A choice, Dario. Come with us now and we'll take you to your father, or stay here in this stinking rat-hole."

Something squeaked and scrabbled in the wall behind the boy. I couldn't have said it—or timed it—better.

Dario looked down at his bare feet sharply. Like the rest of him, they were dirty. But they also bore torn, triangular rat bites.

I closed a hand over one thin shoulder, picking up Neesha's theme. "Choices, Dario, are sometimes easy to make. But, once made, you have to live with them."

He was shaking. Tears gathered in his eyes. Teeth bit into his lower lip as he stared resolutely at me, ignoring Del altogether. "Hamidaa'n tells us women are abominations, unclean vessels—"

He stopped talking because I closed his mouth with my hand. I am large. So is my hand. Most of Dario's face disappeared beneath my palm and fingers. "Enough," I told him pleasantly. "I have no doubts you can quote scripture with the best of them, khemi, but now *is* the time. Now *is* the time for you to make your choice." I released him and rose, gesturing toward Del and the silks.

Dario scrubbed the heel of a grimy hand across an equally dirty face. He stretched the flesh all out of shape, especially around the eyes—an attempt to persuade imminent tears to go elsewhere immediately. He caught a handful of lank hair behind an ear and tugged, hard, as if hoping that pain would make the decision itself less painful. I watched the boy struggle with his convictions and thought him very strong, if totally misguided.

Finally he looked up at me from fierce brown eyes. "I will walk out like *this*. In *these* clothes."

"And be caught in an instant," I pointed out. "The idea here, Dario, is to pass you off as a woman—or at least a *girl*—because otherwise we don't stand a chance of getting you out." I glanced sidelong at Del; her silence is always very eloquent. Neesha also offered nothing. "Decide, Dario. We can't waste any more time on you."

He flinched. But he made his decision more quickly than I'd expected. "*You* hand me the clothes."

That annoyed the hoolies out of me. "Oh, *I* see—from my hands they're cleaner?" I jerked the silks from Del's hand and threw them at Dario. "Put them on. *Now*."

He allowed them to slither off his body to the ground. I thought he might grind them into the soiled flooring, but he didn't. He picked them up and dragged them over his head, sliding stiff arms through the sleeves. The silks were much too large for him, but I thought as long as we stuffed him among us, it might work.

"*Now,*" I said, and Neesha and I each grabbed an arm and hustled Dario out of the cell right behind Del. We reached the nearest exit. I leaned on the door and it grated open, spilling sunlight into the corridor—and came face to face with six large eunuchs. *Armed* eunuchs.

"Hoolies," Neesha muttered, freeing his sword even as I did.

Chapter 9

FOR A MOMENT I THOUGHT MAYBE, just *maybe*, we might fool the eunuchs. But I'd dropped my face veil for Dario. No doubt I was not a eunuch. They each drew a sword and advanced through the door as we gave way into the corridor.

I said, "I think our luck just ran out."

"Something like," Del agreed, and parted the folds of her silken robes to yank her own sword free.

I shoved Dario behind me, toward Neesha, nearly slamming the child into the wall in an effort to sweep him clear of danger. I wasted a moment more tearing the no-longer-necessary silks from my body.

Six to three. Not bad odds, when you consider Del and I are worth at least two to one when it comes to sword-dancing, probably more like three to one. Neesha was close. Sword *fighting*, however, is different, and it showed as the first eunuch pushed past Del to engage me and discovered discounting Del was as good as discounting life. He lost his.

I heard Dario's outcry behind me. I spared him a glance. He was fine with Neesha; my son, bless him, had automatically assumed the duty of keeping the boy blocked from the eunuchs. Dario, peering around Neesha, stared gape-mouthed, in shock, at Del. Grimly I smiled as Del engaged another eunuch while the remaining four came at me. It was my duty to keep them from reaching Neesha.

When involved in a fight that may end your life at any moment, you don't have much time to keep tabs on what anyone else is doing. It is deadly to split your concentration. And yet I found mine split thrice. There was Dario, of course; I was certain the eunuchs wouldn't hurt him, but it was entirely possible he might not duck a sword swipe meant for *me*. But there was also Del, and Neesha. I knew better than to worry about Del—she'd proved her worth with a sword already, even as she did again. So I didn't worry about Del, exactly, but I did keep an eye on her just to make sure she wasn't in any trouble. I'd learned that was all right in the parlance of our partnership; often enough, and even now, she did the same for me. It's an equality two sword-dancers *must* share if they are working together in the circle. Ours was an equality fashioned by shared danger and shared victory, in the circle and out of it. And I'd learned that, in the circle, in the sword-dance, because of Del, gender no longer mattered.

Simply put: You're good, or you're dead.

Neesha, I worried about—but only for a moment or two. The grim determination in his face told me he was ready for what fate threw at him.

My blade was already bloodied; I'd pinked one man in the arm and the other in the belly. Neither wound would stop either guard. So I tried again.

Behind me, I heard Dario speaking to Neesha in a shrill tone. In pain? A quick glance: He seemed to be all right, just shocked and frightened by the violence. Neesha shoved him once again behind his body.

Beyond the eunuchs, I saw Del in rose-colored robes. I heard the whine and whistle of her sword as she brought it across the corridor in a two-handed sweep intended to relieve her opponent of his head. She is tall. She is strong. I have seen her do it before.

I saw her do it again, although it was only in a series of disjointed glances; I had my own head to concern myself with at the moment. It remained attached, but only just; one of the eunuchs parried my sword while his partner slashed at my neck. Braced, I jerked my head aside and leaped sideways even as I used the strength of my wrists to smash aside the other sword. My size is often a blessing.

My shoulder rammed into the corridor wall, sticky, smelling of blood. As I pushed off the wall, I realized I also was sticky and smelled of blood. The beheaded body had drenched me.

"Son of a dog!" one of the eunuchs shouted at me.

He'd have done better to save his breath; Del, working contrapuntally against my own sword-song, killed the mouthy man while I took out his fellow guard.

Six dead, three standing: Del, Neesha, and I.

And one more slumped against the wall though only in shock, brown eyes nearly as wide open as his mouth: Dario.

I spat blood. Mine; I'd bitten my lip. But the beheaded man's blood was splattered across Del's face as well as mine. Dario, blocked by Neesha, had been missed entirely.

Del reached out and caught a handful of the silk that enfolded Dario. "Come." She dragged him toward the open door. When she takes *that* tone, no one argues with her.

We stumbled out into the sunlight, blinked, squinted, determined our precise location in relation to the palace entrance, and once determined, we started running. Even Dario.

Without Del's help.

No more fluttering past the gate guards like a clutch of colorful hatchlings. I took one thin arm in my hand and let Neesha take the other; a moment later we were running again, Dario in tow.

Horses waited for us in the market, but only three. I sheathed my sword and threw Dario up on the rump of Del's horse even as she sheathed and swung up, then I jumped aboard my stud and headed him through the winding alleyways with Del (and Dario) in the lead, Neesha right behind. Hooves clicked against stall supports. I gritted my teeth and waited for the anticipated result . . . and heard the shouted curses of an angry merchant as voluminous folds of canvas collapsed into the alley.

Ahead of me, Dario was an orange bud against Del's full-blown rosy bloom. Silk snapped and rippled as she took her gelding through the alleys at a dead run, putting him over handcarts, bushel baskets, piles of rolled rugs and water jugs. Dario, clinging, was engulfed in clouds of silk. But somehow, he hung on.

Hung on to a woman.

We stopped running our mounts when we left Rez behind and entered the desert between the two domains. We stopped walking them when we reached the oasis.

"Water stop." I unhooked foot from stirrup and slid off the stud, unslung the goatskin bota from the saddle and headed for the spring. "Can't stay for long, Dario. Drink up, now, then we'll go on to your father."

The boy was exhausted. His stay in the dungeon hadn't done much for his color or spirits, no matter how hard he tried to show us only fierce determination. Del, still in the saddle, offered him a steadying hand as he tried to dismount; he ignored it. And I ignored his startled outcry as he slid off the horse's rump and landed in the sand on his.

Del unhooked and jumped down. Sunlight flashed off the hilt of her sword. I saw Dario staring at it as well as at Del. No more shock. No more gaping mouth. Consideration, instead. And doubt. But I didn't think it was *self*-doubt.

Del was at the spring with her own bota. Dario still hunched on the sand: a gleaming pile of orange silk. "You're burning daylight," I told him as I levered the bucket up. "Do your share, boy—water the horses."

"*Woman's* work." He spat it out between thin lips.

"*Boy's* work, if he wants to drink."

Dario got up slowly, tore the offending silks from his bedraggled body and marched across the sand to the well. He snatched the bucket out of Del's hands. An improvement, I thought, in willingness if not in manners. But as he tipped the bucket up to drink, Neesha stepped close and took it out of his hands.

My son said firmly, "Horses first."

Dario was so angry he wanted to spit. But, desert-born, he knew better; he didn't waste the moisture. He just marched back to the horses and grabbed reins to lead them to the spring.

That's when I saw the blood.

"Hoolies, the boy's *hurt*—" I blurted even as Neesha said something similar. I threw my bota down and made it to Dario in two steps. Startled, he spun as I grabbed a shoulder. He lost the reins, but the horse, smelling water, only went as far as Del and the spring. "Where are you cut?" I asked.

"But—I'm *not*—" He twisted, trying to see the blood. "The man she killed spurted all over the corridor—"

"But not all over *you*," I said flatly. "You were behind Neesha—"

"Tiger, stop. Leave him alone." Del was at my side. "Turn your backs. Both of you."

"What—?" Neesha asked.

"Turn your back." But even as we did, she locked her hands in the waistband of Dario's jodhpurs.

"No!" Dario screamed it; I spun back around with Del's name in my mouth as I heard the jodhpurs tear.

"A girl," Del said. "A *girl*—"

Dario clutched jodhpurs against belly. He—*she?*—was yelling vicious khemi epithets at Del. Also at me and Neesha.

"Bascha—" I began.

"I *looked*, Tiger, and unless the khemi have taken to mutilating their boys, *this* boy is not a boy at all." She glared at the quivering Dario. "How in hoolies can you spout that khemi filth, *girl*? How do you justify it?"

"Oh, hoolies," Neesha murmured, closing his eyes.

"I am khemi," Dario quavered. "The Hamidaa'n tells us women are abominations, unclean vessels placed upon the earth by demons. They are the excrescence of all our former lives." Tears spilled over.

"That is no excuse—" I began.

"Tiger." Del cut me off with a sharp gesture. Her expression had altered significantly. Gone was the anger, the shock, the outrage. In its place I saw compassion. "Tiger, it *is* an excuse—or, at least, a reason for this masquerade. And now I want you both to go away. There is something Dario and I must attend to."

"Away—?"

She glared at both of us. *"Away."*

Neesha and I went to the far side of the spring and sat down to wait. He said, "I don't understand. He's a she?"

"I guess Del would know," I muttered, "she being a woman."

It didn't take long. I heard the sounds of silk being torn, low-voiced conversation from Del, muted responses from Dario. He—*she*—had undergone a tremendous change in attitude.

Well, I might, too, if someone discovered *I* was a woman. Especially at my age.

"Water the horses," Del told Dario, and then came over to the well and motioned us a few steps away.

We went. "She's not hurt?" I asked.

"No. Not hurt." She was more serious than usual, almost pensive. She hooked sunbleached hair behind one ear. "Dario is not a boy; neither is Dario a *girl*. Not anymore. Her courses have begun."

I opened my mouth. Shut it. "Ah," Neesha and I said in startled discovery at the same time.

Del's jaw was rigid. "When we get to Hafiz, I'm going with you to see Dario's father."

"You can't, bascha. He doesn't know you're a woman."

Her head came up, and I looked directly into a pair of angry blue eyes. "Do you think I care? His beloved *son* is a woman, Tiger!"

I glanced over at Dario, patiently holding the bucket for two horses in competition for its contents. But I could tell by the rigidity of her posture that she knew full well we were discussing her. It would be hard not to, in view of Del's shouting.

I looked back at Del. "You're sure?"

"What has been done to Dario transcends the need for Southron modesty or beliefs," Del said flatly. "At least it does for me."

I sighed. "I know, bascha; me, too."

Neesha said, "But he—*she*—seemed willing enough to spout all that nonsense."

Del's smile wasn't one; not really. "Women do—and are *made* to do—many strange things to survive in a man's world," she said.

That he understood. "Like you."

"Like me." She unsheathed her sword with a snap of both wrists and automatically I moved back a step. "I want to go with you to see Dario's father because I intend to put him to the question."

I looked at the sword uneasily. "With that?"

"If necessary. Right now, I intend only to tell Dario how I learned to kill."

"Why?" I asked as Del turned away. "So she can learn, too?"

Del's answer was whipped over her left shoulder. "No. Because she asked."

Chapter 10

EL AND NEESHA ACCOMPANIED ME as I took Dario back
to her father. I hadn't bothered to argue the point any longer;
Del's mind was made up. And I was beginning to think she'd made
up Dario's mind for *her*.

It wasn't easy getting in, of course. The palace servants were
men, naturally. Neesha they didn't mind. But the sight of Del's striding defiantly through their halls was enough to make them choke
on their prejudice. I imagine the sight of *any* woman might have
done the trick, but Del—beautiful, deadly Del—was enough to fill
their khemi nightmares with visions of fair-haired demons.

Dario walked between Del and me. In a complete change of
gender allegiance, she'd turned away from me on the ride to Dumaan to give Del her exclusive attention. Poor girl: all those years
spent in a khemi household with no women—*no* women—present
to answer questions.

At first I'd wondered if Dario had even known she was female;
when I'd asked the question, she told me only that a sympathetic
eunuch had admitted the truth after swearing her to eternal secrecy.
It was a khemi rite to expose female children at birth, thus removing
all excrescence from the Hamidaa faith.

"But you exist," I'd protested, "Your father bedded a woman in
order to get you!"

"A son. A son." She'd answered me very quietly. "Once a year a khemi lies with a woman in order to get a son." Brown eyes had flicked sidelong to mine. "*I* am my father's son."

"And if he knew the truth?"

"I would be taken to the desert. Exposed. Even now."

I hadn't said much after that. Dario's muted dignity moved me. All those years . . .

Now, as the four of us walked down the corridor toward the audience tent, I knew what Del intended to do. She stood before the enthroned khemi tanzeer of Hafiz—the richest man in this finger of the Southron desert—and told him she was taking his daughter from him.

He flinched. He *flinched.* And I realized, looking at the expression of abject terror on his face, he'd known all along.

"Why?" I demanded. "Why in the name of all the gods did you never tell *Dario* you knew?"

He was not old, but neither was he young. I watched his face undergo a transformation: from that of a proud Southron prince with an eagle's beak of a nose, to that of a tired, aging man surrendering to something he had hidden from for too long.

His hands trembled as he clutched the arms of his throne. "I am khemi," he said hoarsely. "Hamidaa'n tells us women are abominations, unclean vessels placed upon the earth by demons." His brown eyes were transfixed by Dario's ashen face. "They are the excrescence of all our former lives." His voice was a thread of sound and near to breaking. "I will touch nothing of women, speak to no women, admit nothing of women into my thoughts. I am khemi." Then he drew himself up and, with an immense dignity, stared directly at Del. "How *else* am I to cherish a daughter while also remaining constant to my faith?"

Neesha, behind me, leaned close and murmured, "Does Del mean her to come with us?"

All I could do was shrug.

"A faith such as this *excrescence* does not deserve constancy." Del's tone was very cool. "She is a girl, not a boy; a *woman*, now. No more hiding, tanzeer. No more hiding her. And if you intend to force Dario from her true self, I swear I will take her from you. In the North, we do not give credence to such folly."

He thrust himself out of the throne. "You will take her nowhere, Northern whore! Dario is mine!"

"Is she?" Del countered. "Why don't you ask her?"

"Dario!" The tanzeer descended two of the three dais steps. "Dari—surely you *know* why I never told you. Why I had to keep it secret." He spread both hands in a gesture of eloquent helplessness. "I had no choice."

Dario's thin face was pinched. There were circles under her eyes. "Choices," she said, "are sometimes difficult to make. And, once made, you must live with them." She sighed and scrubbed at a grimy cheek, suddenly young again. "You made yours. Now I must make mine." She looked at Del. "Tell him what you told me—how it is for a woman in the North. A woman who is a *sword-dancer*."

Del smiled a little. She faced the tanzeer squarely. Over her left shoulder, rising from her harness, poked the hilt of her sword. "There is freedom," she said, "and dignity, and the chance to be whatever you wish. I wished to become a sword-dancer, a sword-singer, in order to fulfill a pact I made with the gods. I apprenticed. I studied. I learned. And I discovered that in the circle, in the sword-dance, there was freedom such as no one else can know, and also a terrible power. The power of life, and of death." Again, she smiled a little. "I learned what it is to make a choice; to choose life or death for the man who dances against me. A man such as the Sandtiger." She cocked her head briefly in my direction. "I don't kill needlessly. That is a freedom I do not choose to accept. But at least I know the difference." She paused. "What does Dario know?"

"What does Dario *need* to know?" he countered bitterly. "How to kill? Needlessly or otherwise?"

"In the North, at least she will have a choice. In the South, as a khemi—as a Southron *woman*—she has no choice at all."

Neesha leaned close again. "She means to take her with us."

Dario stared at her father. In a whisper, she asked what *he* could offer.

He stared at Del for a very long moment, as if he tried to decide what words he had that would best defeat her own. Finally, he turned to Dario. "What you have had," he told her evenly. "I have nothing else to give."

Dario didn't even hesitate. "I choose my father."

I thought surely Del would protest. *I* nearly did. But I said nothing when Del merely nodded and turned to go out of the tanzeer's presence.

"Wait," he said. "There is the matter of payment."

Del swung around. "Dario's safety is payment enough."

"Uh, Del—" I began.

"Payment." The tanzeer tossed me a leather pouch heavy with coin. I rattled it: gold. I know the weight. The sound.

Dario stood between them both but looked at Del. "Choices *are* difficult," she said. "You offered me the sort of life many women would prefer. But—you never asked if I thought my father loved me."

I saw tears in Del's blue eyes. Only briefly—Del rarely cries. And then she smiled and put out a callused hand to Dario, who took it. "There is such a thing as freedom in the mind," Del told her. "Sometimes, it is all a woman has."

Dario smiled. And then she threw herself against Del and hugged her, wrapping thin brown arms around a sword-dancer's silk-swathed body.

When the girl came to me, I tousled her matted hair. "Take a bath, Dari . . . for all I know you're a Northerner underneath the dirt."

We left father and daughter together as Del, Neesha, and I walked out into the Southron sunlight. I untied the stud and swung up. "Aren't you even a *little* upset?" I asked, seeing Del's satisfied smile.

Neesha didn't understand either "She made the wrong choice."

"Did she?" Del mounted her white gelding. "Dario told me I'd never asked her if I thought her father loved her. I didn't need to. The answer is obvious."

It was so obvious, I waited for it.

Del laughed and yanked yards of silk into place as she hooked feet into Southron stirrups. "Her father knew she was a girl from the moment she was born. But he never had her exposed." She laughed out loud in jubilation. "The proud khemi tanzeer *kept* his abomination!"

The stud settled in next to her gelding. "As a khemi," I pointed out, "what he did was sacrilegious. The Hamidaa could very well convict him of apostasy and have him killed, if they knew."

Del glanced at Neesha, then looked back at me. "Choices are sometimes difficult to make," she quoted. "But sometimes easy."

This time, Neesha understood.

We were not offered guest quarters at the tanzeer's, so it was back to the big oasis once again. I was beginning to think of it as a second home. Our former tree was taken, but while Del and I watered our horses and ourselves, Neesha once again went off to see what he could find.

This time no Khalid interrupted us. "Maybe he finally got the message." After the stud drank, I scooped water for myself. "Obviously he wasn't impressed by me, but he certainly was by you!"

Del shrugged. "He has talent. But he's wild. He loses focus."

"You tend to do that to a lot of men." I expected some kind of reaction, but there was none. "Well, one of these days he'll meet a sword-dancer who won't put up with him."

Del shrugged again. She drank a little then turned her horse away from the spring. I watched her walk him down the path in the way Neesha had gone. I hesitated, chewing at my bottom lip. She had exulted in Dario's choice to stay with her father. Now she seemed disconnected from it. From me.

I followed and discovered Neesha had found us a very hospitable tree with spreading limbs and well-clothed branches. It was late afternoon and hot. Few people were moving; most slept the worst of the heat away. I thought it was a very good idea. I tended the stud first, untacking and picketing him where webby scrub grass grew in filtered shade at the edge of the tree canopy. Then I spread my blankets and flipped the saddle upside down for use as a backrest. Neesha had done the same but worked mending his bay's fraying rope halter. Del untacked and picketed her gelding, then walked away from us, probably looking for a place to relieve herself.

I stretched out on my back, slumped against the saddle. I was tired. "Was that enough adventure for you?"

Neesha snickered as he spliced rope together. "It's a start."

"We'll try to find you more before we head back home." I watched Del as she walked back. Something about her expression prompted concern. "Bascha, are you all right?"

Del nodded as she knelt beside me and unrolled her bedding blankets.

"You don't look it."

She glanced at me, then concentrated on settling her bed just the way she wanted it. When we washed at the tanzeer's, she had left her hair loose to dry. It fell in a shining curtain, hiding the side of her face as she settled down. She swung it aside, crossed her arms under her head, and stared up through leaves and branches into sky.

I remembered Lena's words. "It's Sula, isn't it?"

Del sighed deeply. "I miss her."

"So do I, bascha." And I didn't say it just to make her feel that she wasn't alone. I did miss the little monkey. "How about we go up to the horse farm, then go back home." I said to Neesha, who was finishing repairs. "You could always go off on your own if we head back sooner than you'd like."

He stood up and went to swap out the bridle and reins for the halter and lead-rope. Returning, he said, "Well, we don't know what lies between here and there. I may be sick of adventuring once we reach the farm." He threw himself down on his blankets, stretching elaborately. "You took him apart, Del," he began. "I'd never truly seen you dance before. That was most impressive. And then when you took that eunuch's head . . ." He shook his. "The North must be a hard place, to train you for such as that."

I winced, wishing his words had been a bit less blunt.

Whether that was the reason, or something else, Del's tone was flinty. "Not as hard as the South, where women are not allowed to do and be what they wish." Then, abruptly, she pressed the heels of her hands against eye sockets. "Oh, don't listen to me. That tanzeer has put me in a mood with all this talk about women as abominations. Unclean vessels. To make a religion out of it! *He* is the excrescence." She turned onto one hip to face us, propping herself up on an elbow. "Tell me, Neesha, were you raised to believe women have no value except to look after the man's wishes? To make him sons? You're a Southroner."

Neesha froze, eyes widening. He flicked a glance at me, asking for help; he got none, so he looked back at her. Carefully he said, "My father gave her more freedom than most men give their wives."

"He *gave* her more freedom," Del said pointedly. "Do you see what I mean? It wasn't something she was raised with. A man had to *give* it to her."

I almost laughed at him. I'd been the target of such discussions many a time.

He was clearly uncomfortable, trying to figure out how in hoolies to say the right thing. "I—well . . . I didn't really pay attention growing up. I just know, compared to what I've seen since, she wasn't so circumscribed. She was free to speak, and she won her share of arguments."

"And you have a sister. How is she being raised?"

Neesha's smile came quickly. "My sister knows her own mind. I don't think any Southroner could convince her otherwise, and that includes our father."

Del grunted. "That's something."

"We used to spar," he continued, "Rashida and I. We'd draw a circle and batter away at one another with dead tree limbs we fashioned into so-called swords."

Del rolled back onto her spine, collapsing loosely with limbs sprawled out. "Maybe she should go to the North. Be a swordsinger. That is, if your father would allow it."

Neesha grinned up into the sky, finding a way through the thicket. "Well, we'll see him the day after tomorrow. Why don't you ask the man himself?"

And that put paid to the topic. Del announced she was going to take a nap and rolled onto her side facing away from us. Neesha and I exchanged grins, and then I settled into a more comfortable position and drifted off.

Chapter 11

AT A LARGE OASIS SUCH AS THIS ONE, it is always possible to buy food from someone if one is tired of travel rations. All three of us decided fresh meat, bread, dates, and cheese would taste much better than what we'd tucked away in our saddle pouches. I cleared dead coals out of the fire ring and built a modest pyramid of sticks, Neesha went looking for food, and Del took our empty coal pot and went to a near neighbor to beg for fresh chunks burning hot. Once she returned I carefully spilled the coals into the fire ring and used a stick to arrange them amidst the kindling. The fire burned warmly by the time Neesha came back with our dinner. In one hand he carried chunks of meat speared on three slender sharpened stakes, two loaves of fresh bread, a hunk of goat cheese to go with the mutton, and a handful of dates. A feast.

As we ate, the sun slid down the sky, dousing itself in a panoply of red, gold, and orange. Bluish twilight settled. The air was redolent with roasting meat, heavily spiced. Around glowing fire rings, people laughed and talked; others sang, played wooden flutes; and some just ate, like the three of us. Neesha and I washed the meal down with aqivi while Del kept to water, after reminding us the aqivi wasn't meant to be drunk, but to aid in disinfecting wounds. Her protest was unconvincing, and Neesha and I merely smiled at her cheerfully as we passed the bota back and forth.

It was as we finished dinner that the man arrived. He wore a burnous of superior silk dyed deep green with copper-colored embroidery along the sleeve hems, a wide, copper-studded leather belt. Matching cuff bracelets glowed in our firelight. Under a green turban with a glinting amber brooch pinned to it, his features and coloring were Southron, but when he glanced at Del he did not assume the pained or outraged expression of a man who wished not to speak in a woman's company. Neither was there curiosity or disbelief; he simply glanced at her briefly, took a deep breath as if to convince himself he should make no comment, then looked down at me where I sat on my blankets.

He spoke Desert with a liquid flexibility. "I am Mahmood. I am a merchant. Others told me how to recognize you because of the scars on your face, and the Northern woman who rides with you. You're the Sandtiger."

I raised my brows to ask a mute question as I finished chewing the last bite of mutton and tossed the bota to Neesha.

He appeared to understand what I meant, and answered me. "They said you hire on to protect caravans."

I swallowed the chunk of meat. "Who's 'they'?"

Mahmood waved a hand apparently intended to encompass the world. "They. People. Just—people."

I nodded at him as I drank a squirt of aqivi. "Yes, we've guarded caravans."

"We're going to the North with spices and silk," he explained. "Saffron and cinnamon, both very costly, and silk threaded with silver. They would be most interested in my goods."

Borjuni—raiders—*would* be interested in his goods. Del was nodding.

"I hired two men as outriders. I lost one to a viper," he continued, "and another refused to finish the journey when he met a woman in a small village. I am left with no guards. If you and the woman come with us, I would pay you well."

At least he understood that if he hired me, he would also have to hire Del. That was a nice change.

"What about me?" Neesha asked, aggrieved. "We'd be three. Better odds, don't you think?"

Mahmood stared at him, sizing him up, then looked back at me as if asking if Neesha was worth the coin. I smiled at him. "Yes, we are three, and the odds indeed would be better."

He bobbed his head and offered a small, soft leather bag. "In advance," he said, leaning down to put it into my hand. "More when we reach our destination."

"Where in the North are you going?" Del asked.

"Istamir. Not far across the border."

She nodded. "Those folk will pay well for your goods."

"Provided we can get them there," he said somewhat gloomily. "I'm told the borjuni are bad this season."

Borjuni were bad any season along the border. The problem was, you never knew exactly where they'd be on any given day. There might be none in your vicinity. There might be many. Mahmood was wise to replace his missing outriders. Mahmood was wise to hire all three of us.

"Four wagons," he said. "Not so many. One driver each, all experienced."

"Do you drive?" I asked.

A nod of the turban. "Lead wagon. I know the way."

Del observed, "So do I." She smiled faintly at Mahmood. "So if raiders kill you, we could still get your goods to Istamir."

He was not exactly sure how he should react to that, coming from a woman. It suggested the possibility of an attack, which would be very bad fortune, and he wasn't certain what Del could offer as an outrider.

"Istamir is a day's ride to my family's place," Neesha said. "We'd just have to drop back down a bit."

"And from here to Istamir, three days." Del nodded at Mahmood. "We will get you there safely."

Faintly, Mahmood thanked her, then looked at me. He was more comfortable looking at me. While he accorded Del more acceptance than he would other women—she was a Northerner, and the Sandtiger's partner—he just didn't know how to treat her. But I gave him credit for trying.

"First things first," I said. "Change out of that expensive burnous and put on your plainest. Leave off the wrist cuffs. Wear a belt with no ornamentation. Take that brooch off your turban."

He was plainly shocked. "But I am successful! No one will know it if I dress like a peasant. They will believe they can haggle me down from my prices!"

Dryly, I said, "Do you want raiders to know you're so successful? And they won't haggle anyway. They'll just kill you and ride away with your costly spices and fabric."

He struggled with it. I was willing to bet it had taken a lot of years and as much effort to reach his current affluence.

After a moment he looked at me worriedly. "I can leave off the ornaments, but I have no plain burnouses."

I shrugged. "Not difficult to fix. Just bring me one. I'll get it wet, then drag it in the dirt."

He wasn't sure if I was joking or not. His voice was weak. "In the dirt?"

"In the dirt. And if the one you pick has sleeve embroidery, smear mud over it."

More weakly still, "Mud?"

"We'll hide your some of your silks under the floorboards, and stuff some into our saddle pouches. The three of us will also carry as many of your spices as we can."

"The dust!" he cried, horrified. "And stuffing them into your saddle pouches? It will ruin the silks, even wrapped as they are!"

"Not unless we splash through puddles, which is unlikely here in the Punja. And if borjuni should appear, they won't assume silk is in our pouches. Better to keep some than lose it all."

"And the spices . . . on your horses, too?"

"Spices smell. They will smell less if they're packed in our saddle pouches." Still seated, I dangled the bag of coins in front of me, offering it. "You don't have to hire us if my requests are too onerous."

Stiffly, he said, "They are demands, not requests."

I displayed my teeth in something akin to a grin but wasn't, quite. "You don't have to hire us if my demands are too onerous."

He looked at Del, at her harness and sword lying next to her on her blanket. He looked at Neesha and *his* sword and harness. Finally he looked back at me. "But you're the Sandtiger."

"Then give me credit for knowing about guarding caravans and fighting borjuni. Don't make yourself an obvious target." His caravan would be a target regardless, but no need to advertise just how much Mahmood transported. "Make your last wagon the lightest. Some silks, some spices, yes. If any raiders appear, they're more likely to cut out the last wagon. You'd lose less."

He was horrified. "Cut out the wagon? But I'm hiring you to guard *all four* wagons!"

"And we will," Del said matter-of-factly. "But sometimes you must throw a dog a bone so he doesn't steal the meat."

"He's the Sandtiger," Neesha put in with a dramatic note of wonder. "A *living legend* would guard your caravan!"

I slanted him a glance and saw that he was trying very hard not to laugh. But it was enough for Mahmood.

"Yes," he said, with a trace of annoyance in his tone. "It will be as you say. But *I* will get the burnous wet and *I* will drag it through the dirt."

Which meant it wouldn't be as worn-looking as I wanted, but I had to give him something for his pride. "Come get us tomorrow morning."

He nodded stiffly and walked away.

Neesha had the grace to wait until Mahmood was out of earshot before he began to laugh.

"That's rude," Del noted acerbically.

Neesha forced words out between blurts of laughter. "But the look on his face! Silks in our saddle pouches? Spices in our saddle pouches? The *horror* of such a thing!"

Del picked up her water bota and squirted him.

"Children," I sighed, and tucked away the little bag of coin. In a saddle pouch.

Del, Neesha, and I were up, packed, and ready to go when Mahmood arrived not long after dawn. His expression was one of a rather morose stubbornness. He had indeed sullied his burnous but not by much. It was yellow made somewhat dull with dust, but there was no mud, even on the sleeve embroidery. No cuff bracelets, though, or copper-ornamented belt, and no brooch on his green turban.

"I picked off every stud from this belt," he announced grimly, "and it took a long time. Do you know what this cost me to buy?"

"No," I answered, "but your being a merchant, I suspect you traded for it and no coin changed hands. Now, let's go to your wagons and portion out the silks and spices."

"You'll ruin the worth of the fabric," he moaned.

"Wrinkles," Del said, "can be pressed out."

She was in harness now, wearing an indigo burnous that set off the blue of her eyes. She didn't need embroideries, cuff bracelets, a belt weighted with worked metal or gems to impress or to raise her stature. She needed only herself. And Mahmood, seeing her in the full light of day, realized it. Many Southroners considered her too blonde, too pale, too tall. Too much of everything, especially self-confidence, self-governance, and a dedication to plain speech. Mahmood was not one of those men. His brows slid up, his mouth loosened, and he stared.

Neesha, leading his horse up by Del, snickered. Del herself made a shooing gesture at Mahmood. "Go."

Apparently it was enough. Mahmood managed to stop staring and led the way to the easternmost edge of the oasis as we led the horses over. Four wagons, as he'd said, and three with drivers on the ground holding the teams. Despite his dress, the canvas-topped wagons were sturdy but unprepossessing; at least he knew to do that much. Nothing of them attracted interest—unless, of course, you just wanted to steal whatever the wagons might carry and discover later if the goods were worth coin or not. Like any self-respecting borjuni.

"All right," I said. "Find the richest fabric you have."

With great reluctance, Mahmood let down the tailgate of the lead wagon, climbed in, brought out a muslin-wrapped bundle. Del unwrapped it to view the costly silk, and indeed it was impressive. All colors, with silver threading worked into the weave. Even Neesha and I, not particularly interested in cloth unless it was worn by a beautiful woman, understood why Mahmood was so worried about losing it. Del ran an appreciative hand over the rich blue length on top, feeling the weave, the nubby richness as Mahmood looked on in worry. She tore up the muslin so the individual bundles would be somewhat protected, then she folded the silk and muslin in half and began to roll it tightly. Mahmood let out a strangled protest but was wise enough not to complain outright.

Del handed out tight silk rolls to Neesha and I. "Here. Our pouches won't hold much, but better than losing it all if raiders find us."

"The cloth will reek of spice," Mahmood said unhappily.

Del looked at him levelly. "Better than reeking of blood. And we're not stupid. We'll put the spice in one pouch and the silk in another."

I felt stupid. That had not crossed my mind.

"Perhaps it will add value," Del observed. "Scented silk."

Mahmood clearly hadn't thought of that. Apparently both of us were stupid.

The merchant considered it, his face taking on a thoughtful expression. "Perhaps so."

Del had now established that she was not stupid. Neesha and I stuffed rolls into our pouches while the drivers watched in interest. For a wonder, Mahmood no longer looked so pained. Del had given his merchant's brain something new to think about.

We parceled out the rolls and spice bags, filling our pouches. With the drawstrings pulled tight, the pouches appeared fairly innocuous. The rest we divided up evenly and found hiding places except for the last wagon, in which we hid nothing. Silk and spices were obvious. Some visible in the other wagons, as well. Altogether, half of the goods were tucked away.

I clapped Mahmood's shoulder. "If luck is with us, all of this preparation will be unnecessary."

His tone was doleful. "If luck is with us, no spices will be spilled, no silk will be soiled."

"Well, yes," I agreed. Or perhaps 'no' was a better response. "Let's go."

Mahmood sighed and looked at his drivers. "We go."

They climbed up on the wagons. Del, Neesha, and I climbed up on our horses. I looked at Mahmood aboard the first wagon. "We'll hope this is a boring journey."

The merchant's tone was glum. "I'll *pray* this is a boring journey.

Chapter 12

WHETHER BECAUSE OF HOPE OR MAHMOOD'S PRAYERS, the first two days were indeed boring. Neesha, who had never before hired on as an outrider, commented on this to Del and me over dinner the second night.

"It's boring," he said.

We sat near the wagons on spread blankets, by our closely picketed horses at the back end of the last wagon. Mahmood and his drivers set up at the front. It wasn't that we were unneighborly; it was a matter of keeping a watch in both directions.

On my advice, we kept no fires. On Del's advice, we untacked, rubbed down the horses, then resaddled and bridled so they would be ready if we had to defend the caravan on short notice. I smiled at Neesha as I tore the flat journey bread into two pieces. "Not much of an adventure, true. Look at it this way: we're being paid for riding north. Which is where we planned to go anyway."

"North-*ish*," my son clarified. "And this is too slow. Can't the wagons go faster? Our wagon isn't this slow." He paused. "And we stink."

"The little wagon we use to haul supplies back from Julah is not as large as these," I pointed out.

"Hunh," he grunted. "I think I'll stick to being a sword-dancer. One who doesn't stink of cinnamon and saffron."

"It's a very expensive stink. Think of it that way. And you can refuse such employment if you wish. Of course once you run out of money, you'll wish for a caravan and a boring journey."

He wasn't convinced.

"Besides," I continued, "no tanzeer is going to hire you yet. Well, except maybe for one who isn't as wealthy as others and makes do with you."

"'Makes do!'"

"Makes do," I affirmed. "You have to establish yourself first."

"How can I establish myself by being an outrider for a caravan?" He paused. "A very slow and boring caravan."

"A successful journey may result in other caravan-masters wishing to hire you. Word gets out."

"Maybe I should go through every domain, visit various tanzeers," Neesha declared. "Let them know I'm for hire. I guess it wouldn't be so bad to 'make do' if I win my dances, and then word will get out about that." He looked at me, frowning. "How long did it take for you?"

I scratched my face through the stubble. "Well, it kind of began when I was at Alimat. I defeated Abbu Bensir. *That* word spread swiftly. Even if it was mostly an accident, and luck." I shrugged. "So, tanzeers heard. I was hired."

Neesha was silent a long moment, twisting his mouth and frowning in concentration. Then he looked at me. "How about I defeat the Sandtiger?"

I laughed. "You can't defeat the Sandtiger yet. Remember? I'm a legend. You kindly pointed that out to Mahmood. With emphasis."

"You could *let* me win. That would establish a reputation."

"And then you'd have to regularly contend with sword-dancers much better than you," I pointed out. "You'd be defeated time and time again, and that's not the reputation you want to build."

"It will come," Del told him. "Be patient. Think of it as an injured horse. Some require many months to be made sound again."

"And some never are," he objected.

It was time I played the father. "Neesha, give it up. Opportunity will come."

Which was not what I should have said as we entered border

territory where borjuni habitually worked their trade, because the very next day, they came.

The caravan was not as slow as Neesha said. But neither was it fast. It was a steady pace determined by Mahmood's wishes and the willingness of the teams pulling the wagons. Though with only cloth and spices aboard, the physical labor of the horses was not difficult.

Del, Neesha, and I traded places frequently. Del on one side, me on the other, Neesha behind. Then we'd swap around. Mahmood, in the lead wagon, kept an eye on the terrain before us. Not truly a road, because sand drifted too often over this hard-packed area, but anyone accustomed to riding or driving teams across the Punja had a good sense of direction. The potential for death—from sun, lack of water, raiders—did that for you.

But now we left behind the Punja and crossed into the borderlands. Sand became soil, vegetation sprang up, scattered shrubs and trees offered shade. Grasslands: pale green and dun, thick enough, tall enough, that the horses grabbed mouthfuls as they walked.

It was Mahmood, in front, who sounded the alarm. "Riders!"

Riders need not be raiders. But they could be. As they got closer, all was answered.

Down from the borderlands they came, threshing grass as they rode. Sunlight flashed off bared blades. My own was now unsheathed, and a quick, assessing glance told me Neesha and Del had unsheathed as well.

Del and I rode on either side of the wagons. Neesha was in the rear. I dropped back briefly. "Keep watch from here; don't come forward," I said. "One or two may try to loop down around us and come in from the rear while we pay attention to the ones in front. Call out if you need help."

Neesha grinned. "And if you need help?"

"If *we* need help, we're in trouble." And I left him with that cheery thought, riding forward. Del and I moved closer to the front of Mahmood's little caravan even as the raiders came boiling out of the grasslands.

Six of them. Not so many for a party of borjuni. But enough to cause problems.

"Raiders!" Mahmood cried.

Really? I thought. I rode up to him. "If I say to, I want you to split off the wagons. You've got four wagons, four directions. You'll divide their attention."

"You said they'd attack from the rear! That's why we lightened that last wagon!"

"That's one technique," I said. "Frontal attack is another. Be ready!"

The raiders were bunched. Then, as they came upon us, they broke apart. A view of Neesha, at the rear, was temporarily blocked by the wagons. It might afford a slight advantage.

The six came at us, blades raised. They hooted and cried ululations, intended to intimidate. Del and I were not intimidated.

I had learned not to divide my attention between Del and battle. She knew precisely what she was doing; my task was to keep myself alive. And as three raiders and I met, that was exactly what I intended.

The stud had done this before. He was nearly as good a fighter as a human. And he screamed back at the borjuni.

Battle is noisy. Blades rang, scraped, screeched, chimed. I rode upright, leaning slightly toward the front. Feet were planted in stirrups, thighs gripped the stud's sides. One hand, on the reins, sent messages to the stud's mouth and neck, guiding him in short bursts, spinning him to take on a raider trying to come up from behind. They realized, now, these borjuni, that Mahmood had hired himself outriders who knew very well what they were doing.

My tangle of raiders became two instead of three. The third looped out away from me, heading, as expected, to the rear. Likely it was the same for Del; she fought two now, with the third reining away hard.

"Neesha!" I bellowed. "Two! Be ready!"

And I prayed that he would be.

A raider came in close. I broke his guard, leaned slightly sideways, and slid my blade between ribs. I jerked it loose rapidly, wheeling the stud to block the second man. As always, my mind divided itself, marking any number of things related to the battle. I noted my enemy was red-haired, red-bearded, clad in dusty brown burnous. He rode a sorrel horse. Not a sword-dancer but lethal enough. He turned his blade on edge, swung it out in a scything motion, managed to cut through my burnous and harness with the tip. Even as I leaned away, his blade tip kissed my ribs. But it wasn't a stab, it wasn't deep, and I knew no real damage was done.

"Tiger!"

Neesha. I shouted to Mahmood as I spun the stud toward the rear. "Split up! Go!" Then, a bellow, "Del, I'm dropping back!"

Two men were on Neesha. He spun his horse in a tight circle, engaging one man, then another. But you couldn't do that forever no matter how well-trained your mount—and Neesha's was—or how steady your seat in the saddle.

From behind, I came down upon the one closest to me, and drove the blade through his spine, yanking it free at once. That left one for Neesha. Then it was my turn to wheel and fend off the raider riding at me from behind. The red-haired, bearded man.

We met, engaged, crashed blades. The stud screamed, came up on his hind legs, and struck out with both hooves. One landed square on the head of the borjuni's mount. Down went the horse, probably dead before he hit the ground, and the man jumped clear even as the horse fell. He scrambled up, throwing reins aside, clutching the sword in one hand.

"Zayid!" came a shout.

On foot, even with a sword, he stood no chance against the stud. But he recognized it and acted. He ran, caught with his free hand the tailgate of the wagon nearest to the fight, used his momentum and swung himself across and down, landing on his feet. Now he was on Del's side of the caravan.

I heard him shout. Saw Del's two men wheel away. One swooped in, put out a hand as he leaned down. The red-haired man caught it, swung up onto the horse's rump. He shouted again, waving his sword in the air in an awkward herding gesture. Even as I turned the stud toward them to charge, three borjuni rode away at a gallop, one carrying double. Neesha lost his adversary, who galloped after the others. Four men. Three horses.

Two men dead. I'd accounted for one. And Neesha had made his first kill.

I yelled after Mahmood's wagons, calling them back. I noted that Del was in one piece atop her white gelding, speaking soothing Northern words, stroking his neck. No blood on her that I could see.

"Bascha?"

She glanced up. "I'm fine. And you?"

I shook my head. "A cut. Nothing serious."

Now I rode up close to Neesha. His bay horse foamed with sweat at the cinch, at the headstall and his neck where reins had rubbed. Neesha himself stared at the body on the ground. Sweat ran down his forehead, but he didn't move to wipe it away with a forearm. Gripped in his right hand was his sword. His bloodied sword.

I rode up. "Are you whole?"

He nodded, looked up from the body and met my eyes. His were filled with a mixture of emotions. He breathed hard.

"So," I said, "guess you're not bored anymore."

The caravan reassembled itself. None of the drivers, including Mahmood, was injured, and no wagons, horses, or cargo were lost. The only dead were borjuni.

It was mid-afternoon, but I had us drive on a bit to get away from the bodies, which would lure predators, then called a halt to make camp. It surprised Mahmood, his drivers, and Neesha, as it was early for it; Del merely nodded. To Mahmood, she said, "Keep the wagons close. Don't chock the wheels. Sleep on the ground beside the wagon."

"It pains me to say it," I told Mahmood before he could protest, "but keep the horses in traces. Unhitch first, cool them down, scrub them, fill the water buckets, give them grain after a while. Then hitch them back up."

He was aghast. "Why? They'll rest better if unhitched and picketed. And we have beds in the wagons! There's no need to sleep on the ground!"

I explained with one word. "Borjuni."

"What if the horses move closer to us? Maybe step on us. Picketing can fail."

"You'll be on the ground next to them," I pointed out. "You can roll aside, and you can jump up and stop them from walking off. Which I doubt they'd do anyway."

He was becoming downright belligerent. "And you?"

"One of us on each side," I said, "and one at the back. Two sleeping, one watching. In rotation." I paused. "And each horse immediately beside its owner. So we could get stepped on, too."

Mahmood stared at Del, at me, at Neesha. He wanted badly to refuse, but he read our faces. With a tight jaw he told his men to make camp for the night as we had described.

"No fire," I ordered. "I'm sure you have salted meat, dried fruit, journey bread. Eat that."

Mahmood's expression was mutinous as he turned to his team. I was fairly certain I heard a swear word or two.

"Do you not understand?" Del's tone was icy as she slipped down from her saddle. "You hired us to keep you alive, to guard your silks and spices. We have done so. We may have to do so again. It's best if the wagons are ready, the teams are ready, and *you* are ready. There is less risk if you're on your wagons swiftly and driving your horses away from the fight. How quickly can you crawl out of your wagon, hitch the teams, unchock the wheels, and drive away? Do you see? Time is important. Time is vital."

"But there is a stopping place," Mahmood protested. "Not far. Best for the horses. Best for us."

"Best for borjuni," I said. "They will go there to see to wounds, human and horse. Do you want to drive your precious cargo right into their midst?"

That, he understood. His face was less tense as he spoke to his drivers, passing along my instructions. For a man who might have been killed at any moment without our guarding him, it was annoying that he wanted to argue with every suggestion. But Del had gotten through to him, and so had I.

I think.

Chapter 13

AT DUSK, AFTER DINNER, I walked to the last wagon, to Nee-sha. He had spent quite some time working on his horse, scrubbing away the sweat stains, checking practically every hair for damage. Apparently he found none. The horse was saddled again, drinking water from a waxed, oil-cloth bucket.

He sat upon a spread blanket. No saddle to lean against this time, as it was on top of his horse again. He was cross-legged, staring out across the grasslands at the rising moon, nearly full. His harness sheath was empty. The sword lay on the sand next to him.

"How's that cut doing?" I asked.

He looked at the forearm where Khalid had sliced him. No longer bandaged, a shallow ridge of stitched tissue was visible. He made a fist, flexed the arm. "It still works."

It probably hurt much worse than he was letting on. I leaned against the wagon's tailgate, folded my arms across my chest. "I don't think they'll be back. Not tonight. But—"

He cut me off: "It's best to be prepared. I know. You've made that very clear. Numerous times."

He had not yet looked at me. He stared out through the deepening dusk. I shifted against the wagon, settling in more comfortably. The cut along my ribs stung from the aqivi Del had washed it with, but it wouldn't hinder me. Especially as no stitches were needed. "There will be others, you know."

He turned his head toward me slightly, slanting his eyes in my direction, then looked back again, not yet facing me. "What others?"

"Men you will kill."

Now he turned, swinging around on his blanket. He stared up at me from the ground. "Is this to be a lesson from my shodo? A talk designed to set me at ease? I know I will kill men. And these deserved it."

"Yes," I agreed.

Neesha sighed heavily, scrubbed the heel of one hand against his brow, eyes closed. "But it doesn't feel good." He let his hand drop, looked up and met my eyes. "It doesn't—and didn't—feel good."

I nodded. "Nor should it."

"I looked into his face," Neesha said, almost in wonder. "I looked into his face and into his eyes, in the midst of all that confusion. He meant to kill me. He *wanted* it."

"Some men do."

"He would have killed anyone he could stick a sword into."

Justification. Rationalization. Easy to recognize. I'd faced both myself, when I was young. When I'd killed my first man. "Yes. But you prevented him from killing anyone. You did exactly what we are intended to do, as outriders. This isn't dancing. This is fighting to stay alive and to make certain those in our care stay alive."

After a moment, Neesha nodded. He looked away from me, watching the last vestige of the sun slip behind the horizon. "There is a lesson in this."

"What is that?"

He rose, brushed soil and sand from his burnous, and faced me fully. "Boring is better."

I grinned, stood up straight, prepared to walk back to the stud and my side of the caravan. "Get some sleep, Neesha. Del will relieve you in a couple of hours."

But he probably wouldn't sleep. I hadn't, that first night so long ago.

We had a minor argument in the morning, all of us, as we gathered at the front of Mahmood's wagon with horses standing by, saddled and ready to go. Mahmood wanted to go on to the stopping place. I did not. Del unnecessarily explained to me that the stopping place offered fresh water, and Neesha reminded us the stopping place wasn't far—both of which I already knew. But my concern was the raiders.

"They might be there still," I pointed out.

"Or not," Neesha said. "Maybe they're out raiding somewhere else."

"That depends on how badly any of them might be injured." I looked at Del. "Did you do any damage that might keep them stationary for a day or two?"

"*If* they're there," Del emphasized. "We don't know if they're there. Maybe they're not there. Maybe they never were there."

Here, there, everywhere. Patiently, I asked again, "Did you do any damage?"

Del said, "A few slices, no more. Maybe needing stitching, but not enough to keep them from riding again. They're probably not there, if they were ever there, which we don't know. "

"They're probably not there," Neesha interjected.

"They could be on their way *here*," I pointed out irritably. "I just don't like it. We've got enough water in Mahmood's barrels to bypass the stopping place."

"Shade," Mahmood insisted.

"Look around," I told him, gesturing widely. "Do you want to risk going in there without knowing if it's safe or not? If it isn't, you would never be able to escape in time."

"Then one of us could scout," Neesha said. "I can go in, find out how things stand."

I scowled at him. "And be killed for whatever you have. Like a horse. A sword. A burnous."

"It's a good thought," Del said, then clarified. "Scouting that is, not killing Neesha."

"I kind of had an idea that's what you meant."

"I'll go," she offered.

"No no no," I countered immediately. "They might be there."

Her brow creased. "That's the point, Tiger. To find out if they're there."

"I don't want you going there alone. Not a woman."

Del stared back at me. I knew that non-expression.

"It has nothing to do with the fact that you're a woman," I said hastily, then realized how stupid that sounded, since I'd just said it was. "Well, yes, I guess it does . . . but not because I don't have faith in your ability to defend yourself. I mean, people _can_ lose. Even us."

"Certainly not," Neesha observed with delicate irony.

"You shut up," I told him. "Del, with a man, all they'd do is kill him. With a woman, you know very well what would happen." Hoolies, she knew. She'd been repeatedly raped by a raider at the age of fifteen.

"We killed three of them, Tiger," Del reminded me. "Three men offer less trouble than six."

"I don't care how many we killed," I said irritably. "Three men are still three men. And we probably made them really angry."

"I said I'll go," Neesha insisted.

Apparently tired of the whole thing, Mahmood raised his voice. "_You_ go," he shouted at me. "No one agrees with you! All but you wish to go to the stopping place. So it should be you who goes to scout."

I wasn't quite certain there was logic in that. I mean, I didn't think we should go, so I was the one who had to?

"And I pay your wages," Mahmood declared obstinately. "You go, or we _all_ go."

Vastly annoyed, I said, "Fine. All right. I'll go. But if I come back with news the raiders are there, we'll go in a different direction for a day and then head north again. No questions or comments allowed. Just do whatever I say."

"That's not exactly fair," Neesha muttered in an aside to Del.

I lost my temper. "Doesn't anyone understand?" I yelled. "I'm trying to keep us safe!"

In the ensuing silence, the only thing audible was a prodigious snort from the stud.

"See?" Del said. "He wants to go, too."

I turned my back on them, put hands on hips, walked about

four paces away, stared south across the grasslands. Beyond lay the desert. The desert where water was worth more than gold. The Southroner in me argued that we should go to the stopping place. But the land was different here. The climate was milder. Grass replaced sand and hardpan. There was likely water to be had from many places in the borderlands. It truly wasn't necessary to put our lives in peril. But Mahmood and his men were from the desert. All they knew was that you don't pass up known water sources. And I guess I couldn't blame them.

I turned and trudged back to the others, still clustered there at the front of Mahmood's team. I wasn't yelling anymore, but I didn't curtail my annoyance. "All right. I'll go. Do what you need to do here. Build a fire if you like, hunt coneys, play in the dirt, build irrigation canals, whatever you want to do. I don't care. But—"

"Irrigation canals?" Neesha asked incredulously.

"Just *be ready* in case borjuni appear!" I took the stud's reins from Del, tossed them over his neck, climbed up into the saddle and glared down at all of them. "I'll be back when I'm back."

It felt rather strange to be alone again with just the stud for company. Going into Julah from the canyon didn't count because that was land I knew. It was home. I hadn't been out in the wide open spaces on my own for years.

As yet, we were in the South, but to me, desert bred and raised, it didn't feel like it. Grasslands, scattered trees here and there, shrubs bursting up from the soil. You could say the same about the portions of the South that were not the Punja, with its deadly crystal sands, but the trees were different, the shrubbery, even the types of rock. Unfamiliarity. And no one at my side, riding a white gelding.

She had told me on several occasions that if I wished to go off on my own, I could. That I should, if I wanted. She explained, too, that this did not mean she wanted me to go. Finally, I figured out what she meant and explained that I was already fully aware of my freedom. I stayed because I *wished* to.

And I still did.

I began to whistle, riding comfortably along on a good horse, happy about where life had led me. Ten years ago I'd have laughed in anyone's face if they'd predicted I would put down roots, especially with a woman and a small girlchild. But at some point you realize it doesn't matter what anyone thinks, that you'll do what it is you'll do. And that included putting down roots with a woman and a girlchild.

I quit whistling. I grinned. Then laughed. I leaned forward in the saddle, speaking to twitching ears. "Hey, old son. Care for a gallop?"

The ears twitched again, trying to sort that out. But he knew exactly what I meant when I leaned down closer and squeezed with my legs.

He trotted. Loped. Then, when I urged him onward, he leaped into a gallop, and we went running, running hard, across the wind-waved grasslands beneath a gentler sun.

There were no borjuni at the stopping place. In fact, there was no one at all, only me and the stud. I swung off, leading him in. It was a considerably smaller well than the one farther south, but there was a low rock surround and a wooden bucket tied to a rope for raising water up. Visits from others had beaten the soil into dust immediately around the waterhole, but it had some substance to it and held foot and hoof prints easily. There was some shrubbery, one broad-leafed tree, and three fire rings. None of the stone surrounds was warm, and all the horse droppings were old. So even if the raiders had been here, it was at least several days ago. And it was entirely possible they had their own encampment elsewhere.

I was in no hurry to return. I pulled the saddle off the stud, wiped him down while he drank from the bucket. The gallop had done us both good. I felt more relaxed than I had for a while. His temper seemed better, also.

Afterward, I stretched, applied thumbs to spine to pop out somewhat noisy kinks, twisted my torso to loosen a few more, and rolled my neck for anything remaining. What I wanted most was a hot bath. I wondered if the horse farm boasted a bathing tent. Neesha wasn't one to build himself up to others, but from a few matter-of-fact comments he'd made, I got the impression the family lived very comfortably.

Speaking of a bath tent . . . well, there was no tent available here, but there was water. I appropriated the bucket when the stud was done drinking, refilled it, then took off burnous and harness and poured water over my shoulders to run down chest and back.

As I slicked water over ribs, arms, and legs, it occurred to me to wonder if Neesha, after taking the trouble to track me down two years ago, would stay with me very long, or return to what he had known as home all of his life. I believed he intended to be a sword-dancer, no question. He had the dedication, focus, skills, and raw talent, but by watching him with the horses it was obvious he cared deeply for them. His departure left his stepfather the only male working the farm, unless he'd hired help—which was entirely possible. But what was also possible was Neesha discovering he liked horses better than dancing. And dancing was all I had to offer.

I caught movement out of the corner of one eye even as my ears registered the metallic chip of shod hoof striking stone. I glanced up and saw a man riding in on a blue roan. A mare, I noticed. He wore a sun-bleached, rust-colored burnous. And from behind his left shoulder a sheathed sword poked the air.

Borderer, I guessed. His hair was sandy, skin tanned but not dark, and his eyes, once he rode close enough for me to see, were blue. I thought it likely that beneath the burnous was a well set-up man, judging by the width of his shoulders. Borderers were just that: born of Southron and Northern parents who lived in the northern South and the southern North. Sometimes they looked all Southron, sometimes they looked all Northern, sometimes, as with this man, they were clearly a mix.

I judged him younger than me, but then, that wasn't unusual among sword-dancers anymore. I'd outlived many, had danced for over twenty years, was old enough to have sired some. After all, there was Neesha.

The borderer nodded at me as I bent down to gather up saddle with attached pouches, blanket, harness, and sword. I hitched everything up on my right hip, leaning away to counterbalance the weight, and walked from the well to give the man room to bring in his horse. I took up residence beneath the lone tree, set down gear, pulled the saddle blanket free and swung it over the stud's back. I did not touch the harness or sword, but anyone intending harm would note that it was easy for me to yank it out of the sheath and engage with an attacker. But this man was a sword-dancer, not a borjuni. Sword-dancers do not as a rule steal; or if they do, they soon find themselves targets of other sword-dancers who send a message loud and clear: It isn't tolerated.

However, if you won a death-dance, you were entitled to anything the dead man had.

I swung the saddle over the blanket, settled it, made sure it was positioned properly. Bent, grasped the dangling cinch, pulled it beneath the ribs, up the stud's side, and ran a long length of leather through it. Then I pulled it tight, doubled over the leather, and ran it through itself. Yanked it snug.

The stranger dismounted, pulled up the bucket hand-over-hand, set it on the ground. Before letting the roan nose her way in, he scooped up water and sluiced it over his face and head. Then he shook water out of his hair and blinked droplets away.

He smiled at me. "I know exactly who you are," he said pleasantly. "You can't hide those scars on your face."

I waited for it.

"My name is Kirit." he said. "Let's dance."

I nodded. Under the circumstances, it had to be asked. "To the win? Or to the death?"

He laughed. "Oh, to the death."

I bent, slid my sword from the sheath. Straightened, grasping it lightly. Modesty had never been a virtue of mine. But then, arrogance has its place among sword-dancers. Why not use what you have? Or what you can affect?

Or what is wholly true?

I met his eyes. "Are you absolutely certain this is what you want to do?"

"Hah! I think so!"

"No," I said levelly. "Are you certain? Are you willing—*ready*—to die?"

Sandy brows rose. "I don't plan to. That's your role."

"This is what you want," I said clearly. "Is this what you can win?"

"Your life? Oh, I think so."

He was arrogant. It had its place, and he knew how to use it. You use what you have. Or what you wish to have.

"Ride out of here," I said gently, "and live another day."

He laughed. The roan mare nosed his shoulder. "Are there people I should tell when you're dead?" His brows rose sharply. "Ah, that's right. There's the Northern woman. Well, the winner takes it all. Even a woman."

I left the stud. Left the tree. Walked out into the sun. "Draw the circle."

Smiling, he agreed.

And eventually, smile entirely banished, he died.

Chapter 14

MAHMOOD'S FOUR-WAGON CARAVAN was right where I'd
left it. A small part of me had wondered if they would set
out for the stopping place without me. But no. For a wonder, they
had actually taken my advice. Though I suppose some might declare
it an *order*, such as Mahmood, Neesha, and Delilah.

The drivers were apparently napping in their respective wagons.
Mahmood, Neesha, and Del sat on blankets on the shady side of the
first wagon. Del's gelding and Neesha's bay, tied behind the wagon,
dozed in the sun but woke when the stud whinnied loudly in greeting.

"No raiders." I halted the stud and swung myself down. "So yes,
all of you may now take me to task for being so stubborn."

Neesha grinned. "Well, we talked it over after you left and decided you were probably right."

"I usually am." I looked at Mahmood, still sitting on his blanket.
"It will be dusk when we reach the well. If we leave now." I glanced
at Del. "How far is Istamir from this place?"

"A day on horseback. Longer with a caravan."

Mahmood pushed himself up, nodding. "I'll wake my drivers."

"Any sign of the borjuni?" Neesha asked.

I dug out the flattened bucket from a saddle pouch, scenting the
air with cinnamon and saffron, punched it open and filled it at Mahmood's water barrel. I set it down so the stud could drink. "No one's
been there for a few days."

Del told Neesha, "Why don't you bring the horses around?"

He nodded, rose easily, and walked toward the back of the wagon.

She came up to me, smoothed a hand down the stud's shoulder as he drank. "What happened?"

"What do you mean, what happened?"

"You're bleeding." She set fingers on my side, pressing burnous against skin. "Right here."

I winced. "No, that's from the raiders yesterday."

"Ah," Del said. "It must have migrated from the other side."

I scowled at her.

She turned from the stud and met my eyes. "A sword-dancer."

"Yes."

"You won."

"Well, yes. Or I wouldn't be here."

"Ah," she said again. "A death-dance."

Neesha came around the other side of the wagon with his mount and Del's. He hadn't heard everything. "You danced?"

I shrugged. "I do try to be accommodating when people ask me to do certain things."

Neesha wasn't smiling. His eyes were serious, as was his tone. "You killed him. Didn't you?"

Grimly, I said, "He insisted on it."

Del's hands were on my burnous, lifting the sheath slit up and over the hilt of my sword. "Let's get this off. I want to see how badly you've been cut."

"Not badly. Honest, bascha. I know better than to try to mislead you. You always find out."

"No, you don't." She tugged emphatically at fabric. "And yes, I do. Now, take this off, or I'll cut it off."

"Don't cut it! It's my only burnous!"

"That's the point, Tiger."

"All right, all right." I unbuckled my belt and dropped it, shrugged out of the burnous, which landed in a pile of cloth. "I told you it's not bad."

Del examined it with careful hands. She was frowning.

"It's not," I said.

Mahmood came up. "Sweet gods!" he cried.

I looked at him, baffled, and saw he was staring at me. I was in dhoti, harness, sandals, doubled silver earrings, and nothing else. It left visible lots of browned skin and multiple scars. The one that caught his interest, as it always does, was the concavity below my left ribs and the gnarled flesh around it.

He looked me in the eyes, clearly stunned. "They say you're the best. Everyone does. But if you have survived such dances as this . . ." He shook his head. "I apologize for doubting you."

I smiled crookedly. "Just a love tap, Mahmood."

Del said, with a slight shrug and delicate irony, "Courting ritual."

Mahmood stared at her blankly.

"Courting," Neesha repeated for her. "You know—man and woman."

Mahmood's look was alarmed. "*She* did this to you?" he asked me. Then, to Del, "*You* did this to him?"

"Well," Del said, "he did it to me, first. But I won't show you my scar because I'm modest." So said the woman who showed a lot of naked arm and leg when she danced. And who thought nothing of walking through our little house wearing nothing but skin.

"Sweet gods," Mahmood said weakly.

Del's attention was back on me. "It isn't bad, as you said."

"As I said," I echoed pointedly.

"So get back into your burnous and let's go. I'll put salve on it later." She slapped me lightly across the cut, inducing precisely the wince she wanted, and reached to take the gelding's reins from Neesha. "We're burning daylight."

When we arrived at the well, the only living thing in sight was Kirit's blue roan. I had untacked her, tied her to the tree on a long halter rope so she could graze freely, put down water and grain, and left her alone with the dead man's belongings. I'd seen no reason to take her all the way to the caravan only to bring her all the way back.

Her presence, alone and riderless, brought home to Neesha and Mahmood just how serious were the challenges of an outcast. Dead bodies. Living horses. Belongings that no longer belonged to anyone.

Mahmood directed his drivers where to park the wagons and to begin dinner. The tree had a very wide canopy and broad leaves, so there was shade for the stud, Del's gelding, and Neesha's bay if we were careful about the roan. The mare was as yet an unknown entity; not possible to determine how she would behave around other horses.

It was Neesha, of course, who went right to her once his bay was picketed in shade, untacked, watered. He spoke quietly as he approached from the front, cupped his hands under her nostrils so she could inhale his scent, then ran a hand down her white-blazed face.

He turned to look at me. "She belonged to the sword-dancer?"

"She did."

"So she's ours now?"

"She is." I nodded toward the pile of tack and saddle pouches. "So is everything else of his."

Neesha nodded, his mind on one thing. "If it's all right, I'll take the mare to my father. He'll decide whether to breed her or not." He glanced around the immediate area. "The sword-dancer . . . where is his body?"

"Out there." I gestured in an easterly direction. "No reason to bring predators to the well."

"No," Neesha said thoughtfully. "I guess not." He slid a hand over the mare's shoulder, bent to run it down a front leg. Then he moved to the rear carefully, keeping a hand on her rump. The mare blinked lazily, swung her head back to look at him briefly, as if to check out the stranger touching her, but swung it back again. She offered no protest whatsoever. When he closed a hand around her hind leg and used pressure to suggest she lift it, she did so. "Well taught," he murmured. "And well put together. All that's left is to see if she's sound and how she goes."

"Take her out now," I suggested. "We've things to do before we can eat."

It took no time for him to decide. She wore a halter over her bridle. He untied the lead-rope, led her from under the tree and away from the other horses, then eased the rope up over her withers as he picked up the reins. I thought he'd saddle her; he did not.

"Forget something?" I asked.

Neesha shook his head. "I suspect she's dead broke. If she tosses me off bareback, then I'll know for sure." He smiled at me. "And I will have deserved it."

I watched my son talk to the mare, then seemingly levitate from the ground up onto her back. He gathered reins and the lead-rope, settled his buttocks right where he wanted them, let her stand quietly with a stranger on her back. He never once stopped talking to her in a low, conversational tone, quietly explaining that she would be his now, and then his father's.

He never said *step*father anymore. Well, the man had been considerably more of a father than I had ever been.

Del came up beside me, watching as Neesha urged the mare into a walk. "You're worried."

I didn't prevaricate. "I don't want him to go. Oh, I know he'll go out into the world as a sword-dancer. But I don't want to lose him to that other man. And yes, I know exactly what you'll say: that other man raised him. Offered him a life, a trade."

"Even as you offer him the same."

"But is it right for him?"

"It's his choice, Tiger. He came looking for you. He's taken lessons from both of us for the last two years. If he discovered he wanted otherwise, he'd have left by now."

"But now we ride back to what he knew. Where he lived for very nearly all of his life." I watched him. "You see how he is with that horse. How he is with all horses. That's a gift."

"Do you remember," she began, almost gently, "that this prophecy my brother spouted was that the jhihadi was a 'man of many parts'?"

I hadn't thought of that for a very long time. "Oh. Yes. Now that you mention it."

"Neesha, too, is a man of many parts. Horses. Dancing. Even women; he takes after you in that respect." She met my eyes and smiled. "There is no reason to believe he must surrender one gift to express the other."

I slid an arm around her waist. "You are so much wiser than I."

As expected, she said, "Of course."

I sighed, pulled her tightly against my side, took care not to wince as the cut stung. "I miss her, bascha. Our little girl who thinks playing in the dirt and mud—and dog piss—is the most enjoyable thing in the world."

Del leaned her head on my shoulder. "Oh, Tiger—more than either of us expected."

Neesha trotted the mare in a large figure eight. As she settled, he asked her to lope the same pattern. She did, making lead changes with a silky fluidity. I was a good rider. Del was a good rider. But Neesha had the *gift*.

I leaned my cheek against Del's head. "You're sure you prefer me to him?"

A quiet, single blurt of laughter issued from her throat. "Most of the time."

Mahmood shouted, "Do you intend to help?"

I planted a kiss on the side of Del's head. "Apparently the 'man of many parts' must also be a cook."

Unexpectedly, Neesha had taken my throwaway comment about hunting coneys literally and provided one for dinner. Mahmood, as usual, ate with his drivers, though I caught him glancing over at me and Del now and again, his expression thoughtful. I think he was still ruminating over the idea that a man and woman could dance against one another without the woman being immediately and utterly overcome; that, and the idea that we had each done serious damage to the other. It wasn't a subject I thought about much, because it still hurt. We had each nearly died; in fact, Del was injured so badly that I was certain she *would* die and couldn't bear being there to see it. I'd left Staal-Ysta, the Northern equivalent of Alimat, in anguish, guilt, and almost paralyzing grief. What I had felt when I discovered Del survived was indescribable.

Neesha, after dinner, was patently, if quietly, troubled by something. It was like an itch with him, waxing and waning. Though dusk was coming on, he said he was going to work again with the roan mare. As he left, Del and I exchanged a look of agreement, and I got up and followed.

He had picketed her some distance from the tree, since the stud was showing an annoying inclination to court her. Neesha used a folded piece of rough sacking and scrubbed her all over with it, then began to use long, soothing strokes all over her body even as he sang to her very softly. Clearly she enjoyed it; if he stopped, she looked around at him as if to ask what the problem was.

Well, that was my feeling, too: wondering what the problem was. "Maybe you ought to use the sacking on yourself, Neesha—get rid of the tension in your body." I waited a moment. "What is it?"

He leaned his head against the mare a moment then lifted it and turned to me. "I don't know that I could ever do it."

"Do what?"

"Kill a man in the circle."

"Only outside of it?"

He was too serious to respond to a feeble joke. "It was different, killing that borjuni. He deserved it; he meant to kill me and anyone else he could. But this . . . it never crossed my mind. I mean, I knew there were death-dances. But I always thought only about defeating an opponent, not killing him."

I grinned. "Neesha, it's extremely unlikely you'll ever be involved in a death-dance. They are very rare to begin with—well, except for the many who challenge me, that is—and I find it impossible to believe you would ever put yourself in the position to accept such challenge. Or to have anyone make it to start with. I know you'd never initiate it yourself."

"No." He sighed again. "I just . . . well . . . I know you have to do it because of *elaii-ali-ma*."

Even now I felt a twinge. So much lost in breaking all my oaths. "A death-dance is nothing I'd ever seek out," I told him. "It's nothing I enjoy."

"Could you have turned down this challenge?" he asked, patting the mare's sinewy neck.

My turn to sigh. "It's difficult to explain. First, he wouldn't hear of it. But also, I declared *elaii-ali-ma* for the only reason that matters: to save Del's life. I'd do it twenty times over. Thirty. I knowingly and willingly broke the codes. But I would like to think there remains a little piece of me who can adhere to what the shodo taught me. Odd as it sounds, it's sort of my own self-imposed code. To accept it."

"It's penance," Neesha said in tones of discovery. "Isn't it? Punishment. And an oath you won't break: to accept such challenges."

I'd come over to sort out what was in Neesha's head. I hadn't expected we'd be discussing what was in mine. I'd never actively thought about penance and punishment, but perhaps he was right. Nonetheless, I was uncomfortable with the idea and turned the conversation back to him.

"I'm a shodo of sorts," I said. "But Beit al'Shahar is not Alimat. I don't ask for oaths. All I do is teach. Students may take what they wish from the training, but I expect nothing of them other than that they fight with honor and integrity, and even then I can't control it once they leave. But if there are no oaths, you can't break them."

"No codes. No *elaii-ali-ma*, then, at Beit al-'Shahar."

"Not ever."

He was quiet a moment, seemingly studying one or both of his feet, then shook his head and met my eyes. "I will never be what you are."

I smiled. "Possibly that is a good thing. No—*probably* that is a good thing. You see, I found a life at Alimat. I wasn't a slave. I wasn't a possession. You were never a chula, as I was with the Salset, and have always had a life because your mother and father made certain you did."

"It's all I ever wanted. To be a sword-dancer."

"And so you are one, Neesha. No, you aren't a seventh-level sword-dancer, but, to tell you the truth, few are. Certainly the man I killed wasn't. But he would have made a good student."

Neesha stared into my eyes, then shook his head. "They'll all die. All those men who challenge you."

I smiled crookedly. "The alternative does not appeal."

"I wonder if they know it. That they'll die."

After a moment, I shrugged. "If you think you might die, you're half dead already."

He spoke earnestly. "But it's your choice to kill them or let them live. Like with Khalid. I heard about what you did. What you said. But you didn't do it with this man, today."

"I knew Khalid would never challenge me to a death-dance again. This man would have. Again and again and again. Perseverance may be admirable in most cases but not in this one." I paused. "I did give him the opportunity to ride away."

"Do they ever do it?"

He cared very deeply. I realized my answer mattered a great deal to him. "I do offer, Neesha. That's the best I can do. Some, such as this man, refuse to accept another way. In which case, all I can do is defend myself."

"Does defense always result in a death?"

Oh, hoolies. How to answer that. "I think you would do best to ask one of the sword-dancers bent on killing me. I don't seek it. I don't desire it. I don't *like* it. But I will stay alive. No matter what it takes."

He nodded, somewhat distracted, still turning things over in his head. And he needed to do it on his own. "The mare wants your attention again," I told him. "Best give it to her."

He knew the subject was at an end for the evening. He turned back to the mare slowly, then began rubbing once again with the sacking. I left him to it.

Del saw it at once. She watched me return from Neesha, stood up before I could sit down. She reached out and took my hand, led me away.

We stood beneath the rising moon. Dusk had become night. Behind us, the fire died to coals. "What is it?"

It echoed what I'd asked Neesha. But my answer was different. "I think I've lost him."

"No. Never. I've told you this before."

"I don't know, bascha. It's different. *He's* different—"

"He killed a man."

"In battle. It's different when a raider is coming at you. Over the past week, he's seen what my life is like. He doesn't seem to understand that it is unlike any sword-dancer's in the South. That it will always be. No one, not a single sword-dancer who lived at Alimat, has ever sworn *elaii-ali-ma*." I raised a hand to quiet her before she blamed herself for that. "What I did that day, and what I do now, is what I see fit to do. But it's nothing the shodo ever taught us."

"You haven't *lost* him, Tiger. He's simply learning his way." We stood very close, hands linked. "You learned at Alimat, driven by circumstances to become the best. I learned at Staal-Ysta because I was driven by circumstances, as well. We've both had hard lives. It wasn't our choices to do so, but these lives drove us to become what we are." She released my hand, slid her hand up my back and stroked it. Rather like Neesha and the mare, come to think of it. "He made his choice when he sought you. You'll never lose him."

It struck me that we'd had this conversation before. But it seemed to be something I couldn't let go. "Two years ago he wasn't in my life. I didn't even know he existed. In most ways, he's still a stranger to me. Why, then, am I afraid to lose him?"

"How long did it take you to fall in love with me?"

That was unexpected. And baffling. "What?"

"How long did it take you to fall in love with me?"

"Uhhh . . . I don't know." Not comforting, but she wanted the truth. "I never thought about it."

"You wanted to *bed* me the moment I walked into the cantina. Later, you loved me."

I was all at sea, and somewhat plaintive with it. "Del, I don't understand what you're saying."

"You fell in love with your son, Tiger. You met him one day wholly unexpectedly, the way you met me. And at some point, you fell in love with him. *Came* to love him. It's entirely normal for you to fear losing what you love." She wound an arm around mine, clasped my hand. "But don't assume you will lose me, lose Neesha. Because you won't."

I thought about that a moment, then let it go and thought of something else entirely. "I wish we were at home. In private."

Del laughed. "We could drag our blankets off into the desert."

I opened my mouth to answer, but Del got there first.

"But you're old. We should get a room in Istamir tomorrow. One with a bed."

I laughed. Then I unwound my arm from her, unclasped my hand, and took her into my arms. Whereupon I kissed her as hard as I could. And she kissed me back.

"Well," Del said once we broke apart. "Perhaps we *should* drag our blankets off into the desert."

I rested my forehead against hers. "Let's."

Back under the tree, we bundled up our bedrolls. Neesha grinned as we did so. White teeth, in the moonlight, glowed against his face. "I wondered how long it would take you. Can't keep your hands off one another."

"And you," I said, "are jealous."

He hooted briefly. "We'll be in Istamir tomorrow. I'll have my itch scratched then." He paused a moment. "Many itches, and many scratchings thereof."

"You men," Del chided. "You must always make it into a competition."

She and I carried our bedrolls some distance away, finding a little privacy by putting the wagons between us and everyone else.

Some time later, our legs entwined, hips touching, breath upon one another's face, I said quietly, "No time at all."

"'No time'? What 'no time'?"

"To fall in love with you."

"Well, I knew that."

"When did you fall in love with me?"

"Who says I did? Maybe you're just—convenient."

I pressed my brow against the blanket. "Sharper than a sword, I swear. Women always wound."

"It took me somewhat longer than you," Del said. "I was driven. Obsessed. There was no room in my heart for a man. For love. Not after Ajani. Not with my brother missing. And you were less loveable at first."

"Wounding, again!"

"You were a pig of a Southroner."

"That's no improvement, bascha!"

"Well, you were," she said matter-of-factly. "And spoiled by all of the Southron women."

"Spoiled?"

"Oh, hoolies, Tiger—they fell at your feet. I was there, remember? I saw it!" She tossed her hair aside as she rolled onto her back. "But mostly . . . I didn't know how to fall in love."

"Or fall at my feet." Belly-down, I rested my chin on crossed arms. "I don't think you ever have, come to think of it."

"Fallen at your feet?"

"Yes."

"Only when I trip."

Chapter 15

ALONG DAY'S RIDE TO ISTAMIR. The further north we went, the more plentiful the trees, occasionally huddling together in thickets. Groundcover, often abloom, was abundant with vegetation, shrubbery, vines twisting around tree trunks. The grass slowly turned from pale green prairie growth to a lush, deep, vivid green, short enough that the wagons moved through it smoothly. Good grazing; I well understood why Neesha's stepfather had built his horse farm in such surroundings.

At one point, as we ate our midday meal in the saddle, Neesha mentioned that if we turned due west, a half day's ride would deliver us to the farm. Later, I rode up from the back of the last wagon to join him and asked if he'd rather break off from us now and go ahead to the farm while Del and I escorted the caravan into Istamir.

A faint frown puckered his brows. "My job is to ride all the way into Istamir."

"I'm sure Del and I can handle things."

"I did kill one of those borjuni, you know."

It wasn't a brag. What it was, I didn't quite understand for a moment, and then I grasped it. It was a subtle defensiveness, an attempt to remind me he had proved his worth as an outrider, as someone who could contribute. Hastily, honestly, I said, "No, no, I only meant it would be less time for you to ride over there from here. That's all."

His brow smoothed as he smiled. "There are women in Istamir."
Oh. That. I grinned at him. "Say no more."

He rode the roan mare, his bay gelding tied to the back of the last wagon. When not watching for raiders, he spent time assessing nearly every step she took, how her ears twitched, how she registered the world, and how often; was she a smooth goer, or so intent on proving herself—rather like Neesha, come to think of it—that she could not relax. All the minutiae that goes into finding out if a horse will work for a rider it doesn't know, and how. Was it war? Was it docility? Was it something in between? The stud was never docile, but not always at war. He could walk out in a long, smooth, ground-eating stride. He just didn't do it often enough.

I shook off stirrups and stretched my legs, popping knees. Then, twisting in the saddle from side to side, I loosened my spine. I hadn't ridden such distance on a daily basis for two years, and my body, on horseback for days at a time, was still deciding if it wanted to remember how all the parts fit together.

And then, for some incomprehensible reason, I looked at my hands. At the stumps of missing fingers.

Is that what it would take to fell the Sandtiger? To recognize and comprehend what it meant for a sword-dancer to have one less finger per hand to help steady his sword and then dance accordingly? I had spent almost every day of my life exercising since I lost those fingers atop the stone spire, among the madmen of ioSkandi. I worked my hands, strengthening fingers and the sides of my palms, training the stumps to close down onto the leather grip with as much pressure as they could. Several men had learned that I remained dangerous despite lacking those fingers. But for all my strength and will and training, I was at a disadvantage if the right man came along.

Or maybe it was more accurate to say, if the *wrong* man came along.

"Riders!" Del called.

I stopped looking at my hands and concentrated on what lay ahead. "Drop back," I told Neesha, and he did so.

Four riders. I unsheathed my sword, knowing that Del and Neesha did the same. I fell in beside Mahmood on the lead wagon, with

Del immediately across from me on the other side. "We're close to Istamir, right?" I asked.

Mahmood nodded. "Not far to go."

"Might these be borjuni?" If so, it was unusual; borjuni did not usually raid so close to a city.

"I wouldn't *think* so," the merchant said consideringly. "But who knows what may have happened here? I've been trading in the South. It's been months since I came here."

The riders came closer. There were no blades flashing in the sun, no ululations, no abrupt change of pace from lope to gallop. Of course all of that could change within a matter of moments. But I saw no tension in the horses, as if set to run.

"We'll halt," Mahmood said. He tipped his head to the sky and let loose with a bellow in Desert even as he began to slow his team, directing the others to stop as well.

I remained next to Mahmood on his high wagon seat, as did Del on the other side. I could not see Neesha, but knew he would let us know if anyone attempted to loop around to the last wagon. So far the four riders showed no signs of doing that.

They came on, then slowed to a trot as they rode close in. Four men, their coloring in hair and skin a mix from Southron dark to Northern light. They ranged in age, I judged, from late twenties to forties. Clothing was simple, unadorned burnouses—though they'd call them "robes"—bound with wide, plain leather belts.

"What have you?" asked the blond man I took to be a Northerner, gesturing to the lead wagon. I decided this was not a raiding party; borjuni never asked what you had, they just stole it.

"Silks and spices," Mahmood answered.

"Ah!" said the blond, "You will be most welcome. We mean no rudeness, but we will escort you into Istamir. We have been beset by borjuni this past month, so now we ride out to help protect the caravans. So many have been lost while approaching town." He looked at Del, then at me. There was no questioning look in his eyes as he saw Del; but then, Northerners were accustomed to independent women. "I see you are well-served already."

"Yes," Mahmood said, "but we would be grateful if you accompanied us as well."

Very diplomatic of him. One man rode to the last wagon, two fell in one on each side, near Del and me, and the fourth took up the point. It was a relaxed ride into Istamir. Few raiding parties, if any, would attack a caravan with seven outriders, three of whom were obviously sword-dancers. Mahmood, atop his wagon seat, looked more relaxed than I had seen him at any point on our journey.

My companion, the youngest of them, Southron-dark, was very diffident. "May I ask a question?"

"You may."

"Are you the Sandtiger?"

I very nearly smiled. Even so far north, the reputation preceded me. "I am."

"Are you aware there's a bounty on your head?"

Oh, hoolies. There went contentment. I gritted teeth. "Yes."

"I only warn you," the young man said on a rush. "There are sword-dancers in town. And there is talk of the bounty."

Inwardly, I swore. "How many?"

"At least six, that I've seen."

More swearing inside my head. "And they all of them know about the bounty?"

"Oh, yes. Tavern talk. They may form a cadre to look for you down south."

Tavern talk. More often exaggeration or outright lies than not, but in this case, as sometimes happens, the truth.

I had two options. I could go looking for the sword-dancers from tavern to tavern, taking the offensive, or hope no one realized I was in Istamir before Del and I took a room at an inn. After all, if I kept a low profile trouble might well be averted. No one would expect me to be in the North.

At Umir's private contest, I had taken on, one by one, more than six sword-dancers, and come out on top. But I'd just as soon not be required to do it again. I was neither foolish nor complacent. The latter had gotten Abbu Bensir seriously injured when I'd danced with him in Alimat, a seventeen-year-old boy with next to no skills. Abbu assumed I would offer no proper challenge. He let his guard down, and because I was big and fast—and lucky—he nearly died of a crushed throat from the strike of a wooden sparring sword.

I would not be like Abbu Bensir. I couldn't afford to. Not when the swords were steel rather than wood.

I knew very well that, when next in a tavern, my newfound friend would be quick to spread the word I was in Istamir. There was always wagering when sword-dancers met; he would want to be the one to dole out the juicy news.

I looked at him, shrugged a little, and said with exquisite mildness that I was not a seeker of fame or wealth but would of course be prepared to entertain any or all of the six. We would not stay long, however, because of business elsewhere.

If all went well, we could shake him off before seeking an inn—preferably a place where we were strangers to the landlord. Sworddancers knew me and I knew them. We were aware of nearly everyone who danced. Those who made their livings in more docile, domesticated pursuits rarely knew me. But with talk of Umir's bounty, it wasn't surprising some word had leaked out, and that word was always coupled with mention of my recognizable facial scars. It was difficult to miss them, just as it was difficult to miss the absent fingers. But that news, I thought, would not have spread so far. I had disappeared upon my return from Skandi. Eventually other sword-dancers would learn of it, but not yet.

Or so I hoped.

Istamir was rich in quarried stone. Unlike Julah with its mudbrick buildings huddling against the earth, this place was made of chiseled stone. It was gray on green earth, or deep brown where the soil was beaten by feet, hooves, and wagons, but featured also pale golden stone and white chunks veined with what appeared to be silver.

These were not the Northern longhouses of Staal-Ysta, Del's home, floating on a lake in the midst of towering mountains. These were stone squares featuring walled privacy courtyards, with flowering tree limbs drooping over the walls to encroach on the roadways.

Everywhere green, in rolling hills and meadows, freckled by flowers of red and white and yellow. Del and I had ridden to Staal-Ysta in winter. But this was summer, and Istamir was glorious with it.

The young man riding with me wished me a pleasant goodbye, said his duty was done, and rode away. The other three departed as well. Mahmood's four wagons once again had only three outriders.

"What now?" I asked the merchant. Our job required us to escort him to wherever his destination, but no further.

"To the end of this street, then right. Not far." He looked at me sharply. "You will be paid the other portion. On my honor."

I stared at him a moment. "Why would I think you wouldn't pay us?"

Mahmood shifted and glanced away from me, clearly uncomfortable. "Merchants are sometimes accused of dishonesty."

"Well, that may be, but I never thought it of you."

He was a proud man. "Thank you." Then he gestured, indicating the street ahead of us. "See the cantina sign? The red one with yellow paint? We turn there. Marketfield is behind it, though at some distance beyond."

Still in formation, we traversed the center of the road. Dirt was soon replaced with hewn stone laid down atop the churned up surface, fitted together into a wide paved street. Shod hooves clopped on stone.

Clearly it was considered perfectly normal for caravans to travel down the middle of the main street. Passersby glanced at the wagons but paid little attention, busy about their own business. "Not much interested, are they?" I observed.

"Oh, they don't bother until marketday," Mahmood explained. "Then everyone comes to see and to buy or trade. Marketfair opens tomorrow; I was late getting started on the journey. My men and I will begin setting up tonight, finish tomorrow at dawn, and people will begin coming shortly afterward. Some will buy, some will look, as always. But I expect to sell out of all goods by the end of tomorrow, or perhaps the day after." He looked up at me. "You will of course return the merchandise carried in your pouches."

I affected dismay. "And now sword-dancers, like merchants, are considered dishonest?"

Mahmood opened his mouth to answer, thought about it, and offered a small smile. "Never."

I directed his attention forward with the jutting of my chin.

"Red sign with yellow paint." In fact, it was a red background and painted upon it was a howling wolf.

"Yes," Mahmood said and worked the reins to begin the turn.

It neared dusk. I was ready for dinner. And some spirits. And a bed with Del in it. And as I smiled to myself, content with my plans, I heard the shout: "That's Kirit's roan mare!"

It was a very loud shout. Everyone in the street stopped talking at once and looked at the man who shouted.

Ah, hoolies.

I twisted in the saddle to look, sighing in resignation. As might be expected, he was a sword-dancer. Dinner, drink, bed, and Del would all have to wait.

Chapter 16

I LOOKED AT MAHMOOD. "I think you'd best move on. It seems we have business, and you're close to this Marketfield anyway. I'll find you later for our payment and Neesha's horse."

The merchant nodded vigorously and called out orders to his drivers. Del and I let the caravan roll on; Neesha held his place upon the roan mare; and once the caravan passed, the three of us gathered together in the midst of the paved street. There was no mistaking what we were, anymore than we could mistake the other sword-dancer for what he was.

He was blond, hair to his shoulders, tall, broad-shouldered. His burnous was a faded green. As expected, the grip and hilts of a sword jutted up from behind his back.

"Northerner," Del observed. "But young. Nineteen?"

Quietly I told Neesha, "A choice. Give over the mare or fight him for her." I paused. "Oh, wait—there's another possibility: Offer to buy her, even though he doesn't own her. We've got the coin."

Neesha looked at me. I discovered he was smiling. Not a mouth-stretching, happy smile, but a smaller, subtler one. I had the feeling he wasn't giving up the mare. Or buying her.

Del, to my right, quietly backed her horse a few steps, rode behind me and fell in on Neesha's left side. It was a silent solidarity and very clear to anyone looking on. Including the Northern-born sword-dancer.

Heedless of the opposition we offered, he strode swiftly across the street and grabbed the roan mare's near rein. He stared up at Neesha, plainly angry. "This is Kirit's horse. What are you doing with her?"

Well, there were several possible answers. Kirit sold her to Neesha, lost her in a wager, or was killed. By me. I wondered which Neesha would offer.

Mounted, my son looked down at the man. His tone was delicately shaded with something akin to sympathy, which I found curious. "Was he your friend?"

That was not what I expected. Apparently neither had the Northerner.

"Is," he corrected. "Kirit *is* my friend. Unless you say otherwise."

"I'm very sorry," Neesha said quietly. "Your friend met with an accident."

Hmm. Was Neesha going to lie his way out of a confrontation?

"An accident," the young man echoed. "What kind of accident would result in the loss of his mare?" He flicked a glance at the sword rising above Neesha's shoulder, then met the rich, honey-brown eyes of my son. "Did you kill him?"

Silence. Well, there was no help for it. "No," I said. "I killed him." I glanced sidelong at Neesha, who looked disappointed. "Well, I can't help it. He asked."

Naturally the young man's attention shifted to me. He released the mare's bridle, took a step toward the stud. The stud didn't like it. He snaked out his head and snapped at the sword-dancer, who leaped back with alacrity, swearing.

"Sorry," I said lightly. "My horse is picky about who his friends are."

The Northerner attempted to recover his composure by yanking his burnous into order. His eyes, a grayish blue, now were empty of fear. Now were full of anger. "Was it a challenge?" he asked curtly. "Or murder?"

It truly caught me by surprise. "Murder? Why in the name of the gods would I wish to murder him?"

The reply didn't amuse him. "Then I challenge you."

He didn't know who I was; he didn't say anything about it,

didn't look or act like he knew. I was, obviously, just a stranger, a sword-dancer like any other. It was rather refreshing. "Well," I said, "I don't think you want to do this. Really. You shouldn't. It would not be a good thing."

"My name is Darrion," he said. "I challenge you."

I winced. "You might want to think again."

"I *challenge* you."

"Who was the better of you?" I asked. "You? Or Kirit?"

He lifted his chin. "I."

I sighed. "Darrion, please reconsider. Kirit and I engaged in a death-dance, as might be obvious. It was fair. He lost. There was no trickery, no murder, no anger in me. It was a sword-dance."

"A death-dance."

"Well, yes. Kirit made the challenge, and that's what he insisted on." I shrugged. "I did give him the option to ride away."

"He would never do such a thing!"

I nodded. "And so he is dead."

Darrion flicked a hard glance at Del. This time he registered what she was. He *saw* her. "Northerner."

"Yes," she replied. Then added, "Trained on Staal-Ysta."

In its way, the statement was a brag. Not everyone was admitted to the island.

"Sword-singer," Darrion said.

Del smiled as the white gelding stomped stone. "I am."

Cheerfully, I added, "I, on the other hand, was trained at Alimat."

Neesha was not to be left behind. "And I at Beit al'Shahar. By the Sandtiger."

I very nearly laughed. More luster for the legend. I managed to repress a grin.

Darrion now looked at each of us more carefully. He appeared to reconsider his position. But he had challenged me. Twice and emphatically. Certainly he could *un*challenge me. But very few sword-dancers did so. There was this problem called pride. And other sword-dancers were in Istamir, apparently. If word was passed that Darrion refused to dance, shame would attach to his name. His reputation, whatever it was, whatever he hoped it might become, would be sullied. To live, he'd be reduced to working for no-name tanzeers in insignificant domains.

Decision made, Darrion lifted his chin. "Do you accept the challenge?"

Oh, hoolies.

Very quietly, out of the side of his mouth, Neesha said, "Tell him who you are."

Equally quietly, I murmured, "I don't think so. Other sword-dancers are in town. I'd like to leave before this turns into a whole series of dances."

Darrion raised his voice. "Do you accept the challenge?"

I sighed very heavily. "I guess." I tossed the stud's right rein to Del, shook my feet free of stirrups, swung a leg across the stud's broad rump and jumped down. I began to strip out of belt, burnous, sandals, harness.

"Well, if *he* doesn't know who you are," Neesha said. "Maybe the others don't, either."

I looked up at him, sword in my hand. "All six of them—well, five, not counting Darrion? And we know from our escorts into town that they've talked of looking for me."

"That doesn't mean they know who you are. No one expects you to be north of the border."

"If a man has heard of me, he's also heard of these." I tapped my scarred check, then lifted a hand with its missing little finger. "Rather easy to identify me."

"Well," Neesha said, "just beat them all."

Ah, such faith my son had in me. I rolled my eyes, shook my head, stepped out into the street. The paved street. How in hoolies do you draw a circle in a paved street?

"Not here," Darrion said. "In the Marketfield."

I glared at him balefully, put my sandals back on, and set off in the direction Mahmood and his wagons had gone. Darrion, astonishingly enough, walked beside me, though not remotely close. Then I realized that he would give no ground that might lessen him in the eyes of others.

Del and Neesha brought up the rear, Del leading the stud. I hoped clothes and harness wouldn't fall off my saddle along the way. The sword, however, was in my right hand; it wasn't going anywhere.

I thought I'd make conversation as we walked. "Nice day."

Darrion said nothing.

"Quite an attractive town, don't you think? Walls strung with vines and flowers. Adds something."

No reply. But his expression was stony.

"I'm actually impressed by this town. Very advanced. I've never seen a paved street." I paused. "Do you live here or hail from somewhere else?"

Finally, he looked at me. Glared at me. "No talking."

I feigned surprise. "Why no talking? I'm just being friendly."

"You are attempting to distract me."

I barked a blurted laugh. "No, no . . . and anyway, a sword-dancer won't allow his opponent to upset his dance. It's one of the rules."

It was no such thing. Just all part of the dance, if a man elected to distract his opponent. Concentration was all. Lack of it lost the dance. Lack of it killed if the dance were to the death.

"I *do* think it's an attractive town," I said cheerfully. "The last time I came north, it was winter. Brrrrrr." I shivered. "Too cold for me. All that snow and ice. I'm just a Southroner. I need warmth in my bones." Darrion ground his teeth. A muscle leaped in his jaw. "It was especially cold at Staal-Ysta," I continued. "I don't see how anyone can live there."

That caught his attention. "You've been to Staal-Ysta?"

I indicated Del behind me. "With her."

"Did they admit you to training?"

"That's not what I was there for." And it wasn't. "Besides, a seventh-level sword-dancer doesn't really require more training." Which was a lie, but all part of my arsenal. Modest, it wasn't.

Darrion's head snapped toward me. "You're seventh level? From Alimat?"

"I have that honor, yes."

"Did you know the Sandtiger?"

My brows shot up. I stared quizzically at the Northerner. "Um, yes. I mean, we met a few times."

"In the circle?"

I supposed it could be said I met myself in the circle. "Sparring, only. Not a true dance. I knew better than to ask it of him."

Darrion nodded. I had him talking now. "I would like to meet him one day. Not to challenge him, you understand—that would be foolish—but to learn from him. He has much to teach."

I wanted very badly to turn around and see Del's and Neesha's expressions, but I didn't. I could imagine them, anyway. Pure, unadulterated, and undoubtedly delighted amusement.

"You seem to know your limitations," I noted. "You wouldn't challenge him, huh? Well, that's wise. He's quite good. The best in the South, in fact. Maybe you'll meet him someday."

Darrion's attention shifted. He gestured. "Marketfield."

We left behind the buildings, the paved street. Marketfield was huge. An ocean of wagons filled the eye. Some folk would work from the back end of their wagons, setting out wares on a blanket. Others raised stalls with canvas sidewalls, awnings. Grass was beaten into a series of paths winding through and around the wagons, creating aisles. Mahmood was here somewhere. It might be a chore to track him down. Then again, there were three of us. And market folk we could ask.

Darrion gestured again. "This way. There is a practice circle pegged out in the grass."

I strode next to him. "Hold frequent dances, do they?"

"It's part of Marketday. People enjoy watching. Some wager on the dances. Do you see? Already we are gaining an audience."

So we were. The residents knew what was up—they saw two tall, broad-built men carrying swords. I heard excited murmurs rising on the air and calls to summon others to the dance. As we approached the circle, more folk fell in.

The circle was, as Darrion had said, pegged out. It was a proper one, though in packed dirt. Inside the circle, the grass had been worn away years before.

At the closest edge, I set down my sword and unlaced my sandals. One at a time, I tossed them to Del. We shared crooked smiles. Neesha didn't bother to hide his anticipation. I guess it no longer bothered him that his dance had become mine.

Sandals banished for the moment, I walked to the center of the circle and set down my sword. Even as I did so, Darrion put down his, then retreated to the side opposite me. I shook out my arms, rolled my neck, hunched and lowered my shoulders a few times. Darrion stared at me as if baffled by my actions. As well he could be at his age; it was long before his body would encounter aches and pains.

I raised my voice to call across the circle. "Who has the honor?" He was the challenger; he could name the person who would tell us to begin.

He looked straight at Del, still mounted. "One of my own kind. A Northerner, trained on Staal-Ysta."

Del nodded matter-of-factly.

My opponent looked around the mass of people surrounding the circle. "My name is Darrion, and I challenge this man." It wasn't necessary to challenge me again or to announce his name, but Darrion wished to be dramatic.

Surprising everyone, I walked across the circle and stood very close to him, leaning in. In a low voice, I asked, "Are you certain you wish to do this? Are you absolutely sure?"

Surprised, he stared at me, pulling his head back from my face.

"You can pick up your sword and walk away," I said. "I'll do the same."

He spoke in a hissing undertone. "I will do no such thing!"

"I'm not going to announce my name. But I will tell it to you." I leaned in even closer, almost speaking into his ear. "You've got your wish, Darrion. You'll dance against the Sandtiger."

It took a moment for him to comprehend. Eyes opened wide. His mouth loosened. Color fled his face. He stared and stared, hundreds of expressions kindling in his eyes, in his face. He looked very young, did Darrion. Young and stricken.

As I backed away, I spread my hands, shrugging. "You never asked."

He breathed hard. He looked at paired swords in the middle of the circle. He looked at the crowd gathered to watch, to wager on, the sword-dance. He saw me complete my trip across the circle. He looked again at the spectators, moistened his lips. I recognized the expression on his face: Darrion simply didn't know what to do.

I took my place across from him. "Ready?"

The crowd had fallen into silence. Darrion looked from one man to another to another. It was too much for him, I knew, to yield before he began. Too many people watching. Other sword-dancers in town. A Northern sword-*singer*, trained on Staal-Yista. The Sandtiger himself waiting patiently across the circle.

He drew in a very deep breath. Shut his mouth. Firmed his jaw. Lifted his head proudly. "Say it."

And Del said it: "*Dance.*"

Chapter 17

THE BEGINNING IS ALWAYS THE SAME. Instead of the fierce beauty of the dance, there is merely the ability to get to your sword first, to take it up, to disarm your opponent if he's slower than you; to defend, if you're slower than he. A fair number of dances have been won and lost in the first few seconds of that charge across the circle, that first grasp and lift of the sword.

We were of a size, Darrion and I. On another day, he might have won the race. But today he did not.

I was of two minds. I could beat him swiftly so I could disappear as swiftly, or I could teach him a lesson more slowly. And I meant that literally: a lesson. As a shodo.

So I compromised.

He came in at me, swinging his sword in a roundhouse maneuver. It was never an effective offense if you're slow, or unpracticed, or if your opponent knows a thorough defense. He was neither slow nor unpracticed, but I was an opponent who knew a thorough defense. I met his blade with mine, with power, with weight behind it. He did manage to hang on to his blade, though he staggered back a few steps. While he did that, I followed, stepped in too close for swordwork, and met him at the very edge of the circle. He glanced down at the pegs, realized that he was precariously near to stepping out of the circle and thus losing the sword-dance.

"Duck down and sideways," I said, holding my blow. "Go

laterally. Not backwards or you step out of the circle. Not forward, because you'll end up too close to your opponent. *Laterally*. Roll if necessary. Somersault if necessary. Just get the hoolies out of way of your opponent's blade as you move away from the edge of the circle."

His balance was completely off. It's difficult to remain in the circle when your feet are nearly on the line and your opponent is in your face. Before he could step outside the confines, I reached out with my left hand, closed it around his right wrist and jerked him toward me, away from the line so he wouldn't forfeit.

Darrion was astonished that I should do so. It kept him frozen.

"Oh, for the gods' sake," I said, annoyed. "Don't just stand there. Or I'll push you to the pegs again, and this time all the way out. I won't save you. You don't learn anything that way. *Dance!*"

He was not better than his friend Kirit, no matter what he claimed. But he was probably better than the dance he offered me. I'd completely undermined his confidence by telling him my iden- tity, by pushing him so hard right at the beginning. Which had been precisely my intent.

We danced a bit more, and Darrion recovered a portion of his composure. He was grimly determined to keep up with me. And as he became more confident, more determined, I guided him into a specific maneuver.

I grinned as blades clashed, and mine went wheeling across the circle. I heard the huge gasp, the indrawn breaths of shock from the crowd. Even Darrion was astonished.

His sword dipped. He hesitated a fraction. I leaped in, clamped my left hand around his wrist, closed my right hand over the hilt, and ripped the sword from his hand. Within a minute it sat in my hand the way it was supposed to.

At arm's length, I placed the tip against his chest, right where his heart beat. "Think ahead," I said. "Think it through. See it in your head before you ever have to use it."

He stood unmoving; wise for a man with a sword tip at his chest. "You released it on purpose," he accused. "Your sword. You planned that."

"That's what you must do. Plan it. Think ahead. Think it through.

See it, and when you must, you will use it. But you have to remember one thing."

He stared at me, asking with his eyes.

"You have to be as skilled, or better, than your opponent. Because someone else who loses his sword and then takes yours may not be as forgiving as I am today." I backed up, put out my left hand without looking, and my sword grip was slapped against my palm. I flipped both blades into the air, crossing one another in front of me. I caught them both, his in my left, mine in my right. "Think it through, Darrion. See it. *Use* it. But only when you're ready."

I tossed him his sword and walked out of the circle.

Mahmood found us, instead of the other way around. He waited politely as I laced up my sandals, dressed, then took the stud's reins from Del. I'd have ridden, but Mahmood was on foot, and I thought it would be rude. He led us to his wagons so we could pick up Neesha's horse, hand over the silks and spices, and get paid the second half of our fee.

The crowd had thinned out, though for a bit I was trailed by kids as we walked through the aisles until one or both parents caught up and dragged them away. Del and Neesha had put Mahmood and me in between them as they rode and we walked, forming a human and equine shield. They knew very well I didn't want to deal with anymore sword-dancers, but the other five would certainly look for me if told I was here. Word would be passed. Istamir's inhabitants didn't need to know my name; all they had to do was describe the claw marks in my face.

Del, Neesha, and I came to a halt when Mahmood indicated that we should. Del and Neesha dismounted, and the three of us began pulling packets out of saddle pouches. Mahmood handled the muslin-wrapped silk rolls as if they were children, welcoming them back. With great care he unrolled the silks, shook them out, spread them across the tailgate of his wagon. Even I had to admit the panoply of colors with a spark of silver throughout was beautiful.

He lifted the top length of silk, smelled it, then looked at me mournfully. "They smell of spice."

Del, standing near, went to look. She lifted a corner of silk to her face, then put it down again. "As I told you, scented silk is not necessarily a bad thing. Charge more for them." Once again she ran a hand over the dark blue length of fabric. Silver thread glittered in the sunlight. "They'll pay."

Mahmood nodded. "Yes, it's possible; I have thought on it. We shall see. And now the spices?"

We dug through the pouches and unearthed the small bags, handing them to Mahmood and two of his men. The scent of cinnamon wafted into the air. Once done packing them into modest wooden boxes, Mahmood handed a small leather bag to me.

"The balance of your fee," he said. "And now I have something else for you." He gestured to his wagons. "You have done us a great service. I would like to return it, even though it is a modest service. My men and I discussed this, and we would like to offer our wagons to you for tonight's sleeping."

I think all three of us were utterly astonished. I certainly was.

"You will be sought," Mahmood said to me directly. "You can't risk an inn."

"Uh," was about all I could manage.

"Sleep the night in the wagons. My men offer to sleep on the ground." His attitude became diffident as he looked first at me, then at Del. "Please, accept my apologies. There is room only for one in each wagon."

Del and I exchanged a glance. "I think we can manage one night sleeping alone," I said dryly. "But—?"

"As I said. You have already danced twice since we left Julah. You are going on in the morning, yes?"

I nodded. "At first light."

"Well then, sleep this night in peace. They won't think to look for you here. But there is one other thing." He was diffident again. "I would advise you tie your horses at other wagons. I have spoken to three merchants I know, and they are willing to host your mounts for the night. If all are left here, it would draw attention. Especially the white horse."

"He's right," Del said. "Neesha's got that sword-dancer's roan, a color not often seen, and I the white gelding, seen even less."

Neesha added, "And even a line-backed dun isn't all that common. Plus he's a stallion. If we tie them elsewhere, sleep in Mahmood's wagons, we'll be safer than anywhere else. However . . ." Neesha raised his brows at Mahmood. "I do have plans for the evening. And it might entail sleeping in someone else's bed, so I wouldn't need the wagon."

Mahmood was taken aback for one moment, and then he understood. He allowed himself a small smile. "Several beds, perhaps?"

Neesha grinned at him. "That would work." Then he caught my expression. "Nobody knows me. And I'll walk to that wolf cantina so there's no horse to draw attention. Though people probably don't know my own horse anyway."

All he said was true. Remove Neesha from my presence—and Del's, since she was well-known as the Sandtiger's woman—and he probably could go anywhere without a second thought. "You might take your harness and sword off," I suggested. "One less thing by which to identify you. Besides, I don't think that's the kind of dancing you mean to do."

Neesha laughed. "Not exactly, no." He smiled at Mahmood. "Where should I take the roan and the bay?"

"Leave the bay," I said. "I think you're right that he wouldn't be recognized. Just take the roan. That way we'll at least have one mount here."

Mahmood said, "My men will take them where they should go."

"Um," I said. "That may not be such a good idea. The stud now and then isn't friendly to strangers."

"I'll take him," Neesha said. "I can do that much before I go in search of lovely women." Thus the stud went with my son while the roan and Del's white gelding were taken elsewhere by two of the drivers.

Del was not a sound sleeper. She woke up as the wagon creaked. "It's me," I said quietly, fighting briefly with the snugged and tied tailgate flap.

There was no light, save from the moon, the stars, and the dying fires throughout the Marketfield. But with the back flap closing behind me, I couldn't see her.

With a note of surprise in her voice, she said, "Why are you here?"

"Couldn't sleep. Where in hoolies are you?"

"The sleeping platform. Where people sleep. Where *I* had been sleeping. That's what it's for." She paused. "It's truly not big enough for two."

I groped my way forward, following her voice. "I know that. I was on a platform in another wagon. But there must be room on the floor."

"You want to sleep on the floor?"

"I want *us* to sleep on the floor—dammit!"

"What?"

I swore twice more. "I just caught my little toe on something. Why is it the most insignificant toe of all ten is the one that hurts the most?" Bent over with arms outstretched, I took smaller, more careful steps. "Say something."

"Why?"

"So I can find you."

She muttered something under her breath. In Northern, so I couldn't decipher it. Once, I was able to; I could read all books and speak all languages when ioSkandi's magic was in me. But not anymore. I'd rid myself of it all.

"Just stay there, Tiger." I heard movement, the sound of rustling fabric. "All right. Bedding is on the floor."

"Are you on the floor with it?"

"If you insist."

"That is why I came over here."

More rustling. "Yes, I am on the floor."

More careful movement from me. I found a leg. Progress. I crawled into a position right beside her, snuggled down beneath the covers and fit myself to her. "Ahhhh. Much better."

Silence for a long moment. Then she said, with a subtle ripple of wonder in her tone, "Could you really not sleep without me nearby?"

"Well," I said, "actually, it was the crying baby in the next wagon."

Del snickered. "A likely story."

"There *was* a crying baby in the next wagon."

"Hah. That's not why you came."

I set my mouth on the flesh below her left ear. "There's nothing wrong with a man wishing to sleep with the woman he loves."

"Even if it means he's crushing the woman he loves?"

I took the hint and adjusted my position. "Better?"

"Somewhat. It will do." She yawned. "Go to sleep, Tiger."

I smiled into darkness. Sleep came softly.

Chapter 18

NOT LONG AFTER DAWN, the crying baby heralded the day. Now Del would know I hadn't been making things up the night before. I untangled myself from bedding, crawled to the back end, untied the flap, and poked my head out. Morning mist slowly dissipated with the measured arrival of the sun.

And then I noticed the body. My son was rolled up in his bedding just beyond the back of the wagon. His bay was tied to it, but showed no inclination to step on his owner. All I could see of Neesha was a tangle of hair poking out from under a blanket. The rest of him was not visible except as unidentifiable lumps beneath bedding.

How many people can sleep with a crying baby next door?

The noise had roused Del as well. She crawled up beside me with her head stuck out the open rear flap. "I'm so glad Sula is past the age of infancy," she murmured.

"Oh, she still has quite the voice," I reminded her. "Especially during her many baths. Baths required because she insists on playing in the dirt, with occasional visits to piss puddles."

She noticed Neesha below. "What is he doing here? I thought he'd stay with a woman."

"Maybe she was crying, too." I undid the pegs of the tailgate and lowered it, crawled out while trying to avoid the bundle of flesh and blood. I stepped around him, put a hand on his gelding's muzzle so as to back him up a step; he was now perilously close to his owner's body. "Though I suppose he might be dead." I prodded Neesha with a bare foot. "Hey. Are you alive?" No reply. Or movement, for that matter. "Up. You can be hung over on horseback. Let's get out of here." I paused, wincing. "And how can you sleep with that baby screeching? It's worse than a rooster."

Del climbed out of the wagon. "He—or she—is not *screeching*, Tiger. That's crying. He—or she—is undoubtedly hungry, or wet. Possibly both." This time it was her foot prodding Neesha. "Up."

The bundle of bedding moved. Neesha peeled back his blanket and squinted into nascent daylight. "Can we stay here another day? I met a woman . . ."

Del and I shook our heads simultaneously in resignation, exchanging wry smiles.

"If you met a woman, why are you here instead of there?" I asked.

Neesha took to rubbing the flesh of his face all out of shape, distorting his answer. "She's married. Her husband came home."

Oh, hoolies. "Not exactly a good thing," I told him. "Husbands tend to dislike such activity."

"Well, she insisted. Kind of." He shoved blankets out of the way and sat up. "Never should a man refuse a lovely woman when she wants him so badly."

"Ah," Del said. "It's in the blood, is it not? Tiger acquiescing to women who insist on dragging him to bed. Now his son acquiescing to a woman who insists on dragging him to bed. Fruit of the same tree."

This required a reply. "Now, bascha, I haven't acquiesced to an insistent woman for years. Well, except for you. And before you, it was never with a married woman."

Del raised her brows, seemingly intrigued. "How do you know? I don't think any woman taking you to bed would *say* she was married."

Oh. Well, there was that. "To the best of my knowledge," I amended.

Neesha scrubbed a hand through dark hair, causing even more disarray. Stubble shadowed his jaw. Time for him *and* me to use a razor. "Anyway, I came back here to sleep," he said, a sentence that transformed into a major yawn. "Didn't want to bother anyone. Especially not her husband, as he came home before his wife expected him." He winced. "Are they even *trying* to shut that baby up?"

"Let's gather the horses," I suggested. "Neesha, you know where they are. Bring them back one at a time . . . I think you leading three horses that are familiar to other sword-dancers would be too much of a risk."

He nodded, rising. After stretching, he went off in search of our mounts.

"Sandals," I muttered to myself. Those, plus burnous, harness, and sword were in the wagon. The morning was a little chill. And my feet were damp and cold because Marketfield was almost completely grassy, holding the dew. I leaned into the back of the wagon and pulled out my sandals. "I think it's best if we don't wear swords and harnesses on the way out of here."

"I doubt any other sword-dancers are up yet, Tiger," Del said drily. "They are probably still in bed. Even if the beds are borrowed."

I sat on the tailgate as I laced up my sandals. "I just don't want to risk it. I really don't want to dance again, here. Too many sword-dancers to spread the word that I'm in the North."

"Didn't Khalid say Umir was arranging another contest?"

I put on my burnous, belted it. "No, just that he'd put a bounty on my head. He wants me to open that book, not dance."

Del climbed over the tailgate and disappeared into the interior long enough to gather her clothes. "I suspect word will spread quickly when you're taken, and many of the sword-dancers would go to Umir's just to see you."

"Excuse me? When I'm taken? Do me the courtesy of saying *if* I am taken!"

"Word will spread quickly *if* you are taken—" She frowned. "Though I suppose word can't actually *be* spread for an 'if.' "

"There won't be an 'if,' " I said. "Not a 'when,' or an 'if.' "

Del buckled her belt. "Then 'might.' "

"No 'might,' either."

"A 'maybe.' "

"You won't win this one, bascha."

Lacing on her sandals, she smiled. Then said, "They'll think you're afraid."

"Who will think I'm afraid? And of what?"

"Who will: the sword-dancers here in Istamir. Of what: your preference for sneaking out of town rather than meeting them."

I snorted. "I'm a legend, according to Neesha. And the jhihadi, of course. Neither of which—or whom—sneaks."

Del shrugged into her burnous. "You are neither legend nor jhihadi if you sneak out of town, which is what you're proposing."

"We are *riding* out of town. There's a difference." I paused, relieved that I was on the verge of being rescued. "And here comes Neesha with the stud."

By the time our horses were packed and ready to go, which took very little time, many more people were awake and working, preparing wagons and market stalls for commerce later in the day. When Mahmood exited his wagon and began giving orders, I went over and thanked him for the use of his wagons.

"But I am grateful to *you*," he said. "My men and I might have died when those raiders attacked, even if my former outriders had accompanied me." He paused. "Perhaps *especially* if my former outriders had accompanied me." He smiled as we clasped hands. "I am proud that the Sandtiger rode with me."

Nice to be appreciated. I mounted the stud, taking a rein from Del. I looked at Neesha, clearly hung over. Still, he was already on his bay with the blue roan to be ponied alongside. "Are you going to be able to stay ahorse?"

He peered at me out of one squinted eye, the other squeezed closed. "Of course."

"Then let's get out of here."

"See? We're sneaking," Del murmured.

I ignored her. "Let's loop around the buildings and bypass the main road." I looked again at my son. "Will you be able to direct us to the farm?"

He scowled at me. "Ride to the end of the paved road and go west. That's really all you need to know right now."

Unfortunately, this was not accomplished. Even as we turned our horses south before going west, someone shouted at us. For a fleeting instant I thought it was Mahmood, and we'd forgotten something, but the actual reason for the shout was very different.

A man dragged a woman out from one of the narrow alleyways. She was in tears, dark hair and clothing in disarray. Her lip was split, and a bruise bloomed on one cheekbone. The man was all Southroner; dark skin, black hair and eyes. He dragged the woman to a stop in front of us, which naturally caused us to rein in the horses immediately.

He was so angry he sprayed saliva. "You!" he shouted at Neesha. "You have defiled my wife!"

To Del, I quietly said, "Uh-oh."

"I should have her stoned," the man shouted, "but I have been convinced this was your doing. She had no wish for what happened to happen! You forced her!"

I knew better than that. It was too easy for women to attach themselves to Neesha. There was no *need* for him to force a woman, even if he was the type to do it. And he wasn't. However, this was a tidy little trap. He couldn't very well admit he'd forced the woman, which he hadn't; but if he *said* he *hadn't* forced her, it would place her in danger of an even worse beating. Perhaps a beating that would kill her.

My son glanced at me. I shook my head slightly and spoke quietly. "You'll have to find a way to settle this."

"Coin?" he asked.

"That could go either way. He might be greedy enough to take it, or it will inflame him further because you're insulting his wife by suggesting she can be paid for."

"Oh, hoolies," Neesha muttered.

"Yup," I agreed. "Best ask him what he wants . . . short of your death, that is."

"Well, yes," he said sourly. "I'd much prefer to avoid that."

"Stop talking!" the man cried. He thrust the woman down hard enough to drop her to her knees. He ignored Del, not surprisingly;

she wasn't capable of defiling anyone. He stared hard at me, then at Neesha. He grabbed a handful of his wife's hair. "Which one? Which one was it?"

Sobbing, she looked at Neesha. It was clear she wished not to indicate either of us. But her husband was too angry, and she'd already had a taste of his violence. "Him," she said. "The young one."

Neesha didn't deny it. A wave of color rose in his face. It wasn't shame; it was anger. "Beat *me*," he challenged. "Beat me instead of her."

"Did she consent?" the man cried. He shook her head by the hair. "Did she consent, or did you force her?"

Either answer was dangerous, for the wife or for himself, and Neesha knew it. But he found a novel approach. "I was drunk," he answered. "Too drunk to remember. Much too drunk. Men in the cantina with me—even the cantina owner—can attest to my drunkenness."

"He was drunk," I put in. "He reeked of spirits when he came to sleep by our wagon."

Del added, "Very, very drunk."

The husband glared at all of us but reserved his enmity for Neesha. "I will have this settled. I will have this *settled*. You will see!"

And so we did. A man came out of the gathering crowd. Borderer by the look of him: brown hair, not black; grey eyes, not dark; skin color close to my own. A sword rode high on his left shoulder. And hired, I realized, by the angry husband.

He looked straight at Neesha. "My name is Eddrith," he said, "and I challenge you."

Without looking at one another, Del, Neesha, and I muttered simultaneously, "Oh, hoolies."

And then another man stepped out from the crowd. He looked straight at me. "And you."

I blinked. "Me?" Here I'd been thinking about Neesha's first true sword-dance, and this man was challenging *me*. Though I guess I should have been glad of the advance warning. It was no longer required that I be given one.

His smile was edged. "I want Umir's bounty. You lose, you go with me."

The stud jangled bit shanks and pawed at the earth as I sat at ease in the saddle, leaning against the pommel on stiffened arms. "And if I win?"

"Then another sword-dancer will have the honor—though it's not truly that, is it?—of hauling you to Umir." His eyes were an icy blue, his hair white-blond. Definitely a Northerner. "But I think that will not happen."

"Rather full of yourself, aren't you?" I asked lightly. But before he could answer, out of the corner of my eye I noticed a third sword-dancer slide out of the crowd. By all the gods above and below—and sideways, for that matter—what was going on?

But this latest sword-dancer I knew.

Darrion was very solemn, but he looked neither at me, nor at Neesha. Only at Del. "I challenge the sword-singer trained at Staal-Ysta."

"Oh hoolies" indeed.

Chapter 19

ARRION, I BELIEVED, wasn't smart enough to look beyond his immediate goal, which was meeting a Staal-Ysta sword-singer in the circle. That left Neesha's man and mine, the ice-eyed Northerner.

Three of us. Three of them. It must have been planned, challenging the three of us all at the same time. "Happenstance," the Northerner said casually.

At my questioning glance, Neesha's challenger, Eddrith, simply shrugged. The mechanics didn't matter to him. Merely the opponent and the outcome.

In an undertone, Neesha asked me, "So, what do I do?"

"You've been challenged. Accept, or decline." Meanwhile, I said to my opponent, "Now? Where—here? Or in the pegged circle?"

"Now. And here will do," he said lightly, unbuckling his belt.

Del observed, "Sneaking didn't work."

"No sneaking!" I said with vigor. "We rode." I swung down from the saddle. "Well, I suppose we didn't actually ride. We *intended* to ride. I think we took two steps, did we not?" I glanced at Neesha. He was not afraid, my son. But I knew his thoughts raced like creek water over stone. I unbuckled my belt and began to take off my burnous. Very quietly, I said, "Remember what I've taught you. You're good enough. You're ready."

Neesha looked down at me from the back of his bay. "I was

never hung over when you taught me anything. Or if I was, I was so drunk I don't remember it."

"Hah," Del said as she dismounted and ducked under her gelding's neck. "You see? You drink too much, and the next day you are challenged. An argument, don't you think, for not drinking at all?"

Neesha sighed. "Ask me when I'm in the land of the living again."

"Enough!" cried the husband. "No talking. Dance!"

A man stepped up beside me. Mahmood. "Must you?" he asked. "Can you refuse?" Color rose in his face. "Should I ask that? Is it an insult?"

"No insult," I said, "but the answer is yes and no. Yes, I must; no, I can't." He looked bewildered. "If you don't mind," I said, "will you hold the horses?"

"But of course!" He held out his hand for the stud and very soon had a clutch of reins in his hand. Del's white gelding, my stud, and Neesha's bay along with the roan mare tied to his saddle.

I poked the stud in the shoulder. "Be kind. He's doing us a favor."

Three of us. Three of them. Obviously planned.

Three challengers drew three circles. Del, Neesha, and I stripped out of burnouses, freed feet of sandals. At my suggestion, we had carried swords at our saddles, not on our backs. Each of us unsheathed from harnesses looped around saddle pommels.

It was anger I felt. Anger, annoyance, aggravation, and frustration. It was so very clever to challenge all of us at the same time, to insist on simultaneous dances. Neesha would doubt himself because he'd receive no coaching from me; I'd worry about him because I couldn't *not* worry; and then of course there was Del to think about, too. And she'd think about me, and think about Neesha; and he about me, about Del. Each of us had more to think about than only ourselves, than only our own dances.

In the meantime, our opponents—led, I was certain, by my challenger—knew we would individually wish to rush our dances to see how the others were doing. And rushing a dance can end in disaster.

What he didn't realize is that I was as good slow as I was fast.

Patience often won the dance. But in this dance, patience would drive me mad.

Inwardly, I swore. Outwardly, I smiled.

My circle was in the center. Planned, too, I was certain. Among us, I was likely accounted the one to defeat as quickly and as violently, as possible; and to distract me with those I cared about on either side of me. Neesha, probably, was given short shrift; he was young, untested, even less experienced than Darrion, who had claimed himself better than Kirit, who'd owned the roan and lost to me. If we were deep in the South, Del would have an advantage. She would always have an advantage there, because Southroners could not divorce the knowledge of her gender from the challenge in the circle.

But Darrion was a Northerner. He understood about Staal-Ysta. He knew what it entailed, to go to the Place of Swords and to return from the island a sword-singer—one who'd made a blade and blooded it in what we in the South referred to as a shodo. Del had made her sword. Made her song. Killed her teacher.

It was Neesha I worried about.

The Southroners present were surprised to see Del challenged and equally surprised when she shucked belt and burnous. She wore only a tanned leather tunic, ending mid-thigh, with slits cut on either side for freedom of movement. She'd never cared about modesty; she wore what she preferred and couldn't be bothered by what others thought. But it was always a shock to those others when she first took off her burnous and showed all those long, lightly-tanned limbs. As she unsheathed her sword from her harness, still fastened to her saddle, a murmur ran through the crowd. Even Darrion, who knew exactly what he'd challenged, seemed slightly startled by what was under the burnous.

In three paces, she reached the southernmost circle where Darrion waited. He, also, had stripped out of belt and burnous, out of sandals, out of harness. He watched as she strode into the circle and lay down her sword. Where I was inclined to talk to my opponent, to begin the dance verbally, Del was always deadly serious and all the more dangerous because of it.

Out of the corner of my eye, I saw Neesha unsheathe. Like me, he wore a leather dhoti, showing lots of tanned skin. He was tall, but not as tall as I. He was maturing into a breadth of shoulder that would serve him in good stead. He was a mix of Southron, from his mother, and Skandic blood from me. One might wrongly call him a Borderer, because he looked neither Southron nor Northern. But were he in Skandi, he'd look all of a piece with the men.

He walked into the easternmost circle and lay down his sword, but before he returned to his place just outside of the circle, he faced his man, Eddrith. "Nayyib," my son said, using his birth-name. "My name is Nayyib."

Eddrith, out of his burnous, showed scars from many dances. I saw him take note of Neesha's unblemished body except for the stitched cut on his forearm. And he grinned, did Eddrith; he counted the dance won.

My turn. I unsheathed the sword hanging, in harness, from my saddle. For a moment memories flashed through my mind: Singlestroke, the sword I'd carried for many years, until it was broken in a dance. And also the blooding-blade I'd made at Staal-Ysta: Samiel. The latter lay in the collapsed chimney very close to our little canyon near Julah. Broken, too, was Samiel, but intentionally done so to free me from magic, to buy me all the years I wanted to spend with Del and my daughter, to know my son better.

I walked into the circle aware, as always, of mutterings and comments about the scar beneath my ribs. I had plenty of others as well, but this one was carved deeply. This one should have killed me, yet I lived.

My pale-haired, ice-eyed opponent watched me walk to the center of our circle. This one knew what he was doing: he carefully marked the balance of my body, marked how I moved, marked my hand upon the leather-wrapped grip as I bent to lay down my sword. And he noticed that I had four fingers, not five, on each hand.

His eyebrows ran up beneath the hair hanging over his forehead. He looked at me sharply to judge my expression. I offered him a serene smile. "You'll notice," I said, "that I'm still alive."

He knew what I meant. I lacked fingers but had survived all threats requiring defense with a sword. I raised my other hand in the air and wiggled fingers at him, calling his attention to the other absent one.

"Still here," I reminded him.

His mouth was a grim line. He came into the circle, set his sword down, and turned his back on me as he walked to the periphery. I departed the circle as well, assuming my usual stance: balanced, comfortable, prepared to explode in a flurry of sand to reach my sword before he reached his. But here, the footing was packed turf. It would power us forward more decisively because, unlike sand, it wouldn't shift beneath our feet. I dug in my toes.

"So," I said, "what's your name?"

"Rafa," he answered. "And yours I already know."

In coloring, in stature, he reminded me of Del. Better yet, Alric. As much as Southroners did, Northerners also looked very much alike. This was a confident man, one not inclined to bluster, to drama, to immature eagerness. He knew what he was. He also knew what I was.

Across the circle, I gave him a cheerful countenance. "Do you regret," I asked, "that this is not to the death?"

"Very much so," he answered without force. "But once you've done whatever it is Umir wishes you to do, we'll meet again. And we'll finish it."

"Yes," I said gently, "that's what so many before you have declared."

Those eyes pinned me in place, even from across the circle. "You've been beaten. They say so."

"Ah yes. The ubiquitous 'they.' I would not have pegged you as a man who listened to gossip and tall tales."

He smiled faintly. "But some of those tales contain information."

"Apparently no information about my missing fingers."

His slight smile faded. "It won't matter. It will be the truth I offer, not gossip, when I kill you."

"Perhaps you would do better to say *if* you kill me. That way no one will consider you arrogant."

"You," Rafa said, "are simply delaying the inevitable. All this talk."

"Well then, I'll let my sword do the talking for me."

Eddrith, in the next circle over, asked who had the honor. Rafa was clearly the natural leader of Eddrith and of Darrion, who was looking younger by the moment.

"I!" a man shouted angrily. "*I* have the honor! Dance! Dance!" Oh yes, the woman's husband. I think even Eddrith had forgotten him. None of us moved. Rafa, as did I, wore a mild smile. I told the husband, "There are customs to be followed."

"Dance!" he cried. He stared hard at Eddrith. "I paid you to dance!"

Opponents we were, but nonetheless all of us were in accord. What he wanted wasn't how these things were done.

Mahmood spoke. "I will," he said. "I will do it." He led the horses as he stepped forward. "Until yesterday, these three were in my employ. I will do it."

Rafa smiled. "Then begin."

Mahmood, merchant by trade, told us to dance.

Chapter 20

BOTH RAFA AND I EXPLODED INTO THE CIRCLE, using the power of our thighs to propel us. We snatched up swords simultaneously, smashed our blades one against the other simultaneously, wasted no time in engaging aggressively. I had initially harbored a small hope that I could control him to some extent; enough that I could listen for the clash and chime of blades in the other circles and judge how things were going. But Rafa was too gods-cursed good.

In this dance there was no finesse, no grace, no initial testing of one another before getting serious. We each of us *needed* to win. And we each of us were so well-matched in power and speed, not to mention size and build, that I knew, and he knew, this dance might last a very long time.

All dances are noisy. There is the clash of blades meeting, the *scree* of metal sliding against metal, the chime of good steel, the chatter and scrape and screech. But in this case the noise was trebled. Three circles, three dances, six swords beating against one another. It set up an almost endless song of steel, all sound knitted together into something akin to metallic harmony.

Rafa and I met again and again. Countless engagements with no subtlety, only strength, speed, and skill. We both understood our bodies so well that finding and keeping balance was a simple matter. We could not knock one another off stride. We fought in the center of the circle, along the curved edge of the circle, nearly over the line of the circle. But we both knew intuitively where that line lay, and neither of us went over it. I moved him across the circle; he moved me. No wasted space. We used all that we had.

Before long both of us sweated. It pasted hair to foreheads, soaked into locks that clung to shoulders. Inconsequentially, as often happens despite most of the brain being focused on the activity, whatever it might be, a memory of ioSkandi swept by. My hair was shorn to the skin and blue tattoos colored my hairline. It was where I had lost my fingers. Where I had been trained in magery.

But this was not Meteiera atop stone spires; this was not even Skandi where the metri lived, the old woman who was my grandmother, who had cast out her daughter because she chose an unsuitable man. That daughter gave birth to a son in the sands of the South, even as she bled to death. Mother dead. Father dead.

But I had a son. And a daughter.

That son was with me, in a circle mere paces away from mine. The daughter, small yet, was at Beit al'Shahar, a home such as I never had. She was more fortunate than I, even than her mother, Delilah, who was raped repeatedly by a raider, family killed save for her brother. A brother who now was dead.

Beit al'Shahar. Where I had defeated Abbu Bensir twenty-five years after our first meeting at Alimat.

What would my shodo think? My shodo would undoubtedly tell me to focus on the dance.

But I had defeated Abbu Bensir. And I could defeat this man.

I was striped bloody by myriad cuts and slices. So it was with Rafa. We stretched our mouths in a rictus of effort, each of us, sucking air, gasping for it, filling our lungs as best we could. Sweat, reddened by blood, rolled down our bodies. I heard the chime of swords in the other circles. I dared not look. Not even a glance. Rafa would have me if I did.

Without an ounce of immodesty, only of acknowledgement, I realized that this must be what it was like to dance with me. Giving no ground, but offering unflagging blows of power coupled with weight, with quickness and agility despite being big.

Then Rafa went after my hands. Not with the edge of his blade, but with the flat. He brought it down in a smacking blow against my right wrist. In that moment three fingers and a thumb were not enough against his strength. The leather-wrapped grip slipped in my hand.

And he leveled another blow with the flat of his blade, this one landing across mine. My fingers, thumbs, and wrists were very strong, because I had worked to make them so, but the goal had never been to fight against the flat of a man's blade wielded with such focused power. Probably no one else would think of it. But Rafa had. What made him dangerous was all the physical skills, which were substantial, but also his ability to think, to adjust, to create a maneuver unanticipated, and terribly effective.

My sword fell at my feet.

And I realized at that moment that Rafa danced to kill. Maybe it had never been about Umir and his bounty. Maybe it had always been about killing me. Maybe he had used the lie to alter my expectations, to buy him an edge when we entered the circle.

I had broken all my oaths. I was subject to none of the codes of honor. Rafa could change the stakes of the dance if he wished, and at any time. I had no chance even to swear. I had time only to lurch aside, diving as I had told Neesha to do; to roll and to rise, to briefly escape the threat of the bloodied blade. I held my arms out from my sides to aid balance, torso bent slightly forward, hands cocked up, one leg somewhat forward, one back, spread, as thighs and calves bunched. He chased me around the circle. He made me scramble, made me roll, made me leap and lunge. But none of his blows landed, and eventually I wound up right where I wanted to be.

I dove again, arms outstretched, reaching for my lost sword. My hands closed on the grip. I rolled away, rose up, defended against a blow coming down from the sky. He had committed himself to that blow, expecting me to either have no sword, or to grip it badly because I'd gone down hard to the soil to fetch it. I was on one knee, my sword stretched over my head. Blades met, scraped, screamed. I thrust myself up from the knee, met Rafa on his level—what should have been, and was again, my level.

Too dangerous, was Rafa.

So I went low with my sword, lower than he expected, and as

his came down I ducked, then thrust with all my might and took him through the guts, hilt pressing belly, the balance of the blade exiting his spine.

Rafa was astonished.

Rafa was dead.

I let go of my sword as he fell. And when he landed flat on his back, dead weight pushed much of the blade back through his abdomen, so that the hilt and the grip stood up from his body.

Gasping for air, I walked away from the body, stood at the edge of the circle. I saw what I hoped to see: Del and Neesha. Their expressions were not alike. Del understood what had changed about the dance, what I'd gone through, how difficult it had been, how difficult it still was. She registered the cuts and slices, the bloody ribbons rolling down sweaty flesh, the ragged cadence of my breathing. Neesha was stunned into silence.

I bent over to catch my breath, hands on my hips. They hurt like hoolies, those hands. But now the gossip, the tall tales, would carry word that the Sandtiger, maimed as he was, still retained the strength, power, and quickness to defeat—to kill—a superb sword-dancer.

My breath ran a little easier. I stood up, still sucking wind, but not as I had before. With a forearm I wiped sweat away from my brow, from my burning eyes. Pushed sweat-pasted hair aside. Then I walked to the body, planted bare foot on its ribs, and jerked my sword from its guts.

I was now able to see, to take note, to examine the reactions of the spectators. The crowd stood in a ring around all three circles, eyes wide, mouths parted. Though I was certain a fair amount of wagering had gone on, no one moved to settle up. People stared. Some were stricken. Some surprised. Some simply stunned.

As well they should be. They had witnessed three simultaneous sword-dances—never done, to my knowledge, anywhere. They had witnessed the Sandtiger, as much in his prime now as he'd ever been. As far as they knew, I was.

I knew differently.

I'd come close to losing.

I'd come close to dying.

I looked for Mahmood in the crowd and found him standing

away from people; undoubtedly the stud had made a few equine comments and gestures that encouraged everyone to give him room. The merchant's face was ashen. His eyes were as wide as I'd seen them. Impossibly, they managed to widen a bit more when I walked toward him. One must guide the spectators away from the truth: that Rafa had nearly won.

"Mahmood, old friend . . ." I rested a hand on his shoulder, suppressed a wince, put a jovial tone in my voice. "I've worked up a bit of an appetite. Could you possibly find me some food?"

His mouth fell open. Then closed. "Of course. For you all. No doubt you have an appetite!"

I nodded. Was aware of them when Del and Neesha came up to flank me on either side. Mahmood backed, then turned the horses to lead them to his wagons.

Del, utterly expressionless, remained calm, said nothing. I noticed her bottom lip was swollen. Neesha, worried, reached out as if to grip my arm. "Don't touch me," I told him curtly.

The snap of command in my voice obviously surprised him. "You're bleeding. And you look like you might topple over any moment."

"Probably I am. But don't touch me."

"Later, Neesha," Del said quietly. "And you have your own cuts to tend."

"Only three," he said.

She sounded amazed. "You counted?"

"Three that I could see."

Gods above and below, my son was counting his cuts.

At Mahmood's wagon, Del took the reins from his hand. She untied the saddle pouches on her gelding, then handed over all the horses' reins to Neesha, except for his bay. "Take them where they were last night," she said.

His voice was full of surprise. "Are we staying?"

"We'll leave tomorrow morning," she told him firmly. "Now go. We'll see to all three of your terrible, gaping wounds when you have returned."

Suddenly concerned, I asked him, "*Are* you all right?"

"He's fine." Del shooed Neesha away, then pointed to Mahmood's wagon as she tied off the bay. "Up. Now."

"I have a better idea," I said, "how about I just sit on the tailgate."

"Up. In."

I climbed up. In.

Del followed. "Sit."

When she was in a dictatorial mood, the better part of valor was to do whatever she said. I made my way to the sleeping platform, turned, sat on the edge. Only then could I plant my elbows, hands held upright, and bow my head, trying to regain composure, to acknowledge and bear the pain. With Del, I need hide nothing.

I swore. Cursed. Gritted my teeth. Fingers—and lack of—throbbed. My thigh muscles quivered under flesh. The strength and power that burned so hot in the circle ebbed once out of it and, eventually, was extinguished. But in the meantime I trembled from extreme exertion ended so abruptly, from the magnitude of the effort. I felt diminished, dull, almost unspeakably exhausted.

"He pushed me." My throat was dry, my voice raspy. "He pushed me to the edge. *Right* to the edge."

"But not over it," said my bascha.

I wiped the heel of one hand against my forehead, scrubbing away crusty hair. Winced as it stung my hand. I examined the stumps of two little fingers. My wrists ached. "No, not over the edge. But closer than I ever want to be again."

After a moment, Del said, "It was beautiful, Tiger. The dance."

Annoyed, I declared, "It was nothing of the sort."

"Well, maybe not near the end. But when you began . . . oh, it was beautiful up till, well . . ."

"When I lost my sword, you mean?"

"You recovered it. I don't think anyone else could have." She rummaged in the saddle pouches. "I have medicaments. Ointment, bandaging. I don't see that you need stitching."

I was, at long last, breathing easily and no longer swearing, cursing, or gritting my teeth. "Why is your lip swollen?"

"I bit it."

"Ah, did Darrion manage to reach you?"

"I bit it watching you dance. At the last, when he brought down his sword so hard, so fast."

For the first time, I met her eyes squarely. I saw in them the simple comprehension of a sword-dancer who knew precisely how hard the dance had been, how close I had come to losing, to dying, and what it had taken out of me. She knew. I had been there before. So had she, on Staal-Ysta, when we'd nearly killed one another.

"I'm fine," I told her. "Cuts and slices heal. And maybe by next year, my hands will stop hurting." I drew in a breath, blew it out sharply. "You won, I take it?"

"I won."

"Swiftly."

"Immediately."

I grinned. "Do you suppose Darrion learned anything?"

She took from one pouch a small stoppered pot. "Oh, he learned a great deal. He learned it's probably best that he find other employment."

I snickered, then let it die. "And Neesha won?"

"No. But he did better than his last dance. He didn't step in any horse piss this time." She pulled a roll of soft muslin out of the pouch. Then she looked up at me, smiling a little. "Eddrith was simply more experienced. Neesha did well against him."

"And the woman's husband?"

"Sit up straight on the edge of the platform. Put your hands on your head. I want to reach all of your cuts." I dutifully put my hands on top of my head. She began spreading ointment on all the nicks, cuts, and slices. I began swearing again.

"Bascha—"

"Be quiet. You say the same things every time I do this for you, and I'm weary of the complaints."

"But bascha—"

"Be quiet." She moved from cut to cut. "The woman's husband was satisfied. Especially as his hired sword-dancer won. He wanted Eddrith to kill Neesha, but Eddrith explained that he'd do no such thing. Honor was served. Here—move a little."

I moved a little. "Is Neesha terribly disappointed?"

"Not terribly, no. And he had no time for it, anyway. As soon as he yielded, he was at the edge of *your* circle. So was Eddrith."

"How badly is he cut?"

"Eddrith?"

"No, not Edd—oh. Hah. See me laugh."

"Turn sideways." She was never gentle unless I was badly hurt, and wasn't gentle now. "No, he wasn't cut badly. He did break most of the stitches I'd put in his forearm before we left, so I'll have to restitch. Which will not please him. The other four cuts will heal on their own."

"Four cuts? He said three."

"Neesha is like his father. He lies when pain is involved. Extremes, always: 'Oh, it's nothing' when it really is something; or 'oh, I'm miserable, see how injured I am' when all you want is attention." She pressed the end of the muslin roll against my chest. "Hold that."

As I did, she fed out the roll and wrapped my torso where the worst of the cuts were. A few bled through slowly, sluggishly, which meant Del would be pulling wrappings off along with scabs. "There. Done. Here's a cloth; you're crying salt tears from the sweat."

I opened my mouth to say something even as I wiped my forehead and face, blinking sweat-scoured eyes, but forgot whatever it was as Neesha climbed into the wagon. He bent to avoid brushing his head against the canopy.

"Horses distributed." He sat down on the plank floor. "And I brought the aqivi." He displayed the bota.

"For medicinal purposes," Del said firmly, scowling at us both. Then I saw the gleam kindle in her eyes. "Your turn," she told Neesha. "There's stitching to be stitched, ointment to apply, wrapping to be wrapped. Your share of aqivi must wait." She took the bota from him and handed it to me even as Neesha protested. "Tiger, get off the platform. Neesha needs to rest his arm on it while I stitch."

"Cruel, cruel woman." Mostly what I felt now was sheer exhaustion, and it was topping pain. I stood up slowly, inventing new curses as I made my way past Neesha to the end of the wagon. "I'm wounded, and I'm old."

"Drink your aqivi," Del said severely.

I sat down carefully and did exactly that. And listened to Neesha swear, which was far more entertaining than when I did it myself.

Chapter 21

DEL HAD COME THROUGH HER DANCE UNSCATHED, which wasn't particularly surprising in view of her opponent. Neesha hissed and muttered now and again as he moved, stretching cut flesh. Del had wrapped his forearm after re-stitching it. It would, she informed him, cause "a beautiful scar," two cuts in nearly the same place.

Mahmood had assigned a driver to build a fire ring for us, to lay kindling and light it. He'd also provided food and water. Blankets down, Neesha, Del, and I pillowed our heads on saddles.

"You said my scar was beautiful," Neesha noted to Del.

"Well, that one, yes. The others are inconsequential."

I lay between them. I felt no urge to speak. In silence, I watched twilight fall, saw the first stars swell into brilliance against the darkening sky. Familiar smells drifted through Marketfield: bread, sausage, roasting meat, onions, beans, potent spices. Familiar sounds—fortunately, the baby had ceased crying. When one has come so close to death, everything in the world seems brighter, richer, more *real* somehow.

With great care, I arranged my hands against my belly. Aqivi warmed me but did not rid me of pain in the finger stumps.

"Inconsequential," Neesha muttered.

"Scars are the mark of a sword-dancer," Del explained. "There is the harness and sword, and the scars. Souvenirs of dances."

"Souvenirs?" Neesha sounded somewhat aggravated. He was tired, more sore than he let on, and out of sorts. Food and aqivi had not soothed his temper. "Why would I want a scar as a souvenir?"

"As I said: scars are the mark of a sword-dancer. It proves you have danced."

"And got cut! I'd think that would tell everyone I danced poorly, to get myself cut."

I couldn't remain silent. "We *all* get cut, Neesha. Why in hoolies do you think Del slathered me in ointment and wrapped me up like a corpse?"

He said nothing.

"Ah," I said. "I see. You believe Rafa is better because he cut me. And that I won merely by happenstance."

"No, *no*—"

I cut him off. "If you wish to believe I'm the lesser sword-dancer, go right ahead. But you're deceiving yourself."

Anger underlay Del's tone. "You should be ashamed, Neesha. Tiger won a dance no one else could have. You saw him. You were standing there with your mouth hanging open."

"*You* weren't cut," Neesha ventured.

"That's because I disarmed Darrion and shoved him out of the circle before he could bring his sword up from the ground more than two or three inches."

"And Rafa had his share of cuts and slices before I killed him," I put in. "You just didn't see them."

"And if you don't want to be cut," Del said curtly, "then you should go back to the horse farm and stay there."

Silence replaced conversation. Neesha said nothing for some time. Eventually, in a chastened tone, he apologized. "I didn't know. About cuts."

I grunted. "Why do you think these terrible scars of Del's and mine aid rather than devalue us? Sword-dancers don't believe we're weak because of them. They just wonder how in hoolies we survived them, and how in hoolies they can defeat us if we can survive that. If you're smart, and if the scars are bad enough, you allow them to work for you. As for what you received today, it's a beginning. Even legends begin as infants."

He considered that a moment. "Will I ever be good enough to defeat a man like Rafa?"

I stared into the heavens, contemplated lying, thought to say: 'Yes. Of course. No question of it.' But I didn't. I told him the truth. "Maybe. It depends on how much you want to be, and how hard you will work to attain it."

Eventually Neesha observed, "He's quite good, is—*was*—Rafa."

I closed my eyes. If I lay very still, nothing hurt. "One of the best."

"But not good enough to defeat the Sandtiger."

I smiled crookedly. "Not many are."

"Nor are many as arrogant as the Sandtiger," Del chided, but I knew she didn't mean it. We were so different, Delilah and I. She was never arrogant, merely truthful. She never bragged; she let her victories speak for her. I, on the other hand, used the arrogance, the bragging, as weapons to shake my opponent's confidence, or focus. Often, it worked. But not against a man like Rafa.

"I'm not good enough to be arrogant," Neesha said.

I opened my eyes. I had not expected such insight in a young man. I smiled into the stars. "I'll let you know when you are."

"Foolishness," Del declared.

"Can I ask another question?" Neesha inquired.

I was puzzled. "When have I ever said you couldn't? Or shouldn't?"

"I wanted to help you away from the circle. You wouldn't let me."

"It was well-intended," I told him. "I thank you for that. But when you're in the midst of convincing other sword-dancers that you are unconquerable—well, that's what you *hope* they think—you don't want anyone helping you from the circle."

"Ahhhhh." His tone rose, then dropped low in sudden realization.

"The mind," I said, "is as important as the skill. The sword is not the only weapon you have."

"I think I'm beginning to see that."

I blew out a long breath. I had a belly full of food, and aqivi in my blood. All of me was sore, tired, aching, incapable of movement. The shakes had died away, but the pain in my hands had not. I wasn't sure which would win throughout a long night: exhaustion or enough pain to keep me from sleep. And without sleep, whatever I felt now would feel worse in the morning.

Del seemed to realize what I was thinking. "More aqivi? For medicinal purposes?"

And for the first time in my adult life, I said no.

Come morning I was close to wishing, though not quite, that Rafa *had* killed me. Hard-fought dances always set up aches within the bones, complaints from overworked muscles, the occasional sharp stab of a cut stretched and broken open. My skills, my talent, had kept me alive, but my age multiplied every ache and pain. I lay very still on the blanket, debating whether I should even attempt to sit up.

Next to me, Del did so. Neesha, too. She made no complaint; he did. He seemed surprised by the protests of his body; he was young, healthy, fit. But he had never tested his body so much, never fought a sword-dancer as good as Eddrith. Being young did not guarantee a pain-free life.

He glanced down at me, noting I was awake. Noting, too, that I showed no signs of moving. Smiling widely, he kicked my left foot. "Up, old man. We are, as you say, burning daylight."

"Neesha," Del said sharply. "Have some respect."

I saw the bafflement in his eyes, the lack of understanding of what his action had provoked. Certainly he had kick-prodded me before, as I had kicked him. As Del had.

Realizing that, Del softened her tone. "You didn't know. Nor even now, do you?"

"Know what?"

"That was a death-dance, Neesha."

Disbelief reigned supreme. "Rafa said it was for Umir's bounty!"

"Rafa lied," Del said.

"But—that's not done. Both of you told me so." He looked down at me, perplexed. "You taught me so."

I expelled a long breath. "It's different with me. I'm not one of them anymore. Any sword-dancer can do anything to me. Lie. Attack without warning. Challenge me outside of a circle. Any sword-dancer may make up their own rules and break them a moment later. There is no binding, Neesha. No oaths, no vows, no codes. Not anymore. I thought you knew that."

And yet knowing is not always the same as understanding.

"None?" he asked. "None at all?"

"None at all."

Neesha thought about it. He looked at Del, looked at me, then prodded my foot with far less emphasis than before. It wasn't so much a kick as a push. "Up. I'll be gentle with you."

Del sighed. "Truly your son."

Neesha bent to extend a hand. "Help, old man? Now that we're not in front of everyone?"

I grunted. " 'Old man' could take you any day."

Neesha hooted a laugh. "Not today!"

"No help necessary." I levered myself up on an elbow. " 'Young man' can go get the horses."

Del waited until Neesha was gone. "*Do* you want help?"

"I'm not getting up without it," I said.

Grinning, Del bent down, heaved me up as I pushed off from the ground. I blessed her size and strength; a smaller, lighter woman couldn't have done that. As I caught my balance, she said, "The ride will loosen you."

"Or kill me," I said in a strangled tone.

Del's amusement faded. "Tiger—he's young. Younger than his years."

I attempted to move muscles that had no inclination to do so. "I know that."

"He grew up on a horse farm where likely the only violence he saw or experienced was breaking horses to the saddle."

Tried another set of muscles. "I know that, too."

"He said himself that his primary sparring partner was his sister."

I examined the bandaging Del had done, noting a few spots of dried blood. "Bascha, what are you trying to say?"

Del sighed. "He's not you. He's not me. We are who we are, you and I, because of what happened to us when we were young."

I stopped doing anything except to look at her. "I understand everything you're telling me. I don't fault him for it. The life he led prior to meeting us was the kind of life you and I should have had . . . hoolies, the life you *did* have until Ajani and his raiders attacked your family's caravan. He's cheerful and happy and full of life. Naive, even. But he learns quickly. And he's steadfast about the things he feels are right. He's an honorable young man." I shrugged. "But that doesn't change the fact that he'll drive us sandsick sometimes, or make us wonder if he's a fool."

Del nodded. "I wish he knew you better. I wish he understood you better."

I grinned. "Just what I said in relation to *you* on that first journey together across the Punja."

"Oh, you did not!"

I let the grin fade. "Listen, bascha . . . I'm not a father to him. I'm not even a man to him. I'm a *name*. He thinks only of the legend, and sometimes he comes up against the truth without actually understanding it: that I am just a man, like he is."

"Hunh." Del looked beyond me. "He's coming now. I'll go help him bring the horses in." But before she left to do so, she said with a furrowed brow and deep consideration, "Maybe I should sleep with him to find out if he's just a man, like you are."

As she walked away, I shouted after her, "That's not funny!"

This time around, we were able to ride out of Istamir without being stopped by sword-dancers, angry husbands, or anyone else. We even rode down the center of the main street, shod hooves clopping, instead of avoiding it. When we rode *into* Istamir people glanced at us with only passing interest, but now many of them stared as we rode out. The three of us had managed to make ourselves famous. And we couldn't even blame the husband, or Darrion, Eddrith, or Rafa. Del was Del, and I was me. Neesha had gained perhaps a smidgen of notoriety, but it was at Del and me they stared—though that was nothing new, after a sword-dance.

The stud, for a wonder, was in a quiet mood. He had never been one to respect my physical condition, being completely self-centered when it came to expressing his mood. But whatever his reason to walk smoothly this morning, I was grateful for it.

Kindness in the skies, kindness to the eyes. Beneath a bright but softer sun, rounded hills rose to our right, preface to mountain flanks. Grasslands were deep green, almost glowing in the light. Trees were more profuse. In the North, scents were different, far different from the South. Here, shrubbery bloomed, and trees rustled in an infant breeze. Foremost, the smells were of rich earth, of new blossoms stolen from branches and lofted on the wind.

A glance at Neesha presented a young man riding with a smile, a looseness in his body. Nayyib was nearly home. And Del . . . her eyes drank in the views, her soul drank in the knowledge that she, too, was home. We had come to the North before, she and I, but in the unkindness of winter, when snow blew bitter-hard and the wind was a bone-deep cold. Not here; farther north, in the frozen fastness of sharp and ragged mountains. Dark, all of them, verging on black, built of bleakness. And if one rode far enough, high enough, a village on the shore, and Staal-Ysta on the island, afloat on freezing water.

The faintest track here, nearly hidden among grasses. Neesha had taken the lead. He rode easily, hips absorbing the rhythm of his mount. The roan mare was again tied off to his saddle. From time to time he closed a hand on the lead-rope and urged her closer to him, clicking with his tongue, speaking quietly. She trotted abreast of him or slowed to a walk. Occasionally she snaked her head out to grab at grass, ripping it, soil clinging, from the earth. The stud did the same, and Del's gelding. Rich grazing here, as my son had said.

I raised my voice. "How far, Neesha?"

He twisted in the saddle to look at me, one hand spread upon his bay's rump as he leaned. "Not long. By midday. Probably just in time for your old bones." I saw the flash of white teeth in his tanned face. "It will be most interesting to watch you and my mother meet for the first time since I was conceived."

Interesting. Hunh. I could think of other words. "Awkward" was foremost, with "uncomfortable" right behind it. But at least I *knew* that we would meet; she had no idea. "Your stepfather knows about me?"

"Well," Neesha said dryly, "he knows that *someone* lay with her."

That deserved a glare, except I wasn't sure he could see it. "But not me precisely. I mean, he won't know I'm your father. That it's me in his house."

"Oh, he *will* know you're my father. My mother never kept it a secret. I think she was proud of you."

That, I could not grasp. "Why in hoolies would she be proud of me? We spent but a single night together. What woman wants to be left like that, who isn't a wine-girl?"

"But you told her, she said. You told her of your life among the Salset. You told her what you wanted, what you dreamed of. She was the first to know . . . maybe even the only one to know, once you were free, before you rode away from Alimat as a seventh-level sword-dancer."

Apparently I'd told her far too much. Among the Salset, I was only rarely allowed to say anything. It was only to Sula, an older and wiser woman, that I could speak of my hopes for freedom. She'd told me any number of times she had faith in me. And it was Sula, for whom *our* Sula was named, who had nursed me back to health after I'd killed the sandtiger, when poison burned my blood.

But freedom . . . freedom was intoxicating. Neesha's mother was my first woman as a free man. She had consented. She had wanted it. And afterward, there were no regrets from her. She had been a virgin but saw a man who warmed her. A man who answered curiosity.

Neesha, still twisted in the saddle, said, "Her name is Danika."

Then he turned back. It was privacy he gave me; once again, more insightful than expected.

Danika. I had not remembered her name. She said it only once, naming herself as we learned one another's bodies. As we made ourselves a son beneath a half-faced moon.

Chapter 22

A TASTE OF SMOKE UPON THE AIR, the scent of burning wood. Before us, a deep gray-black column wound up to the skies, rising from the horizon.

Del and I rode abreast. "Fire," I said.

She nodded. "We burn sick trees. We cut them down, feed them to a bonfire. To keep the others from blight."

But I was uneasy. "Is that what it is?"

Before she could answer, Neesha turned back in his saddle. His tone was urgent, his expression deeply worried. "It's too close. We have to go."

"But if it's sick trees they're burning—" I began.

My son rode back to us, unwinding the mare's lead-rope. "Take her. I can go faster without her."

"Neesha—"

But his face was a mask. "Those are not burning trees." And his bay was wheeled, sent headlong into a gallop straight away from us toward the smoke-clogged horizon.

"Oh, no," Del said.

"Go," I told her tautly, dallying the mare's lead-rope around the saddle pommel. "I'll be slower with her; go on."

But not so much slower. As Del's gelding kicked up clods of dirt, I sent the stud after her, nearly dragging the mare along until she sensed the urgency. She ran sideways to the end of the rope, ducked her head and let loose a buck. She tried to run even with the stud, then attempted to forge ahead. The rope kept her from it, the rough hempen rope that slid angrily across the stub of a former finger.

Neesha was gone. Del nearly so. There were things in this world more important than a horse. I unwound the mare's rope, threw it at her. Hoped she wouldn't trip. Then left her behind as the stud stretched out and ran, chasing Del's gelding.

A house, and all of it burning, though the flames were dying. It wasn't a fresh fire.

Neesha's bay was loose and had taken himself away to stand upon a nearby ridge. Neesha himself, I couldn't see. Del was dismounting, was setting the gelding free. Horses fear fire. Even those well-trained. Even the stud.

I reined in sharply, threw myself out of the saddle. Del was running toward the house. I followed swiftly, barely aware of aches and pains. Neesha was missing.

And then he came around from the back of the building, soot on his face. His eyes were wild. Through heavy coughing, he said, "I can't get in! It's too hot! Oh, gods above, I have to get in there!"

Soot coated his hands, his forearms. He had tried to lift charred timbers away, to tear them aside as he fought to go in. His hair was singed, flesh licked with flame. Coughing continued.

"Swords," I said, even as Del unsheathed.

Neesha was in shock. He didn't understand.

"Swords," I repeated. "We'll knock down some timbers, make our way in. We can do this, Neesha." But inwardly, hiding in my heart, was the knowledge that it was much too late.

We knocked aside burning timbers as if in a sword-dance, sweeping with blades, smashing down charred wood. Three steps inside, we felt the heat. Too much heat. Neesha, frantic, was unheeding of his body, of the danger to himself.

Del, beside me, coughed in the smoke. "We can't," she said hoarsely. "It's too late. Too hot. No one could be alive."

A painful truth but truth nonetheless. Trying to suppress lung-tearing coughs, I took a long step forward, caught hold of the back of Neesha's burnous; closed hands, through the fabric, on his harness. I yanked him backward so hard he dropped his sword and nearly stumbled. I swung him around, pushed him back through charred timbers, through the ruins of the house in which he had grown to manhood.

When he turned on me outside, when he shoved at me, when, with wild eyes, he tried to knock me aside, I tossed my sword away, grabbed handfuls of burnous at both of his shoulders, and threw him down. Threw him down hard.

"You'll die," I said flatly. "The smoke will fill your lungs. You'll die choking to death. You might even catch fire."

He tried to scrabble up. "I have to find them!"

As he gained his feet, I shoved him backward. Once, twice, thrice, slamming the heels of my hands into his shoulders. I backed him away, and away. "If they're in there, they're already dead! Nothing can be done! You'll kill yourself for nothing!"

Neesha got to his feet once more, coughing, voice breaking from it. "I'm going in."

"You will not."

"I have to!"

"No," I said, "you don't." And I knew what was coming, what he would say.

"You can't stop—"

Before he could finish, I smashed a fist into his jaw. He dropped to the ground, limbs all askew. Unconscious. "Yes I can."

"Gods," Del said, voice raspy from smoke as she echoed Neesha. "Oh gods, Tiger . . . do you think they're in there?"

"Tomorrow," I said briefly, suppressing a cough. "We'll look tomorrow. We ought to be able to make our way in. It will be hot, still, but the flames will have died, the smoke mostly lifted. If the bodies are in there, we'll find them."

Her expression was stricken. Blue eyes shone with tears. "I know what it is," she said, voice uneven. "I know what it is, to lose a family."

I couldn't share that. I'd lost my family before I was even born.

"Gods—" she said. "Poor Neesha."

I moved around his body. Squatted. Hooked my arms beneath his and dragged him farther away.

Del glanced around. Said, newly stricken, "Oh, no."

I settled unconscious Neesha, putting loose limbs to rights. "What is it?"

"The corrals. Tiger, look. The poles are all broken."

I followed her line of sight. "Horses," I said heavily. "They came after the horses."

Del looked back at the burning home. She ran two flattened, grimy hands across her skull, front to back, stretching hair taut, then dropped her hands to her sides. When she looked at me again, her eyes were cold. "We must go after them."

"Of course we will, bascha. And we'll bring the horses back. After the raiders are dead."

Neesha roused some while later. In the meantime, as the flames died into charred timbers, as whiffs of smoke rose and coals burned hot, the wary horses returned. My stud, Del's gelding, Neesha's bay, and even the roan mare, who apparently did not like the idea of roaming across the grasslands on her own, trailing a lead-rope. All were bothered by the remains of the fire, but Del and I repaired one of the smaller corrals with a few strategic poles put into place and tied off with leather thongs, and turned the untacked horses into it. They had water from a trough. We pitched to them grass hay that had escaped the fire. Strangely, we found heaps of produce. We tossed that to the horses, too.

As late afternoon grayed out, the day promised an end. I'd struck Neesha hard, and it took him awhile to make his way back to awareness. Already his jaw was swollen. Bruises would follow.

And then he sat bolt upright, saw the remains of the house, remembered all, and scrambled wobbly to his feet.

In two long strides I had him by the arm. "Tomorrow," I said. "We'll go in tomorrow, if we can. It's just too hot, Neesha."

He tried to twist his arm out of my grasp. His face was smeared by soot, and there were some burns upon his hands. "I have to—"

Again, I didn't let him finish. "No, you don't. *Neesha*—if they're in there, they're dead. I don't say that for effect, but because it's true."

"It is true." Del joined us. "Neesha, you must see it. Either they died from smoke or burned to death."

Each of us coughed from time to time, bringing up blackened mucus, breathing through the heaviness in our lungs.

He winced at her bluntness, but his attempt to break free of my hold was now less frantic, and I loosed him. As he stared at the house burned into ruin, his posture was one of defeat, of grief. He linked hands across the top of his skull, elbows jutting out.

"Gods," he whispered brokenly in a tone harshened by smoke. "Gods, gods, gods."

"We don't know," I told him quietly. "They may have gotten out."

"Raiders," Del said. "They wanted the horses."

Neesha's voice was thinned by grief. "I can't wait until morning. Not to know? I can't spend a night like that, waiting for dawn." He lowered his arms, rubbed the back of a forearm across his brow, rearranging soot. "I must go in."

Both Del and I shook our heads. "In the morning," she said gently. "If they're dead, they can wait."

He could not accept it, looking from one to the other of us. His expression was wracked by sorrow, by a painful disbelief. "How can you tell me to wait, when someone may be alive in there?"

I could not imagine what he felt, or how he could believe there was a chance anyone had survived. "Neesha, what we *can* do is walk the area around the house. All sides, at increasing distance. If anyone did manage to escape, he or she may have made it away from the house."

His tone was bitter. "Or died at the hands of raiders!"

I hadn't said it, because it was so likely. The house, I could keep him from but not from anything else. Even if anyone had escaped the flames, I expected the raiders had probably caught and killed them.

"We'll all go, the three of us," I said quietly.

He wrapped both arms around his ribcage and hugged himself,

staring at the ruins. He paced back and forth, struggling with the knowledge of what had come to him. He could not believe it. Could not. *I* could; I'd survived raiders even as my parents had not, born of my mother's womb into Southron sand. Del survived raiders when she was fifteen, when all had been lost save for her and her brother; and she lost him later.

But my son had known only the kindness of life, brought up with no hardships of the body, no hardships of the soul. Del stepped closer to him, taking an arm into her own as she stood by his side. "I do know, Neesha. I know. But let this not change you as something very like this changed me."

"My sister," he said hollowly. "Would they have taken her?"

Oh, hoolies. I hadn't thought about that. I'd been concentrating on the burned house and how to keep him out of it. But I understood the question and the two-edged answer: Had she not burned to death it was because she'd been taken for sport.

"We'll look," Del said. "There will be no answers until we have exhausted a search, in the house and out of it." She paused. "Do you wish company while you search?"

After a moment, Neesha shook his head. "No. Let me be. Let me do this alone."

She released his arm, and came back to me. There was loss in her eyes, a darkness of spirit. She remembered, I knew, what had been done to her. And worried, I knew also, that it might have been done as well to Neesha's sister.

We searched in circles, each growing larger with every completion. Hoofprints aplenty, but human feet had left no impression upon the grass, only in the bare, beaten dirt immediately surrounding the house and corrals. Hoofprints and footsteps had carved narrow trails into the grass. But those small trails were made of frequent passage; someone running from the house, or riding from the house, making their own solitary way would not leave much to mark their going.

A man, a woman, a girl. But none of them was found. It gave us no joy, no relief, because until we could search the house we couldn't know if the lack was good or bad. Hoofprints surrounded the house, led outward in rays from the house, from the corrals.

Neesha mentioned pasturage apart from the corrals. But we could not imagine that any of his family had gone so far; had been allowed to go so far if seen by the raiders. And there were no tracks. Grass grew freely, tightly, and robustly. In it, no tracks had been laid by galloping horses, or by fleeing humans. Nonetheless, it offered the possibility that some of the horses had not been discovered by the raiders. A far pasture provided safety to frightened horses, and with so many mounts close to in corrals, I doubted the raiders would have bothered.

Eventually it was Neesha, as the sun went down, who said we should halt our search. It made no sense to continue looking; we had walked far, farther than anyone trying to escape the depredation of raiders could have managed; and in the dark we would see nothing. What we knew was that the corralled horses had been stolen and that we had no inkling of whether Neesha's mother, stepfather, and sister had escaped or burned to death in the house.

Neesha would not sleep. Throughout the night he held vigil, praying for good fortune. And seeing, I knew, the faces of his kinfolk, the memories of life among them. None of us was hungry. We drank water, chewed journey bread so our bellies wouldn't growl, and thought our own thoughts.

Del set her bedding very close to mine. We lay down together, full of silence. Del turned to me on hip and shoulder, scooting close; I wrapped an arm around her and held her tightly. We knew we could not offer peace to Neesha with simple words. Nor could Del and I banish our memories of hardship. But we lay there entwined, wordlessly sealing ourselves to one another, sharing strength to escape from how we had begun; to remember, now, we had a home between canyon walls, with sweet water and green grass and a life no longer fraught with daily danger.

Neesha, in his way, was being annealed as I had been atop the spires of Meteiera on ioSkandi; as a young Del was annealed on Staal-Ysta. I wanted to take it from him, but I couldn't. It was for him to be annealed or to break of brittleness.

Chapter 23

I AWOKE IN THE MORNING when part of the house collapsed upon itself. Ash drifted on the air. Heat remained but was pallid. Del roused even as I did, pushing hair out of her eyes as she sat up. And Neesha . . . Neesha's bedding was empty.

I swore, rose rapidly, awkwardly, stiff as always first thing. I grabbed up my sword and hastened to what once had been the plank front door and now lay charred upon the wooden floorboards. "Neesha? *Nee*sha!" Hoolies, had he gone in on his own? "Where are you?"

Del joined me, sword in hand even as I held mine. "Did he go in?" she asked

"I don't know," I said grimly. "But we'll have to."

"No. No, you need not."

I spun around and saw Neesha approaching from the corral containing our horses. Tears had left white runnels in soot and grime. He was clearly exhausted.

Del murmured something in Northern.

I asked because I had to, even though I believed it was self-evident. "Did you go in?"

"I did."

I waited for the words. Waited for the grief. I knew what the answer was. My son had cried.

Neesha said, "There are no bodies."

At first I wasn't certain what he'd said. And then I understood. He cried for relief, not in grief. "They got out," I said in surprise.

He nodded. But his expression remained tense. "What if the raiders took them and *then* set the house afire? That's no better, is it?"

"Of course it's better," Del told him flatly. "*I* escaped from raiders. I am proof it can be done."

"Wait," I said, putting a flattened hand into the air. "Wait. Neesha, if they escaped both fire and raiders, is there a place they might go?"

He stared at me blankly a moment. Then, exploding from him, "*Yes*! They'd go to Sabir and Yahmina! Our closest neighbors—eight or so miles away." He gestured. "That way. Gods, I should have realized . . . I saw that produce. Sabir must have found them."

"Then what are we doing here?" I asked. "Let's get tack and pouches and horses and go."

Which is exactly what we did.

We wasted no time riding to the neighbors'. Eight miles was nothing under these circumstances. Del, who took mercy on me and my sore hands, dallied the roan off her saddle this time, keeping the mare snubbed up tight to avoid protests or rambunctious behavior. We couldn't afford it.

The house came into sight as we crested the top of a hill. Neesha, riding point, twisted in the saddle to look at me. I knew very well what he meant to say even before he formed the words, so I waved a hand at him and said, "Go. Go."

He rode his bay hard down the hill as Del and I took the descent at a slower rate. We were not needed, at least not immediately. Neesha should learn the truth of his family without two people flanking him who were strangers to the neighbors, even to his folk.

Neesha was well in front of us as he entered the dooryard. He shouted names while reining his horse into a long sliding stop in which the bay nearly sat on his rump, digging furrows into the soil. In the midst of that, Neesha leaped off the horse, flung reins at him, and ran toward the house. Again he called names, and this time I recognized them: *Father. Mother. Rasha.*

Even before he reached the door a woman hastened out of the house, halted briefly as if in disbelief, then threw her arms around Neesha as he reached her. They clung hard to one another. Del and I were close enough now to hear that she spoke to him, but not what she said. And it wasn't necessary. We knew well enough what a mother would say to a son come unexpectedly home just when she needed him most.

Danika, he'd said. But at this distance I could see no details of her features to recognize her. Just that she was a woman.

Drawing away from the embrace, she took Neesha's arm and led him rapidly into the house. Del and I rode up slowly and reined in. Not very distant, Neesha's loose horse cropped at grass.

Del's gelding shook from nose to rump, hard. She sat it out, grimacing as bit shanks clattered, then looked at me. "What do we do?"

I drew in a deep breath, released it in a heavy, abbreviated sigh. "I don't know. But—we might do best to just stay away, for now. I don't think we should get in the way."

She agreed. "Perhaps we can set up a small camp, just us and the horses. We can wait for someone to get us when they are ready."

"Probably Neesha." I dismounted. "There's a well and a cookfire ring with spit," I noted. "And a very large tree over there. We can make camp under the branches."

Del nodded, dismounting as well. We led two horses apiece to the wide-bolled, spreading tree and found good areas for picketing. We untacked all four mounts, scrubbed off the sweat with hard-bristled brushes, took turns cranking up the well bucket to fill waxed cloth buckets for them, then picketed each. When it came time for us, we once again spread out the blankets, weighting the corners with stones, and set our saddles upside down at one end of each.

Del rummaged in her saddle pouches, came up with more journey bread and added cheese and dried fruit to the meal. Even as she did so, I realized I was hungry. It wasn't precisely a feast, but would fill our bellies nicely. We each of us had botas; we washed down the food with water that tasted of leather. Didn't matter. It was wet.

Just as we finished, the woman who had embraced Neesha

came to us. And I knew her. It had been twenty-five years since we had seen one another, she and I. All she could do, and all I could do, was stare awkwardly at the other. I felt heat in my face. Color shaded hers.

Del hastily brushed off her lap, rose, and said she was off to find an accommodating bush. Whether she really had to do so—and that was certainly possible—I knew it was her way of offering us privacy. I suspected she wouldn't return for a while.

So did Danika, who smiled faintly, crookedly.

I got up less nimbly than Del. Hoolies, I felt like a kid again, not knowing what to say or do that was not circumscribed by the Salset.

Then I smiled, because I remembered what that kid had done, and with this woman. It wasn't purely the physical act; it had been, for us both, a rite of passage. It made her a woman, despite her youth; it made me no more a chula but a free man.

I saw it in her eyes, that mutual memory. I bent briefly to drop bread and bota to my bedroll, then straightened and took the three steps to reach her. I did not embrace her; that was much too intimate after so long. Instead, I took her hands in mine, leaned down, and kissed her gently on the brow.

As I straightened up, I squeezed her hands lightly. "You made us a fine son. You *raised* a fine son." I paused a brief, tight-throated moment. "You and your husband."

She was dark-haired, as I remembered, but now also had strands of silver framing the sides of her face. Most of the hair was wound in a coil against the back of her head, but that coil had loosened to droop against her neck, with straggling locks fallen free. Age had laid a gentle hand upon her, I thought. Happiness in her man, in her children, in her life, softened the more obvious encroachment of ruthless time. Hazel eyes, olive skin—I had forgotten both. Her grandfather had been a Borderer, and she'd told me her coloring took after him, not her father or mother. It would be flattery, if I could say I remembered everything about her, could tell her she hadn't changed. But flattery was not always the truth, and I knew she was worth the latter.

She squeezed my hands briefly, then slipped them free. The moment had passed. And the age I had not seen suddenly mastered her face. Her body went rigid. In her eyes was a great grief. "I would like to hire you."

That was the last thing I'd expected to hear from her. "*Hire* me?"

Her voice shook, though she tried to keep it steady. "They took my daughter. They left Harith and me behind to watch the house burn, the horses driven away, and my daughter taken." Her chin trembled a moment, just a moment, before she regained composure. "She ran. A raider on horseback caught her and dragged her up before him. I heard her screams until the raiders were no more than a cloud of dust." She swallowed heavily. "I would like to hire you. To bring her back."

"No, Danika; no need for hiring." I shook my head decisively. "Del and I had already decided to go after them. After seeing your house, we came here with Neesha in hopes you had survived, and now to talk with you and your husband about the details of the raid. Anything you might tell us is of help." I gestured toward the blankets. "Will you sit down?"

She shook her head. "I can't. I must see to my husband. They beat him badly. One of his legs is broken, and his head is injured."

I grimaced. "I'm sorry, Danika. But we will rescue your daughter and your horses and kill all the raiders. Each and every one."

Neesha's mother nodded as tears welled in her eyes. "Justice."

I nodded. "At the very least."

She gestured toward the house. "Come in. There is room to visit, though not to sleep, I'm afraid. But we can feed you. Sabir and Yahmina have been good enough to take us in."

"We'll do just fine right where we are," I assured her. And we would; Del and I both would be uncomfortable within the house, with so much of worry and pain already in it.

Somewhat hesitantly, she put out a hand. I took it. The awkwardness was gone. We shared much, she and I, in our son. We walked slowly toward the house with fingers entwined. "I'm glad you've come," she said. "For all reasons: Neesha. You. The raiders. But I should have expected it. The gods know what is most needed and when." She glanced up at me sidelong. "Is she your wife?"

"Sword-mate," I answered. "We saw no reason for words to bind us. The gods know we belong together."

Danika said, "She's beautiful."

I smiled. "She is."

"She's a sword-dancer?"

"Sword-singer, as the Northerners say."

"Good," Danika said firmly, after a moment. "When you bring Rashida back, perhaps your woman—*the* woman—would be willing to teach her a few forms. Ever since Neesha left, Rasha has been extremely vocal about her desire to be a sword-dancer like her brother."

I smiled crookedly. "Is that what you want for her?"

"No," she answered swiftly, honestly, yet without annoyance or bitterness. "But it's her choice. You taught me what freedom was, one night so many years ago."

That astonished me. "You were already free!"

"But not as Rashida is, was." Tears spilled over as she turned to face me, letting go of my hand. "Bring her back. Tiger, please . . . bring my daughter back."

Fervently, I said, "I swear it by whatever god you like, Danika. I'll swear by all of them, if that's what you prefer. We'll bring Rashida back."

After a moment she nodded, brushed away her tears, then walked in quiet dignity before me into the house.

Danika's husband, Neesha's stepfather, had been settled in a bed. His left leg was splinted. His head above his eyes was tightly wrapped in muslin, showing spots of blood. One side of his face already exhibited the ugly purple of deep bruising.

The room wasn't large, but we managed to squeeze Danika, Neesha, the neighbors—Sabir and his wife Yahmina—and me into it. Del, who came in later, stood in the doorway.

"Has he been conscious at all?" I asked.

"Occasionally," Yahmina answered. "He knows where he is and what happened, but he doesn't remain awake very long."

I nodded. "Has he said anything about the raiders?"

"A little," Yahmina replied.

"Can you wake him now?"

Yahmina was shocked. Her husband, Sabir, turned an angry face on me. "He needs his rest!"

"He's here, and safe," I said. "So is Danika. But their daughter is not. If Del and I are to find the raiders, we need to know details."

Sabir looked at me, looked at Del. His jaw was set. "Sword-dancers."

Del's voice was cool. "Who better to go after raiders?"

"And ask them to dance?" Sabir shook his head. "I hardly think any of those men would step into a circle."

Neesha, kneeling on the floor very close to the bed, lifted his voice. There was a perceptible edge in it. "I don't believe Tiger or Del would do any such thing as invite them into a circle." He looked at me. "Would you?"

"Well, no," I agreed. "Not exactly."

"I want my sister back," Neesha said flatly. "I can conceive of none better to accomplish such a task and to bring her home."

Sabir looked at Neesha, looked at me again. He inclined his head slightly in accordance with Neesha's words.

"Can you wake him?" I asked once more.

It was Neesha who reached out, who massaged Harith's shoulder. "Father," he said. "Father, it's Neesha. Please awaken. Please speak with us."

The wounded man reacted but not in a helpful way. He moaned, shifted slightly, rolled his head away.

"Father, it's Neesha. I'm home. I need to speak with you."

After a moment, Harith turned his head back. A slight wince gave way to twitching eyelids, to a mouth that trembled.

"Father. I'm here."

The eyelids cracked. Lifted halfway. What lay behind them were dark brown eyes glazed with pain, with confusion.

Neesha took his father's hand into his own. "Yes," he said. "It's me. Neesha. I'm home."

Harith's lips parted. The tip of his tongue extruded briefly, as if to lick dry lips. In a cracked voice, not much above a whisper, he said, "Neesha's gone away . . ."

"No. I'm home. I promise. I'm here. Right here. Feel my hands?" He squeezed flesh. "Feel them? I'm home."

And Harith said, "Rashida."

Neesha glanced briefly at me, at his mother, before turning attention back to his father. "Yes. Rashida."

"Not here . . ."

"No," Neesha agreed, more gently than I might have expected, under the circumstances. "But we mean to bring her back."

"Harith," Danika said quietly. "Harith, we need to know. Is there anything you can tell us?"

His eyes wandered. He saw his son. Life crept back into his eyes. "Neesha?"

"I'm here."

He moistened dry lips. "They took her . . . took Rasha."

Neesha nodded. "We'll bring her back. I promise. But what can you tell us?"

"Follow hoof prints," Harith said. "So many horses . . ." Then he roused a bit more. "Six men. Northerners. Borderers. One was red-haired." Pain took him; he gave in to it. "Follow . . ."

"We will," Neesha assured him. "I swear it."

Harith volunteered no more. Unconsciousness left his face lax.

"It's enough," I said. "Probably this red-haired man is the same red-haired man who attempted to raid Mahmood's caravan. His coloring, plus so many horses, will mark him out."

Danika's expression was bleak as she cupped her elbows in her hands, but her voice was hopeful as she looked at me. "You're sure?"

"I saw him," I told her. "I saw him from close up. I'll know him if I see him again."

She looked at Del, standing very quietly just behind me, and accorded her the honor of being a sword-dancer, not just a woman. "You're sure?"

Del's voice was frigid. "If I do nothing else before I die, I will bring your daughter home."

Neesha carefully settled his father's hand on the bedclothing again, then rose. He glanced briefly at his mother, then looked at me, at Del. "Let's go out."

I had expected it. I turned, Del turned and led us out of the house into the air, into the scent of grasses, of trees, the faintest whiff of near-dead coals in the cookfire ring. Tree leaves rustled faintly on an equally faint breeze.

Neesha paced as Del and I waited. Finally he stopped and looked at us. "I have to stay. She has nothing now, my mother. If he dies—"

Del cut him off. "He won't."

Neesha stared at her. "You can't know that."

"I can," Del declared. "He'll wait for us to bring his daughter home. Hope will keep him alive. And when we bring her back to his side, joy and love will mend his bones and bruises."

Emotions and thoughts filled Neesha's eyes, followed by tears, though he blinked them away before they could fall. "You will bring her back."

It was as much question as it was statement, as much hope as defeat. "Del said it best," I told him. And so I echoed her words, if with one small alteration. "If *I* do nothing else before I die, I will bring your sister home."

Neesha loosed a long breath that vanquished some of the tension. "A two-fold promise. So much power in that."

"Merely the truth," I told him.

"Gods," he said tightly. "I want to stay, I want to go!"

I nodded understanding. "But your mother needs her son."

"I know. I know." He shook his head.

I glanced at Del, then back to Neesha. "You'll know when it's done. You'll hear the thunder of the horses and your sister's voice."

Neesha squeezed his eyes closed. "Gods. Gods."

When he opened them, I stood right in front of him. "Yes," I said.

And for the first time ever, my son and I hugged.

Chapter 24

DEL AND I DECIDED TO SPEND THE NIGHT under the big tree beside the house and leave at first light. I hoped to ask Harith a few more questions when he awoke. Neesha was to let us know when he regained consciousness. By dusk, I learned Harith still had not done so. I had seen my share of broken heads and began to fear he wouldn't wake at all.

I went in search of Danika, found her in the house, and asked her to join me outside. We wandered over to Sabir and Yahmina's corral containing two sorrel geldings and a bay mare. Danika, staring into the corral, said Harith had bred the mare and one of the geldings.

We talked horses briefly; it was what she knew, and it gave her a short respite from constantly worrying about Harith, though I didn't blame her in the least for it. But after awhile her attention left the horses, and we turned our backs on them, leaning against the corral poles.

"Danika. I have to ask this." I glanced at her sidelong. "You said you watched the raiders carry off Rashida?"

After a moment, she answered. "I knew it was happening, yes."

I found that strangely evasive. "She screamed and ran, you said, and a raider swept her up."

Danika didn't look at me but stared at the house. "Yes."

"In which direction did she run? I mean, Del and I can check tomorrow to be more certain of things—we'll look at the hoofprints and footprints if we can find any—but whatever you can tell us would be of great help."

More hair had come down from Danika's coil. A couple of locks hung beside her face. By rote, she removed the clip from her hair and let all of it come down. She busied herself winding the hair into a thick, twisted rope, then coiled it against her head again and re-clipped it. It was, I knew very well, a means to delay her answer. Which of course was answer enough.

"They beat Harith," I said. "They abducted Rashida. Danika . . . I very much doubt they ignored you."

"I was tending Harith," she said quickly. "I couldn't see every-thing. And then . . . the fire . . ."

Quietly, I said, "You're not able to tell us in which direction the raiders went, are you? Because you didn't see it."

Her face, even in profile, was stony. She hugged herself tightly. Then, abruptly, she stood up from the corral poles and faced me. "Why does it matter?" she asked bitterly. "You said it yourself: You can look at the hoof- and footprints tomorrow if Harith doesn't come to."

"And should it rain between now and tomorrow morning? Clouds are coming in. And should Harith not come to by then?"

She was angry as she stared at me, with shame mixed in. "Yes," she said curtly, "they raped me. While two beat Harith outside and one chased after Rashida, the others took me into the house and raped me. I didn't *see* in which direction they rode once they left me, because I was still in the house. I couldn't—couldn't go outside im-mediately. When I did, Harith was unconscious, Rasha was gone, and the house was on fire."

I drew in a deep breath that filled all my lungs and expanded my chest. It was difficult not to get angry on her behalf, but I felt it would not aid the situation. "I'm sorry, Danika. But we needed to know which way they went. Harith will tell us, or the hoofprints will."

She brushed away tears, clearly annoyed that she'd cried again. "Was it necessary to ask me these things? To shame me?"

"Shame has no part in this," I told her. "There is nothing for you to be ashamed of. What they did was against your will. Just as Harith could do nothing as they beat him, nor could Rasha when she was abducted. It was all done *to* you, to all of you."

This time she did not attempt to rid herself of tears. Her voice was choked. "I heard her screaming from inside the house. I thought at first they were raping her, too, but when I got outside, she was gone. And I realized they'd taken her." She drew in a shaky breath, met my eyes. "I could do nothing. I heard it when they beat Harith, I heard it when they stole Rasha, and I could do *nothing*!"

Without emphasis, I said, "Nor were you meant to."

It stopped her tears, stopped the pain a moment. She stared at me.

"Tell me this, Danika, because I know you can. Harith may not recall clearly. Were they Northerners? Southroners? Borderers?"

"All," she answered promptly. "Two Southroners, three Northerners, and one I believe is a Borderer. You don't find red hair often."

People took me for a Borderer because my hair, eyes, and skin were not dark enough for a Southroner—plus I was too big—but not fair enough for a Northerner. I didn't fit. Not here. I was pure Skandic. Born *in* the South but not of it. It could be the same for the red-haired man, that he was from elsewhere. Or his people were. Neesha himself was half Borderer, half Skandic.

"Neesha's staying to help," I told her. "One thing he can do is ride over to the house and pick through it. There may be belongings there that survived."

"That doesn't matter," Danika said dismissively. "It's Harith and Rasha who matter."

"Yes," I agreed, "but it's something he may do. A task. And whatever he finds, if anything, may mean something to you, to Harith, to Rasha, when you're a family again."

That, she had not thought of. After a moment she nodded. "I will, then. I'll send him over there."

I knew better than to offer an embrace. Del had told me it took her a very long time before she could tolerate a man's hand on her after she had been raped repeatedly. In truth, Danika and I were strangers to one another. We'd made us a son one night, we'd shared dreams that night, but twenty-five years was a gulf we couldn't cross.

"Thank you," I said. "And be very certain Del and I will bring her home to you. I can't say when—I wish I could—but it will happen."

I couldn't tell her it had taken Del five years to find her brother. Five years would feel like one hundred to Danika. It was enough, for the moment, that she knew it would be done. Though she would count every day.

Harith did not awaken. Yahmina and Danika began to put together a meal for all. Sabir stayed with Harith after shooing Neesha away, and my son came to the tree camp as Del and I stayed out of the way. He was distracted, but also wanting company.

"Sit," I said. "Have aqivi."

Frowning, still lost in thought, Neesha set out his bedding and unrolled it. His saddle once again served as half-pillow, half-chairback. Del and I lay back, arms thrust beneath our heads, but Neesha sat upright. He took the bota of aqivi and drank absently, then handed it back.

"I'll ride with you tomorrow," he said. "To the house. My mother wants me to see if anything survived the fire." He paused. "I think it's make-work."

"Does it matter?" I asked. "You might well find some things."

He nodded, distracted. "Sabir found my mother and father. He was on his way to Istamir for Marketday; they grow crops, as you see, and sell them in town. But he found my parents, cleared the wagon of produce to make room for them, and brought them here."

"It was well done," Del said quietly.

Neesha's voice was curiously flat. "I think he might die."

That brought silence. Del was not one for attempting to assuage fear with falsehood. I took my lead from her when at last I answered. "He might."

"Even if you find Rasha—"

"*When*," Del declared.

He looked at her. "What?"

"*When* we find Rasha."

It annoyed Neesha. "When. If. It doesn't matter. Once Rasha is home, it will be only my mother and sister on the farm."

"Have they coin?" I asked.

Neesha shrugged. "Possibly. I'll look tomorrow. But most of our coin eats grass and stands on four legs."

"Hire help," Del told him. "They need not be alone. Their crop is different from most and requires more labor, but the end is the same: it's sold."

I knew what was nagging at him. "Hired help frees you," I said.

"Hired help," he said, "is not the same as a son."

"You'll know," Del told him. "When we bring Rasha and the horses home, you'll know the answer."

Neesha took the bota back, unstoppered it and drank deeply. He set it down again, then rose. "I have to go in," he said. "I can't stay out here, wondering whether my father will live or not. I have to be there with him."

"If he rouses enough to be coherent, please let us know," I said. "We need to know in which direction the raiders went when they left."

He scrubbed a hand through his hair. "My mother can tell you, can't she?"

The awkward moment had arrived. It was for Danika to decide whether to tell her son what had occurred, not us. I thought Del might answer, being a woman familiar with rape, but she didn't. It was up to me.

"Well," I said tentatively, "she's got much on her mind. And she was tending your father; it might have been difficult for her to see." Which I knew was a lame answer because any mother would run after a screaming daughter being carried away by raiders. But it was the only one I had.

He was too distracted to parse that out. He merely nodded and headed back to the house.

"He'll know," Del said. "She won't have to tell him. When his mind is clear, he will realize what happened."

I took up the bota. "Maybe so. But let's hope it's *after* we rescue his sister and the horses." Because if he knew now, he would undoubtedly insist on accompanying us. And he would be so full of rage and revenge he could actually harm our efforts. There would be no patience in him to sort out the best way to take the raiders. He would simply get himself killed. And poor Danika would have no daughter, no son, and possibly no husband.

"Something else we must ask of her," Del said, "though tomorrow will do. How many horses were stolen, and is there a way to know them as belonging to this farm?"

"Neesha can tell us the last," I answered, "but he's been gone too long to know how many. Hoolies, I hate to bother Danika again."

"There is another thing she must be asked. Again, Neesha's been gone too long and girls grow quickly. It must be Danika."

"What must be asked?"

"Is there a way to know Rasha when we see her? Alive—or dead?"

"Hoolies, Del, that's cold!"

"It needn't be phrased that way to Danika, but it's what is needful. And you know it, Tiger."

So it was. And I hated it.

I woke up at some foul point of the middle of the night; foul because I hate it when I can't sleep through until morning. And then I can't go back to sleep right away, either. So I lay there staring up at the night sky, aware that Neesha's bedding was still here, but he was not. I suspected he was in the house, sitting by his father.

Then I realized that Del's breathing was not of someone asleep, either. "You awake?"

She didn't sound in the least groggy. "I am."

"Did I wake you?"

"Oh, no. I'm thinking."

I rolled over onto hip and elbow to face her, even though I couldn't see much of her face in the darkness except what the stars illuminated. "Thinking about what?"

"Thinking," she said, "about how I'm going to kill the raiders."

I stroked her arm, slid my hand down to draw designs on the back of her palm. "Well, you can't have all of them. I want at least half." I lifted her hand, threaded fingers into hers, kissed the back of it. "That's three for me, three for you."

"How many doesn't matter," Del said. "It's how they will die."

Since I knew very well it wasn't always a decision we could make about how someone died—they usually had an opinion about it, too—I humored her. "How, then?"

When she spoke, her tone was incredibly casual considering what she actually said. "First, I will cut off the hands. Then the feet. And as he realizes what has been done to him, and that he is dying, I will cut off the head."

Chapter 25

FOR A LONG MOMENT I was too stunned to speak. Even to move. Then a wave of fear swept through me. My scalp prickled. "Bascha . . . bascha, no. Please don't do it."

"Don't do what? Kill the raiders?"

It was difficult to say. I had never expected this to come up. "Make yourself into what you used to be."

She sat up, removing her hand from mine. I sat up as well. We faced one another in the starlight, physically close, but very far apart in certainty of mind.

Her eyes were hollows made of shadow. "I will do what needs to be done."

"Del, *please*. You can't do this to yourself."

The stars were kind to her face. Always. Whatever she said, they were kind. "I will do what needs to be done."

I wished very badly for daylight. For torchlight. A lantern. Hoolies, even a coal. Just to see her. Just to look into her eyes, to see Delilah. "You won't need to *butcher* them, Del. Just kill them. That's all that needs doing. Not a deliberate, step-by-step plan."

She was silent.

And I knew that silence. "It's not necessary, Del."

"Oh, it is very necessary."

I tried with great effort to keep my tone level. "This is not about you, Del. This is not what happened to you ten years ago. The circumstances are different, the people are different—"

The heat of her anger replaced icy self-control. "What is different about a young girl being kidnapped by raiders? About a man who was beaten nearly to death . . . about a girl's mother who was raped repeatedly by multiple men. *What is different*, Tiger, from what I experienced?"

"Del—"

"No. *No*, Tiger. You can't know. You're a man."

A man. It wasn't me that mattered. It was my gender.

I couldn't help being sharp. "Bascha, we fought that battle five years ago. Or *began* that battle five years ago, and finished it some while back. I'm not the same, you're not the same, the circumstances are not the same. Don't erase those five years. Don't become what you were. How many times must I say it? This is not the same."

"Tiger—"

I put it into words a Northerner trained on Staal-Ysta would understand. "This is not your song."

She began to stand. Before she could, I grabbed an arm and pulled her down again.

All of her went stiff. "Let me go." She tried to twist her arm out of my hand. "Let me go, Tiger."

It would have been easy to be angry, to use that anger to underscore anything I might say. But I didn't do it. "We have a daughter, Del. We have a life at Beit al'Shahar. We have friends there in Alric and Lena, in Mehmet and his aketni. We have a business partner in Fouad, who will cheat us whenever he can, thinking we don't know. We have circles under the sun, watched over by a ruin of rocks where our blooding-blades lie broken: your Boreal, my Samiel. Hoolies, we own goats and chickens! Our daughter spends far more time dirty than she ever does clean. And we are *happy* there, Del. Contented. Certain of our course. Any songs we had, any songs we once sang in the circle—even me, who can't sing to save his soul—are finished."

"Tiger—"

I raised my voice over hers. "We are not the same, neither of us, as we were five years ago, when you walked into a cantina searching for a guide to lead you across the Punja in pursuit of your brother. We are not the same. And you are not Rashida, not stolen by *these* raiders. You are you, and you are whole, and to become what once you were is to turn your back on me, on our life . . . and on your daughter."

She hissed in anger then fell silent. I knew to wait, not to continue to spew words even if I badly wanted to. You can drown a person in words, in reasonings, in your own fears and angers and biases. I had to let her think. Even if sometimes my words, and my silence, did not immediately plant a crop.

At some point, I had loosened my grip on her arm. Now, she twisted that arm free and rose. She walked away.

Ah, hoolies. The remains of the night, I knew, would not be spent in sleep. By either of us.

Shortly after dawn, on a gray, heavy day, I got up to see to my needs and to begin the bucket run for the horses, but found Del had already done the horse chores. Her gelding was saddled, bridled, haltered, pouches on board, ready to go, and the stud was still picketed under the tree. Taking that as a message, I got my gear together and prepared the stud for the journey. I didn't see Del and assumed she'd visited a nearby shrub. Eventually, when she did not appear despite my being ready to go, I headed to the house, and found her about to come out the door. I stepped aside and let her pass.

No sign of our argument reached her face as she spoke to me outside. "Harith hasn't wakened. It's possible he never will. We won't get any information from him."

"And Danika can't provide what we need, either." I scratched thoughtfully at beard scruff; I really needed to shave. "So, we go to the farm and hope to find hoofprints."

In silence, Del pointed to the sky.

I followed her finger with my eyes and saw what she meant:

The clouds had significantly darkened and were now hanging quite low, fat with rain. "No. No, no. Oh, hoolies, that's the last thing we need. Rain will wash tracks away."

"That's why I got the gelding ready and brought the stud over. But you were still asleep, so I let you be."

I found that amazingly unlike her, considering our goal. "Why?"

Del sighed. "First, because I hoped Harith could provide an answer. Second . . . well, because of last night." An uncharacteristic darkness shadowed her eyes. "I understand now what you meant. But Tiger—it needs doing. Those raiders should all be killed for what they did to Neesha's mother and father, and Rashida."

"I wasn't arguing that. I agree with you. I was scared to death I'd lose you back into the constant coldness and anger that defined you when we met. It was a hard journey for you, becoming a kinder—but not a *weaker* woman—and I didn't want you to go through it again."

She nodded, looking past me to the sheltering tree. "But I still might take a head."

It was almost, but not quite, worth a laugh. "Hey, if a head ends up in front of my blade, I'll take it myself." I touched her on the arm. "I'll go see Neesha. And I need to ask Danika a question."

Del nodded again and walked toward the horses. I went into the house and found the cluster of people gathered near the bed. Harith's breathing did not sound normal. Like Del, I felt it likely he'd never wake. Danika glanced up as I entered the crowded room. I gestured with a lifted chin, and she got up and came to me. I led her into the kitchen area.

She was exhausted. It showed in her face, in every line and posture of her body. But I knew better than to suggest she get some rest. She wouldn't until she collapsed from exhaustion. "What does Harith use to mark the horses as belonging to your farm?"

"He shears the mane to the neck." She saw my brows go up. "You can't disguise them as someone else's horses that way. If we tied something into the mane or tail, it could be found and removed. And he won't burn a mark because that, too, can be altered. Only time will alter a shorn mane."

Well, yes. I hadn't thought of that. Rather clever. "And what should we tell Rashida when we find her? She's not likely to trust us any more than the raiders, after what she's been through."

Danika smiled wearily. "She'll know you. How many sword-dancers have sandtiger scars in their faces? Do you forget? She and Neesha used to spar. He spoke of you often, saying one day he'd find you and tell you he was your son. She'll know."

"And how will I know it's her?"

She blinked. "She'll be with raiders. Won't you be able to tell? Besides, she can certainly tell you who she is."

A dozen answers went through my head. Raiders often kidnapped and kept women with them, which meant Rashida could be one of several. Some captives were sold. There were no guarantees Rashida would still be with them, depending on where they were bound. And no guarantees they would not have removed her tongue.

Danika saved me from having to say such things. "She has Neesha's eyes, all warm and cider-colored. Her hair is brown, but the sun streaks it gold in places. She was wearing a yellow tunic and skirt."

I opened my mouth to say something more, but heard the sound of raindrops on the roof. Danika and I both looked up, then at one another. "Yes," I said. "I'd better go if we're to make the farm before rain washes away the prints." I leaned forward, kissed her briefly on the brow, and told her we'd bring home her daughter and the horses.

Danika shook her head. "Just bring my daughter home. Don't worry about the horses."

"Neesha," I called, "we'll be back." He barely had a chance to nod before I left.

Outside, Del had the stud ready to go. She wore her hooded oilcloth coat, belted around her waist. She had once insisted we needed these and I had disagreed. Now I was glad I'd lost the argument. I pulled on mine, buckled the belt, then grabbed the stud's rein from her. I stepped into a stirrup and swung a leg up and over hastily. The rain was falling harder.

"Wait!" It was Neesha coming after us. "There's a horse fair. In Istamir, on Marketday."

A horse fair. And here we'd thought to learn details from a badly injured man, rather than from my son who actually knew the answer.

Del and I looked at one another. Now there was no need for us to go to the burned farm, to look for hoofprints. Merely to ride to Istamir.

I very much wanted to ask Neesha why he hadn't told us that earlier. Del read it in my face. She eased the gelding around so his back was to the house, to Neesha. Very quietly, she said, "Let it go. Too many distractions for him."

To my son, I said, "Go back in, get out of the rain. We'll return as soon as we can."

He nodded, lifted a hand, but was too distracted to offer anything else. He disappeared inside.

"The raiders might go elsewhere," Del suggested. "The horses will be known here."

"But we'll have to look in Istamir first. Ask a few questions."

We exchanged nods and set both horses to a hard gallop.

Chapter 26

THE BURNED FARMHOUSE WAS ON OUR WAY TO ISTAMIR, but well before reaching it the rain began to fall harder. Both of us wore our hoods up, but the rain didn't particularly care about that; it slanted in different directions. The ground now was soggy, and the horses' manes and tails hung in soaked strings. There was much shaking of heads by both Del's gelding and the stud, and whipping tails meant to express irritation. Occasionally the stud swung his so hard that it slapped against my coat and soaked strands stuck there until I peeled them off. Hooves brought up mud, splattering sandaled feet and the hems of our coats.

Del and I rode abreast. I slid my hood back partway. "How long is this going to last?"

She didn't look at me. "Until it stops."

"Bascha—"

"I don't know, Tiger. Truly." The hood was aimed upward, as if she looked at the sky. "The clouds are still heavy."

"I don't like this," I complained. "This is too much water."

"Well, the South has too much heat and sand."

"You could drown in this!"

Del pushed her hood back into place. We were practically shouting at one another because of the rainfall and the sounds of the horses. She said something.

"What?"

"I said, I don't think so!"

"Well, it feels like it!"

"It's more pleasant than a sandstorm."

"I'm used to those. I know what to do."

"You should know what to do in the rain, too: get out of it. And if you ask me, the South could stand a few rainstorms now and then. There would be streams and rivers, and everyone could eat fish."

"I don't need to eat fish."

"You eat fish regularly, Tiger. You are being foolish."

"Yeah, I know." I pulled my hood up farther. "I wish Neesha were coming with us. It would be a help with Rashida and the horses."

"He's best staying there right now, to aid his mother. And if Harith dies, Neesha will be all Danika has. He knows horses. He could do the work Harith was doing."

And so she said what I'd begun to fear in the back of my mind. Yes, Neesha wanted to rise through the seven levels of sword-dancer training, but he was a dutiful son. Danika and Rashida would both need his help.

"But Harith may not die," Del said.

Sometimes she knew exactly what I was thinking. I was never certain how to take that. "No, he may not."

"If he recovers, Neesha may come back home," she said.

He might. He might not. But I didn't want to talk about mights and maybes. "Is that the house?"

Del peered ahead. The rain was so heavy it was difficult to see much through it. "I think . . . yes. It is."

"No more fire, no more hot areas," I said. "We might be able to find shelter. This rain will stop the raiders, too. They'll hole up under oilcloth, or, if they're in Istamir, under a roof."

The house was a massive pile of burned timbers and planks, most collapsed upon one another. Del and I rode to the corral we'd repaired for temporary use, untacked the horses, and turned them into it. Rain had already filled the water trough to the halfway point. We hauled saddles, bridles, supplies, bedding, to the remains of the house, where we set them in front of what had been the door.

Then we made our way in, kicking wet wood aside, and hunted for some portion of the house that might keep off the rain.

"Ah," I said. "Neesha's sword. I forgot he'd dropped it when I threw him out of the house." I bent, picked it up. Peered up through what remained of the framework, all wood charred. Rain hit me in the face.

Del was in another room. "Tiger—a little shelter here."

I made my way to her through burned planking and fallen timbers. I discovered a section of wall not burned through. Del was wrestling with planks that had not succumbed entirely to the fire.

"Here." I set down Neesha's sword and grabbed one of the planks. "What are you doing?"

"Leaning them up against the wall. I think we have four that will stand. We'll make a lean-to." She heaved at a plank. "Such as it is."

We did manage to lean four planks against the partial wall still standing, though they were of different lengths. As shelter it wasn't much, but would still shed some of the rain.

I stripped off my coat. "Give me yours. I'll go wrap the tack and our things in them, best as I can. Not perfect, but better than *more* rain getting to them."

I picked up Neesha's sword and crunched back through charred wood to the front of the house, where I wrapped saddles, pouches, bedrolls, and Neesha's sword in the oilcloth. He'd need to clean and hone it, but at least he'd have a blade again.

With the sun occluded by the clouds, I couldn't sort out what time it might be, but I thought probably late morning, not yet midday. That left a fair amount of time to make our way to Istamir by evening, if the rain stopped. I peered up at the sky, shielding my eyes against the rain as best I could. I had no experience with rain clouds, but I saw no promise that the rain might halt anytime soon. I thought for a moment, weighing crude shelter against riding in rain. And I wondered if Rashida were wet, wherever she was.

Ah, hoolies. I made my way back to Del, sandaled feet blackened by wet, charred wood. I leaned down beneath the slanted planks. "I don't like it."

She was seated, leaning against the wall. "The rain? Yes. You already said that."

"No. Staying here while the raiders are doing who knows what, where they are doing it, and to whom they may be doing it."

Del squinted against the fractured rain that made its way through the leaning planks. "I thought you wanted to stop. You said the raiders would look for shelter, too."

"Well, I could be wrong." I raised a finger. "Mind you, I said '*could* be.' "

Del rose, bent, ducked out from under the lean to. "Or they could be in Istamir."

"They could."

"Nothing to stop them keeping the horses some distance away from Istamir, then bringing them in for Marketday a few at a time, per man."

"No, nothing," I agreed. When Del picked her way past me, I followed. It was true I'd wanted shelter, but all I'd do is sit there twitching, wanting to be on my way. Rashida's welfare depended on it. I did not want to imagine what she might be going through while Del and I sat under planks set against what could be the last standing portion of a wall in the house where she grew up.

Outside, Del said she would get the horses while I unwrapped our belongings. Neesha's sword might present a slight problem, since there wasn't room for two blades in a sheath—in the rain, we wore our swords as usual with hilts poking through a seam, but with a flap of oilcloth fastened over them—but I improvised. I dug out a roll of muslin bandages and wrapped it around and around the blade. Once Del was back with the horses, I readied the stud, held Neesha's sword in one hand, and mounted. The wrapped sword I slid through the top leather strap of my stirrups, then settled my thigh over it. The hilt poked free of my leg.

Del, as she mounted, looked a little bedraggled. Her soaked braid hung out of the hood, and droplets ran down her face. While the rain wasn't terribly cold, we were nonetheless wet and it robbed us of body heat. I could imagine I didn't look much better than Del. She climbed into the saddle, cast me a glance that asked a question.

I shrugged. "Sooner there, sooner done."

Once again, we galloped east toward Istamir.

As we approached the town, I felt somewhat relieved that it was raining, despite my complaints. No one would be out of doors, going about their business. Those free to escape the rain inside a tavern, house, or rented room, would stay put. Which meant it was unlikely any sword-dancers were out where they could see and recognize me.

We were here for Rashida and the horses, not sword-dances. But I could be challenged at any moment. Rafa was dead, but Eddrith wasn't—Darrion didn't count—which meant the other two rumored sword-dancers could be hanging around, whoever they were. I suspected word was passed that I had departed, but as Danika had said, it was hard to miss me with the scars on my face. A fair number of people knew me by them: sword-dancers, tanzeers, tavern keepers, and possibly others I couldn't count. For now the hood would hide me, but once the storm broke and the sun came out, there'd be no need for the coat, and a man who kept his hood pulled up in the sunlight would be even more noticeable.

We entered the town, horse hooves clopping on paving stones and splashing through puddles. Water ran swiftly in a miniature stream down the center of the street. We passed two cantinas—taverns, here in the North—including the one with the red-and-yellow sign, and an inn.

"I can go into the taverns," Del said. "I'm not so out of place here as I am in the South. I'm one of many Northerners. You could wait for me." I began to object, but Del rode right over the top of my words with a raised voice. "We have no time to waste," she reminded me. "You being challenged to a dance wastes it. I'll go into taverns and inns, ask a few questions about a red-haired man."

It sounded unlikely. "You believe borjuni will be staying at an inn? Really?"

"It's not impossible. And who's to stop them?"

I still found it unlikely. "You could be recognized by one of his men," I reminded her. "They saw you at Mahmood's caravan when they attacked. Once seen, no one forgets you."

"They will if I'm not wearing harness and sword. In a burnous, I'll be just another Northern woman."

My hood slid back. I pulled it forward again. "Bascha, trust me—you could *never* be just another Northern woman."

She turned her head and shot me an irritable glance. "You know very well what I mean. You go to Marketfield and talk to Mahmood—he may have seen the red-haired man if the raiders have brought the horses in. I'll see what I can find out in taverns. It shouldn't be difficult. Men are willing to talk to me."

That resulted in me laughing aloud, and loudly. When most of the laughter died away into the occasional chuckle, I shook my head. "Gods, Del, you have a true gift for understatement!"

She scowled, worked her way out of her coat, took off the harness with its sheathed sword. She moved her horse closer to me and thrust the harness and sword into my hands. "Take this to Mahmood. He can keep it for me." She pulled her coat back on and tugged it into place swiftly before she got too wet. "I'll meet you at Mahmood's camp."

"I don't like it," I told her. "You without a sword."

She hitched one shoulder in a slight shrug. "Without one, people are less likely to recognize me. And they certainly won't challenge me."

"Darrion did. I'll bet Eddrith would."

"Not if I have no sword."

Well, she was right. By the codes, sword-dancers need not accept challenges if, by their own free choice, they were not wearing a sword . It didn't matter for me, but it did for Del. I knew what she said was the truth.

"Well, I still don't like it."

Del's smile was faint. "You don't have to." She turned her gelding and rode away from me.

I scowled after her. You just couldn't change Delilah's mind once she had it set on something. Sometimes that was a good thing. Other times, such as this one, it annoyed the hoolies out of me.

The clouds began to break just as I tracked down Mahmood's caravan. His wagon was all closed up, silks and spices tucked away; himself as well, if he weren't at a tavern. I rode up to the back end and used the pommel of Del's sword to knock on the wagon. I heard a body moving around, some activity. After a moment, Mahmood stuck his head out.

"Oh," he said in surprise. "You're back."

And before either of us could say another word, the stud let loose with a spine-rattling, lengthy shake, spraying water in every direction. Poor Mahmood received much of it in his face. He scowled at me, disappeared a moment, then stuck his head out, wiping his face with a cloth.

"Will he do that again?" he asked, aggrieved.

I sighed deeply, trying to settle my bones back into their accustomed places. "Who knows. He does as he will. He's stubborn that way."

"Teach him better manners!"

The rain had let up. I pushed my hood down on my shoulders. "Speaking of horses, I understand there's a horse fair here on Marketday?"

"There is. Every Marketday."

"Have you seen any of the horses to be offered?"

Mahmood pushed open the snugged-down canvas. "How should I know? Horses are horses."

"These have shorn manes. And Mahmood, it's important. They were stolen from Neesha's parents. Along with his sister."

Mahmood stared in shock at me a moment, then shook his head. "I've seen none as you describe. Is Neesha here?"

"No, he's staying with his mother. His father—well, stepfather—has a serious head injury and may not live. If you see any horses that suit, let me know." I displayed harness and sword. "And can you put this in safekeeping? It's Del's. She's checking taverns for that red-haired raider; I'm looking for horses with shorn manes."

Mahmood took the harness and sword. "The red-haired man who attacked my caravan?"

"The same. He won't be doing it much longer." I gathered reins. "Del's meeting me back here, if that's all right."

"Of course! Of course!" Mahmood made a shooing gesture. "Go! Find this man!"

The stud and I set out to do just that.

Chapter 27

MARKETFIELD WAS FULL OF WHEELED CONVEYANCES. Now that the rain had stopped, merchants began to open up their wagons again. Clouds broke apart and allowed the midday sun to strengthen, warming the air. But the earth was saturated, and puddles and rivulets didn't dry up immediately. The stud splashed through, mud sucking at his hooves.

I wore sandals; I was not going to dismount unless I had to. I did, however, shrug out of the oilcloth coat and drape it across the saddle in front of me. My burnous was quite wet at the neck and hem; the latter was freighted with mud as well. I considered taking it off altogether, but that would make it obvious I was a sword-dancer. I'd just as soon not advertise it, though I knew there was a good chance I would be recognized. My facial scars did indeed identify me.

I rode slowly through the wagons, making no sign that I was looking for anyone specific. And in a way I wasn't; what I sought now were horses with shorn manes. Even if I came across any, I wouldn't confront anyone. Del and I would do that together. Six-to-two weren't superlative odds, but we'd handled six before.

Hmm. We had fought six at Mahmood's caravan, and killed four. Whoever was leader—and I tended to think it was the red-haired man, since he'd done all the shouting—must have replaced them, unless Danika had miscounted. But perhaps they were more than six, while each raiding party was kept to a smaller number. It didn't really make any sense to me, but then I wasn't a raider to think of such things.

Though perhaps I'd better think of such things if Del and I were to overcome the borjuni—especially if they had more men to draw on as needed. That suggested a tougher enemy than originally expected. An endless supply of men, all dedicated to killing whoever so they could take whatever they wished.

I rode onward, wandering idly through narrow alleyways, between wagons, in front of or behind various lines of conveyances. Horse teams were picketed here and there, close by their respective owners. The stud got snuffy and whipped his tail, stuck his head up in the air, developed a slight hump in his back as he pulled himself into a compact bundle. I swore. This was his there's-a-mare-in-season-nearby-I-want-her behavior. It certainly wasn't surprising in view of the fact horses were picketed all over, but neither was it appreciated.

As I rode I had conversations with the stud. I told him it really wasn't necessary to show off, that certainly all the other males were geldings and offered no threat to his magnificence. He was unconvinced. The scent of mare—or mares, plural—turned his brain to goo. Only one thought remained in his head, and it had nothing to do with riding slowly through Marketfield.

"I don't need this," I told him, sitting loosely in the saddle so my body could adjust to whatever move he might make. "Really, a calm walk would do. The goal here is to not make ourselves obvious. We don't *want* people noticing us, particularly if they happen to be attached to horses with shorn manes. This is reconnaissance, not a hunt."

He was unimpressed.

"Honestly, every human knows you are the finest horse here. They have only to look at you to see your handsomeness. Even all the horses are impressed. Geldings, remember? No threat."

Still unimpressed. He knew very well there were also mares present—which made perfect sense for a horse fair—and he wasn't about to listen to me.

If I dismounted and attempted to lead him, he would be less

controllable, and I stood a good chance of being stomped on, intended or no. Best for me to stay in the saddle and guide him. Well, *try* to guide him.

Try didn't work. Eventually the only action that did accomplish anything was to turn him back the way we had come. The search would have to be done on foot. Or else by Del, when she returned. Which didn't please me. It was risk enough for her to walk into taverns, alone and unarmed. She was correct about being less noticeable here where there were more Northerners present, but how many Northern women sword-singers, trained at Staal-Ysta, were present? Probably all of one, whose name was Delilah.

The stud, realizing we were now riding *away* from whichever mare, or mares, he'd scented, was not cooperative. He danced a little, tested my grip on the reins, bobbed his head, lashed his tail, gave me an altogether uncomfortable ride. I gritted my teeth, swearing I'd castrate him when we got back to the South. Between then and now, I needed him intact.

Of course he didn't take my threat seriously. He knew better. I'd been making that threat for at least a decade.

When Del and I rode our mounts, we did so with rope halters over leather bridles. Lead-ropes, tied to the saddle pommels, were used only when we picketed the horses or tied them to trees. At present the stud was unlikely to stand quietly when picketed, so I'd have to tie him to a nearby tree with that lead-rope rather than pounding a peg into the soaked ground. I didn't want to imagine what he'd do to a wagon if tied to one. Probably attempt to drag it to the mare, wherever she—or they—might be. Mahmood, I suspected, would not appreciate that. Especially if he were inside.

I fought my way back to Mahmood's four wagons, looked around for a tree, and found a possibility not terribly far away. As the stud had not acted up until some distance from Mahmood's little caravan, he probably wouldn't behave terribly here. Then again, it might make no difference, now that he knew an in-season mare was somewhere within, oh, a hundred miles.

We splashed our way to the tree, the stud and I, where I untied the saddle pouches and slung them away, wincing as they landed in the mud. It squelched up between my sandaled toes as I dismounted and looped the lead-rope around a very stout limb, tying it firmly. I pointed to the ground. "Grass. See? Grass. You eat it."

At the end of the rope, he paced back and forth, testing it with little jerks of his head. I grabbed the bit shank closest to me. I held it firmly, giving his head a tug back and forth to remind him I had ways of controlling him.

He rolled an annoyed eye at me, bared his teeth. As he tried to swing his head at me, I made a fist and bashed it into his muzzle. He jerked his head away, tail whipping again, hooves sucking mud.

With a few twists of the lead-rope, I fashioned a slip-loop and wound it around his muzzle, tugging it tight. If he tried to set back and break either halter or tree, this would put pressure on more sensitive flesh. A last resort but usually effective.

"You're bigger, stronger, and could stomp me into the ground, given a chance. But I'm *smarter* than you. I travel with hobbles, remember?"

One did not waste any time when hobbling an irritated stallion. He was tied to the tree and the slip-loop would help, so I ducked down, put the hobbles around his fetlocks, knotted the ropes *very* hastily, and took two long steps away from his mouth.

"Your fault," I explained. "Bad manners will not be tolerated." He blew a huge and wet snort of annoyance, but I was distant enough that not much reached me. I pointed to the ground again. "Grass. See? Eat it. I'll get you water and grain as well. For now, just settle, would you?"

The stud gave me a look that would freeze the flames of hoolies. Thwarted by rope at nose and fetlocks, there was little he could do.

Well, that was the theory. One never knows with a stallion, especially when mares are around. Particularly in-season mares.

I looked down at my feet. I stood in several inches of mud, and most of my sandals were invisible, except for the tops of my feet and laces. I swore, grabbed the saddle pouches, and splashed my way back to Mahmood's wagon. There at the tailgate I took off and spread my coat on the ground, placed the saddle pouches in the middle, and leaned against the wagon to unlace my sandals. In this muck, bare feet would do best.

I shook as much mud as I could off the sandals, dried them

slightly with a sleeve of my coat, dropped them on top of the heap. Now I wore burnous, harness, and sword. And I wasn't about to go without a weapon. There were other sword-dancers in Istamir—or had been. Why did I have to be me? Recognizably me?

I bent and scooped up mud, dragged some across my facial scars. Not much, but enough, I hoped, to fill in the depressions and divert the eye. I splattered some on my burnous as well. After all, my horse was very difficult to ride. Mud in appropriate places told its own story.

Barefoot and muddy, I took myself off to go walking, hunting Harith's horses again. Only one was necessary. That would lead us to the others.

The stud, watching me go, flung snorting, squealing insults at me. Good thing I didn't understand horse speech.

I found no horses with shorn manes anywhere near the Market-field. Of course it was entirely possible I missed one or more, but the state of my bare feet, calves, and the bottom of my burnous, heavy with mud and water, proved my efforts. And no one recognized me.

I squished my soggy way back to the stud, thinking about Rashida, and discovered he was somewhat calmer. He still gave me the Ugly Eye, but I promised him grain and water, and went off to get both out of my saddle pouches. When I returned, I decided he was calm enough to remove the slip-rope and unsaddle him. I'd have to leave the bridle on him because the halter was fastened over it. In order to remove it I'd also have to remove the halter, fasten it temporarily around his neck, then remove the bridle and let him drop the bit from his mouth, whereupon I'd slip the halter back on. A well-trained horse is generally quiet during this process, but 'well-trained' was not a term I'd attach to the stud. Besides, he'd wait for the exchange, for a chance to jerk his head away, thereby tearing the halter out of my hands and departing at high speed to find the mare he'd scented earlier. Or any number of in-season mares scattered here and there. Life is never boring when you ride a stud-horse.

I removed Neesha's sword from the stirrup strap and placed it carefully in my armpit, then pulled the saddle and blanket from the stud's back. I was in the midst of arranging blade, blanket, and saddle when I heard Del's call. I turned to it, hooking the saddle against one hip. And my jaw nearly hit the ground.

A man was with her. A sword-dancer. Blond, blue-eyed, tall. A Northerner.

The first thought that ran through my mind was that Del had accepted a challenge and had come for her sword in Mahmood's wagon. But that shouldn't apply, because in lacking her sword she wasn't expected to accept a challenge. Which left the other possibility.

He'd come for me.

Well, I had two swords. One, wrapped in muslin, tucked under one arm; the other in harness across my back. He was far enough away that it was a simple matter to drop saddle and blanket and arm myself before he could reach me, and I think he recognized it also.

I looked at Del, tilting my head just a bit and giving her a wide-eyed, extremely pointed, questioning stare.

She smiled. "This is Eddrith," she said. "Remember him? He danced with Neesha."

"And defeated him," Eddrith said.

I didn't look at him. "I remember Eddrith," I told her coolly, "but what is Eddrith doing *here*?"

"It's not a challenge," she explained.

"Well, not *yet*," Eddrith clarified.

Del frowned at him. "You didn't say that in the tavern."

He smiled, first at Del, then at me. "You didn't ask me in such a way as to require a complete answer."

I dropped saddle and blanket into the mud, took Neesha's sword from under my arm, and sliced through the muslin wrappings to free the blade. I looked a question at Eddrith, waiting for the challenge.

"No," he said, alarmed. "No, no. That's not what I'm here for, here. Not now. Wait. I promise. Let me draw my sword."

"That's a good indicator of a friendly intention," I said dryly.

Del stood next to him. Together, they were so similar in coloring, two tall, pale-haired Northerners. But carefully, deliberately, she took the number of steps necessary to remove herself from Eddrith's reach. My bascha was not happy, not happy at all. In fact, she was coldly furious. Probably more with herself, bringing a challenge to me when I was supposed to be elsewhere.

Eddrith showed me his palms. "No challenge," he said. "No challenge. Let me remove my sword. I'll drop it into the muck. Or hand it to her." His eyes slanted to Del.

I smiled broadly. "Yes, give it to Del, why don't you? It puts you close enough to attack an unarmed woman."

That appeared to have never crossed his mind. Thoughtfully, he looked at Del, as if tucking away in his brain the action I'd suggested. Then he looked back to me. "In the muck," he said. "I'll toss it out of my reach."

I smiled at him. And while he watched, I tossed Neesha's sword to Del and unsheathed my own.

"All right," I said. "Now you can remove your sword and toss it aside. In the muck. But be careful when you do so. Very, very careful."

Eddrith was very, very careful. The sword slapped down into mud, well out of reach. Then he stood very still and looked at me. His demeanor had changed to worry. He was now facing the best sword-dancers in the South. Even if we were presently in the North.

"Now," I said lightly, "why in hoolies are you here?"

Eddrith licked his lips. "I wish to help you defeat these raiders."

I had expected nothing like that. "You what?"

"I wish to help you defeat these raiders."

I looked at Del, once more asking a pointed question with my eyes.

She shrugged. "That's what he told *me*."

Eddrith said, "I hired on as a caravan outrider, once. Raiders attacked. One of them managed to stick a sword in me, jerk me off my horse. They thought I was dead. *I* thought I was dead. And while I lay there, waiting to die, they killed everyone in the caravan I'd been hired to protect."

Chapter 28

I EYED HIM UP AND DOWN. "You do not appear to be dead."

"Well, no. It wasn't a killing strike, it just looked like one. And another caravan came along not long after."

I nodded. "All right, let's back up a little, shall we? Something you said early on. You know: about this not being a challenge yet. *Yet*."

"Oh," he said.

"Yes, oh." I smiled at him cheerily. "Well?"

"Not a *real* challenge," he said hastily.

"How do you make a challenge that isn't a real challenge?"

"Yes," Del said grimly. "How do you do that?"

Eddrith seemed somewhat puzzled by our ignorance. "Well, I challenge you to dance. But it's not to the death. Practice, mostly, because I know you would defeat me."

I'd decided Eddrith was younger than I'd thought at first glance. "You mean sparring."

Eddrith nodded. "In exchange."

"In exchange for what?"

"Help with the raiders."

My eyebrows shot up. "Oh, there's a *price* for your help, is there?"

Del took two steps toward him. He was now in range of her blade. In an icy voice, she told him, "You mentioned no price in the tavern. You simply offered to help."

"I think it's fair." Now he was on the defensive. He looked at me again. "Don't you think it's fair?"

Neither Del nor I said anything. Color filled, then drained from his face.

What Eddrith didn't realize was that he had actually put Del and I in the position of having to pay his price for his help. It wasn't that we needed help, particularly, but if we chased him away, he might just go to the raiders and tell them where we were. I didn't *think* he would, because of his story; then again, it would be a clever man to tell such a touching story, all to win our favor.

Maybe Eddrith was brighter than I'd thought. Or else a very good actor.

I glanced at Del. Her expression said she was leaving it up to me, probably because it was me Eddrith wanted. "All right," I said. "You can help us. Afterward, you and I will spar."

He nodded once, attempting a dignified acceptance, but the light in his eyes was pure anticipation and excitement.

Del remained in reach of Eddrith, though she spoke to me. "I stabled my horse. I took a room in an inn."

I glanced briefly at Eddrith. "Did he recommend the inn?"

Del knew better than to do such a thing, but it was worth asking in front of the young man. "Oh, no. This was done before I began going into taverns."

I looked again at Eddrith. "Meet us here tomorrow. We'll discuss plans."

He nodded, but remained where he was. Warily.

Ah. I walked over to his sword, slid my blade under his, and flipped the sword in his direction. Del was already in position to defend or attack, as was necessary.

But it wasn't necessary. Eddrith caught the sword awkwardly, shook it to clear some of the mud, but did not sheath it. The blade would have to be cleaned, first. He backed up, then turned and walked away, attempting to avoid the deeper puddles.

"Why?" Del asked.

"My shodo once told me it's better to keep potential enemies close, rather than distant. So you know what they may be planning."

"Ah. My *an-kaidin* just told us to kill them."

Mahmood once again offered us his wagon for the night, but this time I politely declined. He'd done quite a bit for us already, and he was certainly entitled to sleep in his own bed. Del took her sword and harness out of Mahmood's wagon, while I put tack back on the stud, loosed his tie-rope and the rope around his nose, and led him away from the tree. I suggested to Del we ride double through all the muck so as not to wade through it.

She shook her head. "I don't think we should be seen together. You ride, I'll walk."

I wanted to object, but she had a point. "All right. Where am I going?"

She provided directions and description for the inn; the small livery in which she'd stabled her gelding was in the same row of buildings. It was nowhere near the main street through town, nor where many men drank, she explained. Spirits were not allowed in the inn.

"Not allowed?" I asked.

"Not allowed," she confirmed.

"Well, no wonder you chose that one!"

Del merely smiled in satisfaction.

"I hardly ever drink anymore," I protested. "I don't even know the last time I was drunk."

"Approximately five days ago, when you and Alric sat by the stream sucking down ale."

Oh. Yes. We had sucked down ale. And yes, I'd felt it. Time to change the subject. I asked if she'd learned anything about the raiders while visiting taverns. She said she would tell me at the inn.

I watched her go, then gathered up the tack and gear resting on my raincoat, which now would be even muddier than before. Once the stud was ready I worked my way back into the mud-coated oilcloth, mounted, and rode away in a direction different from the route Del took.

The sun, hidden above dark clouds for much of the day, began its journey down the ladder of the sky. Now was the time the taverns would fill up. Marketday would draw from miles around. The end of the day signaled time for food, spirits, even wine-girls, were a man not married. Caravaners who brought wives with them could avail themselves only of food and drink.

Hoolies, *I* couldn't avail myself of drink, thanks to Del finding what likely was the one inn in all of Istamir that neither sold nor tolerated spirits.

The mud on my face had dried and now itched, caught in beard scruff. It took great effort not to scratch all of it off. I remained barefoot, riding with sandals tied together and draped across the pommel, wearing the bedraggled coat in hopes of looking nothing like a sword-dancer, despite my sword jutting up over my shoulder. I'd covered it with the flap of oilcloth, but mostly it made me look like a hunchback. A very oddly shaped hunchback. So after consideration I took my mud-caked sandals off the pommel and tossed them over my shoulder, one dangling in front, the other in back, attempting to disguise the hilt.

So. A hunchback with a very muddy face and muddier coat. Well, it might work.

I drew a few idle glances as I made my way around the wagons, looked for a way into the town that wasn't part of the paved main street. Nothing about me looked particularly prepossessing. And no one commented or called out to me.

Eventually I found my way to the small, extremely narrow street Del had described. It was indeed well away from the main part of town and its paving stones. Here, dirt ruled, which, of course, had transformed itself into serious mud. Livery stables and smithies often were built adjoining one another; I followed the sound of a blacksmith ringing down a hammer upon an anvil. As I rode closer, I saw the shower of sparks, smelled the acrid tang of coals burning in the forge. And there was, indeed, an adjoining livery.

The blacksmith glanced up as I reined in the stud. He nodded his head toward the open double doors of the livery. "Wanting stabling, then?"

I nodded, untangled myself from sandals and coat, and stepped down into mud. The black-eyed smith, arms and shoulders overdeveloped from years of pounding iron, smiled through his dark beard. "A soft day, wasn't it?"

I shot him a morose glance. "If that's what you call unremitting downpours up here in the North, then yes, it was 'soft.'"

"Not a Borderer, then?"

I decided the better part of safety lay in saying nothing about me being a Southroner. I wanted to give no one the puzzle pieces of my presence and appearance. "Borderer," I said. "Just not from this area."

"You've got the look." He used tongs to pick up the horse shoe from the anvil, inspected it, dumped it back into the coals. "How long are you wanting to keep your horse here?"

"A few days. Is there an hostler here?"

"Oh, that'd be me," he said comfortably. "Both places, you see. I'll see to your mount. By the looks of that crest on his neck, he's a stallion."

"He is."

"Stallions cost extra."

"He's a very well-behaved stallion."

The smith looked at him again. He grunted. "Doubting that. Extra, like I said."

I sighed and agreed. Then a thought struck me. A smith would know more about what horses came through town than anyone. Even if they hadn't seen them in the flesh, smiths undoubtedly spoke of their trade and customers—human and equine—in taverns.

"I'm here for the horse fair," I said. "Harith—you know Harith? East of here?—asked me to pick up two head, if I found any good ones. Mares, of course."

The smith pulled the horseshoe out of the coals, set it on edge on the anvil, gripped the tongs tightly closed, and began banging away to shape the shoe properly. He nodded, watching his work, not me. When he paused for a moment to examine the shoe, he spoke. "I know Harith. Good horseman. Hasn't been running so many head now that his son's away. Gone two years, I think it is. No matter. Young men wanting travel. Though I don't know as how being a sword-dancer is an honest day's work compared to raising horses." He cast a knowing glance at me. "But no offense. You're either that, or a hunchback. And I don't think you're a hunchback."

I ignored the unsolicited comments. "Harith just hired me on. Said his son was gone, and he needed the help." I paused a moment, watching him; made the question idle. "Have you seen any horses with shorn manes? Wildcat got into a corral, broke one of the poles down. A few horses got out. Someone might have picked them up."

"Someone might have. I haven't seen any." He once again stuck the shoe under the coals and laid down his tongs. "Well, shall I be taking this brute, then, or will you put him in a stall yourself?"

I assumed a blank expression, just held out the reins. He was a big, stout man who likely took no guff from recalcitrant horses. He might be a match for the stud.

He indicated a table piled with bridles, straps, bits of iron, horse shoes and nails, a rasp. "Be putting it there." And he told me how much I was to be putting there. He grinned, displaying a missing front tooth, as my eyebrows shot up. "Extra for a stallion."

I glowered at him, then pulled the saddle pouches down, dug through one, and came up with a modest leather pouch. From it I took his price, laid coin on the table. I decided I preferred that the stud be difficult, successfully difficult, just to show the smith he was right not to make exceptions.

Grinning again, he took the reins from my hand. "Extra if he's mean."

"More 'extra?' Hoolies, you're not a smith *or* an hostler. You're a thief!"

"Others have claimed the same," he said agreeably. "But there'll be no other liveries with room so close to Marketday."

I figured he told the truth. But I glared at him anyway, watched him lead the stud into shadow. I changed my mind and decided I wanted the stud to be meek. Otherwise he was going to cost me more.

With the sun nearly gone, the mud under my feet was growing cold. I walked hastily, wanting to reach the inn before I had to stop and put my filthy sandals back on. Keeping the smith's comments in mind, I'd hung the saddle pouches over my shoulder, hiding the hilt poking up beneath my coat. I found the inn Del had described and went in.

I made it two strides inside, whereupon a woman shouted at me. "*Stop!*"

Startled, I stopped.

She wore an apron over black homespun tunic and full skirts; a woman no longer young, with bony shoulders, thin frame. Hair, gathered into a thin coil fastened with pins, was gray-to-white, and her skin was heavily creased. Her fingers, I noticed, were beginning the characteristic twist of joint-ill.

"I run a tidy inn," she declared. "I'll not have you tromping in here bringing street mud with you. Go outside, shake off that filthy coat, and wash your feet."

I was taken aback. "Wash my *feet*?"

"There's a pot out front on the bench and cloth. Shake off that coat, I said; wash and dry your feet, and then we'll talk about a room while I decide whether I want your custom or not. And wipe those sandals."

"*Whether* you want my custom—?" But I let it go. I turned around, walked the same two steps outside, saw the bench she meant. Pot of water, folded cloths.

"Shake that coat!" she called from inside.

Shake the coat, shake the coat. I yanked it off my body, sleeves now inside out.

Another command was issued from inside. "And shake it in the street, not on my porch!"

Hoolies. Why had Del decided we should stay here? I had to wash my feet *and* there were no spirits.

I shook the coat in the street. I beat the coat with my hand. I brushed off the coat as best I could. Then I planted my butt on the bench, grabbed a cloth, dunked it in the bowl, and began washing my feet.

When I was done, I turned to step into the inn and found her waiting on the doorstep. "Show me," she ordered.

Dutifully I held out my raincoat. As dutifully I displayed my feet one at a time. I let the sandals dangle from one hand.

"Very well," she said. "Now, you'll be wanting a room. How many nights?"

"I'm not sure. But I'm here for the horse fair, if that helps."

She nodded once. "Extra if you can't say how long. It affects my business, you see, not knowing who's staying and who's not."

Extra. *More* extra? "Are you related to the blacksmith?"

She knitted gray-white eyebrows over brown eyes and her mouth went flat. "An odious man."

I wasn't quite sure what 'odious' meant, but I assumed from her demeanor and the tone in her voice that it was not a good thing. I was just on the verge of saying I'd share the room with Del, but it crossed my mind that doing so might make me an odious man.

"I've one room left," she said. "It's small but will do." She examined me from head to toe. "Your feet may hang off the end of the bed. Just double up your knees. The mattress is clean, as is the pillow. There's a ewer and pitcher on the stand with a towel and a nightcrock underneath. Wash up before you get into bed."

I nodded, sighing in resignation. "Where am I?"

Brows lowered. "Standing right here in front of me."

"No—I mean, where is my room?"

"End of the hall. Blue curtain. And don't bother that lovely young woman in the room next to you. Green curtain. She needs her rest, she told me. Mind, I don't approve of those swords, but a young woman will be wanting to protect herself." She squinted at me. "If you bother her, she's likely to skewer you. Leave her be."

We stared each other down. "And the other men here?" I asked. "Did you give them that speech, too?"

"No other men but you have come in since the young woman did. But I'll tell them when they come back from their carousing."

"Then you don't mind your lodgers—carousing?"

"Of course I mind it. I won't tolerate it in my inn. But I don't make any coin if I turn away every man who arrives on my doorstep. A widow's got to live. So they may go elsewhere for their spirits, then come back here *after*." She squinted her eyes at me. "Well?"

"I won't bother her," I offered meekly.

"Very well." She gestured. "End of the hall, on your left. Blue curtain."

I tried to sound harmless and grateful. "Thank you." I took a step, but she remained planted. I paused, backed up a step.

"Do you snore?" she asked. "I can't abide a man who snores."

I stared back at her. "I do not snore." Which, of course, I did; at least, Del told me I did. I'd never personally heard it.

"Extra if you snore," the old woman said crisply. "You'll wake me and any number of other lodgers."

Gods above and below. Again, extra. But I did not call her a thief, as I had the blacksmith. She was likely to charge extra for name-calling. "I don't snore."

"And wash your face. You've mud all over it."

I waited for additional orders. This time, she stepped aside. With great care, I scooted my way past her and escaped down the indicated hall on the left. Even as I walked to the end, I braced myself for yet another order.

And it came. "Don't put those filthy saddle pouches on my clean bed!"

Blue curtain, pulled aside in the doorway. I ducked in as quickly as I could, yanked fabric across the opening, then dropped my pouches and sandals—on the floor—with a sigh of great relief. Hoolies, what a termagant!

I divested myself of coat. Of burnous. Of harness and sword. Fell down flat on my back on the bed in dhoti, a string of claws, doubled silver earrings, and nothing more. I lay there for a long moment contemplating things. And remembered that I was paying for a room I did not intend to sleep in. Del was, after all, right next door.

Hoolies. I'd have to sneak!

Chapter 29

I WAS HOPEFUL, but Del did not appear. I badly wanted to go to her room, but the landlady had me worried about even glancing in that direction. I sat on my bed and thought about why I was reluctant to cross a small, mean-minded, old landlady, but nothing came to me. I was annoyed, frustrated, and irritated all at once with myself—and a little trepidatious. She might decide at any moment that my eye color would cost extra.

I checked the wall between our rooms in hopes of finding a knothole, or a crack between the planks. And it was as I was squatting, examining the wall, that Del slipped into my room. She put a hand on my shoulder and startled me so much that I tried to stand up too fast, bashed a knee as I ricocheted off the bedframe, and landed on the floor in a most inelegant sprawl of arms and legs.

Del slapped both hands over her mouth to stifle laughter, staggered away two steps. I thought she might collapse onto the bed, she was working so hard not to laugh. I climbed to my feet, brushed myself off, and gave her my best green-eyed Sandtiger's glare. Del had mastered herself, but nearly went off again.

I kept my voice very low. "Why in hoolies did you choose this place?"

"Because of Tamar," she answered as quietly. When I looked blank, she added, "The landlady."

"*Why?* She looks like she hasn't cracked a smile in, oh, two hundred years."

"Did you have to wash your feet?"

"Of course I had to wash my feet! And brush off my coat, too, and wipe down the sandals—which is a good thing, I guess, as otherwise it might be difficult to get into them tomorrow. Oh, *and* she wants me to wipe the mud off my face." I paused. "Did you have to?"

"Wash my feet? Or wash the mud off my face?"

I scowled at her. "Both."

"Yes. I had mud up to my ankles. My face was clean, though."

"Is she charging you extra for various and sundry things?"

Del frowned, perplexed. "No."

"Hah!" I said emphatically, then winced because it was louder than I wished. Would that bring Tamar-the-landlady?

"She likes me," Del added.

Suspicious, I asked, "Did the hostler-smith charge you extra?"

That frown again. "No. Why would he?"

"Hoolies." I was utterly disgusted. "They're all picking on me."

Del nodded, smiling. "You are eminently pick-on-able."

"That's not even a word." I scratched at my face, then began brushing hard at the disguising mud.

She said, "Use the ewer, Tiger. She's left washing cloths for us."

"You're on *her* side." I walked around the bed to the tiny table that held ewer, pitcher, cloths, and a mostly-melted candle set in a cup. "Once again, why did you pick this place?"

"Once again, because of Tamar. Consider, Tiger: Will she allow sword-dancers?"

"She allowed you. She allowed me.

"I told her my man insisted I play dress-up games, but had left me in the last town for an itinerant actress. She was most upset on my behalf."

I grunted. "I'll bet. And me?"

"I saw you come in. You looked a little like a hunchback. I think she took pity on you."

"*Pity?* The damn woman doesn't know the meaning of the word." I dipped the cloth into the filled ewer, began wiping my face. "And she doesn't serve spirits!"

Del sighed. "The medicinal aqivi is in my saddle pouches."

I brightened. "So it is!" I scrubbed at the dried mud over my scars. "It saves us having to go to a tavern for it."

"*As* I was saying, Tamar will guard the door. No one is going to sneak in and challenge you."

"You snuck in."

"To your room," she said. "Not through the front door—no; you missed some. Here, let me do it." She extended her hand. I put the wet, muddied washing cloth into it. "Sit."

I sat, ruminating on the fact that the two women currently closest to me thought nothing of ordering me around. No wonder Tamar liked Del.

Del wiped at my face, then stopped and looked at me. "Do you have your shaving things?"

"In my pouches somewhere."

"Good." Del stuffed the wet cloth back into my hands, knelt, and began rummaging through my pouches. Eventually she came up with my folding razor. "No soap? I didn't find any."

"It was down to a sliver. Not anything to salvage."

"A dry shave, then." Del opened the blade right in front of my face. "I'll neaten you up. Tamar will approve."

"Hoolies, Del, I don't care what that woman approves or doesn't!"

"You'll care if she decides to throw you out. You'll be sleeping with the stud if she does. Now—hold still."

I squinched up my face. Del poked a finger at a furled cheek. "Stop that. Do you want more scars?"

"Don't *you* have soap?"

"It was down to a sliver. I thought I might buy more while we're here."

"Young lady!" A gnarled hand yanked the curtain aside. "Young lady, why are you in this reprobate's room?"

'Reprobate?' I wondered if the word had kinship with 'odious.'

"He's filthy," Del said. "He asked me to neaten him. Since I grew up with five brothers, I agreed. I know how you like clean, tidy lodgers. He'll pay extra, of course."

In the doorway, Tamar nodded. "Very well. Shall I stand watch for you? I should hate to see him take advantage of you."

"Oh, I don't think so." Del smiled at her. "I have the razor."

Tamar bobbed her head once. "Very well." She fixed me with a minatory eye. "If I suspect you are making unsavory plans for this young woman, I'll hand you over to the Watch. They know me, know my rules. You won't see daylight for two weeks."

I stared at her. "Two weeks?"

"Two weeks. That's the minimum sentence."

"Well," I said, "I have no unsavory plans for this young woman. I'm sure five brothers taught her many ways of beating off overeager admirers."

Del's smile broadened. Tamar thawed the tiniest bit. "See that you don't become one of them." She looked disapprovingly at the sword and harness resting against the tiny table. "Since you aren't a man with a crooked shoulder, it will cost extra for your sword. I can't abide weapons in this place."

"Extra! Is there anything in this town that *doesn't* cost extra?"

The old woman stared at me narrow-eyed. "Be grateful you've got a room at all."

She had a point there. "I am," I said in a conciliatory tone. "Very grateful."

Tamar bobbed her head. "That's as it should be." She looked at Del. "Are you sure you don't wish a witness?"

Del smiled her sweetest smile. "I'll slit his throat if he even moves."

"Ah. Very well." Tamar yanked the curtain closed again and took herself away.

I stared at the door curtain a moment, suppressing the urge to rip down it and every other curtain in the place, just to drive the landlady to insanity, but dismissed it with regret as Del poked again at my face.

"Now the jaw," she said. "I'm sure you see why we need not fear other sword-dancers a-hunting you here."

My eyes crossed as the razor came close to my face. "I suspect she'd take every coin they had before they stepped foot into this place."

"That's the point," Del said. "Now, shut up. I don't want to nick you."

Some while later Tamar served cider, fresh bread, strong cheese, and portions of the stew bubbling in the pot that hung from a long iron hook in the kitchen fireplace. There was, however, no place to sit in the small common room just off the kitchen. I asked very politely if we were allowed to take the food and drink back to our rooms.

She was stirring stew in the fireplace with a large ladle. "No, you certainly may not. I like to keep an eye on my lodgers while they eat."

In an intentionally meek tone, I asked why.

"So they don't steal my bowls and spoons. Some would, you must know. Some *have*."

I examined the bowl and spoon set upon a metal plate. Short of them being pure silver or gold, I couldn't think of a reason anyone would steal them.

"Eat," she ordered. "Then off to bed with you."

I forgot to use my meek voice. "I don't generally *go* to bed right after dinner."

"I want you out from under my feet. If you'd prefer, you may go outside to walk, to waste coin in a tavern. But if you're here, it's off to bed with you."

And then all the inner amusement about the woman's manner peeled away. Beneath that layer, buried partway because I felt so helpless, was the knowledge that with every passing moment it would become more difficult to find Rashida.

"Listen. Del and I are here together." I was aware of Del's surprise that I should say so. "We're here together, in Istamir, because my son's sister was stolen by raiders. We're not here to carouse, we're not here to make life difficult for you—though I don't know why you operate an inn when you dislike people so much. We are here to track down these raiders. Nothing more, just to find the girl—and the horses, if we can; they took those as well. And while I usually have respect for women of your age, you're making it very difficult. We're here for one very serious reason." She stood in front of the hearth with her back to it, mouth open, ladle clutched in one hand. She appeared not to notice stew and grease was dripping on her plank floor. Frozen in place, she just stared at me. "I realize Del made up some cockamamie story about masquerading as a sword-dancer, but she *is* a sword-dancer. Trained on Staal-Ysta. And if it takes killing to get the girl back, then we will kill."

Tamar's eyes were very wide. After a moment she looked at Del, seemingly for confirmation. Del didn't smile, but neither was she rude. She nodded once, confirming my words. Tamar stared at her a moment longer then looked back at me. "Young man, if you're riding with a Northern woman trained on Staal-Ysta, the very least you should know is that she's a sword-*singer*."

It was my turn to stare. But Tamar turned back to her stew, breaking up a floating layer of grease with her ladle. Her spine was utterly straight. I looked at Del, who shrugged. Then looked at my plate.

As if she could see with the back of her head, Tamar said we could take food and drink to our rooms. Fresh out of words, I walked from the kitchen swiftly, carrying mug in one hand and a plate full of stew, cheese, and bread in the other. Del followed.

"Fetch that girl home!" Tamar called.

Del and I, after eating and returning plates, spoons, and mugs, dragged my mattress off the bed and put it in her room on the floor, along with my things. Her mattress joined it. Now we could sleep closer to one another than an entire room apart. I no longer cared what Tamar might say.

While it was not our habit to go to bed immediately after dinner—at home, Sula wouldn't let us anyway—this time we took Tamar's advice, 'advice' being a kinder word than 'order.' We lay down side by side. I shoved arms beneath my head and stared at the ceiling.

Del snugged herself close to me, hips and shoulders touching. "You're worried,"

I released a heavy sigh. "We've got to find her soon."

Del's sigh matched my own. She pressed hands against her face, then ran them over her hair to the mattress and let her arms flop down against it. "Yes."

"Raiders didn't kill *you*."

"No. I thought they would. They killed everyone else save my brother. At first, I was too young to know what they saved me for. Just like Rashida." I recalled then that Rashida was fifteen or so, the same age as Del when she was abducted. "But I learned, and so will she. If she hasn't already."

"They'll come for the horse fair tomorrow. They must, if they mean to sell any of them, and they certainly won't want to keep all of them. What did Neesha say? The horses were 'coin on four legs'? Well, that's what these raiders want. Coin in exchange for horses." I stretched a lid out of shape as I rubbed an eye. "We should have found her."

"We've done what we could today," Del said. "We even gained assistance, with Eddrith. I saw no red-haired man in any of the taverns I visited, and you saw neither man nor horses. We can't conjure her, Tiger. But we have clues: a man with red hair—as I said, that's not common—and horses with shorn manes."

"But they may not come here precisely *because* there's a red-haired man among them and horses with shorn manes. They may go to another town, another fair, if they know Harith's horses are identifiable."

Del thought that over. "And they might even go south."

"What?" I levered myself up on an elbow to look at her more easily. "That's a long ride from here."

"And no one there knows a red-haired rider, probably. Certainly no one knows Harith's horses. Not so many, at least."

I swore and flopped back down on the mattress. "But do they know where the oases are? Have they any idea about the Punja?"

"It's too bad they saw you with Mahmood's caravan. You could hire on as a guide and work from the inside."

I thought about that a moment. Unfortunately, what Del said was true. I remembered the man. He would remember me. "I don't think it's possible."

"No," she agreed regretfully. "It was only a wish."

I went very still. I didn't even blink. "Wait . . ."

"What?" Del asked. "What are you thinking?"

"If you were a raider," I began, "and you wished to come to Istamir, would you keep yourself to the main part of town? Would you go the smithies and liveries there, where passers-by would see you? Or would you find a smith and an hostler where no one would think to look for raiders or stolen horses?"

Now Del was still as well. "I did ask him about a red-haired man," she said. "I said I was trying to avoid him."

"And he told me he hadn't seen any horses with shorn manes."

We thought about that for a moment.

"Tomorrow," she said.

And I, "First thing."

Chapter 30

THE BLACKSMITH WAS DRINKING ALE and eating bread and sausage for breakfast. He sat on a section of a sawn tree stump, set between smithy and livery. Black hair needed washing, and he took no care whether he dripped ale down his shirt by taking too large a swig. But black eyes were watchful, taking in passers-by, grinning to himself if he found one amusing.

Del and I wandered up. I went to peer into the as yet unfreshened coals, while Del stood on the other side of the smith, studying something else. He glanced at her, nodded his head hello, stared a moment longer, then returned his attention to the street. He ate the last chunk of crusty bread, drank down the final swallow of ale, set the mug on the ground and rose.

"Well now," he said. "You don't have to be a blind man to know you've got business here other than shoeing and stabling horses."

"Business, yes," I agreed. He looked again at Del, at me, and grunted. "Together then."

"So we are," Del said lightly.

"I see you're not hiding that sword anymore," he told me. "Makes me wonder why you did at all. A good reason, maybe. For you."

Del unsheathed her sword. In the doing of it, she diverted the smith's attention from me just long enough for me to bury a fist into his belly and shove him down onto the stump. The mug bounced off and made a whacking sound as it struck the wall. Del took two steps closer, tapped his throat very gently with her sword.

"A red-haired man," she said.

And I added, "Horses with shorn manes."

The blacksmith glared at us over the glint of bared blade. "I told you yesterday I don't know any such man, and I haven't seen horses with shorn manes."

"You lied," Del said quietly.

"I did not—"

But he broke off as I unsheathed my sword. "You know," I began, "few men, maybe none, would set up custom hidden away back here if they wanted to make a living. Sure, you'd have a few horses to shoe, people looking for oddments, repairs. And the same applies to the livery. It's too far from the main street. I suspect most of your stalls are empty most of the time. You don't make much of a living this way. Unless, of course, you have customers who would rather not be known and pay you for silence. Raiders, perhaps."

Bread crumbs clung to his beard. "I run honest establishments."

Del set the tip of her sword just beneath his chin, tapped it. "You do not. No such thing."

I crossed my arms across my chest. "I imagine a man like you wouldn't say no to more coin. Another 'extra,' you might say."

He gave up any pretense of being an honest, if unpleasant, man. "They'd kill me. They'd kill me certain-sure."

I smiled at him. "They can't very well do that if they're dead."

That startled him. "You can't kill them! Not Zayid's men!"

Del asked, "Does Zayid, by any chance, have red hair? Red beard?"

The smith's mouth was tight. "Yes."

Underneath at his neck, Del shaved some hair from his beard. "We might kill you. But we'd rather pay you."

"Where?" I asked.

"I don't know right where they are." He stiffened as I rested my blade on his shoulder. "They don't tell me! And I don't go looking! They've a camp somewhere. They only stay here sometimes."

"There's a horse fair tomorrow."

Small, dark eyes shifted from my face to hers.

"It wasn't a question," Del told him. "They've got horses. Stolen horses. And a stolen girl."

I tapped his shoulder with my sword. "Her mother and father would like her back."

"And the horses," Del added. "It's a shame, don't you think, that men would covet another man's things so much as to beat that man near to death, rape his wife, and steal his daughter."

"They'll be at the fair, won't they?" I waited. "That *is* a question."

"Yes. *Yes.* If they've got horses, they'll be here later today. Over at Marketfield."

Del and I were thinking the same thing. Easy enough for him to send a messenger boy to Zayid. I drew from behind my wide belt the small leather bag containing the rest of the coin Mahmood had paid us. I tossed it into the smith's lap. Del had also prepared for this; she dropped a second small bag into his lap.

"Silence," she said. "No messengers. Your mouth stays closed. We've bought that mouth, after all."

"Best to take it," I suggested. "Because after today, you'll be missing some of your regular customers. And somehow I think you never asked them for extra anything."

Del leaned back against the wooden wall next to the smith, hooking up a foot. She did not sheath her sword. "Tiger, why don't you get the horses. I'm enjoying the beautiful morning speaking to my good friend the blacksmith."

The small black eyes blinked rapidly.

"Tamar's right," I said. "You are an odious man." Smiling broadly, I went into the livery.

Del and I rode to Mahmood's wagon, which apparently had become our official meeting place. He and merchants at all the other wagons had their wares out on tables, wooden barrels, planks, tailgates, blankets on the ground, baskets, iron rods rising from the earth with small display arms, even a few women—wives or daughters— wearing the merchandise. Marketfield was a mass of ordinary things such as pots, knives, mugs; cookfires hosting spits cranked by children; flatbread cooked over a tabletop coal fryer; cider, ale, other drinks and spirits. Music sounded from several directions.

The field slowly took on the mixed aromas of various foods. Some merchants had hired women dressed in sheer veils to slip through the crowd, enticing men to come to their employers' wagons. Other men shouted out what they had to offer. Women and children carrying full baskets wound their way, offering ribbons, pastry delicacies, even flowers. Produce was available, as were fresh meats hanging from racks. Adding to the noise were goats, chickens, lambs, pigs; the gods knew what else. It seemed everything in the world was for sale in Istamir on Marketday.

Mahmood had set up cleverly constructed multi-tiered wooden racks over which he draped fabric samples, and on a wide table made of individual planks laid down across his water barrels, he offered woven baskets full of spice. Each of his four wagons was arranged the same way. A great deal of time had been spent, probably by his drivers, pouring spices into small, tightly-woven fabric bags wrapped at the mouth with colored yarn. Amber for saffron, orange for cinnamon.

Mahmood himself had discarded the drab clothing I'd made him wear as we traveled; he was dressed for a meeting with the wealthiest tanzeer in the South. (Which reminded me of Umir, damn him and his bounty to hoolies.) Peacock-blue burnous, belted by silver-studded leather, and a turban made of his silver-and-blue cloth. It was intricately wrapped, and a peacock feather was pinned to the front of the turban by a chunk of raw turquoise. Multiple cuffs of silver studded with turquoise hugged his arms, matching rings on his fingers.

Del and I dismounted, tied our horses to the tailgate. I put the nose-loop on the stud, but there was enough confusion going on, coupled with a myriad of smells, that I doubted he would scent whichever mare it was who'd taken his interest before.

We slipped between wagons to Mahmood, standing behind his table. Already there was a crowd of women present, dazzled by the silver-threaded fabric. Some had already put spices in their market baskets and now had time to please their eyes. He glanced up, saw us, and immediately cried out.

"Del! Del! You must come! Come!" He worked his way from behind his table. Ignoring customers, he put his hands together, bowed the tiniest degree, then grabbed one of her arms and dragged her close to his table. "Here! Here! You must!"

"Must what?" she asked warily.

Mahmood glanced at me briefly. "You will see! Del, here . . ." He grabbed a length of fabric on display, swiftly and neatly swirled it around her, tucked folds here and there, then dropped the end over her head to hang to her shoulder. Her arms were bare, but from head to toe the blue-and-silver fabric swathed her without hiding her curves. Her single braid hung free of the cloth across her head. Because of the Southron sun she wasn't as pale as the Northern women, but the glow was understated. Her blue eyes almost seemed to blaze.

Mahmood instantly turned back to his customers, deftly moving his hands to indicate how he had draped and wound the cloth. Of course the sword hilt poking above her shoulder gave the vision an incongruous look, but Mahmood had known better than to ask her to take off harness and sword. When Del reached up to slip the fabric from her head, he stopped her hand.

"No! Please. A moment longer. Perhaps two moments . . . three?" He draped the fabric over her head once more, did something with his fingers that made it fall gently to her shoulder. Again he turned to his crowd. "You see what this cloth looks like on a woman. Beautiful! See how it brings out the blue of her eyes? See how rich it appears with just a touch of silver threading? A husband would be neglectful if he did not wish to see his wife in cloth like this. And look! Other colors as well. Go! Ladies, go and find your husbands, bring them here!"

Del glanced at me with her mouth hooked wryly. And then the wry look was banished, replaced with a look so intense that I knew something was wrong.

"*Tiger!*"

She unsheathed, scattering the women like a flock of chicks, took two steps as I ducked out of the way, cut the air with her sword, stilled it, and allowed the man to spear himself on her blade like a piece of meat on a kabob skewer. Del jerked it out of him, tried to lift a leg to push him over, but the cloth draperies got in the way. By then the man—a sword-dancer—was down anyway. She stood over him as her sword dripped blood. "*Not* from behind," she said, angrier than I'd seen her in some time "*Not* in the back when he doesn't know. There's no honor in that!"

The sword-dancer gazed up at her, blood staining his burnous. He gasped, "*Elaii-ali-ma.*"

"Not from *behind*," Del told him. "*Elaii-ali-ma* doesn't mean you can kill a man from behind. To do so could well result in *you* being called an oath-breaker. And now you have paid the price for it."

Well, she didn't exactly have that right. He could kill me however he liked, though taking me through the back wouldn't add any particular luster to his name. But he didn't hear the last of what she said. He was gone.

One-handed, Del began trying to tear the beautiful cloth from her body. "No woman should be cursed to wear this if she has to *move*! You can't do anything dressed like this!"

"Oh, I don't know." I shrugged. "You can kill a man."

Del stopped pulling at fabric. Her expression and tone was pure exasperation. "He would have beheaded you!"

That made me rub the back of my neck, of course. I noted the crowd we had drawn came from neighboring wagons as well as Mahmood's. A glance at Mahmood's face showed an expression of horror.

Del became aware of it, too. And an astonishing thing happened: she blushed. She handed her sword to me and began to unwrap the cloth with a kinder touch. Once done, she put the bundle into Mahmood's hands. She raised her voice so that most could hear. "It's very pretty."

Well. It had been. Before blood stained it.

Del brushed by me, slipping between the two wagons. I followed to the tailgate. There I handed back her sword. "I think I forgot to say 'thank you.'"

"How many more?" She shook the blade to shed blood droplets, then grabbed a section of her burnous to wipe it clean. "How many more to fight before they give up?"

"I don't think they *will* give up, bascha."

She sheathed in a practiced movement. "We should go home. We should find Rashida, find the horses, and just go home."

I had never heard that tone from her. She saw my surprise, tossed her braid behind her shoulder, and asked me why I hadn't known the sword-dancer was coming up from behind.

"Because I was looking at and appreciating a beautiful woman."

She made a dismissive gesture. "Tiger, tell the truth."

"That *is* the truth! Besides, who can hear in all this noise?"

The tension was leaving her body. She nodded. "Yes. All right." She looked past me, eyes intent again. I swung around, a little on edge. Another sword-dancer.

"It's Eddrith," I said. "He was to meet us here."

Del relaxed. "Yes. I remember."

I waited until Eddrith reached us. Before either Del or I could speak, he said, "It's already being passed around all of Marketfield."

"What is?" I asked.

He halted, looked at Del. "How a Northern woman in a *gown* killed a sword-dancer."

Del scowled. "I'm better when I'm not in a gown."

Eddrith's brows ran up. I just grinned. "Too bad you missed it."

"Horses," Del said, impatient. "A red-haired man."

Eddrith nodded. "I've found the horses."

I was startled. "You've found—? Well, let's go take a look. We'll come back for *our* horses after we've figured out what we need to do."

Eddrith said, "Follow me."

And follow we did.

Chapter 31

HARITH'S HORSES, EDDRITH EXPLAINED, were not the only ones present, but five of many. The horse areas were at the far end of the winding double line of wagons, which formed a huge semi-circle. There were no markers to direct the horse traders to specific areas; everyone, as they came in, simply took the spot they preferred. Apparently, most knew one another; there were friendly arguments over who had the best horses, and outlandish claims about what the horses could do.

Eddrith led us to the last wagon before the horse area. The three of us gathered there, trying to look as if we were in a casual conversation. Already customers walked the horse lines to see what was available before they began asking questions and haggling.

"Only five horses?" I asked. "I'm certain Harith had more. The corrals and paddocks were empty, their poles and planks broken in places. Any number of horses may have been driven out."

Eddrith nodded. "But they would be fools to bring all of the horses to one fair. It would look too suspicious. A few this time, a few next time."

That was probably the smartest thing Eddrith had ever said. I eyed him. "Have you seen this band of raiders before?"

He shook his head. "To my knowledge, no. But not all men draw attention to themselves with hair color, height, or memorable faces. You would be remembered. But I may even have met one or two on earlier visits. How can I say? It's only your red-haired man who might be noticed."

"Is he likely to come?" Del asked. "Surely he knows people notice him."

"But how many are aware he's a raider?" Eddrith asked.

"Well, that's true," Del agreed. "They stable their mounts in a livery well out of the way. It is likely the men don't stay together while here. They are just men. People in town for Marketday."

I looked beyond Del and Eddrith. Horse-boys, at their employers' orders, walked out specific horses when asked to do so by potential customers. Some mounted, rode the horses in tight patterns. "Where are Harith's horses?" I asked.

Eddrith indicated the direction with a lifted chin. "Four places down. The red-haired man I have not seen."

"Go there," Del suggested. "Ask about the horses. Tiger and I are too memorable, as you say. But if those men are engaged in haggling with you, they will be blind to us until our breath is in their faces. We need only one. He can tell us where Rashida is."

"Zayid," I said. "That's the man we want. The others are incidental. But I expect we'll have to kill them."

"Divide them," Del told him. "Have one bring out a horse. Ask him to show what the horse can do. But lead him in this direction. When he's close enough, we'll take him."

"And have a little conversation," I added. To Eddrith, I said, "Where is your horse?"

"Tied at my uncle's wagon. He's a tinsmith. He always sells wares on Marketday. He does well. I used to be his apprentice."

" 'Apprentice?' " I echoed.

"Istamir is my home," Eddrith explained.

"Is it likely these men are camping here, or elsewhere?" I asked.

"Here," Eddrith answered. "They'll hold the horses close."

"Do you know where that happens to be?"

He shook his head. "Close. But if we capture the one man you mentioned, he'll tell us, won't he?"

"Maybe," I said grimly.

"Let's go," Del said. "We've been here too long. Two of the men with Harith's horses have already noted us standing here. It may be nothing, but we shouldn't risk it."

No. We shouldn't. I looked at Eddrith. "Walk ahead of us to Mahmood's wagon."

Eddrith sighed deeply, then turned and began walking. Del caught my eye and nodded very slightly. Eddrith might be exactly who he claimed he was, a resident of Istamir once apprenticed to a tinsmith, but he was also one of an uncountable number of Northerners present. And all of them looked similar with pale hair, blue eyes, height matching or approaching mine. He was definitely a sword-dancer, but that didn't mean he couldn't be a raider.

Del and I kept our distance from him as he walked. We wanted room to unsheath should Eddrith swing around and attack. But to carry bared blades as we walked would draw too much attention, so we left them riding above our shoulders. Anyone looking at us would see three sword-dancers; it was not worth comment that we were together. Probably we knew one another, they'd assume, just as merchants knew one another.

Eddrith stopped at a wagon. A sorrel horse was tied to one of the rear wheels; as we did, Eddrith used a rope halter. Pulling on the end of the rope would quickly undo the tie. With the stud, I didn't have that luxury; I had to use a more assertive tie.

"This is my horse," he said.

"Bring him to Mahmood's," I told him. "Walk, don't mount."

One tug undid the halter tie. Eddrith was beginning to look resentful. It was an expression a man would show when he wished only to help, yet was treated like a potential opponent. He was young. I doubted he was experienced enough to portray himself as an innocent when in truth he was a raider.

We arrived at Mahmood's. Del and I untied our mounts as Eddrith waited with his horse. I flipped the lead-rope over the stud's shoulder, tied it to the pommel. The odors of various meats, bread, spices, and pastries served notice that my belly was unhappy, and I remembered Del and I had not had any breakfast.

Later, I told my belly. After.

"Wait," I said to Eddrith. "Wait until Del and I have mounted."

The last thing I wanted was for him to be above us holding an unsheathed sword.

His expression now was mutinous. He glared at both of us. He mounted after Del and I were settled. "I'm here to help you!" he said in a simmering anger. "Did I not find the raiders? Did I not take you to them?"

"You did," Del said, but nothing more.

That did not satisfy Eddrith. "I told you what happened to me, to that caravan! I told you about the raiders and what they did! Why won't you trust me?"

I leaned forward, palms on the pommel, stretching my back. "A girl's life is at stake. Would you trust us if it were the other way around?"

He opened his mouth. Shut it. "No."

"Then let's *go*," Del said. "All this talk-talk-talk."

She had a point. "Remember," I said to Eddrith. "Distract one of the raiders. Once he is distracted, mount. Ride down the line and cut the lead-ropes on all five horses wherever you find them. Send them away. As they go, other men may appear from Zayid's encampment, and we'll be able to see where it is. That's where Rashida will be."

What I didn't say, what Del didn't say, was that we hoped Rashida *was* there and had not been sold away. But this was our best opportunity of locating her.

"That wasn't what you said before. You wanted a man to question."

I smiled at him. "I thought of a better plan. Go. Del and I will be watching."

"You can't see the horses from here," Eddrith said, frustrated.

Del asked lightly, "Who said we'd stay here?"

He glared at us a moment. Then turned his horse and walked down the front line of wagons. Del and I rode behind the other row, shielded by conveyances. At the end, we halted, watched.

"So, you changed the plan because you don't trust him?" Del asked.

"I figured it wasn't a bad idea. If he is trustworthy, he'll do what we suggest."

Eddrith, leading his sorrel, walked to one of the raiders. By his gestures, it appeared he was indeed discussing horses. And as the discussion grew quarrelsome, the other two men holding horses watched as well.

"Now," I said quietly, watching Eddrith closely.

And as if he heard me, he turned, began to walk away. The raiders watched after him a moment. Then he was moving, swinging up into his saddle. He spun his horse back toward the men as he unsheathed his sword, and rode right at them. The blade swung in morning sunlight as Eddrith rode the line and cut the lead-ropes. He shouted like a maniac to drive the horses away.

"There," Del said.

A tent we had not seen the previous day disgorged two men who ran to help. Only three of the horses had run at Eddrith's behest. Two were left behind and two of the raiders quickly knotted the free end of the halter ropes to use as reins and swung aboard. Bareback, they unsheathed swords that had been hanging at their waists.

Eddrith made his horse dance in front of them, easily avoiding the raiders. But that only lasted a moment. With the five men mounted, he'd lost most of his advantage. Wisely, helpfully, he wheeled his horse and rode away into the line of wagons, shouting for Marketday people to get out of the way. One of the raiders went after the loose horses; the coin on four feet were worth too much to lose.

"And now," I said.

From behind, Del and I rode up to Zayid's tent. Many of Zayid's horses were picketed there. Del took one side, I the other. We cut the picket ropes and sliced through tent guy-lines, where saddled horses waited close to the door flap. But there was some kind of interior framework; the tent wobbled but did not collapse.

I gestured. Del nodded. Behind the tent, she swung off her gelding. With infinite care, she made a hole in the oilcloth, then cut a line through it from top to bottom. She ripped fabric aside.

I took the front, doing much the same thing. I could not trust the door-flap; it's what Zayid and anyone else inside the tent would use to exit. So I made a new opening. As Del went in the back, I jumped down from the stud and broke through the front.

Zayid had a knife at a girl's throat.

As he intended, Del and I stopped moving. Our swords were ready, but so was Zayid's knife. He had not run out with his men. Why should he? They could always steal more horses, and the girl was his protection.

She had, as described, gold streaks in dark hair and Neesha's eyes. Young, but on the verge of womanhood "Rashida," I said. "Rasha."

With a knife at her throat, she did not speak aloud. But her eyes said all that she wished to say. Tears ran down her grimy face, making narrow white rivulets. Zayid had tied her wrists in front of her. He held her close against his body, one arm wrapped tightly around her shoulders. The knife was in the other hand, poised at her neck, free to bite into flesh.

Zayid did not waste his breath on words. He knew why we were there.

Del stood lightly balanced at the cut she had made, at least two long strides away from Zayid. I was closer. I could take him if he held no hostage.

From outside, I heard men calling out to one another. A flicker in Zayid's eyes, a twitch of his lips told me what I needed to know. Eddrith's distraction was no longer a distraction; the others now returned to report to Zayid.

He watched us closely. He assessed us. He had seen us work at the caravan, witnessed our skill, our competence. Yes, his men had returned, but he was one, and we were two, and if he killed his hostage he'd be dead the next instant. He knew it. We knew it.

Zayid put a hand on Rashida's back, and shoved her toward my sword. Then he dove out the doorflap.

Del was there. "Go!" she said. "I have her."

I went out the opening I'd cut, not through the doorflap—that's where they expected me. Zayid was on horseback, already galloping away. I swore, thrust my sword through one man and jerked it free. I heard Del say something urgent to Rashida, heard a man cry out, then another. The stud was a step away. I took that step, mounted as hastily as I could while holding a sword, and kicked him hard. He leaped forward, running as the lead-rope beat against the ground. I had one hand full of reins, the other full of sword. His lead-rope had come untied. It was dangerous to ride with the lead-rope or reins hanging. If the stud stepped on either, he might go down, and I with him.

Eddrith had gone down the central walkway. Zayid had gone through the wagons. The people, thanks to Eddrith, had moved, pressing against wagons and trade stalls. I took that route, faster, free of flesh-and-bone impediment. I wanted to kill Zayid. I did not wish to kill innocent people.

The ground was mostly dry on top, mud stiffening beneath the sun. But horses are heavy, and the stud, as he ran, dug up clumps. It slowed us. More fair-goers had walked here, digging hollows. The stud broke through into damper mud beneath. I could feel it in his gait: a heaviness in his hooves, occasional slippage.

Zayid broke out of the wagons well ahead of us. I swore as the stud stepped on the lead-rope. It didn't foul his legs, it didn't jerk his head down when he came to the end of it. He did not fall. But it slowed him nearly to a stop.

Swearing, I leaned forward, set my blade under the lead-rope as he moved, and tossed it toward the saddle. I took no time to tie it to the pommel; I grabbed it in my left hand and added it to my reins. Now we were free.

We had lost momentum, and Zayid was farther ahead of me. He glanced back once, saw me, quickly turned his mount back into the wagons. I did the same, hoping to catch up to him if he emerged again. I held the sword crosswise over the stud's neck, keeping it out of the way, yet close enough to swing it back at need.

Three wagons ahead, Zayid once again took a sudden turn between two of them. I heard a crash of metal pots, bowls, mugs and couldn't help but wonder, oh so briefly, if that wagon belonged to Eddrith's uncle the tinsmith.

I rode one more wagon down, cut right, sent the stud down the main avenue again. Zayid crashed through wares for sale, but the stud had gained on him by a length. Across the walkway Zayid charged through stalls on the other side. He, too, held a sword in his right hand, guiding his horse one-handed as he dug into his mount's ribs with his heels. Unlike me, he wore boots; kicking would have greater effect.

"Go on," I told the stud. "Go on, boy. Let's catch that son of a Salset goat."

The stud responded. I reined him right, rode through two wagons, broke out on the other side. We'd gained a length. I saw the flash of Zayid's face as he glanced back. He dug in heels again to gain more speed.

"He's yours," I told the stud, who had killed a man before. "All yours, old son."

Zayid once again rode through the tight spaces between wagons, this time to the left. I did as well, swearing as the stud made a misstep and crashed through stacks of wooden fruit basket containers, all full. We were back on the main walkway. We cut the corner closely and my head collided with hanging windchimes; some came down while others rang crazily.

By that sound, Zayid knew where we were, knew how close. We had gained yet again, the stud and I. I lifted my sword, holding it up in the air.

The red-haired raider reined in sharply. He spun his mount toward me, lifting his sword as well.

Too close . . . too close to stop . . .

Zayid dropped off his horse. I knew what he meant to do. From below, he could take the stud by driving his sword up into the chest; going right through ribs to the heart; cutting viscera to pieces. The stud would collapse, and as I tried to save myself Zayid would have me. But he had to take the stud first, or his plan wouldn't work.

I did not want the stud to stop. I kicked harder than ever, drove him on with words. I did not intend to avoid Zayid.

I shook my left foot free of stirrup. Clamped left hand on the pommel. Leaned down to the right, riding sideways, left leg a counter balance across part of the saddle's seat. One hand held most of my weight, some in the right stirrup. It was a precarious position because of my size, but the chance was worth the risk. Suddenly, Zayid didn't have the advantage of using his blade on the stud. I was in the way.

We thundered down upon him, my boy and I. I swung the sword like a scythe.

I took Zayid's head.

Chapter 32

THE STUD RAN ON. I pulled myself up, settled back in the saddle properly. It was then I eased the stud toward a slower gait. When we hit it, I reined in, turned him. Down the walkway, running wild, was Del's white gelding. Running with him, surprisingly, was Darrion on a gray horse.

Darrion?

"Ease off!" I shouted as they both ran right by me. And to Darrion: "Don't chase him!"

And then I forgot all about Darrion and the gelding and thought only about Del. Either she was fine and the horse had been startled away—neither he nor the stud had been tied as we dismounted at Zayid's tent—or she was in trouble.

Zayid's body lay in the street. I spent no time examining it. I rode by it at a lope, not wishing to duplicate my mad rush down the middle of the walkway. Marketday folk in shock still pressed back against wagons and trade stalls. I caught the sound of a horse behind me, twisted in the saddle, saw Zayid's loose mount coming up beside me. Loose horses all over, what with those Eddrith had run off after he cut their lead-ropes, and Zayid's, and now Del's. I wasn't worried about any of them; horses are herd animals and, given a choice, will go to other horses once fear faded.

At Zayid's big tent I heard the sound of swords clashing. While part of me wanted to drop down right in the middle of battle, I knew better. There was yet something to be done, someone Del protected.

I dismounted at the back of the tent. Zayid's horse shied away, kept on going at a trot, reins dangling. A dead man lay there. I stepped over the body, yanked open the long slit Del had cut, and found Rashida immediately inside, pressed into a near corner as Del fought one of the raiders. Not a good place for a swordfight—too many things to foul a blade or your feet. But often you had no say in the matter.

"Rashida," I said.

Terrified, she pressed herself harder against the corner. Brown hair, tinted with gold, was loose and tangled. Her clothing was torn. Neesha's eyes, so large and melting, the color of cider, were fixed on me. "Rasha." I gestured. "Come away. Let's get you out of here. Del will deal with him."

She hesitated a moment. While I wanted to shout at her to get out of the tent, I knew better. The last thing she needed was yet another stranger shouting at her. "Will she kill him?"

That caught me off-guard. "Probably."

"Good," she said fiercely. "What about the others?"

"Our plan is to kill all of them."

And again, "Good."

"Rasha. Your mother and father are with Sabir and Yahmina. They're safe."

I saw immense relief. Then recognition filled her eyes. "You're the Sandtiger!"

"I am. Now, let's go!"

This time she came. I sheathed my sword quickly, guided her hastily outside as blades rang, cut the rope at her wrists with my knife, then swung her up into the stud's saddle.

"The reins," she said, reaching. I grabbed the dangling reins and pushed them into her hands. I wanted her away from here as swiftly as possible. "Don't forget to cut the lead-rope."

She'd grown up on a horse farm; I figured she could handle him just fine. But I asked. "He's a stallion. Will you be all right?"

She took offense. "I've ridden every stallion we've ever had at the farm!"

I had to laugh as I cut the rope. I should have known she wasn't likely to be a fading flower. Not someone who matched wooden blades with her older brother. Knife put away, I unsheathed my sword again. "Go," I said. "Doesn't matter where. Just get away from here as quickly as possible. Go to the wagons." A thought struck me. "I take that back . . . find the man with the beautiful fabrics and spices. Mahmood. He'll hide you." I gave her directions, then slapped a hand on the stud's rump and sent him away.

I heard a blurt of shock even as I pulled aside the cut flaps of the tent wall. Del's opponent was down, dying on the matting. Rasha would be pleased and I didn't blame her.

Sword raised and ready, Del spun to face me as I came through the slit. Recognized me and lowered her blade. "Rashida?"

"I sent her to Mahmood's." Her face was tense, but she was unharmed. "Any others?" I asked.

"This one," she said. "One behind the tent, and the one you killed in front."

"And Zayid's dead. That's four."

"Where's Eddrith?"

"I don't know. He cut the horses loose, and then I lost track of him."

She shook her sword, found and used a cloth to clean her blade. We have to go after them."

"On foot, then. Your white boy ran off—last I saw Darrion was chasing after him down the middle of the street—and Rashida has the stud."

"On foot, then," she said grimly. "We must find them all."

"What we *must* do," I said, "is get Rashida to safety, back with her parents."

I heard the sound of hooves approaching at a smart trot. "Go out the back," I told her. "I'll take the front."

Del nodded, ducked out. I went through.

The man on horseback rode with his sword unsheathed. Blood ran off bright steel.

"Oh," I said.

Tautly, Neesha asked, "Where's my sister? Where's Rasha?"

"Safe," I told him. "She's on the stud, heading to Mahmood's."

He looked immensely relieved; tension bled out of body and voice. "I killed one. I recognized him from the caravan attack. And I saw Eddrith drive his sword through another."

I added that to my mental tally. "Six. To my knowledge, that's all." Then, "What are you doing here?"

Del had recognized Neesha's voice. She came around the tent. "What are you doing here?"

"Your father," I said abruptly, envisioning death.

"Awake again," Neesha answered. "In pain, but better than he was. My mother told me to come here. Apparently I was underfoot."

"You must have ridden hard."

"The hardest I ever have." And indeed, his bay showed white lines of sweat, foam along the sides of his neck. Neesha twisted in his saddle to look down the line of wagons. "Is Mahmood where he was?"

I gave him directions, and he rode away. Del sheathed her sword. "We've accounted for all of them," I said.

Del wasn't so certain. "All of them unless Zayid has a camp elsewhere."

"Zayid's dead. If he doesn't return, and the other five don't return, either, whoever's there will sort it out. Once they do, they'll scatter."

Del wasn't happy. "Yes, they'll scatter—to raid again."

I shook my head. "We can't rid the world of them all, bascha. Not even if we had a hundred men. We accomplished what we came for. Now let's get Rashida home and settled. And then *we* can go home. I think Neesha, if he stays with them, will understand why we head back so quickly." I sighed, grabbed the door flap, and ran an edge down my blade, rubbing it free of blood.

"What do we do about Harith's horses?" she asked.

I looked around, searching. "They'll be here somewhere. Neesha may have an idea. They should wander back at some point."

"Bodies," she said.

Two not far from us. Another behind the tent. Zayid in the middle of the street. And wherever Neesha and Eddrith had killed theirs. "I'm sure Istamir has a graveyard," I said. And I was fairly certain Istamir also had a burial detail for inconvenient deaths.

"So, are we spending the night?"

I shrugged. "Guess that depends on Neesha. He may want to take Rashida home right away."

Neesha did not wish to go home right away. It was late in the day, and dusk would arrive just about the time we reached the burned farmhouse. I could think of better places for Rashida to spend the night, and agreed with Neesha's decision. Besides, while I had the stud and Neesha his bay, Del's gelding was still missing—probably running farther than he might otherwise have done because Darrion had chased him. Del was seriously annoyed and wanted to borrow the stud to go see if she could track Darrion down, but there was Rashida to look after, female to female.

Tamar, to my surprise, said nothing at all to Del about washing any portion of her body before she entered the inn, nor anything to Rashida. However, Neesha and I did not enjoy the same reception. As Tamar directed Del to take Rashida to her own private room, she turned her customary testiness on us.

"Wash your feet."

Neesha, who had not had the pleasure of meeting Tamar before now, blinked and stared. "What?"

Tamar narrowed her eyes at him. "You have been in mud. I see it on your sandals. Wash your feet, young man!" She glanced at me. "*He'll* tell you."

I sighed. "We wash our feet if we want to enter the inn."

"My feet aren't that dirty! I was on horseback most of the time!"

"But not *all* of the time," Tamar insisted.

He scowled at her. "I have never, in my life, had to wash my feet before entering an inn."

"That's because no one *cared*," Tamar said. "My inn is clean, unlike all the others."

"Might as well just do it," I told him. "You can't win this battle."

Tamar nodded approval of my comments. "I've got supper on the hearth. Clean up, and I'll serve you."

Neesha frowned. "Where's my sister?"

"I've sent her to my room with Del." She glanced at me, then looked at Neesha again. Her tone of voice changed to something approaching sympathy. "She needs time to talk to another woman."

I understood. Neesha did not. "I'm her brother. She can talk to me."

Tamar's momentary kindness evaporated. "No, she may not. My rules, or you can take a room elsewhere."

Neesha was completely nonplussed, but also growing angry. "I'm not leaving my sister."

Tamar stared at me. Her message was clear.

I touched Neesha's arm. "Let's wash our feet. Rashida's in good hands with Del."

"I don't understand—"

I closed a hand on his upper arm, swung him around. " Trust me."

Tamar gave me a brusque nod and went back to her hearth.

I pushed Neesha to the bench, then shoved him down hard with a hand on his shoulder. He set his feet preparatory to standing up. I tightened my hand and pushed him down again.

"Think," I said. "Just—think."

He didn't. "I have every right to see my sister. Gods, Tiger, she's spent the last three days with raiders!"

"And that's exactly why she needs to be with Del, now."

"But—"

"*Think*, Neesha! Your sister with six raiders!"

I saw the dawning of realization in his eyes, followed immediately by horror. "Oh, gods. Oh *no*. Not Rasha!" He looked as if he might vomit.

"Del will talk with her. Tomorrow, she'll be with her mother. I'm not saying you should ignore her, nor treat her as if she might break. Just let her come to you."

Tears stood in his eyes. He pressed his lips together, fighting not to let them fall. "Will she be all right?"

"She's your sister. That means she's strong. Very strong."

Neesha, at a loss, sat in silence with a world in his eyes.

He needed distracting. I picked up a clean washing cloth and dropped it in his lap. "Wash your feet."

Amazingly, Tamar sent us to a different room instead of making us eat while standing up. There, Neesha and I perched on stools, holding plates, bowls, spoons, mugs, and the same kind of stew I'd eaten before. I wondered if she ever cooked anything else for her lodgers.

Del and Rashida did not join us. Neesha was clearly concerned by this, ready to protest, but I shook my head at him. He settled, but not before he aimed a ferocious glare at Tamar. If she saw it, she gave no sign.

After we finished eating, she took plates, bowls, mugs back and set them on a workbench beside the hearth. Then she turned to us, smoothing her hands down the front of her apron. "I have never, ever suggested this to anyone before." She looked at us both. "Go get drunk."

It startled Neesha, but not enough. "I want to see—"

"Not yet." I caught his arm. "Let's do as she says."

Neesha yanked his arm out of my grip. "Will you *stop pushing me around*?"

I met his angry glare benignly. "Probably not."

Neesha clamped his mouth closed. He brushed by me and went out the door.

Before I could follow, Tamar asked, "Your son?"

"Yes."

She nodded. "Thought so. But the girl isn't yours, is she?"

That startled me. "How can you tell?"

"Because if you were her father, you'd tear my door down to get to her."

I digested that a moment, decided she was right. And it would not have been for the best.

"There's a decent tavern at the end of the street," Tamar said. "The owner is a friend of mine. Tell him I sent you."

A friend. Tamar? "I take it he's not an odious man? Or a reprobate?"

She fixed me with a sharp glare. I promptly went out the door to find Neesha.

Chapter 33

THE TAVERN WHERE TAMAR SENT US was so different from our cantina in Julah that I very nearly gaped. The tabletops were buffed to a gloss—albeit scars in some of them, which is to be expected in a place where drink is served. The bartop was made of many different kinds of wood, dark and light, filled knots, age rings, stripes wide and narrow, striations and whorls cut into small sections then pieced together into an intriguing pattern. Yet there appeared to be no unevenness in wood that didn't match. All had been planed smooth, then buffed. The room had a warm, comfortable glow about it. Most of the illumination did not come from candle cups and lanterns on each table, but from twisted iron sconces hung up on the walls. As far as I could tell, each one was capped with pierced tin. Long, fat wicks rose from them. These were oil lamps, not candles with short wicks and meager flame that too often went out, or were knocked over.

We, of course, were strangers. Everyone stopped talking and watched as Neesha and I walked in. No one missed our swords. I saw looks exchanged and heard quiet comments, but none so loud as to be decipherable.

The wine-girls were not dressed in skimpy clothing. Tunics and long skirts, mostly, though waists were cinched tightly in bright scarves to show off admirable curves. But no tassels. Unlike the South, where Del was so different, here all three of the girls were fair-skinned, blue-eyed, and very blonde.

One of the open tables was tucked into a corner beneath a sconce. I wended my way to it through other tables. I was surprised to see that the bench I intended to claim was actually covered with leather. And, as I sat down, I discovered it held padding *under* the leather. I began to see why Tamar had recommended this tavern over others. I began to see why the owner was a friend. Obsessively tidy woman and what appeared to be an obsessively tidy man.

I sat. Neesha followed more slowly. He sat down with his back to the door. I shook my head in resignation; he wasn't paying attention. But then, Neesha didn't need a clear line of sight the way I did. I couldn't truly relax as long as we were in Istamir, because the gods knew how many sword-dancers were still around. Didn't have to worry about Darrion, certainly, and Eddrith now simply wanted to spar, but there might be others.

A wine-girl arrived, unbound hair falling in a glorious pale shower nearly to her waist. She bestowed faint smiles on both of us, but did not plant an arm on the table and lean down to show off cleavage. Whatever cleavage she claimed was hidden behind a rich purple tunic. Her skirt was striped purple-tan-yellow beneath a ruby-hued belt. Amber beads ringed her wrists, dangled from her ears.

Her eyes were calm. "My father runs a clean house," she said in a slightly husky tone. "The food is excellent, the ale superb, and the spirits strong. We will be most pleased to serve you enough food and drink to fill you for a week. What we will *not* serve you is me or my sisters. We don't mean to deny men their needs, but there are many taverns that suit that purpose. If you want women, please go elsewhere."

I looked at the other two blondes. They stood at the bar, calmly watching their sister as if waiting for our decision. I began to smile. "I don't think Tamar would send us here if it were that kind of cantina—er, tavern. I'm here for some superb ale and have absolutely no designs on any of you."

Her own smile blossomed from slight into wide. "Tamar only sends safe men here. Be welcome."

Safe. I'd never heard that word applied to me before.

Neesha, on the other hand . . . but then I changed my mind

about teasing him. He was barely paying attention to a beautiful young woman. "Ale will do for us both."

She turned briefly and nodded to her sisters, who visibly relaxed. One of them, having drawn two tall mugs with foam spilling down the sides, delivered them with a smooth efficiency before moving away to tend another table.

Del would approve of this tavern. Fouad would not.

Across the table from me, Neesha brooded. I watched the play of expressions across his features. "What?" I asked, when I thought he might actually answer.

He looked up from the table, came back from a far place. "What?"

"I asked first."

He sighed, ran spread fingers through his hair, then scrubbed it into a landscape of tufts. "I want to help her. But what can I do? What can anyone do?"

He sounded lost. I tried to steer him away from it. "I think we've done quite a lot, actually. We killed all six raiders."

"Well . . . yes." He contemplated his ale. "But that doesn't undo anything that happened."

I raised my own mug, drank, lowered it and wiped foam away. "No."

Neesha shook his head. "I don't know what to do."

I smiled. "Just be her big brother. The one she's always looked up to."

That nearly brought him to tears. He grabbed his mug, spilled some ale, drank down nearly half, I judged, before he took a breath. When he did, he set the mug down with an audible thump. "All dead. Yes. But Rasha—gods. *And* my mother." And then he ran out of words to express what he was feeling and just stared at the mug.

For some reason, I thought of Eddrith. I hadn't seen him since he sliced all the lead-ropes and chased after the five horses the raiders had put up for sale. "You saw Eddrith kill one of the raiders, you said."

Neesha blinked hard and looked up. "Yes. Or, I think he killed him. I didn't check to be sure if he was dead. But Eddrith spitted him through the belly."

Dead, then. "And Eddrith was all right?"

Neesha frowned at me. "Why do you care? What has he to do with anything?" He sat up straighter, finally giving me his full attention. "You said he chased off the horses?"

"Five of your horses, yes. Shorn manes. He cut them free and chased them off, so they could get away from the raiders. We wanted them on foot." Well, come to think of it, Eddrith had chased off three horses; two had been recaptured by raiders, but then they got loose again as the raiders died.

Neesha was totally baffled. "Eddrith *helped* you?"

"I didn't believe he meant it at first, but he did indeed help us."

"Why?" he asked bluntly. "Why would he want to?"

"To spar with me." I shrugged. "We came to an agreement. If he helped, I'd spar with him."

Neesha was shaking his head vehemently from side to side. "You can't."

I raised a brow. "Why can't I?"

"He defeated me. Shouldn't you support *me*? Your son?"

"That has nothing to do with this. Or this has nothing to do with that. Whichever way you like it."

Neesha scowled at me. "It matters."

I drank more ale. Neesha waited for an answer. Wiping at foam again, I said, "I agreed. I won't go back on my word."

Tight as drawn wire, he stared hard at me. He did not drink again. He was very, very angry, and I knew it had nothing to do with my agreeing to spar with Eddrith. Well, almost nothing. He did care about that. What he wanted was to put things back the way they had been. No attack on the farm, no father seriously injured, no mother raped, no sister abducted and violated. He'd killed one of the raiders, but it wasn't enough. There wasn't enough in the world. It was grief, for the loss of what he'd known. Grief for his family. Grief, though he didn't know it yet, for the young man who would never be the same. The light-hearted, cheerful young man whose life had been so undemanding, had finally come up against a painful hardship.

Neesha abruptly pushed his mug toward me. "I don't want this." He stood up, scraping his bench away from the table. "I'm going to see my sister."

"Neesha—"

"No." He leaned down, planted his hands on the table top. He stared hard at me. "No more from you. You are not her father to say what she needs. I'm her blood kin. *I* say what I do when it concerns her. You have no say." He pushed himself straight. "No say at all."

I watched him walk to the door. Watched him walk out. Made no move to go after him. I knew very well that he'd left something unsaid. I was his father, his blood kin, but I had no say over *him* any more than over Rashida. I hadn't earned it.

It hurt, knowing that. But I couldn't fault his feelings. I knew what he was thinking: This journey, which he himself had suggested, was no longer an adventure.

When I departed after several mugs of superior ale, I discovered Del's white gelding tied just outside the tavern. In fact, not paying any attention, I nearly ran into him. I went over him with eyes and hands as best as I could in dying light, and he seemed fine. I wondered why Darrion hadn't come in to tell me. But I untied him, led him down to the livery, and did not find the smith there. I thought about it a moment, then walked the horse into the barn, figuring I'd pay the smith in the morning. I was greeted by a series of very loud snorts, a demanding nicker that contained all the arrogance in the world, and repeated thumpings against the wall, thanks to shod hoof connecting with wood.

"Hey, old son." I should have expected it. Neesha had found Rashida at Mahmood's, aboard the stud. He would have tended him. I unsaddled, unbridled Del's horse, turned him in, fed and watered him, then stepped next door to the stud's stall. He promptly turned his back on me and stood with his head in the corner, one hind hoof cocked up as if he meant to kick me, were I foolish enough to enter the stall. I was not. "I knew you'd take care of her. Did she give you a good ride? She's Neesha's sister, and I know you like Neesha."

He refused to talk to me. He had water and hay, so I picked up saddle, bridle, halter, and blanket and hauled everything inside. Unsurprisingly, Tamar met me at the door. "What are you doing with that? Do you think you're bringing it inside? Gods only know where it's been!"

"On Del's horse. And I don't trust the smith. Since I didn't see the stud's tack anywhere, I'm assuming Del brought it in?"

Her lips compressed. "Very well. But you and the boy will share that small room. Del and Rashida will have the larger one."

"Well, all right." It didn't sound promising to me. That room was too small for two grown men. Then again, Neesha might spend the night elsewhere. Maybe he *was* paying attention when one of the sisters laid down the rules, and sought a woman in another tavern. "Oh, and it was quite a nice tavern, as you said. I met the young women but not their father."

The faintest of spasms ran across Tamar's face. "He's very ill. The healer says it's only a matter of time. Sometimes he stays in the common room for a bit; the rest of the time he rests in bed while the girls run the tavern."

"Well, one of them made it very clear that we should go elsewhere if we wanted more than food and drink. But ale was all I wanted anyway. Neesha left; I don't know if he's coming back tonight, or not."

She sniffed eloquently. "Fools, those young men. They'd do better to keep themselves away from whores."

It shocked the hoolies out of me that she used the word. And Tamar clearly saw it, because color crept into her face.

I broke out into a wide smile. "I finally outgrew it," I told her. "Eventually. I have to think my son will also."

"I lock my door at nine of the clock," she said. "If he's not back by then, he'll have to sleep elsewhere."

A vision of Neesha bedding down in the livery amused me. Besides, it left me more room if he stayed out all night. But the amusement spilled away. "How is Rashida?"

Tamar's face tightened. "She's had a scrubbing with soap and water. Actually, three scrubbings; she says she can't get clean. But that will pass in good time. Del is helping her a great deal. No false sympathy because she doesn't—can't—understand. Just matter-of-fact tending with the occasional kindness."

"That's because Del *does* understand." Tamar looked at me

sharply, and then shocked realization flared in her widening eyes. To change the subject, I said, "We'll go tomorrow. Then Rashida will be with her parents. That should help."

Tamar's shock dissipated. "Not necessarily if she goes right back to where the raiders abducted her!"

"No," I said. "No, we won't do that. There's nothing left but a heap of burned timber."

She shook her head. "I'll pray those raiders will be caught and given their own just desserts, but all the men in town are afraid to take them on."

"No worry," I said. "Zayid—the red-head—is dead, and so are his five men. Several of us played cat and undertook the job of getting rid of the vermin permanently."

She was startled. "*You* did?"

"Me, Del, Neesha, with help from Eddrith and Darrion."

Her voice climbed to a new register. "Darrion? *Darrion* helped?"

"He did."

She shook her head, eyes glistening. "Well, perhaps my grandson will come to something after all."

I stared at her in surprise, then smiled widely. "He did well."

She flapped her hand at me. "Go to bed. Go on."

"Blue curtain?"

"Blue curtain."

I hitched up the saddle and tack once more and walked on down the hall. Maybe Del would sneak into my room again.

I had long since given up on Del's coming to my room, and when she *did* I was so sound asleep my heart nearly burst out of my chest from surprise. "Stop doing that, bascha!"

There was no light, so I couldn't see her. "Doing what?"

"Scaring the daylights out of me!"

"Hoolies, Tiger, I'd think you'd be a bit more alert when there are sword-dancers after you!" I was amused to hear 'hoolies' coming from her, until she finished the thought: "Then again, that's what happens to older men."

I realized then that Neesha was not in the room. Well, there had always been a good chance that he wouldn't return until morning. "Then if I'm old, you might have taken pity on me." I sat up. I'd put the mattress on the floor because, as Tamar had once warned me, the bed was too short for someone of my height.

"I didn't say 'old,'" Del noted. "I said 'old*er*.'"

I felt the presence of someone very close to me. Hearing, feeling—didn't matter. You just kind of know when someone is close, even if it is pitch black. Then hands patted my leg, moving from knee to mid-thigh.

I nearly quivered. "Are you trying to send me a message? If so, I have definitely received it!"

I heard soft laughter. "No, no message. Truly, I'm just trying to find you. I'd stay to take advantage of you, but I want to get back to Rasha."

She sat down close as I levered myself up on elbows. "How is she?"

Del sighed. "Difficult to know. She walks from anger to fear to sadness and shame, then back again."

"Shame! Why shame?"

In the dark, she was silent a moment. "Women are taught they should maintain their maidenhead until they marry. She no longer has it."

I sat up next to her. "That's hardly her fault!"

Del's tone was delicate. "It doesn't matter, Tiger. It's rare that a man will forgive his bride's lack of maidenhead. She's now considered a whore."

I was astonished. "Rashida is not a whore!"

Del said nothing a moment. When she did speak, it was with an undertone of sadness. "No. But men will believe so."

I said something very rude about a certain number of males. A large number.

"Well, yes," Del agreed. "But you and I are hardly like others. You didn't expect me to be a virgin since I'd already told you what happened. You also weren't looking for an unsullied bride."

"Hoolies, Del . . . you don't mean she can never marry, do you?"

"It depends on the man. Here in the North there are considerably more freedoms than women experience in the South, but a woman without virginity—unless she's a widow—is always suspect."

"Suspect for what?"

Del sighed. "Sleeping with a man not her husband."

I mulled that over. "I didn't expect you to be a virgin even *before* you told me what had happened."

"Thank you very much!"

"Well, think about it, bascha. You spent how many years training on Staal-Ysta, surrounded by men? You rode alone across the Punja. And you took up company with me."

Her tone was exquisitely dry. "The last being the most damning."

I couldn't come up with a good answer for that. I took the conversation in a new direction. "Did Neesha come to see her? He said he would."

"He did come, but Tamar chased him out. We were helping Rasha bathe."

I remembered how Tamar had said Rashida bathed three times because she felt so dirty. I knew it wasn't dirt and grime and mud she was referring to. "So he left?"

"Yes."

"Did he say where he was going?"

"No."

I sighed. "So, about Rashida—what do we do?"

"We take her home."

"Her home is gone."

"Ah," Del said on a note of realization, "so it is. Well, maybe that's not a bad thing. We'll take her to her parents. That's also 'home.'"

I found a thigh and cupped my hand over it. "Can you stay the night?"

"No. I suspect she will have night terrors. I should be with her."

I'd sort of expected that. "Then you'd better go, because otherwise I'm going to do my best to talk you into carnal activities."

Del laughed, though she restrained it so as not to disturb Tamar. "'Carnal activities.' I like that."

"So do I. But I guess they're out for tonight."

"Sadly, yes." She leaned, kissed me briefly, then rose. "Goodnight, Tiger. I'll see you in the morning."

By the time I wished her goodnight, she was gone.

Chapter 34

NEESHA WAS SITTING OUTSIDE ON THE BENCH on Tamar's porch when I finally awakened and went out to look at the day and its weather, carrying the tack I'd collected from Del's room. Seeing him made me pause a moment. Tied at the porch posts were the stud, Del's gelding, Neesha's bay.

He sat on the bench next to the basin of water for washing feet, slumped against the wall. It made me look down at my feet. My poor sandals were stiff from water and mud, though I'd cleaned off most of the leather because of Tamar. Either they'd soften as I wore them, or I'd need new ones.

"Feet all clean?" I did not want to venture onto the uncomfortable ground we'd walked the night before.

"They'll do." Neesha rose. "I ran into Eddrith at a tavern. He, of all people, had the five horses. He didn't know where to take them. And he doesn't know where the raiders may have taken the rest. For all we know they've already been sold."

I knew that was a bitter and painful realization for him. So many years put into developing superior breeding stock, and now only five were left. I went to the stud and began getting all the pieces arranged in order. "Any of them a stud horse?"

Neesha shook his head. "Two of the mares are obviously in foal. If the other three were bred, it's too early for me to know."

"So no stallion."

"We—well, my father, providing he can—will need to find a good stallion elsewhere and breed the three mares to him, if they're not in foal."

"I'd offer my stud, but I hardly think he's what you want to breed." He had never been a particularly attractive horse, but I couldn't have asked for a better one in so many ways.

Neesha's lips twitched wryly. "Well, no." He sighed. "So I guess they're starting over. After thirty years."

"No, you're not," I told him. "You have five good mares. Two are in foal. You know what good brood mares are worth. And they're not the first mares your father ever bought. He'll know a good stallion for them. And you could get a stud colt from one of the two mares in foal. You aren't starting from the very beginning where no one will sell you a good mare." I brightened. "And there's the roan mare I inherited from Kirit. Six mares will help get the farm on its feet again."

After a moment, he nodded. "That's true."

"So we ride to Sabir's and Yahmina's today."

"Yes."

"Do you want to run the mares loose, or pony them off of our mounts?"

He thought it over. "Easier to let them go on their own. They'll look to your stud to make the decisions."

"Oh, *that* could be a problem, if he decides to pitch a fit."

"He only pitches a fit with you. He knows you expect it, so he gives it to you."

That sounded more like the old Neesha. "Will Rashida ride double with one of us, or ride a mare bareback?"

He shook his head. "I don't know."

"Let her choose," I suggested. "Give her something to think about."

He nodded. "Yes."

"Where are the horses now?"

"In a corral at the livery." He rose. "I'll go over there. Once you and Del are ready, we can turn the mares loose and send them out of town. I think they had enough of freedom yesterday. They'll stay close."

"Well, if you see Eddrith, tell him we're leaving town. He's not going to get his sparring session unless he finds me on the trail. I'm not waiting for him."

Neesha nodded absently as he stepped off the porch, mind on the horses and the journey.

"Don't you want breakfast?" I asked.

Neesha's smile was very faint, but recognizable. "Well, no. I already had breakfast."

"Elsewhere?"

"Elsewhere."

"With female companionship?"

"With female companionship."

I grinned and went back into Tamar's inn. I remembered my days at Neesha's age. No responsibilities except in the circle. And women who did not expect you to stay. Though it was best, as Neesha had learned, not to go to bed with married ones.

That is, I *hoped* he had learned it.

Since I didn't know Rashida prior to the abduction, I couldn't compare her behavior now to what it had been. But she walked out of the inn with composure, hair combed and tied back, clothing clean and neat. I'm sure Del had told her all the raiders were dead, so she need not look for them around every corner every moment. I wondered, however, if it was possible not to look. I could not imagine what it was like for any woman, let alone a young girl, to go through what Rashida had.

Tamar gave her some clothing and mentioned in passing that she wore the outfit when she rode many years ago—I had trouble picturing her as a carefree young woman.

Rashida wore a long rusty-brown tunic with split sides, a long skirt also with split sides, and a doubled leather belt, though Tamar said the buckle had broken a long time ago. It was now tied off like a latigo on a saddle. The end dangled to her knees. She was, however, barefoot; Del said no one had any boots or sandals that would fit.

Rashida shrugged. "I'll ride barefoot. I ride that way around home all the time."

Then it struck her, as it did us, that she would not be riding around the home she'd known all of her life. And Neesha, who'd been refused several times when wishing to see her, wrapped his arms around her in a tight embrace. He just hugged her. Hugged and hugged. Rashida clamped her arms around his waist and pressed her head into his chest. She was trembling.

I glanced at Del. I had no idea what had been said among the women yesterday, and I don't know if Rashida cried then, but she did now, holding onto the only one spared the fire and outrage done to her family. I thought it was probably a very good thing.

When Neesha looked over her shoulder at me, tears were visible on his face. He was not so self-conscious as to try to hide them. "We'll go see the horses," he said. "Rasha can pick which she'd like to ride." Before any of us could say anything, he set her down and turned away from us. With his hand resting gently on the back of her neck, they walked down the street toward the livery.

Watching that, I said grimly, "It's a good thing those men are already dead. Because I'd kill them again. And more painfully."

Del met my eyes, understanding completely. Her face was tight, her tone tighter still. "I think we should have done as I suggested. Cut off arms, legs, let them bleed, then take the head."

This time I didn't argue her out of it.

Tamar looked at Del's face, then at mine. Her mouth was compressed, her eyes fierce. "It's too bad *she* can't kill them. The girl."

Del looked at her sharply, clearly surprised. And in Del's eyes I saw the memory of what she had experienced; how, after five years of training, she had killed Ajani, the man who had done to her what had been done to Rashida.

Then Tamar smiled thinly. "Take her home." She nodded at us both, then went inside and shut the door.

Rashida ended up riding her brother's bay, rather than any of the mares. Del's idea. When I got the chance, I asked her why.

"Backbone," Del said quietly, as Rashida and Neesha rode close together a little ahead of us. He was bareback on one of the mares who were not obviously in foal.

"What? What about a backbone?"

Del looked at me a moment, as if trying to find the right words. Finally she said, "She was raped repeatedly. A saddle is . . . more comfortable."

Neesha's saddle wouldn't fit any of the mares as well as the horse who usually wore it, true. But then I realized what she meant. Oh, hoolies. "You know, I understand a little better now how you dedicated yourself to learning the sword. The oaths you swore. The obsession—yes, bascha, that's what it was. Don't look at me like that—you followed through to completion. And I think for Neesha's sake, it's good the raiders are dead, too."

Del thought for a long moment, staring ahead at my son and his sister riding side-by-side. Her expression was strange. Finally she looked at me. "It will make him a better sword-dancer."

It stunned me. For a moment I couldn't speak. Then, as I started to, Del cut me off with a gesture.

"I know," she said levelly. "I know perfectly well what that sounds like and how it would shock others to hear it. I didn't say it for effect. I said it because that's what Neesha wants to do with his life. Sometimes it takes the obsession you mentioned, or a potent will to overcome a dangerous and deadly challenge, or just giving oneself over completely to what one most wants to do. I don't know what the future holds for Neesha, whether he'll stay with his family or come back to us, but I do know that this will make him a better sword-dancer. It's difficult to be as good as he wishes when one is not driven by demons. You and I know about those demons. Neesha didn't; now he does. It just depends on what he wants of life *now*."

I held my tongue, thinking all of that through before saying anything. Finally I nodded. "I understand. I don't want to, but I do. Yet in a way, I wish he could have avoided this. Tempering is difficult. Tempering is painful."

"Tempering is necessary, Tiger. For us. For people like us. He's not like us, and he won't be, I don't think, but he can't be a sword-dancer, a *true* sword-dancer, without understanding how it lives in us. And now a little of it lives in Neesha. Now he must decide."

Neesha's decision was to remain with his family. He told me after we'd put the mares back into a corral at Sabir's and Yahmina's; after he'd lifted Rashida down from the saddle and walked her into the house. Del and I heard Danika's cry all the way outside. After a moment, Neesha walked back out and came straight to us.

"I can't be in two places," he said evenly. "I have to choose which. It will take my father a long time to heal, and there is a house to rebuild. Mares soon to foal. They need my help. But you—" He looked straight at me. "You don't need my help. I know you'd say you did, but you don't. You have plenty of other students. I've been with you two years. You've taught me so much. But you don't *need* me."

He wasn't cruel. He didn't say it to hurt me, to disrespect me, to make me angry. He said what was in his heart at that particular moment. And he was right. They needed his help more than I needed his company.

I managed to summon a faint smile. He believed what he believed. There were all kind of remonstrations I might make, all manner of protestation, but I couldn't say anything to him. I couldn't say a word. I let him believe what he believed.

Neesha said, "Yahmina is cooking a huge pot of stew. Sabir has ale." He smiled. "It will be cramped, but I think we can fit everyone in the house."

I intended to thank him and say Del and I needed to get back on the road, but she spoke before I could. "That will be good, Neesha. We'll put our mounts over at the tree again, set up a small camp as before."

He smiled at me. "Come in and get some ale."

Del and I rode over to the tree and began the usual tasks of untacking, picketing, watering, graining, setting out bedrolls, sorting through saddle pouches. When we were done, Del stepped close and took my hand. "I think even I will have some ale."

After dinner, after Sabir's ale, I slept for several hours. Then I woke up. I wasn't going back to sleep any time soon, so I crawled out of bed, took care of business, walked out from under the thick tree canopy to look up at the stars, at the half-faced moon, and think about my son.

I heard Del as she came to me. She stood very close by my side, saying nothing. Listening to the night. Then she stepped around to face me, to wrap her arms around me. Mine went around her. I hung on to her for the saving of my soul.

"I'm sorry." She stroked the back of my head. "Oh Tiger, I'm so sorry."

I nodded against the silk of her hair. I had no words in me. Nothing adequate. Nothing at all.

Of course he had to stay. It was best for him to stay.

For Rasha. His mother. His father.

Chapter 35

NOT LONG AFTER DAWN, Del and I were up and tacking the horses. The stud was just about ready to go. Bedrolls and saddle pouches were onboard, as were collapsible water buckets, food, botas, all the bits and pieces one carried on the road.

It was as I was hooking the halter around the stud's neck that Danika came outside to us. I caught Del's glance and her plan to lead her gelding away to give us privacy.

But Danika put out a hand. "No. Stay. Please." She swallowed heavily, as if trying not to cry. Brown eyes glistened. "There are no words. There are no words. What you did . . ." She shook her head as the threatened tears spilled over. "It had to be the gods' doing that you came when you did. Because otherwise Rasha would be lost to us. Hired men would not have tried hard enough to find her, to rescue her." She gazed at Del a moment, then walked to her and reached out for a hug. Del hugged her back, murmured something in Danika's ear. Danika nodded, then managed to get the words out: "Thank you for bringing me back my daughter."

Del smiled, nodded, and then as Danika stepped back from her, she led her horse away. Danika did not stop her this time.

She stood beneath the tree staring at me, with a kindness in her eyes I would not have looked for. She came close, took both my hands in hers. "The best gift I ever had was the son you gave me all those years ago. Now you give him back, a better man than he was. And Rasha—" She shook her head. "There are no words, Tiger. You have brought both of my children back to me."

I nodded, my hands clasping hers.

Her voice shook. "Thank you for those twenty-five years. Thank you for these few days. No other man could do so much."

She stepped close. We embraced. I set my cheek against the top of her head; she was shorter than Del. "It was you who gave me the gift," I told her. "You raised him right, you and Harith. I am so proud of him." We broke the embrace. "Will you be all right?"

Danika nodded. "We'll hire men to help rebuild the house. Harith won't be able to help, but he can direct them. That will be enough. Until then, we'll stay here with Sabir and Yahmina. Neesha is going to put up a tent for us beside the house so we don't get too much in the way."

He was going to fit right in, my son. Home again.

Danika sensed my thought. "His spirit is too big to remain on a horse farm. He's not ready to settle down. You'll have him back. I promise. I just don't know when."

I nodded, finding a faint smile. "And I thank you for that."

"Come back," she said. "Come back some day."

I promised it, but we both knew it wouldn't happen. Time would pass. Any intent to return would die away. Only memories would remain.

Danika's smile wavered. She thanked me again, then turned and walked back to the house.

I finished readying the stud. Led him over to Del. She was mounted, and I swung up as well.

Her expression was startled. "Aren't you going to say goodbye to Neesha?"

I looked away from her, gazing across the gentle hills. "I don't know if I can."

"Oh, Tiger . . . wait. There he is."

I looked back at the house. Neesha stood in the doorway, leaning against the doorjamb. Across that distance we stared at one another, though not close enough to see the details of expression.

Then he raised his hand. I raised mine. And it was enough.

"Let's go," I said.

Del nodded. We turned our horses and headed out.

When you've been with someone long enough, there is no need to talk all the time. You need put no effort into carrying on a conversation. You are content and comfortable in one another's company, even in the silence.

Del and I didn't speak for a long time. I suspect it wasn't so much unnecessary as we were both lost in thought about life without Neesha; about how his family would cope with the significant changes and hardships; about Rashida's future. Del had more insight into the latter, but her explanation about people's views of Rasha post-rape had made me realize that women faced more challenges than I'd believed even after Del had already done much to educate me.

In the South, a woman who is raped either says nothing about it for fear of punishment or, should she let it slip, is punished by being whipped. And if the woman who says nothing is found to be pregnant later, she is fortunate if married because it could be passed off as her husband's. If single and pregnant, she was killed so she would no longer tempt men or bring a child into the world who might well grow up to be a raider himself.

Being in the North again reminded me how difficult and sometimes cruel was the South. And a question occurred that hadn't been asked for a long time: "Do you miss it, bascha? I mean, now that we've been in the North again?"

Del just looked ahead. "Sometimes. And yes . . . more so because we've been here again among the trees, the grass, the hills."

We rode a little farther. I had to ask it. "Would you want to stay here? Make our life here?"

That brought her head around. "Why are you asking? You've said the South is your home. I'm happy in our canyon."

"Because it reminds you of the North."

"Well, certainly more so than the Punja does!" Del shrugged. "Alric is happy as a Northerner in the South. Why can't I be?"

I was quiet a moment. "I don't want you to feel that I'm insisting."

Del frowned, bewildered. "Is it Neesha? Do you want to be closer, now that he's staying here?"

"There's Kalle also."

We had not spoken of Del's daughter in years. She had been fostered to a good family in Staal-Ysta when Del left the North to find her brother.

Del shook her head. "No. As you saw at Staal-Ysta, Kalle has real parents, not a mother who deserts her."

"The exile is over. You could go back to Staal-Ysta if you wished. To see her."

"I don't wish," Del said quietly. "We've got Sula, you and I. You didn't know Neesha even existed until two years ago. And Kalle doesn't even know I *am* her mother. Neesha has done very well; I'm sure Kalle has also." She met my eyes. "I'm happy where I am. It's you who matters, not the place."

I nodded, frowning. "But you'll tell me if you'd like to go back, won't you?"

Del's smile kindled. "I'll tell you, yes. I vow it."

I couldn't hide the relief in my voice. "All right, then."

We spent the night at the small stopping place, then rode on in more haste. Now that we were bound for the canyon, our urgency was different than it had been going north. Quite apart from it being our home, Sula was there. She was deserving of a settled place, but if Del wished to move to the North at any time, I'd do it.

Without Mahmood's caravan to attend, we made much better time. South again, we arrived at the big oasis with a few hours left before dusk. As always, plenty of people were there, but more yet would arrive with the sunset. The spring was thronged by people trying to fill buckets or water animals, so Del and I hunted down a tree and found a sparse-limbed one with modest shade.

As had been my habit in the past, I rode the stud around the perimeter of the oasis, through the tents and wagons. I saw no sword-dancers. I went back to Del and, as she had already done, completed the usual horse and human chores. I grabbed up two of the water buckets and went to the spring.

Where a sword-dancer had just arrived.

Ah, hoolies.

I very nearly turned to go back to our tree. But he had already glanced at me briefly, noted the sword above my shoulder, and nodded matter-of-factly to acknowledge a fellow sword-dancer. Apparently nothing alerted him to my identity. He watered his mount, then walked away. As I filled our buckets, I reflected that it was arrogance to assume that *every* sword-dancer knew me on sight. Many did, but probably there was a fair number of them who either hadn't heard of me or did not recognize the scars on my face. Many of them were young. Alimat no longer existed. Other than by rumor, the younger men might not even know what *elaii-ali-ma* meant or that I'd declared it.

Then again, Khalid knew me. Kirit had known. Eddrith knew. Even Darrion was aware.

Other men crowded forward at the spring to fill buckets of their own. None were sword-dancers, merely family men driving wagons, merchants such as Mahmood, solo male riders. I saw no harnesses, no swords sheathed in them. Tension began to melt away. I had not yet taken off my harness and sword, which had marked me to the sword-dancer; I intended to, but were I unarmed, others could attack.

I moved away from the crowded spring and walked back with full buckets, trying to keep the water from slopping over the rims. I wasn't entirely successful, but most remained in the buckets when I set them before the horses. Maybe later, in the dark, I'd lead the horses back to the spring when it was less crowded. Just now it was a mass of jostling as animals crowded to water, and the stud usually let everyone know he did not approve when he was in the middle of such things.

I found that Del had already laid a fire and was coaxing tinder. She nursed a flame carefully, and once it was established, she carefully laid larger branches on it.

As I arrived, she glanced up. "We have stew makings. We could boil one on the fire."

I screwed up my face. "Stew again? I think that's all we've had for days."

"Well, short of begging for food at other fires, this is what we've got. Tamar sent the makings with me."

"Tamar's stew? Is that all we'll ever eat for the rest of our lives?" I sighed heavily, feigning deep regret, and stripped out of my burnous. The harness and sword followed. I set the sword, unsheathed, immediately beside my blanket. "I suppose it will do."

She then suggested I go to other fires and beg a pot. Apparently this was different than begging for food. When on the road we carried dried foodstuffs and hoped now and again to catch a sand coney, wild fowl, or, if we were fortunate, cattle or goats that had escaped their herds; even, occasionally, snakes. But many animals were scarce as we camped on the edge of the Punja. Del and I had a little cumfa meat left, journey bread verging on stale, fruit that was starting to spoil. But Tamar had sent more dried meat, tubers, herbs, onions, and potatoes. Mixed with water and heated over a cookfire, it would do nicely. We lacked a spit so we'd set the pot right down on the rock ring. That is, if I managed to borrow a pot.

"I have a better idea," I said. "*You* go."

She was tending the cookfire once more. "Because I'm a woman?"

Uh-oh. I turned on my heel and went off to scrounge a pot.

Chapter 36

THANKS TO AN ACCOMMODATING NEIGHBOR ONE TREE OVER, Del and I were able to eat Tamar's stew—or at least an approximation of it. In addition, Del put out slices of softening apple, hardening journey bread, and some thick-rinded cheese. This time I drank water, not aqivi.

After eating, I lay back on my blanket with arms shoved beneath my head and sighed a heavy sigh. It felt good to be on the way home. Neesha's desire for adventure had been fulfilled, if not quite in the way he expected, and Del and I had a chance to recall what our lives had been, and to know what they were now. Now was better.

"Your turn," Del said.

"My turn what?"

"I cooked."

"I found the pot."

"You should return it, too. But best to clean it first, don't you think?"

Ah yes, the legendary Sandtiger, given the task of cleaning a pot. Definitely added luster to the legend. I got up from my comfortable sprawl, took the pot from the cooling rocks set in a ring around what now were glowing coals, and grabbed a handful of sand. The easiest way to clean a pot in a desert is to use sand to scour out the bits of food a spoon or fork couldn't quite get, and not waste water while doing it. As I scrubbed, gritty sand scratched against the metal. Eventually all that was left was a rime of sand dust, which I blew out, then ran my hand around the interior once again.

"All right." I rose. "I'll be back in a bit. I'll take the horses to the spring before it gets too crowded again."

The sun perched on the horizon. Daylight was gone. Now the evening slid up from the earth with dusk in accompaniment. I un-picketed the horses, led them away as I went to the next-door tree again and returned the pot with effusive thanks. Then I took the stud and Del's gelding to the spring.

Del's horse, as sunlight disappeared, took on a kind of glow, as if his coat gathered up what little light was left. He drew attention as we walked but less for that, I thought, than for the narrow strings of leather swaying against his face.

More and more wagons came in for the night and also a handful of men who rode alone. I quickened my steps and managed to stake out a good place at the spring before the onslaught, letting out lead-rope so the horses could drink. A large bucket was available, and while some used it to dip up water for animals, most let their animals drink directly from the spring. A few brought with them waxed canvas buckets like those Del and I carried.

As more animals were brought in, the jostling began. The stud pinned back his ears and slewed an eye sideways to take the measure of the horse next to him.

"Hey." I snapped a finger on his muzzle with intended sharpness. "Not here and not now." He offered me the equine equivalent of a scowl. "Don't give me that. Now, quit. Just settle."

He did not. He jerked his head sideways to nip at his sorrel neighbor, though he never made contact because I gave his halter a jerk. When that didn't have much effect, I grabbed the bridle by a bit shank to insist with added vigor that he mind his manners.

The sorrel's rider ducked his head down beneath his horse's neck to see me. He was grinning. "Opinionated, isn't he?"

"More than is good for him," I grumbled. "And for me, too." More horses began to come upon us. "All right," I told the stud, "we're going. Just keep your teeth and heels to yourself until we get out of this mess."

We couldn't turn because of crowding, so we had to back out. Del's gelding was perfectly willing to do so. The stud was less so. Finally, I bent down and set a shoulder into his chest even as I tightened my grip on the bit shanks. "Back up, you son of a Salset goat!" And I put all of my weight to the shoulder against his chest, leaning hard. I muttered all kinds of imprecations, and at last he backed up, and we were free of the throng.

The man with the sorrel had waited to see who won the battle. He was still grinning. Now that I was done arguing with the stud, physically as well as verbally, I got a better look at the man. Shorter than I, but not by much. Brown hair, pale eyes. Younger than I. And I got a good enough look to see the sword rising from behind his shoulder. Hoolies, there were sword-dancers everywhere I went! But my harness and sword were back at the tree. I shouldn't look like a sword-dancer to anyone.

"Aren't you the Sandtiger?"

I could lie. Lying might be good.

"I recognize you by the scars," he said.

I glared at him. "You will note I am not wearing harness and sword. You're supposed to leave me alone."

He cupped a hand lightly over his mount's nostrils as the sorrel breathed noisily. "Ordinarily, yes. But not in your case."

I waited. He didn't say anything.

"And—?" I asked eventually.

He shrugged. "Just looking."

"Not challenging?"

"No."

"Looking to kill?"

He frowned. "No."

"Hunting a bounty?"

"What bounty?"

Hmmm. A sword-dancer who didn't care about *elaii-ali-ma*, and knew nothing of Umir's bounty. How refreshing!

"Never mind," I said and led away the gelding and stud.

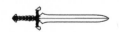

Now that darkness had fallen, Del built up the fire for light. Scattered throughout the large oasis were twenty or more cookfires, lending a smoky glow to the area. Pockets of darkness remained, but it was easy enough to see folk as they moved around. Buckets were carried to livestock, while some mounts were led to the spring. Children refused noisily to be put to bed. The usual music and singing began. It was a comfortable evening.

Well, it was comfortable until the sword-dancer from the spring—the second sword-dancer from the spring—showed up. He was on foot, barefoot, still in harness, and I began to get a bad feeling. Though certainly nothing could be done now, in the dark.

He carried a bota. "If I'm not intruding, may I join you?"

Del sat up even as I did. She looked at the stranger, then glanced at me, asking a silent question.

"We met, sort of, at the spring," I explained. "The stud tried to take a hunk out of his horse. Other than that—" I looked at the man, "I haven't the faintest idea who he is or why he wishes to join us."

"To share a bota." He lifted it. "Mostly I want to ask questions." He paused. "Oh, and my name is Tariq."

Del's hand was on her naked blade, lying close on her blanket. I was in the same posture on my blanket, with my sword.

Tariq looked from one to the other. Some of his friendly smile faded. "I don't care," he said. "Truly, I don't care about *elaii-ali-ma* or what other sword-dancers have sworn. I go my own way. Whatever bounty exists for someone to kill you . . . I don't *care*."

"Easy to say," Del observed.

I did find it interesting, though, that he apparently believed the bounty was simply for killing me, not something put up by Umir.

"Here." He dropped the bota, stripped off the top part of his belted burnous to reach his sword, and with great care slid it out of his sheath. Slowly he set it on the ground and gathered up the bota once more. It dangled from its thong. "I have questions," he said, "because I wish to learn. No more than that. Who wouldn't wish to do so, given the chance?"

Who wouldn't wish the chance to challenge me, or to actually kill me?

Tariq waited expectantly. Del left the decision to me, since I was Tariq's goal. After a moment, I nodded.

Very carefully, Tariq sat down out of his sword's range. He could only recover it by making a mad lunge, but it wouldn't be quickly enough to stop me or Del. Smiling, he unstoppered the bota, took several swallows, then offered it to me. So now Del and I knew the drink was safe, not a way of drugging us into insensibility. On the side of safety, I had to assume he did intend to take me for the bounty, or to challenge me to a dance. But likely he would not.

Once, I would have been happy to share my fire with another sword-dancer. Now, I couldn't afford it without being on my guard, or assuming the worst.

Tariq slung the bota to me on one side of the fire. In courtesy, he waited till I drank before beginning his interrogation. As was customary, Del refused; if she drank spirits, it was rarely. I tossed the bota back.

Tariq caught it, set it aside. "May I ask questions?"

Del shrugged. I nodded.

And thus began a spate of questions that threatened to go on until dawn. He wanted to know about technique. He wanted to know about maneuvers. He wanted to know what I'd done to certain sword-dancers in order to defeat them.

Finally I stopped him. "The questions you have can't all be answered in words."

It was full dark now. His face was illuminated by the glow of the dying fire. He was perhaps Neesha's age. "Then can you show me?"

"Here and now?"

"No, no. In the morning. Would you have time for a lesson?"

"You said you didn't intend to challenge me."

He was honestly taken aback. "No! I want no such thing. Only a lesson."

I looked at his hopeful, eager expression. "We're going home," I said finally. "We'd just as soon get there without delay. I thank you for your interest, but we'll head out at first light."

Disappointment was obvious. It appeared as though he'd try a different tack, but he gave it up. He gestured to the bota. "Please. Keep it. You would do me a courtesy. Thank you for answering what you could." Tariq smiled faintly, got to his feet, collected his sword. With an odd little bow, he backed up, turned, and walked away.

After a moment, Del said, "That was strange."

I grunted. "He may be exactly what he says he is, and he may truly want a lesson. But . . ." I took up the bota, aimed for the foot of the tree. "I'll stick with our own water or aqivi, I think."

Del's eyes had followed the bota as I tossed it aside. Now she looked back at me in some consternation. "Do you think it's drugged?"

I shook my head. "Tariq definitely drank, and I tasted nothing odd in it. I feel fine."

"You're sure?"

I lay back down on my blanket, crossed one ankle over the other. "You didn't drink anything. If necessary, you can protect me." I smiled up at the stars. "Perhaps you should stay awake all night, be a guard."

"Perhaps I should," she replied with some asperity.

Grinning, I interlaced hands over my chest and closed my eyes. "Then good night, bascha."

When I woke with the dawn, Del was curled up against me, mostly hidden under a blanket. "Ah-hah!" I cried. "You slept! So much for protecting me!"

Del's voice had its customary morning huskiness. "I only went to sleep a few minutes ago."

"Uh-huh. Right." I peeled back my blanket and looked around at the world. A faint film of moisture touched almost everything.

I yawned prodigiously, stretched from a sitting position, then stood up for an additional stretch. Across the oasis others were beginning to move. Livestock awoke and began their noisy morning pleas for food. Behind me, picketed on the other side of the tree, the stud snorted loudly and pawed at the ground, raising dust.

"Oh, stop," I said through a yawn.

The stud dropped a certain equine apparatus and began peeing emphatically. Fortunately the river did not find a channel through our bedding. Steam rose, along with a pungent scent.

"So?" I asked. "I can do that, too. Even if I'm only human-sized." And I walked off to a shrub to prove it.

When I returned, Del was in the midst of rolling up her bedding. Saddle pouches were over by her gelding. She grabbed saddle blanket and saddle and took both to her horse, where she set the blanket across his back one-handed, swung the saddle up into place and cinched it up. Then she went off to have her own communion with a bush.

When she returned, pretty much everything of mine was on board. I donned harness and sword followed by burnous, belted it, waited for Del to finish readying the gelding and herself. A normal start to the morning. We never cooked breakfast on the road, just ate what we had in saddle pouches.

"A few more days," I said as we led the horses through the middle of the oasis, bound for water. "Then we'll be home where we can once again look after a determined and opinionated two-year-old. And train young men to become sword-dancers."

Del smiled. "So we can. Though I'd like to see a woman student come to us."

I shrugged. "It's the South."

"Maybe some day."

"Maybe."

As we approached the big rock surround where the spring bubbled up, we heard the sound of swords, of spectators shouting approval for one blow or another—obviously wagering was in progress. Since this gathering was directly beside the track Del and I wished to follow, we mounted our horses once watering was done and rode over there, intending to pass on by. But then we saw the circle, the men inside it. Tariq, and the sword-dancer I'd seen at the spring on our arrival.

Del and I watched a moment—we couldn't help it—then headed out. Or we were, until I heard a shout.

"Sandtiger!" I should have known: Tariq. Then I heard, apparently said to his opponent, "Yes, yes, it's the Sandtiger. I met him last night. We shared a bota. Wait—where are you going?"

I had a very good idea where Tariq's opponent was going. Swearing under my breath, I swung the stud around. The man strode steadily, sword gripped in his hand. Older than Tariq, now that I could see him in daylight, dark-haired, tanned. His eyes were blue. Probably a Borderer.

He stopped short of the stud. "When I acknowledged you last night, I didn't know who you were. Trust me when I say I would never have done you the courtesy had I known. I didn't see the scars in the dusk." He stood even straighter. "I challenge you."

I released a rather noisy sigh. "You know," I said to Del, "I'm getting really tired of this. Maybe I should just kill everyone who challenges me."

"I am Hamzah," the man said. "Come down from there and step into the circle."

Del was at my side, relaxed but watchful. "We have somewhere to be," I told Hamzah, "and it isn't here or in a circle. I won't accept your challenge."

He was outraged. "You must! It's required!"

Well, it sort of was. "Death dance?" I asked.

"No. To defeat."

Well, that was something.

Tariq looked thrilled. "Yes! I would pay to see this!"

If I defeated Hamzah, he'd never challenge me again. It was attractive. "Then let's get this over with," I told Hamzah. "We do have somewhere to be."

He nodded once, walked to the circle and into it. He set down his sword in the middle, took up a position outside the line, and waited for me.

I swung off the stud, undid belt, took off burnous and sandals. All these I draped across my saddle. I handed the reins up to Del, who had a better vantage point from horseback than from the ground.

"Do hurry," Del suggested.

I grinned crookedly. "I'll do my best,"

I walked into the circle, set down my sword, and noticed how avidly the crowd watched. I suspected they'd prefer a death dance, but we weren't offering that today. Probably a little blood, though, which should please them to some extent.

On my side of the circle, I looked across at Hamzah. Tariq stood at an edge, nearly quivering with excitement. "May I?" he asked of both of us. "May I have the honor?"

Hamzah shrugged. Resigned, I told Tariq he could say it.

"Dance!"

It took a little longer than the 'immediately' I'd planned. Hamzah was talented. Whether he considered me past my prime, or at its peak, he did not let it show. He just danced. So I let him have a taste of what I could really do. I laid on, he defended. We spun, ducked, blocked, clashed blades, scraped steel, leaped apart only to go back in again. I drove him to the edge, he drove me to the edge.

Then I heard Del shout. She never did that. Never. She knew what focus was all about. I put a hand in the air in Hamzah's direction. "Wait!" This was allowed. The opponent was to halt. And halt Hamzah did, smiling.

Smiling.

I turned toward Del. I saw that she had been yanked down from her saddle. She was sprawled on the ground with a man sitting atop her, holding a knife to her throat.

I wheeled around, expecting Hamzah to be coming up on me with his sword. But he stood there, blade hanging from his hand, and shook his head. Then I felt a hand lock into my harness from behind, and a knife point delicately pricking a few layers of skin over a kidney. Not a good place for the recipient.

"Drop it. *Now.*"

Tariq. His voice was no longer young or eager. And he made no threats about what would happen to Del if I didn't drop my sword. There was no need. He knew, I knew. I dropped the sword.

"Wise." He jerked me out of range. Pressed the knife deeper. I gritted my teeth against it. "Stand very still."

"Del," I said tightly.

"Oh, she's coming, too. Umir wants you both,"

I let out a long string of vicious epithets. Umir. *Umir.* And we'd walked right into it, thanks to Tariq's assurances that he didn't know about any bounty.

Hamzah came close. "There are six of us," he said. "Look around."

I looked. Four men stood forward from the crowd, dressed in

the kind of clothing that made them inconspicuous. They wore no harnesses, no swords. They looked like every other man standing with the spectators. Two stood by Del, still pinned down.

Hamzah stepped closer yet. "We have great respect for you," he said. "Be glad of it."

Something very hard came down on the back of my head. I nearly went to my knees, but managed a staggering turn toward Tariq even though my head was full of flashing light. A second hard blow collided with the side of my head, and the world winked out.

Chapter 37

I REJOINED THE LIVING IN SHEER MISERY. My head hurt so badly I thought I might throw up, which would have made things worse, of course. But my abdomen was hurting, too. And wrists and ankles. The world was wavering back and forth.

I opened my eyes a slit. I discovered myself in my saddle, atop the stud. My abdomen hurt because I was lying forward across the pommel, upper body stretched out along the stud's neck. When I tried to sit up, I discovered my wrists were shackled together under the stud's neck. It was impossible to sit up. And my legs, when I tested them, were locked into shackles as well. The connecting chain ran under the stud's abdomen. If I made a significant attempt to loose my legs, the chain would shorten and very likely send the stud into a temper tantrum with me stuck aboard. That, I did not wish to experience.

Hoolies, they were using my own horse against me!

Tariq had the stud's lead-rope, ponying him off his saddle. I turned my head very carefully and discovered Del was attached to her gelding the same way I was locked onto the stud. Her face was turned to the other side. Hamzah was leading her horse. "Bascha?"

Del shifted, managed to look at me. Relief flooded her voice. "Thank the gods, you're all right!"

"Well. Kind of. I wish they'd just chopped off my head."

She grimaced, resting the side of her face against her gelding's mane. "I didn't see what they did to you. Someone was sitting on me. But you should be gratified to know it took four men to get your dead weight into the saddle and chained."

"Then gratified I am. We'll celebrate later. How are you?"

"Uncomfortable."

Understatement. I closed my eyes. The rocking motion of the stud coupled with an abdomen on top of a pommel and a head throbbing from two blows, not to mention the chiming of the chains, rendered me nauseated. With small shifts of my weight, I attempted to lift myself off the pommel just a bit to relieve my abdomen. I was unsuccessful. I couldn't remember the last time I had felt so sick or hurt this much.

Well, the latter might be an exaggeration. I'd been the victim of too many captivities, maimings, and wounds to know for certain. They kind of ran together. But it was nearly impossible to breathe with so much weight pressed over the pommel. At the rate we were going, that pommel might well rub itself through my belly and out the other side.

I heard Del muttering to herself. Her face was turned away from me again. "You all right?" I asked.

"No." She repositioned her head to look at me. "No more than you are."

"But you were swearing. You never swear. I distinctly remember hearing a bad word in there."

She gulped. Her face had taken on a grayish cast. "That man . . . he squashed me nearly flat. And now this." She closed her eyes. "What's wrong with throwing us sideways across a saddle? That's an effective way to control us."

Hamzah, ponying Del's horse, laughed. "This is the way Umir wanted you transported."

"Then *he* should have to ride this way. Just once." I was as belligerent as I could be under the circumstances.

"No, Umir's giving the orders, not taking them. I think he'll skip riding in this position."

"Can we?" I asked.

Hamzah glanced back, grinning. "I take orders, too."

"Can we at least stop? For a moment? Let me settle my belly? I really don't want to vomit all over the stud's neck."

"Vomit all you like," Hamzah said cheerfully.

Del said, "There may be two of us getting sick. Would Umir wish us to arrive with vomit all over our horses and all over us?"

It was Tariq's turn to laugh. "Umir doesn't care how you arrive, so long as you do. Vomit as much as you'd like."

He wasn't joking. Neither was I. My mouth flooded with saliva and last night's dinner began a slow crawl up my gullet. I *really* didn't want to throw up in front of these men. And the stud deserved better. I swallowed, tried to remain just as still as I could. Didn't want to make even the smallest movement. Inside my head, I began to sing a ridiculous little song I'd made up for Sula one day. She liked it so much and demanded I sing it so frequently that I was sorry I'd ever invented it. But that ridiculous little song might be the saving of me. Or at least of my head and belly.

When finally, *finally*, we reached Umir's big desert palace, I had indeed been sick to my stomach. My head hurt so damn much and with that pommel digging into my belly, I'd really had no choice. All I could do was try to avoid splattering the stud and myself. To my surprise, I was fairly successful.

Hamzah had taken Del's gelding up in front of the stud, so we couldn't even talk anymore. She shifted position as best she could several times, but I don't know how successful she was at easing the discomfort. I'd begun sucking in my gut as best I could to relieve some of the pressure on my abdomen, but it was impossible to do so for very long because of the stud's motion. I wondered why Umir had seen fit to ask we be transported in such a painful way. But then, we had managed to defeat him several times; maybe this was a sort of revenge. He'd never been inclined that way whenever we met; Umir was an elegant man who liked to collect very rare items. He wasn't one for torture. He hadn't even referred to me as a captive when I very much was; I was his 'guest.' Of course my putting a spell on the book so he couldn't open it had likely infuriated him. I could imagine him trying every day to find a way to open the book. Which wasn't possible. Such frustration. Possibly even fury.

At some point he'd decided that as I'd locked the book against him, I could unlock it. And here we were, Del and I.

The problem was, I couldn't open the book anymore. I'd surrendered all my magic. I couldn't read the book, couldn't cast any spells, couldn't do anything at all that involved magic. I was empty of it. I'd poured all of it into Samiel, my jivatma, my Northern blooding-blade, and then I broke the sword. It lay within the fallen chimney near the canyon, along with Del's Boreal, equally broken.

Samiel's destruction meant my freedom. Empty of the magic that would have killed me in ten years, I would see my daughter grow up. I would see Neesha marry and raise children, no matter what he might think now. The future lay before me, and it would be a long one.

Well, if no one killed me before I actually experienced that future.

Walls surrounded Umir's white-painted palace. Once through the iron gates, we entered a lovely courtyard, thick with blooming gardens, trees, vines; exquisite tile, and a fantastical fountain. The place hadn't changed.

Hooves clopped on pavement. Del and I were stopped. One of the men dismounted and went into the palace, came out not long afterward. He spoke to Hamzah, who was, apparently, the leader of this expedition.

Hamzah nodded, looked at his men. "He wishes us inside. We're to take them into the larger reception room. We're to get them off the horses, but keep them shackled." He dismounted and turned to Del. He unlocked the chain running beneath the gelding's neck and the one beneath his belly. Del did not immediately sit up. Hamzah caught an arm and jerked her down out of the saddle.

It was then we saw the blood. The saddle was soaked with it. Del, as she was manhandled, nearly fell to the paving stones. Hamzah and another caught her by the arms and held her up. Her legs folded beneath her.

"Get me down!" I shouted. "Get me down from here. She's hurt. She's bleeding. Get me off this horse!"

Del's head lolled. Her face was very pale, even her lips. Ah hoolies, bascha! "Get me *down!*"

Hamzah and the others were clearly shocked. As they held her on her feet, blood dribbled down her legs. But Hamzah looked up at me, then switched his gaze to Tariq. "Leave him there. Don't unshackle him yet. And *keep hold of that stallion!* Don't let him loose, or he'll be as hard to handle as his rider."

Tariq followed orders. "What's wrong with her?" he asked.

Hamzah shook his head and shrugged, then handed Del over to another man. "Not ours to worry about. Take her inside to the reception room. *Then* we'll haul the great and famous Sandtiger down from his horse."

I called Hamzah every foul name I could think of. In the midst of it they unlocked the neck chain, the belly chain, and I was able to sit up for the first time in hours. And I nearly cried out because of the pain in my abdomen. Too soon going upright when I'd been down for so long, and the pommel had indeed done some damage. I just hoped it was the kind that could repair itself. No wonder Del was bleeding!

They unlocked the two long chains from me, but I remained shackled at wrists and ankles. I bent over slightly, trying to undo the cramping of my gut. I wasn't sure shackles were necessary. I didn't think I could mount any kind of escape.

I stood there half bent, breathing noisily through clenched teeth. "Get me in there. I want to see Del."

Hamzah gave orders to the others to tend the horses. Then he took one elbow as Tariq took the other, and pushed me toward the entrance. Hoolies, but it hurt to move. And it wasn't particularly helpful when the chain between my ankles barely had enough slack for me to approximate walking. Though that certainly didn't affect how Hamzah and Tariq handled me. They probably would find it a good joke if I tripped and fell face-first on the stones.

Into the palace, as beautiful as I recalled. I was taken through several rooms and at last arrived in what was, apparently, the large reception room. And I saw Del, and I saw Umir.

She lay curled on her side upon tiles, limbs still contained by shackles and chains. Her legs were drawn up to her belly. Umir, standing over her, was the picture of horrified distaste.

I tried to throw off Tariq and Hamzah. They hung on. "Let me go to her!"

Umir looked at me. Then he nodded to both men. I nearly fell as I crossed the floor to Del, but managed to kneel down beside her, chains and shackles clashing. Hoolies, but she looked bad.

"Del? Bascha?" Despite the chains, I grabbed her wrists. "Bascha?"

She opened her eyes. Pain glazed them. "I'm sorry." Her voice was so weak as to be nearly a whisper.

"Sorry! Bascha, what on earth—"

"I've lost it," she said.

"Lost—" And all the hair stood up on my skin. A chill ran through my body. I looked at Umir. "Get her help," I told him. Umir kept a healer on his premises. "*Now*. She's losing a baby!"

Umir's expression as he stared at Del was nothing less than sheer disgust. It made me so furious that I pushed myself up. But between the chains and Tariq and Hamzah, who moved to catch me, I could not throw myself at him as I wished.

"If you want me to open that thrice-cursed book, you'll get her help. Right *now*!"

Umir made a motion, and I saw his steward come forward. "See to it," Umir said.

I stood there in chains, held in place by Hamzah and Tariq, and watched as slaves came, collected Del, and carried her away. I had no idea where she was going. But I didn't intend to let her go there alone. "Until she's recovered, the book will remained locked," I said coldly. "You'll get no magic from me."

Umir examined me. He was Southron-dark, grey-eyed, and always clad in the richest of fabrics. His hands were elegant. He cared little for women, little for men. All he wanted was to build his collection. Apparently that was enough for his needs.

"Let me go to her," I said.

Umir smiled. "I think not." And he told Hamzah and Tariq where to take me.

Chapter 38

I WAS FAIRLY CERTAIN I'D BEEN IN THE ROOM BEFORE. If not, in one exactly like it. Same small, squared windows high in the wall; same door with hinges and lock on the outside, a lip over the jamb so nothing could be inserted; and a wooden cot. A night-crock.

Tariq, again, shut one hand very tightly into my harness and let the flesh over my kidney once again make an acquaintance with his oh-so-delicate knife. Hamzah squatted, unlocked the ankle shackles. Even as he did so, Tariq pressed the knife point slightly more deeply. I knew very well what he was doing. While the repeated wounds were nothing more than slices, they were also promises. Umir's men wanted no surprises from me as they took off the shackles.

Next, the wrists. This time Tariq didn't use the knife. Instead, a knuckled punch struck me hard right where the knife had been, immediately over my kidney. I arched backward, fighting the pain, and Hamzah took off the wrist shackles before I could do anything. As he and Tariq let go of me, as they went out the door, chains and shackles clanking, the best I could do was fall to hands and knees. No fight from me.

For some time I knelt on the floor, willing the pain away. Slowly I got to my feet. A burst of pain slammed me in the kidney and all the muscles tightened. I swore, gingerly tried to stretch. But not such a good idea.

I strung together some of the vilest curses I could think of or invent, and walked carefully to the cot. I sat down. Waited for the worst of the pain to pass. Once most of it did, I stood up again. I threw the cot over onto its side. Sat down on one of the topmost wooden legs, and bounced. Twice, and the leg cracked right off the frame.

On my most recent visit a couple of years ago, I'd used a broken cot leg as a sparring blade, to make myself fit again. This time I'd employ it as something else.

I stepped to the door. Knocked gently on it to measure the thickness, the sound. Then I began bashing the leg into the door over and over again.

The exercise would not harm or open the door on its own, but it would make it impossible to ignore me. And then a person would open the door.

Bash—bash—bash—

Bash—bash—bash—

After a few more bashes the leg cracked lengthwise and fell apart in my hands. I tossed the pieces aside. Went back to the cot. Broke another leg off it, returned to the door.

Bash—bash—bash—

My lower back hurt like hoolies with the exertion so soon after a kidney punch. I ignored it by bashing the leg against the door all the harder.

I heard voices outside. I stopped bashing long enough to set my face against the door. I shouted. "I can do this all night!" *Bash—* "Really I can." *Bash—*

"Stop!" someone shouted from the other side of the door.

Bash—bash—

"My master says to ask what you want! Other than your freedom, of course!"

Oddly, that made me grin. *Bash—bash—bash—*

"STOP!"

I stopped. "Take me to Del. That's all I want. Take me to her."

Silence.

"All right," I called. "Here I go . . ."

"STOP! STOP!" The tone sounded frenzied. "I'll ask my master!"

I waited until it was likely he'd gone. I rested a couple of minutes, panting, then began again.

Bash—bash—bash—

The master apparently did give permission for me to be moved to wherever Del was because not long after my request, the door lock rattled. I knew how the game was played; I'd played it here before. I walked to the far wall, tossed the cot leg aside, and waited peacefully.

Hamzah first. Tariq next. Shackles and chains.

"Are you his favorites?" I asked. "Does he have you do any additional services for him other than catching people? You know—*services.*"

They were too professional to get angry. In fact, they looked almost bored.

"Take me to Del," I said.

Tariq smiled. "We may just clear the room of all furniture, even the nightcrock. Then what would you do?"

"Yell. Want to hear me?"

Hamzah shook his head in mild disparagement. "We'll take you to her. But if you try anything, you'll never see her again."

"Umir wouldn't kill her," I said sharply. "He's never been that kind of man."

"No, no," Hamzah said. "I meant exactly what I said. You'll never *see* her again. That does not necessarily require killing either of you."

No, it didn't.

I put out my hands. Hamzah locked shackles over my wrists again. The connecting chain was exceedingly short. "Try us," Hamzah suggested.

I shook my head. "Just take me to her."

They did.

Del was in what appeared to be the healer's quarters. She was not in a cell but an alcove that adjoined a larger room containing cabinets of herbs, pots and bottles, rolled cloth, rolled paper, any number of other things I could not identify. A table was nearly as crowded with various items, including candles, oil burners, lamps. Herbs hung from strings stretched across the room. All of them lent the air an odd mixture of astringency, sweet spice, and something that made me cough.

Tariq and Hamzah stood on either side of me. A man came out from the alcove, a question in his face. He looked at them, then at me.

"He's to stay with the woman," Hamzah said. "Someone will wait outside the door. He's a prisoner."

The healer said in a surpassingly dry tone, "I rather assumed that when I saw the shackles."

"Del," I said curtly, staring at the man.

The healer made dismissing gestures to Tariq and Hamzah. "Go. Go. This is not a place for swords and knives. This is the place where I repair what swords and knives have done." And before I could once again demand to see Del, he held out a beckoning hand, indicating the antechamber.

It was small, low, arched. A narrow cot was pushed against the wall. A lantern hung from the ceiling on a chain.

She lay on her back beneath two blankets, a pillow under her head. She remained very pale, but there was faint color in her lips again. I knelt down beside the cot. "Oh, bascha . . . I'm so sorry."

The healer stood behind me. "Did you know she was pregnant?"

I wanted to stroke her head and hair, but to do so would likely result in shackles and chain striking her. "No," I said. "She hadn't told me. Will she be all right?"

"She lost a lot of blood. Did it come on suddenly?"

I related what physical insults Del had suffered, from the man sitting on her to the pommel pressing hard against her abdomen all the way to Umir's from the oasis. And the blood when they took her down from the saddle.

The healer's expression was grim. "It's not unusual for a woman to miscarry. But the cause of this was probably everything that happened today. She needs rest, water, broths to eat."

"Did they tell you she's a prisoner, too?"

"I assumed it."

I was disgusted. "And yet you willingly serve Umir."

His face tightened. "You had best be thankful I do, or I would not be here to render aid. You'd still be shackled like a beast, and she would be dead of blood loss."

I bent forward, pressed lips against her brow. "Heal well, bascha. Rest well. There's no need to leave just yet."

The healer emitted a dry cough of a laugh. "You won't be leaving until my master says so." He paused. "My name is Wahzir."

I turned from where I knelt on the floor, looked up at him. He was a small man, slight of frame, most of graying hair missing from the top of a brown skull. A beak of a nose dominated his face. His eyes were the rare shade between brown and green. Thin skin stretched tautly over pronounced facial bones. The robe he wore was of an excellent weave and weight, dyed gray-blue.

I restrained an angry response and swallowed back the taste of fear. "Will she live?"

"She should," Wahzir replied, "but I make no promises. I do what I can do and leave the rest to the gods."

The gods. The gods. Always the gods. I didn't believe in them. But then, I'd never believed in magic, either. So, just in case, I asked within my head that the gods heal Delilah.

I moved to the end of her bed and propped myself against the wall there so I could watch her face. Shackles clinked.

Wahzir frowned. "Stand up."

"What?"

"Stand up. The way you moved bothers me."

"Why should I?"

"Because I've asked it. If you like, I'll add a 'please.' Please get up."

I got up. Ow. Wahzir moved behind me, set a hand on the small of my back right where my kidney was. Since I was only in dhoti and harness, I felt his dry touch. I winced.

"Well, you'll be pissing blood for a few days."

"I know that!"

"Or you'll die."

"Die?"

His tone was quite matter-of-fact. "Oh yes. You can die of a hard blow to the kidney. The organ rots inside you. It poisons the blood—"

"Stop," I said, feeling queasy again. "I don't need to know the details." I moved away from the healer and resumed my place against the wall, upper body propped up as I sat. It stretched the insulted muscles in the small of my back.

Wahzir disappeared a moment, then returned, dragging a stool into the alcove. He sat down, very much at ease. But he looked thoughtful. "What is it about you that makes my master want you? What are you to do?"

I shrugged. "He did not take me into his confidence."

The healer thought a moment longer, eyes narrowed, lips twisted. He was turning something over in his head. And then he began to laugh. "It's the book! The *Book of Udre-Natha!* So, the rumors are true! Now it fits together—the puzzle is solved!"

"What rumors?"

Wahzir showed small, even teeth briefly in an amused smile. "That you had locked it against all others and only a mage can do so. Only a mage may open it." The smile remained, crinkling the corners of his eyes. "You gave the book to my master knowing he couldn't open it, because you—a mage—closed it. Locked it with spells. Then you disappeared before Umir could do anything about it. But a man recently brought word where you lived, and that you were going north. Umir knew you'd return to the South. And he knew how to find you on the way. No one bypasses that big oasis."

No. No one did.

"I'm sure Hamzah and Tariq were growing very bored, waiting for you." He laughed again. "All is explained."

There was no reason to deny it. "You've seen it? The *Book*?"

"Oh, yes. My master *likes* people to know what he owns; he doesn't hide all away. His pride is his collection. We're all allowed to see it."

It crossed my mind that he might be lying. Umir was a subtle man. "Describe it for me."

"I don't need to." Wahzir rose, left the alcove. I heard him rustling papers, moving pots around, shoving things aside. Finally he returned with a large book in his hands. "Is this it?"

It was a plain, leather-bound book. No inset gemstones, gold or silver scrollwork, no burned-in knotwork designs that might set it apart from other books. Hinges and locked latch and hasp were made of patinaed copper, and time-darkened gut threaded the pages onto the spine.

I looked from the book to Wahzir.

He smiled. "I thought perhaps it might be a copy. But it isn't, is it?"

"What are you doing with it?" I made a gesture to encompass the larger room, astonished that Wahzir not only had it, but that a book of such power, a grimoire, would be jumbled together with everything else in an untidy room.

"Trying to open it," he said lightly. "I'm a mage."

"A mage?"

"Mage-healer."

I'd heard of them. I'd never met one before. "But why here?" I asked. "Shouldn't it be kept in a safer place?"

"I told my master I could not be expected to sit alone in a reception chamber and open it. I required what I was most accustomed to, and that is here in this room. The book was brought to me."

I played over something he'd said. I was very careful with my words and intonation. "*Trying* to open it."

"And failing."

"But you're a mage."

He sighed. "We are not infallible."

I began to be a little concerned. I'd always detested magic, and most of what was claimed to be magic, wasn't. But I'd learned. I'd been taught that lesson atop the stone spires of Meteiera. "You said you know something now. That you understood the puzzle."

"I know why my master has done what he's done, yes. And why. The rumors about you are true. My master wants you for the magic in your bones."

Ignoring him, I got up again, moved back to Del's bedside and sat once more. "Bascha?"

"I gave her a draught," he said. "She won't waken for quite some time."

Bitterly I asked, "Umir's idea?"

"No. Mine. She needs to remain very still or the bleeding might begin again."

I turned, leaned my back against the edge of the bed. My kidney stabbed with pain, and I couldn't suppress a grimace. I closed my eyes, sighed very deeply. Shackles rattled in my lap.

"He wishes very badly that the book be opened, does my master."

I grunted.

The book lay on his lap. "Would you do me the favor of pushing your hair back?"

I stared at him in bafflement. "Push my hair back? What in hoolies for?"

"Will you?"

"There's no reason I should do any such thing."

"Please."

We stared at one another a long moment. I was angry, frustrated, and he knew it; he was calm, patient, and I knew that. So I skinned my hair back from my forehead, baring the edge of blue tattoos that ran all along my hairline.

"Ahhh." He smiled. "Thank you. I'd always heard of the mages of Meteiera, but had never met one."

I let my hair flop back over my brow. "Yes, I'm very unique." And kept the tattoos hidden with hair. The mages of Meteiera shaved their heads.

"Is it true that you'll go mad and die in ten years?"

I had seen men leap from the spires in the moment before the madness overtook them, killing themselves so they would do no harm to people they loved. Not all had the will to leap. Some had indeed gone back to families, thinking they could control the madness—and slaughtered them when the magic overwhelmed their minds.

I told Wahzir the absolute truth. "I'm a sword-dancer," I said. "That's all. A long life lies ahead of me."

Wahzir smiled sadly. "The book must be opened."

"Hunh. Umir should know by now that I don't surrender quite so easily."

"You must," he repeated. "Please."

I scowled at him. " 'Please' isn't going to work this time. I don't know what Umir's paying you, but it's not going—"

He broke in. "He's not paying me. I'm part of his collection."

It stopped me cold. I stared at him.

"Part of his collection," he repeated. "There aren't many of us left, you see, we mage-healers, so here I am." He shrugged lightly, as if resigned. "But when I tell you the book *must* be opened, it has nothing to do with me, or even my master. It has to do with you and your future."

That was odd. "My future?"

Wahzir's eyes were kind, but also sad. "Umir has your daughter."

Chapter 39

BUMPS ROSE ON MY FLESH. Hair stood up. I felt cold, so cold. I shivered from head to toe.

"Yes," Wahzir said, before I could deny it from disbelief. "It's quite true. I've seen Sula. She's approximately two years old, has hair not quite as blond as Del's, blue eyes, and she frequently announces her name to anyone within earshot."

My lips felt stiff. I couldn't speak properly. "How did Umir find her?"

His expression was apologetic. "I don't have that answer. I'm sorry, Sandtiger. All I was given to know was that Umir wished to use your daughter to force your hand. Then I knitted together the rumors I'd heard about you being a mage. Though I'm not sure anyone believed it."

He knew her name, Sula's. That he knew mine, knew Del's, meant nothing. But *Sula's*. The Sandtiger had a daughter. People in Julah knew. It was no secret. But neither was it something that came up in conversation except with people Del and I knew well. We didn't hide it. I could think of no reason why anyone would ride out of Julah all the way to Umir with such knowledge.

Del and Sula. Two hostages.

One would have been enough.

Gods. *Sula*.

I rose to my knees and turned to Del, who was insensible to all.

I bent down over her, putting my head against hers. "I'll make her safe," I told her. "I promise. I'll do whatever he wants. She'll be safe. And we'll all go back home together."

"Sandtiger."

I kissed Del's brow. "I promise."

"Sandtiger."

On my knees, I turned.

Wahzir held out the *Book of Udre-Natha*. "Here. You can do it right now, right here, and all will be over."

I stared at the book. My eyes burned, but were dry.

"It will be over," the mage-healer repeated. "All you have to do is give Umir what he wants."

I collapsed back against the bedframe. I was empty, so empty.

"You closed it. You can open it." He stepped forward, bent, pushed the book into my hands. I'd forgotten how heavy it was. "*Open it.*"

It crossed my mind briefly that Wahzir was being very aggressive about me opening the book. It bore thinking about. But I had no focus to do so.

The *Book of Udre-Natha*. I stared at the cover. I touched it. Ran fingertips across the unadorned leather. Touched the hinges, the hasp, the latch. It looked like any other book. But this one would never open for anyone but me.

The me I'd once been, but wasn't anymore. I had made sure of that when I poured my magic into Samiel and broke the blade.

A great grief rose up as I met Wahzir's eyes. "I can't."

"He'll let you go," Wahzir insisted. "All three of you. He just wants the book."

"I can't."

"Sandtiger—"

"I can't. I gave all the magic away. "

Wahzir sank down, eyes wide with shock. "You gave—?"

"I gave it away. I couldn't face having only ten years left to me. Not when my life was so full."

His face was pale. "You gave it away?"

I tossed the book aside. No pages fluttered. The cover didn't get caught on anything. The book was locked. No harm was done.

"I gave it away."

Wahzir stared at me. The pupils in his eyes grew and grew. Lips peeled back. He displayed gritted teeth. *"You gave away what I would kill to have!"* He leaped to his feet. "Do you understand? All that magic!" He swept up the book I had tossed aside. He hugged it to his chest. "Gods! Gods! All that is in here, and I can't open it. *You* can't open it!" He dropped to his knees, rocking, keening, as if he'd lost a child.

I looked back at Del, who had just lost a child. The other one, the living one, was now at risk. What could I tell my bascha? That *both* children were dead?

Wahzir sobbed on his knees.

"You're a mage-healer," I said. "This book is nothing to you."

He lifted his head jerkily, meeting my eyes "This book is *everything* to me!"

I felt numb. Sluggish. That my thoughts were too dull, too jumbled, to put anything together. The puzzle pieces.

But slowly, they came.

"You want the book for you. Not for Umir. You knew he had it. You allowed yourself to be taken, to become part of his collection so you could reach the book. But you couldn't open it. So now— there's me. Umir wants me to open it. You *need* me to open it."

He stared at me, then put out a shaking hand and pointed behind me toward the alcove. "If you tell Umir, I will kill her. All I must do is nothing. Nothing, and she'll die."

Another puzzle piece. "You're not worth anything, are you? Not to Umir, if he knew. You've lost your magic."

Rage suffused his features. "And you *gave yours away!*"

Umir wanted the book opened, but mostly just to have it so. A locked book in a collection, when what lay beneath the lock was the greatest knowledge a mage could ever have, was not valuable. Particularly when it was such a plain thing to look at. So he wanted what was on the inside. And he threatened my daughter to get it. He was not called Umir the Ruthless for nothing.

"I can't live this way," Wahzir said. "I'm empty. *Empty.* Nothing is in me. I can't live as an empty man!"

And all I wanted was to *be* an empty man.

Wahzir trembled. "Umir will kill your daughter when he knows you have no magic. Just to punish you."

So he would.

"And I'll kill her mother, *just to punish you!*"

He and I both heard a rattling in the larger room. A door boomed open. Men came to the alcove: Hamzah. Tariq. Others.

Umir, too, came to the alcove. "Has he opened it?"

Wahzir shook his head.

"Did you tell him of his daughter?"

Wahzir nodded.

"And he still refuses?"

"He can't open it!" Wahzir cried. "He gave it all away. He gave his power away. He's an empty man, like me. And the book stays closed!"

Umir looked at me. "Is this true?"

I didn't bother to look at Wahzir. "He's lying. The book can be opened."

"Are you quite certain?" Umir asked. "Wahzir has been of help to me. I have never known him to lie."

"Three things," I said, "and I'll open the book for you."

Umir remained, as always, icily calm. "Three things?"

"You will harm neither my daughter nor her mother. You'll let me see Sula. And you must let me go free."

And Umir smiled. "Do they mean so little to you after all? You'll use *them* so you can be free?"

I raised a delaying hand. "Wahzir is correct about one thing. I am what he calls an 'empty man.' I have no magic."

"You see?" Wahzir shouted.

I looked only at Umir. "But I can get it back."

Even Wahzir fell silent. The only sound in the alcove, in the room, was the chiming of my chains.

"Give me the stud," I said.

Umir forbore to point out that made four things. "Either you're lying, and won't return—"

"In which case you're no worse off.

"—or you will use the magic against me."

I shook my head. "Not while you hold Del and my daughter. I'll open your book. On their lives, I promise. And then we leave here. All three of us. *Alive.*"

Umir smiled very slowly. "But if you have your magic back, I might wish to keep you. For my collection."

"But I won't *have* any magic if I put it into the book."

One brow rose. "You can do that?"

"I put it into a sword. I can put it into a book."

Wahzir's eyes lighted. I knew what he was thinking. The magic in the book was powerful enough, but augmented by the magic I'd brought home from ioSkandi? He knew what that power was. He knew of the mages atop the spires. He knew I'd had that power.

"Trust me," I said, "I don't want the magic. I'll be happy to let you have it. Why do you think I stuck it in the sword to begin with? The cost is too great. I have too much to live for." I indicated Del. "Her. My daughter. Me. We leave here alive and unharmed."

"You will leave now," Umir said with quiet emphasis. "Waste no time. You have two days."

I was stunned. "Two days! Are you sandsick? I need more—"

"If you don't return within two days, I will assume you have no intention to."

I shook my head vehemently. "I can't do it in two days. Not across so much of the Punja!"

"Hamzah," Umir said, "have his horse readied."

Hamzah inclined his head in acknowledgement and departed the room.

Umir took two steps to me, another past me, and stopped at Del's bedside. He looked upon her, then turned to face Wahzir. "See that she survives. On your head be it."

He moved past me. Wahzir followed. I knelt down at the cot and kissed the side of Del's head just above her ear. "I promise, bascha. Nothing will harm her."

Hoolies. Two days. I'd counted on more.

"Stand up," Tariq ordered.

I stood. Turned. Held out my hands. The shackles were removed.

"My daughter," I said pointedly.

Umir said, "Tariq."

Tariq indicated the door. I walked out of it.

The stud was waiting as I was led through the front door into the colorful courtyard. Umir did have a taste for beautiful things, beautiful surroundings. And of course he very quietly underscored his wealth by making a fountain the centerpiece. In a desert, water was worth more coin than most could claim. Even other tanzeers.

A stranger held the stud. He was saddled, bridled, ready to go; had full botas on the pommel. He stomped on paving stones noisily, employed a conversational tone in nickers and squeals. Mostly he was swearing.

I turned away from him and looked at Umir's steward waiting on the entry steps. "Where's my daughter?"

He indicated a second floor window. And there my daughter was, held in a stranger's arms. She slept. She did not know I was here.

I have never done a thing so hard as to ride away from Umir's. And to my death.

Chapter 40

I T WAS ONLY AN HOUR OR SO before the sun set and the moon rose. In sand and soil, the stud and I need not worry about rocks and snake holes lying in wait to trip him, as they would do once we left the Punja. So we ran, the stud and I, racing as far as we could before the light changed, before the footing did too.

We'd left the North behind. Here it was hot. I stopped reluctantly because I so badly wanted to go on, but the stud needed water. I had no bucket. I peeled an upper lip back and shoved the bota's spout up into his cheek. I squeezed. The stud, completely startled, jerked his head away and backed up, ears rigidly forward.

"Water." I shook the bota. "You need it. Drink."

He was not at all pleased to have the bota anywhere near his mouth, after what I'd done with it. I was not at all pleased to argue with him. The law of the desert is to drink *before* you're thirsty. If you wait until you are, it might be too late. People die of too much sun, not enough water. So can horses.

But every moment I wasted trying to convince the stud was time away from Del and Sula.

One day there, one day back. And magic to recover in between.

In desperation, an answer occurred. Umir had ordered I be given a burnous. Now, faced with a recalcitrant stud and needing to ride on, I tore off the burnous. I dug a hollow in the sand, spread the burnous over it. Squirted all of the bota's contents into the cloth-lined basin, emptied a second as well.

"There," I said. "*Drink*. And hurry up before the water soaks through!"

The stud, of a wonder, drank.

"Should have thought of this first," I muttered.

The stud's water was gone quickly. The last sips remaining in the two botas ran down my throat. Not enough, but I wasn't doing the work. The stud was.

I grabbed the wet burnous from the sand, slung it up and over the saddle. The bota strings went over my shoulder. I swung up hastily, botas flapping against my ribs, and kicked the stud back into a run.

"Sorry, old son. Just no choice."

The sun went down. The moon came up. Light was muted, but I could see well enough. Now Punja sand was intermixed with rocks, scrub, low trees, dry and stickery grass. Snake and vermin holes. But there was also a track, a well-worn track with better footing, because this was the main route across the Punja.

Sweat lay on the stud's neck, reins rubbing it into white foam. Sweat rolled down his flanks. He wasn't laboring yet—he was much too fit—but I didn't doubt that he felt the exertion.

I halted him. Jumped off. Dug a basin. Threw burnous across it, emptied two botas. This time I didn't need to tell the stud to drink.

I drank, too. A live horse with a dead rider would do me no good, especially if I was the dead rider. Four of ten full botas remained, but it wasn't much under the circumstances. Umir had thought of water for riding. He hadn't thought of water for running.

Sweat rolled down the stud's face. The hair beneath his headstall and halter was soaked. As I stood before him, he pressed his head against me and commenced to rub. I nearly fell down.

It wasn't affection. He was wiping off his face.

Burnous across the saddle. Botas flapping against me. Back up and into the saddle.

"Sorry, old son. We've got to."

And on we ran.

The next time we stopped, his nostrils worked like bellows. The interiors were very pink. He shook his head up and down. Shook his entire body. Nearly pushed me aside before I could fill the burnous basin.

He drank it all, then peed.

I hadn't needed to pee since we'd left Umir's palace. And that was dangerous.

I unfastened another bota. Sucked a third of it down my throat. Realized how badly I needed it.

The sun was down, the night was warm, not hot, but our pace was what mattered under the sky, not the temperature.

I rested my forehead head against the stud's sweaty face. "I know. I'm so sorry."

Trot. Walk. Lope. Over and over again. Trot. Walk. Lope. Julah was far away. The canyon father yet, and the broken stone formation that housed a broken sword.

I watered him. I watered myself. Both of us needed more. But the moon was far gentler than the Southron sun. I urged him onward. Not far, not far, I said. Not so far, I lied.

Sunrise. Heatrise.

Gods above and below, my back was killing me. And when I finally peed, the blood in it was bright.

He was winded. He labored. We had somehow wandered off the track. I couldn't remember why or when.

I reined in. Practically fell out of the saddle. Got down. Dug the basin. Emptied two botas. Kept some sips for me. He plunged his muzzle down as deeply as he could into the shallow hollow, sucking water. Under the circumstances, a pitiful amount.

"I'm sorry," I said again, from a throat that felt dry to bleeding.

He drank the basin dry. He swung his head into me as I sat upon the ground. I collapsed backward into the dirt, the rocks; the scrubby, stickery grass.

"No more," I told him. "Not until tomorrow." I could barely move. "Tomorrow. For now, a short rest. Catch your breath. I'll catch mine."

I woke when the stud moved. I had tied his halter rope around my wrist so I wouldn't sleep too long. He was stretching to reach another hummock of grass. By the sun's position, it was past time for us to go.

Too long, too long, I thought. No time was ever enough.

I climbed up into the saddle, swearing at the pain in my lower back. That punched kidney was mightily offended. I bit into my lip, settled down into the saddle, and told the stud it was time to go again.

Once again, we ran.

The choppiness of his gait roused me. I'd fallen asleep in the saddle. The halter's lead-rope hung down to the ground. Just about the time I was coherent enough to understand, the stud stepped on the rope. It stopped him dead, and I nearly came off.

He fought the rope. He didn't realize that he was standing on it. Until he moved, *it* wouldn't. I swung a leg over the saddle, let my weight follow it down, and ended up on my butt. I pounded a fist on his fetlock. "Move it. Move it."

Outraged, he lifted his hoof. I yanked the lead-rope from under it.

No stopping now. No delay. We had to reach Beit al'Shahar. Had to reach the sword.

"—sorry," I gasped.

I dug, I poured. The stud drank it up.

Not enough. Not enough.

And I realized, all of a sudden, that we were not upon the track that cut the Punja in two. We were entirely elsewhere, and I had no memory of going there.

I grabbed the stirrup. Pulled myself mostly upright. Changed my grip from stirrup to saddle. Breathed hard, then stuffed my foot into the stirrup and hauled myself up. Butt in the saddle, reins in my hands, I sat very still. There were no words for the clenching, the cramping of my back.

"Let's go," I said. Nothing more was in me.

The stud's gait ran ragged. I roused, realized he'd been carrying me without direction. Now he wanted direction. Now he needed it.

I reined him in. Dragged my right leg across the saddle. Crossed his rump with a flopping foot. Tried to lower myself carefully. Instead, I fell.

The reins were in my hand. The halter rope as well. Sudden tautness in leather, in rope, pierced the fog in my head. And I watched, in stupefaction, as the stud surrendered.

He stood with all four legs spread. He tried to equalize the weight, to prop himself up. Instead, his knees gave twice. Snapped back into place. Then he canted forward, folded his forelegs, and awkwardly went down. The hind legs followed where the front legs led.

The expulsion of breath was loud. The stud bobbed his head, then let the weight of bone take him. His muzzle went into soil and rock. He propped it there, blew dust from the soil. After a moment he heaved himself up partway, splayed front legs, then rolled onto his side.

Gods gods gods.

So little left in him.

I peeled back his upper lip. Set the bota between cheek and teeth. Pressed it, squirting what liquid was left into his mouth. He did not protest this time.

I lay on my belly. Swung an arm across his neck. Into the soil, I laughed for no reason I could think of. Small clouds of dust puffed up.

In the stone, fallen down; in the ruined, fallen chimney, I knew what I must do.

I knew, too, what I needed now to do.

Two more fat botas. I drank a few swallows from one, dug a haphazard hollow, and emptied the last of the water into it. Removed halter, bridle, put the halter back on. Tied the long lead-rope so it wouldn't trip him when he got up again. *If* he got up again.

I knelt there beside him a moment longer. "Old son," I rasped. "Good old son. I could never ask for better."

I pushed myself to my feet. Wavered a moment. Then turned my back on him and began to walk.

From behind me came a faint nicker. I shut my eyes and walked on, praying—yes, praying—that someone would find him. Or that he would find someone.

I ran, I walked, I jogged. Tripped a few times. Fell down once and got cactus spines in my left forearm. Jerked them out one at a time, cursing between my teeth, and then went on. It crossed my mind to search for the track, but to do so would use time I didn't have. I knew my directions; I was heading the right way. I just had to keep going.

An inner sense told me I was close. I knew I was when I came across the sandy riverbed that never ran with water. It was choked with stones, sand, and flat, chunky boulders, hedged by scrub trees. Del and I had never been exactly here, but it was the same riverbed. If I crossed it and held to my direction, I should come across the regular track we took into Julah.

Which was, as I kept going, exactly what happened. I ended up between the high bluff with its lean-to, and the mouth of Mehmet's canyon. I stopped long enough to drain the last of my water from the bota. Then I went on, jogging awkwardly again. Because the track was worn, the footing was better. I still managed to trip now and again because I was just so tired, but the going was easier.

Close enough to run, I ran. Mehmet's aketni all came out to greet me, but I gave them a ragged wave and kept going. I passed out of Mehmet's canyon, found the narrow mouth of ours, ran and ran.

High overhead, an eagle spiraled. I aimed for the natural pool that Alric and I had since improved, splashed through the shallows to the deeper portion, and fell face down in it.

So cool . . . so wet . . .

I scooped up several handfuls and drank, then splashed back out of the pool and ran again. This time to Alric's. As usual, their children were running around everywhere. I was relieved to see they were all right.

Lena met me in the doorway. She was so startled her mouth fell open. "Gods!"

"Is Alric alive? Are you all right?"

Tears ran down her face. Through her hands she said, "I'm so sorry! I'm so sorry! They just took her!"

I caught her shoulders to stop her trembling. "I know. Lena, I know. I've seen her. Sula's all right. What about Alric?"

"Tiger?" It came from the other room, their modest bedroom. "Is that you?"

I slid by Lena and went to the bedroom opening, pulling the curtain aside. Alric was struggling to get out of bed. His face was in the first bloom of ugly bruising, and it appeared Lena had stitched closed a long cut on one cheek. His left arm was splinted. The right leg was wrapped.

"Stay in bed," I advised. "And Sula's all right. She's all right. I've seen her. Are *you* all right, you and Lena?"

Alric gave up the fight to stand. He sat on the edge of the bed, left arm and splint cradled against his chest. "Yes. No harm done beyond this, as you see. But Sula—you're sure she's all right?"

"She's at Umir's. I saw her . . ." I paused. "Yesterday, I think it was." Lena was at my elbow, offering a mug of water. I thanked her, drank it dry in a few gulps, gave the mug back.

When I looked at Alric again, his face was ravaged. "They just rode in here and took her. Tiger—"

I cut him off with a gesture. "I know. I *know*. Don't blame yourself. Either of you." I paused to catch my breath. "There's something I need to do, and then I must go. But I'll need a horse. And there are no guarantees you'll get it back."

"Where's the stud?" Alric asked.

I sighed deeply, feeling a hard twinge of regret. Of grief. "Somewhere between here and there. I'm not sure. He couldn't go on. I had to leave him."

Alric's mouth dropped open as he stared. Then he closed it. "Gods, Tiger. What's happened? Is Del next door?"

"Del is at Umir's, with Sula."

He was astonished. "*Umir's!*"

"It's a long story," I told him. "There's something I must do, something important, and then I'll need the horse. I have to go back to Umir's."

"You're exhausted!" Lena protested.

"No choice. The horse?"

"Yes! Yes! Of course," Alric said. "You'll take mine. He'll be ready to go when you are."

I nodded, blowing breath out between pursed lips. "All right. I'll be back for him . . . well, when I'm back."

Lena put out her hands. "Give me those botas. I'll fill them. I'll pack some food. And a clean burnous—"

"Lena. Stop. Thank you, but . . . stop. The water will do." I pulled the empty botas off and handed them to her. "I must go."

This time neither protested. Neither asked questions. But I saw both reflected in their faces, in their eyes. I nodded in thanks, in acknowledgment, and walked out of their house.

Chapter 41

TWO YEARS. Two years since I had been up to the fallen chimney. Then, I poured all the magic within me into the sword. And then broke the blade, banishing power I'd never wanted. Now, as I ducked to enter the tunnel-like opening made of tumbled rocks, I recalled that here, too, Neesha had told me I was his father.

The tunnel was not a proper one. As the chimney crumbled, large slabs had fallen in such a way as to create something very like a tunnel. The interior chamber that had been a circle collapsed partway as well. Originally it had been open to the sun; rounded, striated walls climbing to the sky. Now there were fissures and cracks in tumbled slabs fallen in a heap. These allowed sunlight, but not much, and in no kind of pattern that was easy to recognize as what the chimney once had been.

I walked carefully and slowly through the tunnel, ducking my head. I hated this cavern-like formation. Hated creeping below fallen slabs. Such close confines always made me nervous.

By the time I reached the huge boulder blocking almost completely the way into the chamber, I was panting. Exhaustion was sapping my strength, my balance, my endurance. I needed sleep badly. But no time, no time at all, for human frailties. For mine.

Between the huge slab and the broken wall lay a narrow chute from uneven stone floor to what passed for a ceiling. I examined the chute with eyes and hands. Neesha had gotten through with only a few strips of skin left behind; the first time, I simply couldn't fit. The last time, I'd brought a pot of grease to ease my way. I'd left more skin than Neesha, but the grease had done its work. Unfortunately, I had no grease with me now, and I had no idea if I had gained or lost weight over two years.

After a lengthy inspection of the chute, I finally took off the harness with its empty sheath, unlaced sandals and kicked them away. Sideways, I slid an arm through to lead the rest of me. I followed up to my shoulder. It was flesh and bone I risked now. Rather than take and hold a deep breath, which expanded the rib cage, I blew out all my air. The trick was to get deeply enough into the passage that I could begin shallow breathing. But before then, I would not fit.

I inserted myself into the chute and began to work myself through. I found it easier in the narrowest areas to scrape through as quickly as I could. But it meant I left more skin, began to bleed. I felt horribly compressed.

Before me lay shafts of light. The remains of the circle were *just* there. I blew out breath again, steeled myself, forced my way through. Momentum dropped me to hands and knees in pale sand. Chest and back stung from bad scrapes, but as I started to move, pain in the kidney area flared so excruciatingly that it dropped me face-first into the sand.

The picture in my head was what Wahzir had told me. *The organ rots inside you. It poisons the blood.* The kidney rotting, spreading poison throughout my body.

"Not now," I murmured. "I have things to do . . ." Gods, it hurt, and so badly the sweat rolled off my body.

I lay there with teeth gritted, fists clenched, breath hissing into and out of my mouth. When at first the pain began to diminish I didn't believe it. But slowly it lessened, degree by degree. Sweat dried. Breathing steadied. I could lie there no longer.

I eased myself up to a sitting position. About a foot away lay the blade portion of a broken sword. Close by lay the other half: hilt, pommel, grip, and approximately a foot of amputated blade.

Samiel.

Not far from my broken sword lay Del's Boreal. Named blades.

Blooding-blades, keyed by us in the blood of a living being. I had come home from Skandi brimming over with magic foreign to my bones. Foreign to my blood. I, a mage, annealed and tempered atop a towering spire of stone on ioSkandi, island of the mad.

No time. I needed this done.

I reached, took up the blade half. Moved a little farther and took up the other. It was dead in my hands; sundered, stilled, damned.

Sand and blood caked my chest. For a moment I held both halves in one hand, then scraped a swath of blood from my skin. I painted both halves with it. I closed my right hand over the grip. The left over the blade. I thrust both into the air, pointing up, out of the chimney, pointing to sun and sky.

Come, I told it. *Come home.*

The interior of the chimney exploded with light. Bursts like shooting stars raced up, raced down, spun themselves around the interior. A whirlwind of light painted the chamber, spinning, spinning, spinning. It never had disappeared. Never dissipated. It would not desert its host. But it was wild. It was angry.

Come home, I said. *You are needed.*

A whistling began. Each time a burst of shooting star was born, sound accompanied it. A high, keening sound, loud with its whelping, trailing off as the burst grew a tail and shot through the air—up, down, around. A deep throb came into the chamber, trembling beneath my legs. I reared up, braced myself on knees and calves, let my head fall back as I thrust the two broken halves even higher into the air. Up to the sky. Up to the stone-blocked sun.

The chamber was wreathed in light of a hundred colors. The whirlwind spun, humming. The newborn bursts streaked in numberless directions, shrieked, fell into the whirlwind, added meager light to the whirlwind glorious in power, in the spinning of its children. It climbed the broken walls of the chamber, spun high, higher than my head, higher than Samiel, whirled up the chimney. The keening of its song, the humming of its power, the deep throb under my body grew in volume. And the whirlwind spun down. It dipped, touched, pull sand into itself. Glittering crystal sand. I tasted its grit in my mouth. Heard the added song, the almost-painful throb.

It had not been this way when I broke it. Maybe because I had killed the sword by forcing everything into it.

Bursts exploded into existence, tiny, brilliant shooting stars, alive with light, with sound. Each reveled in freedom briefly, then fell into the whirlwind to add one more blazing streak.

And the whirlwind, built with light, pregnant with its children, spun itself down and down, over my body.

Inside, all was quiet. Light spun and spun, but didn't touch me. Sound pulsed in me, but I couldn't hear it. All was still. All was silent. I knelt in the chimney with broken Samiel in my hands, offered to the light.

Come home, I said. *Come home where you belong.*

The whirlwind spun itself up. No longer was I shielded. I felt the stinging of the sand, saw the blazing of the starbursts, heard throb and roar and hiss. A keening, half-mad song of magic's grief, mourning its desertion.

The whirlwind climbed. It jerked both halves of the sword out of my hands. They were spun into the whirlwind, flashing in meager sunlight bleeding down through fissures and holes. Though half-deafened by the wind and its wailing, I thought I heard a click. Metal on metal. Tumbling down from the whirlwind, wreathed in light, Samiel fell. I realized I was there in its path and threw myself aside as the sword came down and planted itself in the sand, whole once again.

The whirlwind spun and spun, climbed to the sky, fractured into fragments. In countless colors light rained down with a hundred thousand voices. It struck me: painless. Bathed my face. Ran off shoulders. Rolled down back and flanks. And the lights winked out.

Sand and dust settled. I was blinded by darkness at first. But vision cleared, and once again the sun crept through crevices. In its touch, Samiel's new-made blade was blinding.

I stood up. I reached out, closed my hand around the grip, and pulled the blade free. It slid easily from sand, shed glittering crystal, was clean and bright and whole.

But Samiel wasn't the magic. Samiel was merely the harbinger.

The sun was banished. Darkness reigned. And from every crack and crevice, every slot and fissure, light crawled out. It ran down the chamber walls, welled up from the marriage of stone to sand. Magic pure and potent. Power incarnate.

"Oh, hoolies," I said. "This is going to hurt."

Light crawled across the sand, trickled down the walls. I watched as it quested in the sand, like a puppy hunting milk. I stood there, waiting, breathing noisily. Then I drove Samiel, blade first, deeply into the sand. I sank down slowly. Gripping Samiel was all that kept me upright.

Come on, I said. *Take me.*

Light came. Touched. It crawled all over me, bathing naked flesh. I felt it creep slowly into every pore. My mouth, my nose, my ears. Lastly, my eyes. Tears ran backward. I tasted them in the back of my throat.

Magic kindled. Deep within my soul, within my sense of self, the spark grew larger. Breath blew upon it. Tinder caught. The fuel of my body burst into conflagration. I threw back my head and screamed. A hundred thousand voices sounded.

My flesh was unmade then knitted back again. Skin sloughed away, taking with it scars and the aches of age. Heat wreathed my bones, then transmuted into ice.

Take me, I said. *Come home to me.*

Joyously, power leaped within me.

I was what was needed.

I knew when all was done. I had ten fingers again.

I stood. Pulled Samiel from the sand.

"Bascha. I'm coming."

Chapter 42

WHEN I GOT BACK DOWN TO THE MODEST MUDBRICK houses, I found Alric sitting on a bench outside his doorway. He kept his bandaged leg stretched and cradled his splinted arm. Tied to a leg of the bench was a buckskin gelding.

I stopped dead. "Not *your* horse! Alric, I don't know if he can make it back. It's hard riding I'm doing." And harder yet because of time lost in the broken chimney.

Alric's eyes were on the hilt sticking above my left shoulder. He looked at me, his expression oddly blank. "You didn't have a sword when you went up there."

"No."

"That's why you came back? To reclaim Samiel?"

"Yes."

His gaze was quite steady. "Tiger, what's going on?"

"I don't have time. Truly. I have to go back to Umir's to get Del and Sula." I looked at the buckskin again. "Are you sure?"

"I'm sure." He bent somewhat, untied the lead-rope with his good hand. The horse was ready to go. All the botas I'd brought with me, plus several more, all filled, hung from the saddle. "I was not effective in watching your daughter."

"Alric! It's not your fault!" I stepped forward, took the lead-rope from his hand. "We'll talk about this more when I'm back. In the meantime, just rest. Heal. Do you hear?"

He took a breath, let it out. "I hear."

"Good." I tied the lead-rope to my pommel, climbed aboard, untied the reins that had kept them out of the horse's legs.

"There's food in the packet," Alric said. "Lena insisted."

That did not surprise me. I shook my head, smiling, raised a hand briefly to Alric, turned the buckskin, and left at a swift lope.

I would not ordinarily get to know a horse—and have him get to know me—on a mad gallop across the desert. The buckskin was a willing goer, but because he was good at heart, not because I asked it of him. We did come to an agreement. I wouldn't use my heels, and he wouldn't add a hitch to his gait when I least expected it.

We rode through scrub trees, cacti, shrubbery, dodged rocks large enough to catch a hoof and roll. Down into the dry riverbed, clopped across slabs of stone embedded in the sand, a gallop with footing that wouldn't harm his hooves, shod or not shod. Then it was up and out of the riverbed, onto the track that led to Julah. But I didn't go into town. I swung the buckskin onto the northbound track and asked—*asked*—for more speed.

The earth beneath had been beaten to a fine dust over the years as people went northwards across the Punja or south to Julah or Haziz. It was safe now to gallop as fast as we could, moving aside when southbound wagons came to us from the north. People in wagons often raised a hand to me or called out a greeting. Some, grinning, asked me what the hurry was. But I had no time to wave or call back. I wondered if a vastly exaggerated tale would be born out of my gallop through the desert.

I eased the buckskin to a trot, then a walk, headed him off the track. I dismounted and dug a basin, threw my burnous over it and filled the hollow with the contents of two botas. The buckskin looked at me as if I were madman, offering too little water in a too-little trough. But he didn't scorn to drink it. I drank some as well, then threw the burnous across the saddle and climbed back up on Alric's horse. North again.

But oh, I missed the stud. He was not far from my mind. Perhaps on the way back I could spare the time to look for him, though it was unlikely he'd be where I left him, unless he was dead. I hoped he'd had the strength to make his way to the track.

The magic once again had stripped me of pain. No cramped muscles, no fire in and over my kidney. I felt fit, almost younger. I had forgotten what it was like to have magic in my bones, keeping its host whole. Yet again, it had not removed either the cavern Del had carved against my ribs, or the sandtiger scars on my face. But all others were gone, and I had ten fingers.

On. And on. Several times I stopped to water the buckskin as well as myself, let him have a breather. I had risked the stud far more than I would this one, who was Alric's horse. Watered him more frequently, gave him breathers. And as we went on, my mind again filled with the vision of the stud, down in the dirt. I hadn't ridden him to death, but closer to it than I liked. My hope now was he'd been found, maybe taken up by people in one of the wagons. He'd been too exhausted to cause trouble. They'd think he was docile. Then they'd learn the truth.

We left behind the scrub desert and entered the Punja. More frequent stops allowed us to continue the ride even at night. I did not stop for sleep as I had with the stud. The pain, the sapping of strength by the sun, was not a factor; that made the difference.

Alric's horse was a good one, but I missed the stud. He was an extension of me. Stubborn, intractable, opinionated, certain he's right about everything, prideful, domineering, and any number of other attributes. In fact, he was too much like me. Or I too much like him.

Walk. Trot. Lope. Punja sand flew up as we loped, as we trotted. Footing was soft, but also gave from under hooves. It required more effort from the horse, tired him more quickly, but I had no choice.

With the sunrise, I said, "Bascha, I'm coming."

For her, and for Sula.

As we neared Umir's palace, the buckskin began to falter. His gait lost its rhythm. Breathing was loud. With grim determination, I unsheathed Samiel, used the flat of the blade, not the edge, and slapped it down on the buckskin rump. Three times. It startled the horse into greater speed again, much as I hated to demand it. Sweat foamed, ran down his body, darkened yellow-white hair into wet sheets. Black tail lashed, black mane flopped against his neck.

"Almost," I told him.

I don't know if he heard me. I don't know if he cared. I was merely the demon upon his back.

White walls heaved out of glittering sand, blinding bright beneath the sun. So close now.

I used Samiel on the buckskin again. Heartlessly, I said, "You can rest when we're there," and hated myself for it.

Through gates into courtyard. Alric's horse skittered across stones, too tired to fight for footing. I thought he might go down, but he stayed upright. I threw myself off, led him to the fountain. Could not, much as I wished to, allow him to drink and drink and drink. He was too weary to protest. Otherwise I'd never have won. Brief drinks only. Flesh quivered, muscles trembled. He was soaked with sweat.

I was here in the time allotted me. But Umir could wait while I tended the horse.

At last the bellows of the buckskin's breathing eased. I let him drink more. And as he drank, I plunged my head beneath the surface, shook water out of my hair, scooped up handfuls for me to drink. The two remaining full botas were on the saddle; easier just to scoop up what was in the fountain.

I led Alric's horse to a tree, one weighted with rich yellow blossoms. I tied him there, patted a shoulder, thanked him for his spirit and will. Then at last I turned to enter Umir's palace, and I found a man upon the steps.

I knew him. The kid from Julah, who'd picked on Neesha. Khalid, whom I had defeated so badly before all the watchful eyes in Julah.

More of the puzzle pieces fell into place. It was Khalid's doing, that Sula was here.

I paused, comfortable with the weight of Samiel slantwise across my back. "All this, because you lost? Because I made you angry?"

Khalid smiled. "Don't discount the bounty. I was glad to do it, yes, but more pleased to be paid for it."

He did not know what I was now. What I could do. To him, I was just a man. An aging sword-dancer with fading skills. Nor did he know what Samiel was. A named blade, blooding-blade; called here, jivatma.

I was dusty, sweaty, wet. But underneath it all, I was not tired to the bone. I wasn't younger. I wasn't better. I was me. But I was also no longer, as Wahzir had named it, an empty man.

"Let's go," I said. "I have business in this house."

Khalid stared at me. "Do you really have magic now? Can you really open this book?"

I stared back at him. "Come and see."

Khalid turned his back on me and walked into the palace.

Smiling, I followed.

Come and see.

Inside, I headed straight for Wahzir's quarters and Del. Not surprisingly, several men appeared almost immediately to prevent me from doing this. I didn't protest. I held out my arms so they could grip them tightly and keep me from moving in any direction. Also not surprising, Tariq and Hamzah arrived.

"*I* know," I said, "you're his pets. Or maybe part of his collection."

Hamzah's smile was slight. "We are what you once were. Sworddancers."

"With honor," Tariq put in.

"You call this 'honor'?" I asked. "I wouldn't be so certain." Khalid was behind me. He yanked Samiel out of the sheath.

There was a note of wariness in his voice. "Is the magic in this sword?"

I smiled at Tariq and Hamzah, answering Khalid. "It's just a sword. I forged it in the North when I had nothing better to do. The magic you refer to is in *me*."

Khalid moved. Two strangers held me. Tariq, Hamzah, and now Khalid stood in front of me. Tariq looked at the sword. Hamzah did not. He looked at me—of the three, the cleverest, and thus the most dangerous.

"Khalid," I said lightly, "don't be so certain you're getting the bounty."

He look up. "What?"

"You told Umir where I was. You did not capture me. That took Hamzah and Tariq. Umir will pay them."

"He said he would pay me."

I grinned. "Umir lies."

Khalid looked uncertain. Then angry. He glared at me.

"Now," I said, "let's go to Del, shall we? Before I open that gods-cursed book, I have a task. And you can tell Umir that, Khalid. *After* you ask him about the bounty."

Khalid hesitated, then gave Samiel to Tariq, turned on his heel and walked off, stiff through spine and shoulders. Hamzah laughed quietly. "He's a fool, that one."

"Del," I said pointedly.

Tariq looked up from inspecting blade, hilt, grip, and pommel. "*Is* it a magical sword?"

I laughed at him. "Magical swords only exist in stories."

Hamzah was watching Tariq. He appeared to be amused. "Here," he said. "I have an idea. Just in case." He took Samiel from Tariq, gestured to one of the men to release my arm. He presented him with the sword. "Umir will likely wish to put this in his collection." His amused glance slid to me. "Just in case."

And so Khalid gave up the sword, Tariq gave up the sword, Hamzah gave up the sword. Hamzah also closed a firm hand over my arm. "I realize you know the way," he said lightly, "but allow us to escort you."

Wahzir was bent over items on the long table. He glanced up as I was brought in with Hamzah and a stranger attached, trailing Tariq. Wahzir jumped up so quickly he bashed his thigh on the edge of the table and upset a bottle of ink. Or a bottle that looked like ink. Still the dry little man but with hunger in his eyes.

"You have it?" he asked. "You have the magic?"

"Del."

"Alive. I have kept her so." He stared avidly at me. "You have the magic?"

"I did. But they took it away from me."

It completely baffled him. "Took it—?"

"The sword," I said calmly. "Of course it holds the magic. That's the way it always is in stories."

"*Who* took it?"

"Ask Hamzah. He's the last one to have his hands on it."

"Oh, stop," Hamzah said. "Now you're boring." He let go of my arm and gestured for the stranger to take himself away. He knew I wasn't going to escape, or even attempt it. Del was here, and Sula elsewhere.

"Umir has the book," Wahzir said. "Can you open it?"

"Of course I can open it. I closed it." I walked away then, went into the alcove. Del still lay beneath covers, her head atop a pillow. Her color was normal. "Bascha." I knelt down on the floor beside the cot. "Del. I'm here."

She stirred. A glow began in my heart, a small, growing spark of relief and joy. As she opened her eyes, the spark became a flame. Delilah saw me. Delilah smiled.

Chapter 43

I PUT MY HEAD DOWN VERY CLOSE TO HERS, spoke so softly I knew no one else would hear what I said. "Bascha. Whatever happens, pretend you're still very ill."

Awareness and understanding flickered in her eyes. Still on my knees, I turned to Wahzir. "You said she was better. This isn't better."

"I said she was *alive*," he clarified. "That's all that was expected of me."

"She can't leave like this," I snapped. "And we certainly aren't staying here once I've done what Umir wants. What do you recommend? Can't you heal her?"

The hunger in Wahzir's eyes was replaced with a smoldering anger. "I kept her alive. I can kill her also."

"Umir wouldn't like it." Still on my knees, I looked at Tariq and Hamzah. "One of you had best go get my sword."

"Nonsense," Hamzah said curtly. "There's nothing in that sword. You just want it close enough to use if you get the chance."

"Then ask—oh. You're here."

Umir came in. He carried the book almost reverently. Khalid, accompanying him, had my sword. Very helpful of him.

"That's not wise," Hamzah warned. "Breaking codes and oaths does not make him any less dangerous a sword-dancer."

Umir looked at him. "You have a sword, as do Tariq and Khalid.

But it doesn't matter if the blade is here. His woman is ill, and I hold his daughter. Use sense."

I stayed on my knees.

Despite the dimness and shadows of Wahzir's quarters, I saw color come into Hamzah's face. He was angry, angry and embarrassed to be ridiculed for his concern. I very carefully kept my expression blank. Annoying him was one thing, angering him was quite another. Hamzah was not impressed by Umir the way Tariq and Khalid were. That made Hamzah dangerous. And Umir, I thought, didn't know it.

"Is my daughter safe?" I asked the tanzeer.

Umir was insulted. "Of course she is!"

"Let me have a moment with Del. Then I'll open your book."

"Hurry!" Wahzir cried.

I'd been kneeling and I remained so. I turned back to Del, saw her watching me expectantly. She didn't know all the answers, but she knew what the questions were. I smiled at her, then pulled back the covers. She still wore her short leather tunic. I placed one hand over her belly. Something inside me leaped. It made me gasp. This was no kindly power.

I leaned down, rested my head against the cot frame. Shut my eyes tightly. Felt a spark of something coiled down deep unwind itself. It found my spine. Ran up the cord to my neck, then down over shoulder to arm and the hand spread beneath it. I thrummed with it. Throbbed.

I saw Del's face. Wonder filled it. But she recalled what I'd said. She lay very still, closed her eyes, did nothing they would expect of a recovered patient.

"Finish!" Wahzir shouted.

Umir turned on him. "Be silent, or I will send you from this room, and you'll see nothing of the book. Nothing of the spells."

Wahzir closed his eyes, nodded. Lips trembled. I thought any moment he might faint from expectation.

"Open it." Umir's eyes were very cool as he looked at me. "You know the cost if you can't. Or won't."

I drew in a deep breath. Stood. Gestured to the table. "Put it there."

Wahzir leaped to the table. He pushed aside everything, knocking various bottles and other impediments out of the way. They fell to the floor, spilling contents, shattering, rolling away. Umir quietly set the locked book down. Tariq and Hamzah stood by the door. Khalid was near Del's alcove. Umir was closest of all. Wahzir hovered.

I sat down on the bench. Touched fingertips to smooth, aged leather. Once I had read the book; once, when I had power. I knew if I opened it, I could read it again. That gift was Meteiera's. What had been forgotten in the crumbled chimney as I poured out the magic was now remembered.

Umir's tone was no longer as calm. "Open it!"

I put fingertips on the lock, on the hasp and latch. I let the words come up out of my soul. Spoke them very quietly.

The lock clicked and undid itself. The book fell open. As it did so, Del was up from the alcove, yanking Khalid's sword out of its sheath. Of the items Wahzir had sent spilling from the table, one remained: a knife. And as Del killed Khalid, I grabbed the knife, flipped open the *Book of Udre-Natha*, dug the blade deep into the gutter between pages, and sliced down through the gut stitching holding pages to lambskin. A hard, heartfelt toss into the air sent pages flying.

Umir and Wahzir screamed in unison, terrible, stricken screams of shock, horror, denial.

Light rained upon us, blinding bright. Bursts grew tails, flashed into darkness. Pages were caught as the light began to spin, to spin and spin. The whirlpool was of writing, not of light. Words flying in the air.

Del crossed swords with Hamzah. Tariq was so taken aback by the suddenness of events that he hadn't yet unsheathed. Khalid was down, dead. Beneath the body lay my sword. I shoved Khalid's body aside, grabbed the sword, and took on Tariq as he finally unsheathed. He fell back out of the doorway, bleeding badly from the gut wound that would kill him.

Hamzah was good. But Del was better. She left him unarmed, wounded, and spun to face Umir. "No more!" she shouted. "*No more of you!*"

Delilah took his head.

All dead now, save Wahzir. He was grabbing page after page, holding them close to his chest as he bent and bent, trying to grab more. He chanted something under his breath. Somehow, he looked pitiful.

Then the chanting stopped. The clutching at pages stopped. He opened his mouth in wonder. And then he screamed with joy. *"Whole again!"*

Oh, hoolies.

"Run," I told Del, who wasted no time doing precisely that. She leaped Tariq's body, half-turned to look for me. I leaped as well, aware of singing in my bones.

"—*not empty*—!" Wahzir shouted.

Del and I ran down the corridor to the large, domed entryway.

"Sula," she gasped. "I know where she is—"

"Go. I'll get horses for us."

Del ran, sword blade flashing. I turned toward the massive front door. Just as I reached for the heavy latch, something caught me and threw me down. I slammed into the marble floor. Every bone in my body felt shattered.

I made it to hands and knees. Everything in me was filled with light, with sound. Hair rose up on my flesh. Fingernails bled light instead of blood. My eyes burned in sockets.

"Tiger!"

Del was back. I tried to see her, but the light wouldn't permit it. I saw nothing but blinding bursts. On hands and knees, I shuddered. The light within was singing.

"Tiger!"

It was difficult to hear her through the song.

I felt her hand on my shoulder. "I've got Sula. Tiger—let's go!"

I vomited. Light fell out of my mouth.

"—I want it all—" Wahzir screamed, echoing down the corridor. "Don't go to him!"

Don't go to him. Don't go to—*him?*

Magic attracts magic. Wahzir knew the only person in the palace who had any magic was me. Some of the power he'd tried to claim while clutching at pages had escaped him. Wild magic, coming to me. Strings of words, writhing through the air.

"Go!" I shouted hoarsely at Del. "Get out of here!"

Del yanked open the heavy front door. Through a scrim of brilliant light I saw Sula in her arms. Then both of them were gone.

The *Book of Udre-Natha* was a grimoire, a compendium of magic, of arcane knowledge and spellcraft written down over centuries. I'd learned as I read it two years before. Learned so much. But now the power in the book, attracted to magic, came flying to the foreign magic born of ioSkandi. Words. Lines of printing. Diagrams. I had an idea now why mages went mad and leaped from spires.

"*Come back!*" Wahzir screamed.

"Fight later," I said breathlessly to both the magics within me. "If I'm dead, you're dead."

Inside my body I felt a pause. Light winked out of my eyes. I grabbed my fallen sword, scrabbled to my feet, ran through the open doorway. Del was on her white gelding with Sula in front of her. She ponied by lead-rope a buckskin already saddled and bridled. The spray of the fountain put droplets in his mane. Both horses bore saddle pouches and botas.

"Alric's horse?" she asked.

"He can't go," I said. "Not again. I'll have to take another."

Del looked beyond me. "I don't think that's a good idea."

I turned. Wahzir stood in the doorway. His eyes bled light.

Oh, hoolies.

I ran to Alric's horse, threw myself into the saddle, and turned him hard toward the gate. "I'm sorry," I said. And to Del, "Go!"

Go she did.

I knew when we were free: Del, my daughter, and I. I felt Wahzir's questing attenuate, die. He claimed magic now, was no longer an empty man. He wanted what I had, wanted the rest of the magic, but we were free of him for now, and he had other things to deal with.

I told her we were free. And so Del wanted to know everything, and everything took us all the way to the big oasis. There we went about our usual chores: found a tree, untacked the horses, unrolled our blankets, watered the horses, relieved ourselves, sorted through pouches. What we had never done before, at the oasis, was keep an eye on Sula.

You would never have known she'd been abducted. *She* didn't know she'd been abducted. She was fine. She was Sula. She spilled the water I gave her and proceeded to play in the resultant wet sand. Well, a considerable improvement over horse piss.

Del sat cross-legged on her blanket, watching our daughter's sheer joy in becoming dirty. I tended Alric's buckskin. He was tired clear through, not unexpectedly. We had only galloped away from Umir's palace a brief distance, as I knew the buckskin couldn't do more. After that we walked. Khalid and Tariq were dead. Umir was dead. Hamzah may have survived, but he was wounded, and there was no reason to chase after me. No Umir meant no bounty.

I scrubbed and brushed Alric's horse. As much as I could, I rid him of salty sweat stains and walked him around. When he felt cool and his breathing eased, I took him to the spring and repeatedly poured water over him with the communal bucket, which resulted in more than a few people expressing annoyance because mud and rivulets now surrounded the spring. I considered explaining that I'd just escaped an evil tanzeer who wanted my sword because of the magic in it, but decided I didn't really feel like making up a story for people to embroider as it was passed around. I just finished pouring water over the buckskin and walked him back to our tree. Picketed him, collapsed upon my blanket.

Once collapsed, I saw Sula staggering off toward another tree. Someone had a dog. Sula liked dogs. Del went after her, caught a hand, turned her around and brought her back. Sula had no plans to stay with us when a dog was nearby, so Del dug through pouches and came up with a twist of stick cinnamon. She gave it to Sula, told her she could only have it if she stayed on the blanket, whereupon our distractible daughter became very well-behaved.

Del moved close to me. She leaned a shoulder into mine. "Tiger."

I shifted, putting that arm around her. "What?"

She dropped her voice to a whisper. "I think we should get her a dog."

I found that utterly baffling. "Why?"

"Because if we don't, we'll never keep track of our daughter. I can't carry cinnamon and sweets with me everywhere she goes. Neither can you."

Well, no. That was true.

"It can stay outside."

I remembered Alric telling me their new dog would stay outside. She eventually slept in a big tumbled pile with all the children. Inside.

"Alric's bitch has puppies."

"I know Alric's bitch has puppies. They keep coming over to our house."

"If Sula had her own, maybe the others would stay away."

"I don't think—wait. Wait a moment—" I got up, took three long strides, caught our daughter as she left the blanket at as fast and steady a run as she could manage. Which wasn't very fast *or* steady. I bent down, swept her up, carried her back to the blanket. "Your mother said you should stay right here, remember? She gave you a sweet for it." I looked at Del. "You know, that's bribery. Do we really want to teach our daughter about bribery?"

"Either that, or put a lead-rope on her." Del paused. "Or get her a puppy and put a lead-rope on *it*."

I set Sula down, looked for the cinnamon stick. Found it in the puddle she'd made earlier. I wiped it off on my burnous, blew at granules, but the sand was too wet to be completely evicted. I sighed and tossed it to Del.

She stretched out on her back, ankles crossed, arms thrust under her head. "Why don't you take her for a walk?"

"Why?"

"Wear her down so she'll go to sleep. There's too much for her to look at here. She's too excited. She'll never sleep. Which means *we* will never sleep."

"Can I put her on a lead-rope?"

Del laughed. I took my daughter's small wet hand and led her off the blanket. She fought the restraint and eventually I released her, planning to scoop her up if she headed for trouble. My legs were considerably longer than hers. She did attempt to run off here and there because something caught her eye, thereupon received multiple rescues by her father. It was not a terribly productive walk. She was, as Del had observed, too excited.

But when her steps finally appeared to be a bit more unsteady, I picked her up, cradled her, lugged her back to our camp. I set her down between us and told Del, whose eyes were closed, that she was right.

Del opened her eyes. "Right about what?"

"She needs a dog. Of her own. So she doesn't try to make friends with every damn dog at every damn oasis."

In the deepest hour of the night, I woke up. Del slept. Sula slept. Except for insects and snuffling from various types of livestock, it appeared the whole oasis slept. I got up carefully, quietly, looked down at Del and my daughter, then walked off into the darkness.

Out from under trees I saw the entire night sky. Black and black, and so many stars. Thousands and thousands of them. But only one moon. Tonight, it was full. A single baleful eye, glaring down at me.

I drew in a deep breath. Tipped my head back. Closed my eyes.

"I'm just a man," I said. "Just a sword-dancer. Why in hoolies do you want *me*?"

A starburst was born behind closed lids. I saw it slash across my vision, trailing smoke and light.

"Why do *both* of you want me?"

Writing rose within my eyes. Blood-red ink, yellowed page, scratches shaping words. A list of ingredients. A spell to cast.

I had a *book* inside me. And whatever else was sharing space with it. Light and darkness. Silence and sound.

I closed my hands into fists. Felt all ten fingers where eight used to be. That, I found good. But the rest? Who could say? I couldn't. I am not a god. I'm just a sword-dancer.

The magics within me laughed.

Epilogue

ON THE REST OF THE RIDE HOME, Del and I traded off putting Sula in front of us, in our saddles. She wasn't big enough to interfere, and was too light for the horses to notice. The only problem was that Sula wanted to ride with whomever she *wasn't* with. This occasioned much back-and-forthing as we continually traded her, until finally Del grew annoyed and suggested that spoiled little girls might not get for their birthday what it was they wished for. Sula subsided and fell asleep with her back against my chest.

"That's blackmail," I said. "First you condone bribery, and now you descend to blackmail?"

"Do you have any suggestions?"

"Well, no."

"Then be quiet."

We left the desert behind and entered Mehmet's canyon. Just seeing high stone walls, lush green grass, and a stream running through brought a sense of peace. As always, Mehmet's aketni was scattered here and there doing chores. As always, they waved and shouted greetings. We waved back and rode on, then turned past the rocky shoulder to enter our canyon.

Del, who had taken Sula again, tipped her head back to look up into the sky. "Eagle."

I looked up. A second eagle joined the first. "Must be a clutch up there somewhere."

"Remember the first time we came here? Eagles flew."

I smiled. "So they did."

Alric's and Lena's corral lay ahead, their house just past it. "I need to give Alric back his horse. I'll be home shortly."

Del nodded, rode on past. Sula asked something in a high-pitched voice. Del answered, but I don't know what she said. I watched them go, thinking about the baby she had lost. Wahzir, when he was merely a healer, had said it was likely she'd have no others. I hoped Sula was enough to ease that pain.

In front of Alric's and Lena's house, I reined in and stepped off the buckskin. I called to them both. Lena came out immediately. Alric came more slowly, favoring his leg.

I smiled. "We're back. All of us. Even this big boy."

Alric visibly inspected the horse. "Used him a little hard, did you?"

I shrugged. "He had something left."

"Ale by the pool?"

I nodded gravely. "Ale by the pool would be almost the very best thing I can imagine."

"You can't go there," Lena protested to Alric. "So far on that leg?"

"Ale," Alric said, "has medicinal properties."

Lena scowled. She reached inside the door. "Then use *this*."

I shouted with laughter. "A cane! A cane!"

Alric glared at me. "Coming?"

I heard Del's raised voice. She was calling me. It wasn't from fear; just a summons. "Go on ahead," I told him. "I'll see what she wants, then join you."

"Tiger!"

"I'm *coming*, bascha!" I walked on over, found her standing outside the front door. "What?"

"Come with me."

"Come with you where? We just got home."

She grabbed a hand and yanked. I followed. She took me around behind the house to the small corral.

Out of shock, I stopped. "Where did he come from?"

The stud, seeing that I had at long last arrived after so many delays, exhaled a noisy, prodigious snort. I didn't mind. I was too relieved to do so. I went to the corral and put out my hands. The stud came up, snuffled at them.

Tears stung. And I didn't even mind if Del knew it. "Did he make it here on his own?"

A voice other than Del's answered the question. "No, he didn't make it here on his own. I found him in Julah. Someone's young daughter was riding him."

I spun. Saw Neesha. Who grinned at me in a mixture of delight and triumph.

He answered the unspoken question. "My parents talked me into coming. They hired two men for the farm and told me to go on back to my lessons. Rasha wanted to come, but they said no."

I felt a strange little lift in my heart. "They may have talked you into it, but is it where you want to be?"

After a moment of overdramatic consideration, he told me yes. "I'm only third level. And barely that. Besides, you'll need help with the students."

"I apparently don't have any students at the moment, remember?"

"Two," he said. "Besides me. Eddrith and Darrion."

"Who?—oh. Those two from Istamir."

Neesha nodded. "Eddrith says you owe him a sparring dance."

I had some memory of that.

"Darrion says his grandmother sent him."

And I definitely remembered that grandmother: sharp-tongued Tamar.

"They've taken one of the little houses by mine."

My grin was slow, but huge. "Then go get them. We'll *all* drink ale."

Del's tone was elaborately resigned. "Sula wants to eat. It appears that *once again* the woman must do the work while the men drink spirits."

Neesha went off to gather Eddrith and Darrion. Smiling like a fatuous fool, I began a comfortable stroll down to the pool where Alric, and Alric's ale, waited.

Del's voice followed. *"Save some for me!"*

Author's Note

I HAVE THE GREAT AND GRAND LUXURY to write what I love to write. And I love writing about Tiger and Del.

First, it was only to be *Sword-Dancer*, back in 1984. But by the end of the book, I couldn't walk away from Tiger and Del. So I wrote three more volumes, thinking that was the end of the story. But no. It wasn't. And I wrote two additional volumes, *Sword-Born* and *Sword-Sworn*.

But those volumes turned out not to be the end of the story, either, even though in the *Sword-Sworn* Author's Note I said it might be. So here I am again with a seventh volume, and an eighth to follow.

Tiger and Del obviously have their own ideas about how and when their tales are told. I now acknowledge that they are in charge. Certainly I am not!

—J. R.
Tucson, Arizona
November 2012